UNLOCKED

KINGDOMS OF YRIA

Ashyre's Story

ALEXA E. WOODIWISS

Princeton, Minnesota

Printed in the United States of America
Woodiwiss Books, LLC

Unlocked/ Alexa E. Woodiwiss

ISBN 978-0-9826583-3-8

To my mother,
Denise
With all our love,
Grandmama and me

CHAPTER ONE

'Tis forbidden, 'tis forbidden....

Navali, princess of Lynaria, silently reiterated the phrase that so often preceded the laws of her countrymen as she stared across the expanse of light blue silk carpet separating her from her father, King Naran.

She clasped her hands tightly together, hidden as they were from her father's sight in her lilac and pearl-dipped skirts, and desperately fought the unseemly and wholly irrational urge to scream at the injustice being thrust upon her as she composed her features into a smooth mask, carefully hiding the emotion roiling just beneath the surface. All the while, firmly stifling the ridiculous impulse to flee the apparent insanity swirling in the room and hide in the relative safety of her bedchamber.

Straightening her spine yet a degree more in its already rigid stance, Navali stiffly perched on the seemingly delicate wrought iridescent glass chair that bespoke of the wealth and position her family commanded in the region. She dared not forget her place in the world, though she felt she would indeed perish if she were to be forced to continue to sit motionless and listen to what the king was commanding of her.

Her father's deep blue eyes, the only color in his otherwise pale countenance, betrayed none of his thoughts as he sat comfortably on the matching chair opposite her. Only a small amount of illegal impatience lit the cold luminous orbs, and Navali drew in a steadying breath, bracing herself for the words she knew were about to emit from her sire's mouth.

"You will do as I request for the wellbeing of your people, Navali," King Naran stated his *request*, which was by far more of an edict, in a calm, even tone. For the king of Lynaria never raised his voice. That would have been considered exceptionally ill-bred, and her father would never give anyone credence to speculate as to his lineage.

"You are as aware as I am that our race is losing the ability to bear children and that we are slowly heading towards extinction. All of Lynaria, and mayhap all of Yria by now, knows the last child born of our race is six cales of age. And if they have not drawn that conclusion as of yet, they shortly will. That is something I simply cannot allow the world to know."

King Naran internally sighed at the mere thought of what he was requiring of his daughter, for though he never gave voice to his affection, he loved her greatly. But he experienced a blinding agony at the contemplation of his race extinguishing, and the sacrifice of a little of his daughter's dignity and comfort was, he felt, comparable to the benefits of the world believing they were not completely barren—even if she must wed and bed a Dareknay barbarian to do it.

The Dareknay as a race were absolute polar opposites of his people, boisterous and uncouth and quite prone to displays of emotion and fits of temper, and in King Naran's eyes could never compare to his near-perfect subjects. Navali's sire was completely certain that governing his countrymen was never a difficult or trying issue, as they individually commanded themselves with decorum and courtesy at all times, remaining outwardly unfazed in any situation. Every Lynarian knew his place in society. From the lowest drudge in the city streets to the highest noble dining with gilt cutlery, no one ever dared complain, and followed their duty to their country with single-minded diligence and loyalty. King Naran would countenance no less with his daughter, even if he must stoop to explain his reasoning for his outrageous request.

"The Dareknay are flourishing while we slowly die off. The council and I are hoping that with the joining of their blood and ours, it will allow us to conceive, and bear children once again.

At this point in our existence there is no other feasible way our healers can find that will cure our barrenness."

"Father," Navali interjected smoothly, the defiance glittering in her downcast silver eyes hidden as best she could manage given the present circumstances. She knew it would not bode well for her if the king saw the emotion, and she stamped it further down with the little control she had left, before raising her gaze to collide with that of the distinguished man sitting across from her.

"I understand we must join with other races to be able to exist. Though why the Dareknay?" She felt a tiny, forbidden wrinkle of distress crease her forehead as the hated word left her lips, but could not help revealing that small telltale of emotion as her panic rose forthwith at the very mention of those blackguards. "What of the Vetuai or the Selenacans? Surely they are far more civilized and would propose a better match as they are our closest allies?"

Navali would give anything not to have to marry a coarse, ill-mannered Dareknay, and she allowed her eyes to briefly convey that message before firmly restoring herself back to controlled sereneness. *Of course,* she admitted to herself, *she had never met one face to face, but she did not have to encounter one of their kind to know they were the worst sort of ruffians.*

Rumors of their exploits traveled faster than the speed of gossip in the downstairs kitchens, and Navali's nursemaid had never considered it the better part of valor to keep her mouth closed. Indeed, she had informed Navali often enough when she was a child what would ever happen to her if she misbehaved. The thin-faced woman had relished her story of an unkempt, foul-mouthed Dareknay creeping into the princess' bedchamber at night and lying in wait beneath her bed to take her back to his lair and make her his overworked and frequently tortured slave.

Now that she was older and a great deal wiser to her nursemaid's schemes, Navali knew otherwise and felt quite secure in the knowledge of how well her personal guards were trained. However, she had heard other tales of the Dareknay, and reflecting back on some of them, she could not quite suppress the inward shiver of icy dread that raced up her spine.

She could not marry one of them, she cried out in silent anguish. Not even if she must indeed defy her father's commands and unleash the torrent of emotion in her breast would she ever consent to marry one of their unsavory ilk.

King Naran rose smoothly from his comfortable position and began pacing the length of the carpet, snaring Navali's attention away from her rebellious thoughts. Her sire only paced when he was *truly* and unambiguously agitated and she was undesirous of causing any further displays of uninhibited action. Not that she was wary of him ever physically striking her, for he never had, but he was entirely too ingenious by half, and one could never be entirely certain what he would declare in this presently displayed disposition.

"The Vetuai and Selenacans are experiencing the same quandary that we are, Navali, and we simply do not have the time to discover what is causing it," he explained to his only child and then hesitated momentarily before presenting the next piece of distressing information. His pale even-toned skin pulled tautly over his harsh cheekbones, accentuating his thin, slightly overlong nose and his lips formed a tight, compressed line, before he forced the words of what he considered his ineptitude past them.

"The Pitan are harassing our eastern border near Wiscane and we do not have sufficient troops, even with the aid and surprise of Trickster's Basin, to keep them at bay if they decide to launch a full-scale war. The Dareknay are the only ones who possess enough seasoned warriors capable of defeating them," her father finished, his long, straight white-blonde hair swinging ever so slightly against his ramrod stiff shoulders as he strode back and forth across the vast study.

King Naran's gaze swept over the furnishings in the room as he attempted to keep his mind from wandering to exactly how desolate their circumstances really were. But nothing caught his attention for very long, for everything was stunning and in its usual place.

This particular study was generally his favorite chamber in the entire palace with its huge bookshelves and massive balcony that overlooked the capital city of Lynaria, but at this moment he knew he would never look at it in the same way again. Not even the sight of Truan glowing beneath them with an otherworldly light, could dispel the gloom of their predicament and the king made his way to stand in front of the balcony doors to gaze down at the city he knew he could not personally defend anymore with only the assistance of Lynarian men.

From her seated position across the room, Navali's eyes narrowed in vexation. *All he ever concerns himself with is his precious subjects,* she thought unkindly and with a large amount of accompanying disgust, her gaze following her father's regal form as he resumed his pacing. *Couldn't he care, just once, about her instead?*

The firm grip she had on her emotions was slipping rapidly, and Navali bore only a faint hope that she would be dismissed from the king's presence before the rage simmering inside her broke forth. But even with the imminent threat of becoming inappropriately expressive she could not stifle her voice or her questions just yet.

"So you will trade me to the lesser of the evils just to defeat the greater?" Her voice gained in volume as she spoke, even though she strived desperately to control it as she finally broke the silence that had descended and thickened between them like fog before the arrival of a vast storm.

"Navali!" Her father's voice held a sharp edge of reproof. "Lower your voice at once. This is not something to become hysterical about," he commanded, looking up suddenly from his intense perusal of Truan, his dark blue gaze filled with disapproval. Lynarians never lost control of their emotions, if they did, there were ruthless consequences, even for a royal princess.

"King Avar and I have settled upon an arrangement that is beneficial to both our kingdoms, and all of the other northern regions have agreed as well." He paused briefly and then said very firmly, "You will marry King Avar's eldest son, and he in turn will provide protection against the Pitans. We all get what we want. The Lynarians, protection and the ability to conceive; and the Dareknays will once again enjoy an alliance with us and the other kingdoms in the northern region."

Navali was well aware of the fact the Dareknays desired an alliance, as it would allow them to trade peacefully with the north as they had before. But surely she need not be condemned to a life of wretchedness just so they could trade legally once again. Her father could accomplish that with a single brandishing of his bejeweled hand.

Unable to hold them back any longer, angry words spilled from Navali's lips. "Then let one of the other regions put forth the sacrificial bride. For I refuse to marry that savage king's revolting son," she said vehemently, one slender hand making a downward slash of denial. "And have you completely forgotten that I am already betrothed to Theon, the High Counselor's son?"

King Naran's patience with his daughter was beginning to wear thin. *Could she not see that he had no other choice in the matter? Couldn't she conduct herself like the dutiful, obedient daughter she had been raised to be?*

"My memory has not gone lacking," he said, his deep blue eyes staring hard at Navali. "The High Counselor has agreed with dissolving the betrothal in favor of our people's continued existence. Not only has that been taken into consideration and resolved, but King Avar has demanded that *my* daughter be the one to wed his son, for I hold greater power than all the other northern rulers," he explained, holding up one hand to command silence as Navali opened her mouth to try to reason with him yet again.

"I will hear no more on the subject. You will not dishonor me. You will conduct yourself with grace and courage and in a manner which befits your station as a royal princess of Lynaria," King Naran demanded, having had enough of his daughter's unruly show of emotion and her disrespect for his decisions.

As the king concluded the discussion between them, a servant knocked discreetly on the heavy white oak door, and then quietly entered the study. At the king's acknowledgement, he informed the ruler that one of his ambassadors required his immediate attention.

King Naran went to Navali and offered his hand to assist her from the chair as any gentleman would do, his manner a courtly show for the servant in the room and those out in the hall. "I have faith you will do the right thing, Navali, even if it is not for yourself, but for all those concerned. You may go to your chambers now and prepare for the journey to Dareknay lands."

Coolly accepting the hand he offered, Navali rose to her feet, her chin held high, silver eyes never straying to the right or left as she exited the room with as much decorum as she could muster. Once out of view of the others, she then had to run in the corridor to make it to her bedchamber without completely losing all grasp with composure and sobbing in front of anyone. A Lynarian never cried in the presence of others, no matter the circumstance or provocation.

Her thoughts whirled in her head, one of her main objections to her arranged marriage coming to the fore. She would never admit to a single soul that she fervently longed for a man to love and to be loved by, for it was an incredibly foolish and child-ish fancy, better suited to those of another race. However, that was exactly what Navali secretly hoped for in the middle of the night when no one was around and she could allow herself the freedom to dream. If she were ever to give voice to that desire in the presence of others, it would be tantamount to running stark naked about the room, screaming her lungs out.

Her people would think she had gone mad! Navali reflected bitterly, as she closed the door to her chamber and fell across the white four-poster bed, her entire life looming before her as a bleak and empty existence tied to a man she had no hope of ever being able to love. Feeling as though she would be ill at the thought of her impending nuptials, she curled into a tight ball on top of the heavily embroidered silken lilac coverlet.

A ferocious race of people who beat their women, battled amongst themselves continuously, and stank because they did not know how to bathe oneself properly. She had heard all this and more from the kitchen servants. A small moan of utter despair emitted from Navali's throat, for surely she was to be sold in marriage to the worst of the lot! A warrior prince, rank with the stench of sweat and horse, one who would curse, yell, and make her life a living hell. And now, at the very pinnacle of all those horrors, Navali realized she had not even had the presence of mind to ask her father what the prince's name was!

Suddenly Navali raised her head, a swiftly forming idea rising to the foreground. She would escape before they reached Chimea, the Dareknay capital, then she would not have a need to know the cur's name. Surely she could find somewhere to live with the amount of coins she had surreptitiously saved. She was young and strong, and would certainly be able to find work easily, then she would not have to wed that loathsome prince.

Navali breathed a deep sigh of relief as her plan of escape began to take shape.

Ashyre, heir to the Dareknay throne, was in the midst of a knockdown, all out brawl.

"Addison—*Oomph!*—Hellfire! Get off me!" Ashyre grunted and growled, his handsome face contorting, as one of his younger, but heavier, brothers attempted to flatten him into the stone floor.

He used the hold he had on the arm that Addison had wrapped about his neck to his own advantage. One hand curled around Addison's fist and he squeezed and twisted the appendage, careful to avoid snapping the bones, but exerting enough pressure that his brother's weight shifted to the right. Ashyre then threw his shoulder into Addison's midriff and shrugged him off and over to land on his back before him. Ashyre glanced about quickly, taking note of how close the rest of his four brothers wrestled in respect to his own position, before launching his body at the downed and now chuckling Addison.

"A hesitation like that could cost you your life, Shyre." Addison chortled, mimicking their old master-at-arms, totally unconcerned that his elder brother now held the upper hand.

"It wasn't a hesitation, fool. And with you as my opponent, I could wink at a pretty maiden and win a kiss afore you were even finished wallowing on the floor." Ashyre quipped and then demonstrated by smacking his lips on his brother's forehead and jumping lithely up to stand a few paces away.

With a thunderous roar, Addison leapt to his feet and began circling Ashyre, searching for any openings in the elder's defensive stance.

"Cease, all of you!" A sudden, good-natured bellow interrupted their brotherly disputes and Ashyre heard one of his brothers give a playful groan of dismay as he was forced to release his opponent.

"Father, I nearly had Ashtyn ready to beg clemency." Aakin bemoaned the loss of his supposed victory, as he arose from his place beneath his elder brother.

"Not only is the pup a braggart, but he's a tale-spinner as well," Ashtyn retorted from where he sat cross-legged on the stone floor. His retort brought a round of laughter from all gathered in the great hall, with the exception of Aakin, who merely looked on in mock derision.

"Is this how the heirs to my kingdom conduct themselves once my back is turned?" King Avar asked gruffly, gazing fondly at his six grown sons as he strode into the inviting great hall. Numerous globes of light were strung from the intricately carved rafters of the room, giving the vast area an inviting glow, while each wooden beam spanning the width of it depicted an important turning point in their country's history.

"No, we do it in front of you as well, father," Ashtyn, second in line to the throne and Ashyre's identical twin, returned good naturedly, rising from the brown, gold, and green stone floor that radiated warmth from the vast furnace-like workings that weaved their way throughout the entire castle. The Dareknay were notorious for despising the cold and preferred everything to be warm and inviting, a stark contrast to their rigid neighbors in the north.

The rest of Ashyre's brothers straightened from the tangle of arms and legs, slowly stretching their bruised muscles, each communicating silently with their identical twin to see how they had fared in the wrestling match.

"King Naran has finally sent word that he accepts all the conditions put forth in the treaty. He will arrive within the fortnight to deliver his daughter, Princess Navali, and assure himself that she is properly wed to Ashyre and the rest of the formalities have been concluded to his satisfaction," King Avar informed as he and his sons took their places at the table for the evening meal. As soon as he was seated, Avar looked at each of his strong sons as they bantered amongst themselves. When blessed with male children, the royal Dareknay line typically bore at least one set of identical twins, But Avar had been unusually gifted with three sets, and the only way to tell each male apart from their twin sibling was the color of their multi-hued eyes.

The royal heirs were the picture of Dareknay princes, each carrying on the over six foot tall frame that made them feared Drocuns; highly trained warriors of their people.

First there was Ashyre. Responsible and rock solid, heir to the Dareknay throne, with his striking green eyes swirling the many hues of the forest, and his gleaming black hair pulled securely away from his chiseled face. He was blessed with a toned muscular build, and was undefeatable on the battlefield along with his identical twin brother, Ashtyn, whose only physical difference were eyes the color of the sun, which practically blazed from his handsome face. Ashtyn also favored his hair a shorter length, the ends of which curled just over his collar, there was less chance of an enemy grabbing it and using it to his own advantage, or so he informed his brothers.

Next in the procession of male heirs came Addison, his gray eyes reflecting the lights, and Adam, with eyes that churned the many blues of the sea. Each had dark blond hair bleached lighter by the sun, massive broad shoulders, and both adored teasing everyone. Addison was known as the family clown and prankster, while Adam tended towards more scholarly pursuits, knowing every law, regulation, and custom of their country, and those of the neighboring kingdoms as well.

Aaron and Aakin were the last set of males born to King Avar. The deep fiery red hair they sported should have warned of the two dashing rogues that lurked beneath the surface, but the maidens of the land were hard-pressed to keep from staring totally engrossed at their handsome visages and couldn't have been less concerned with the inner characters of the youngest twins. This caused Aaron to be slightly aloof and Aakin to be the exact opposite.

The elder of the two, had eyes the color of a black night with a smattering of silver stars. He was not known for his social graces, though one could not lay blame at the feet of the ladies of the court for not attempting to further his education in that regard, but he possessed a way with animals that was completely legendary. The second twin had eyes that could take on any color he wished. They were the only brothers able to be exactly alike, occasionally inspiring their mother's frustration. Also giving her concern, was the fact that Aakin had a propensity towards rakishness. It was not that he purposely set out to seduce anything in skirts, he just had this disposition about him that drew women like flies to honey.

It was this very trait that also made him fiercely protective of his sisters, and the king and queen quickly realized they would not have to worry about a lecherous man getting within twenty feet of their three daughters when they came of age, as Aakin would see to it that all unsuitable riffraff were quickly inclined to take their leave.

Melodious laughter drifted from the massive stone stairway outside the great hall's wide double doors and pulled King Avar's attention away from his musings. His wife, Queen Kalista, descended gracefully down the steps accompanied by their three youngest children. After six robust sons, his wife called herself tremendously blessed to now have three young girls giggling about the castle.

The men stood courteously as the women of their family came into the hall to join them for the evening repast. As the smallest sprite toddled past his chair, Addison growled playfully in his throat and swung her high in his arms, before bringing her down and taking pretend nibbles with his lips from her soft neck.

"Ah, my little love, where do you think you're traipsing off to, hmm?" Addison settled her more securely in his arms, as she chortled at his tickling. "You get the honor of sitting next to me, the champion of the day!" He boasted, his triumphant gray gaze flickering over the purported losers as Kiriah squealed in delight.

"Pay him no heed, Kiri. You know he can't possibly best me." Ashyre stated, as he reached over and easily plucked her from his brother's arms. Kissing her forehead, he placed her on the high seat between himself and Addison, where she promptly took one long masculine finger from each man and gripped it in her chubby little hands, smiling contentedly. Her burnished gold ringlets bounced and her blue eyes shone in delight at the teasing attention.

"Were you boys scuffling in the great hall yet *again*?" Queen Kalista inquired, lifting one brow imperiously at the six grown men only she would dare call boys. "You're going to teach the girls appalling manners if you don't conduct yourselves more accordingly. I simply won't stand for it any more!" She said sternly, though a smile danced in her golden eyes, exposing her true feelings on the matter.

"Are you going to sit for it then, Mother?" asked Kyturah innocently, having noted her mother's amusement. She was the eldest daughter, and at the age of thirteen tended to take things a bit seriously.

"See there, Avar, they are already corrupting my sweet little angels!" Kalista teased with a smile directed at her husband, and then joined in the laughter that rang out as one of her 'sweet little angels' chose that moment to do something decidedly unladylike, by burping rather loudly.

"Really, love," Aakin merrily interjected, seated next to the now blushing, petite eight-cale-old Kisana. "I can scarcely believe a sound like that came out of such a tiny package. Good for you!" He tossed a mischievous glance at his mother, who decided to completely disregard his comment, thinking that the better option before her. No need to give them any more ammunition to use against her.

"Say, 'excuse me,' young lady," the queen instructed her daughter gently.

"'Scuse me," Kisana said, hiding her bright red face in Adam's arm. He reached one hand over to tenderly squeeze hers in reassurance, and she flashed her dimples up at him at his comforting touch, almost immediately forgetting her embarrassing episode.

King Avar sat back in his large, burgundy velvet-covered chair, his eyes taking in the sight of his handsome family engaging in a moment of merrymaking as the food was brought in by the castle servants on large wooden platters, reflecting to himself that life was good, not perfect of course, but very, *very* good.

CHAPTER TWO

N avali," her father greeted, offering his arm as she glided down the numerous steps of the castle into the crowded courtyard below. It appeared as though all of Lynaria were gathered to witness their departure.

The pastel-attired masses gazed at Navali, allowing a minute amount of pride for their princess, who was sacrificing herself for their greater good, to show through their normally placid expressions.

"Father." Navali acknowledged the king with a small dip of her head, delicately laying her fingertips upon his, as they turned to continue making their way down the polished pearl-like stairs. The salutation she afforded him was everything her people expected of her—calm, reserved, and perfectly poised.

However, beneath the cool exterior they could not perceive her railing against him inside the confines of her mind. *How could he subject her to something like this!* she shrieked mentally, as he handed her up into his most expensive coach. The conveyance gleamed brightly in the light of early dawn, the pearl and crystalline materials interwoven in an intricately elegant design. Four matched unicorns, their heads bobbing gracefully in the morning sun, were harnessed to the front, eagerly awaiting the coachman's order.

Her father had probably chosen the ostentatious riding carriage to flaunt his vast wealth. The reason that surely preceded this particular decision was to demonstrate to the people of Dareknay that although he had requested and bartered for their help, he did not really need them. He had just chosen to use them for his own purposes at the moment.

Like he was using her! Navali's anguished reflections on the matter nearly broke the fragile hold she had on her composure and she felt her tranquil visage slipping. *She was a bargaining tool, a royal wife for a slavering dog! She did not know how she could bear it another moment!* Desperately calling upon her strict Lynarian upbringing, Navali was able to once again restore herself to outward sereneness as she settled back against the firm, lavender squabs encasing the inside of the coach. For all the radiance that was exhibited on the exterior, the interior felt considerably dreary and cold. And that was exactly how Navali felt at that very moment, cold, and very nearly lifeless.

Her undesired fate was sealed. *One that was far worse than death,* she contemplated miserably, completely missing the shadowed figure of a woman seated in the opposite corner from herself. She would soon be shackled to a huge, hulking beast of a Dareknay for a husband, one that probably still wore animal skins and ate with his fingers. *Disgusting, she could scarcely contain her joy at her good fortune,* were her sarcastic musings in light of her imaginings.

The coach lurched forward and Navali tensed her muscles against the jolt of motion. Her father spoke abruptly from between clenched teeth, smiling tightly at her from where he sat by a window. "They're saluting you, daughter, raise your head and acknowledge them. You're first and foremost their princess. You're not allowed to sulk like a common—" King Naran cut off the rest of his tirade, having realized just how far his emotions had carried him away.

"Like a common what, father?" She nearly hissed back, knowing he would not even deign to reply. Nevertheless, she did give a small smile and raise her hand in acknowledgement of her people as the coach was driven through the castle gates.

Despite the fact that Navali had just goaded the king in private, something she had never before attempted to do, she was not emboldened enough to do so in the presence of others. But as surely as she had goaded him before, she now felt it did not matter if she disobeyed the laws forbidding emotional displays. For what more could he possibly penalize her with? They were outside the castle, soon they would even be on the other side of the Lynarian border. And if the council had their way, Navali would be married before the week was out, a harsh punishment in and of itself, even if they had not intended it as such.

Navali swallowed hard, despising everything about her circumstances. She fervently wished she could hie away now, right at this very moment, but her escape would just have to wait a little longer, the timing was not quite right. She clenched her hands tightly in the fabric of the beautiful, pristine white gown her maidservants had dressed her in.

Her father had ordered she appear her best for their people and her attendants had certainly obliged his wishes as best they could, having brushed her hair till it shimmered and firmly pinched some color back into her pale cheeks. Glancing down at the now crushed silk in her hand, Navali thought sackcloth and ashes would have been a more fitting garb, for it would have complemented the mournful, sacrificial event taking place far more than the rich silks and perfumes she had been adorned in.

She felt like a well-dressed harlot, one whose services had been bought and paid for. True, she had not been purchased with money, but her father and country had still sold her to a people who paid in warriors and the illusion of protection. Not to mention, her father's hope of her being swiftly able to conceive.

Navali could not quite suppress the shudder of revulsion that ran through her before she slammed the door shut on that potentially disgusting contemplation and forced herself to remember the coins she had sewn, while the palace occupants slept late last eve, into one of her traveling gowns. Those gold coins would be her escape, her ransom from a life she had not chosen.

Thinking of the plan she had concocted the previous week, hope bloomed anew in her breast. She would wait for a night when the sentries had consumed an excess of the wine that her father always insisted on traveling with, then she would slip through the camp undetected, and make her way to a destination where no one would think to find her; Dareknay. Her father would never deduce that she would hide in the very country of her despised betrothed.

That was the magnificence of her plan. While everyone was occupied with searching for her, she would be under their very noses, laughing in triumph the whole time. Navali had thought of everything. She would succeed! She had to. Or her life would end tied to an ugly, mongrel beast of a prince.

What she could not foresee was that her father could be just as devious as she when needed. And he had great need at the present time. For he knew his daughter better than anyone, and was quite aware that she was unhappy, and if given half an opportunity would do something foolhardy and drastic to escape what he had commanded of her.

So he had acquired the services of a woman, a fierce-looking matron with ice in her gaze, and one with experience in this sort of situation. Mademoiselle Tabitha came with high recommendations from several of his most prominent lords, who had betrothed their daughters to men not of the girl's own choosing.

The initial requirement the woman had put forth upon her hiring was that a thick chain be secured around the center pole of his daughter's tent every night. When Avar had questioned her methods, she assured him the padded manacle that would be placed around his daughter's ankle as she slept would not chafe her skin, and was just an added deterrent should Navali attempt to flee in the night when everyone was asleep.

Naran now glanced from the corner of his eye over at his daughter as she sat rigidly against the seat, her face turned away from him and her eyes staring blindly out the window, and he swiftly decided the introductions between the two women could wait for a more opportune moment.

Navali's own thoughts at that precise instant would have been less than pleasing to her father if he could have somehow divined them. For the first time in all her twenty cales of life, she was coming to the realization that she was capable of hating someone with all of her heart. Her life was ruined!

Several hours later Navali had been completely apprised of their mysterious companion's occupation and been properly introduced to the woman her father had reportedly brought along to be her lady's maid. However, Navali knew the truth, the woman was more akin to a dungeon guard.

Her *dungeon guard to be exact*, Navali thought, her eyes assessing the tall, thick woman. She even looked the part with her hair scraped severely back from her forehead and secured at the nape of her neck in an unadorned bun, her gray gown so tightly laced in the bodice that the fabric could barely contain her more than generous midsection.

The woman's face had deep-set frigid blue eyes and her mouth was forever pinched into an unattractive frown, and Navali had been haughtily informed upon their meeting, from the woman's own lips no less, that her name was Tabitha. *Mademoiselle* Tabitha, to be precise.

Which Navali had secretly and swiftly altered to Tabitha the Terrible, as the woman continued to apprise her of exactly what would befall Navali's person if she ever dared to rebel. The riding crop the woman had flicked sharply against her own well-padded thigh had emphasized her malicious point.

The improvised disciplinary tool had snapped horribly in the silence as the woman had closed her fleshy lips, and Navali's father had just sat there, looking like he had not a care in the world. Not that he did at that precise moment.

No, it was Navali that would have to watch her step with this hawk-eyed woman.

The old crone was quickly turning into the princess's own personal nightmare. One that Navali was beginning to fear would never end, and this was only after several hours in the woman's abominable presence, and there were still several days left of journeying before they reached Chimea.

Navali had never met anyone so unpleasant as Tabitha, and she was quite certain she would have remembered if she had. For what was swiftly becoming annoyingly apparent was that the woman had no intention of removing herself from Navali's presence. Tabitha had succeeded so well in that regard that Navali had likened her to ticks on a dog; big blood-sucking ones. All the woman needed, in the princess' opinion, was a good pair of fangs and she would blend right in with the lot of them.

So Navali adjusted her plans of escape and moved the estimated time of her departure up to that very night, there was no way she would suffer that woman's presence for any longer than was absolutely necessary.

As her father finally called a halt to their travels, Navali quickly descended from the carriage and, under the guise of stretching her legs, walked about the clearing, seeking the most inconspicuous place to flee the encampment. Tabitha huffed along noisily beside her and Navali was certain it would not be too difficult a task to elude her. The woman was no champion of exercise and she informed Navali of that very fact.

"I don't see why 'tis necessary for us to walk the entire length of the clearing," Tabitha wheezed, grabbing one of her meaty sides as a cramp clamped down on the heretofore undiscovered muscle there.

"I'm just working the lethargy from my limbs," Navali supplied, her eyes espying the perfect spot to make her dash for freedom later in the evening. She abruptly turned to the heftily-figured woman, her intentions for this excursion fulfilled. "Shall we make our way back to my father?" She asked, hoping to curry the woman's kindly regard, if Tabitha were even capable of experiencing such a thing, and give her reason to believe Navali would not be mutinous of her father's edicts. "You appear to have received all of the benefits of our walk, mademoiselle, and I am currently famished for some of our cook's delightful creations."

"There is a cook journeying with us?" Tabitha inquired, her blue eyes not quite able to disguise her delight at the prospect.

"Of course," Navali replied. "My father wouldn't conceive of traversing the countryside without his most talented chef close at hand."

"Indeed," Tabitha declared eagerly, now setting her own hurried pace back to the center of camp. "I would presume no less from our most illustrious majesty. Don't dawdle now, 'tisn't at all good for your lethargy, you know." She swept the riding crop in a beckoning gesture and Navali hastened her stride.

"As you wish, mademoiselle." Navali nearly smirked at the woman's brisk canter towards the source of her one ultimate enjoyment.

Navali wouldn't begrudge the few moments she would be able to glean with her father's chief cook either. The hearty man was a kind, jolly soul, and one of the few non-Lynarians Navali had contact with. Eugene's easygoing comportment had a way of evoking the urge to smile, which she seldom permitted herself to indulge in, but nevertheless the sensation of the smile beneath her cool façade felt immeasurably pleasurable and she rarely missed a chance to benefit from either his culinary creations or his witty, lighthearted banter.

As the two women swiftly approached, Eugene lifted his attention from the pot of fragrant victuals he was stirring in a lazy manner, and quirked a grin at the princess. "That hungry are ye?" he asked, his brown eyes a-twinkle with mirth.

Navali parted her lips to give a quick retort and then felt the overly interested stare of the Lynarian woman beside her and reconsidered her response. "We could do with a bit of a biscuit to tide us over till the evening meal, Master Eugene. Though only if it isn't too much of an imposition."

Tabitha's eyes were now riveted on the burly hand the cook placed on the cover of a shallow pan beside the pot he was stirring, and Navali allowed a small smile to play along her lips to make recompense for not bantering with him.

Eugene winked in understanding, and raised a bemused brow at the woman who accompanied Navali. "Not a bit of an imposition, yer highness. Just so long as ye can recall everything I taught ye about makin' 'em."

Her appointed shadow's eyes widened in dismay as she stared at the fluffy biscuits the man displayed for her pleasure and then shot a quick look at Navali, clearly hoping the princess had not forgotten any instruction this man had allotted her.

"How could I forget, when you made me perform the service for fifty ravenous men?" Navali asked, recalling the adventuresome incident with puckish relish. It was one of the few times she had been permitted in the kitchens without a handmaiden to observe and report her every move and spoken word to her father, and it was also one of the few that she remembered ever letting herself act with such carefree abandon.

"Aye, they were indeed ravenous." Eugene chuckled at the memory. "Since they ate yer biscuits with nigh a complaint to be had amongst them." He stroked his stubbled chin contemplatively. "Though I've of a mind to believe it was more yer comely face and figure about the kitchens that had them gulpin' down biscuits as quick as ye could turn them out, rather than the burnt and doughy blobs ye managed to offer their bellies."

"Really, sir!" Tabitha rebuked sharply, her spine straightening with an almost audible crack. "I know you aren't a Lynarian and for that I'll forgive you your lack of proper comportment, but I cannot lightly dismiss the fact you just mentioned the princess' figure. And named it comely, no less!"

"I'm an unmarried man, woman. And not a bad looking one to boot, if I do say so meself." Eugene's eyebrows waggled at the rotund harpy and he rubbed one hand over his burgeoning stomach. "What did ye suspect I was; a monk?"

"Certainly not!" Tabitha blustered. "No one could consider *you* a chaste man!"

"Thank ye kindly, madam. But just so's we're clear on one matter, a man would have to be blind not to notice the charms of the princess. Aye—" He held up the spoon he had been employing in the victuals to forestall any more nonsense spewing from the woman. "That includes Lynarian men."

"Well, I never!" Tabitha flounced disgustedly, and peevishly spun away, completely meaning to forego the pleasures to be found in a hot, fresh biscuit if it were to be prepared by this sinful wretch. "Come along, your highness. We shan't spend another moment with this mealy-mouthed lecher!"

Eugene rolled his eyes at the woman's branding of what a lecher comprised of, and Navali gave him a brief smile of shared derision. "For what it's worth," she said very quietly as she passed alongside him. "I do recall everything you ever taught me."

His return smile was very gentle as he replied, "That's good, me dove, for there will come a time when yer man will want to thank yer instructor for it, and I very much want the reward he will bestow upon the man who shared such wondrous knowledge with ye."

Navali's eyes became pensive and her face smoothed into the cool visage that normally frequented there, and she dared not reply beyond a brief nod as she hurried to accompany her unwanted watchdog. There was no need for this man to be acquainted with the travails that were soon to befall her. It was better by far to let him believe that someday her husband would enjoy her cooking, rather than crush his merry misconceptions by informing him of the truth; that there was absolutely no way a savage like her future husband could ever come to appreciate the finer things of her culinary tutelage.

"You took a lengthy enough time in returning yourself to my presence," Tabitha criticized sharply as she swept aside the flap of the tent Navali and she were to occupy and waited for her charge to enter.

Navali grit her teeth in annoyance at the woman's shrewish tones. *Was it even possible that Tabitha was a true Lynarian?* "'Tis never my intention to leave someone without so much as a by-your-leave when I have not been insulted," she replied honestly and then bore witness to Tabitha's face turning an impossible shade of outraged purple. *Nay,* Navali thought as rage suffused the woman's jowly features, *there was not even a remote possibility of her being numbered among the Lynarians outwardly composed ranks.*

"If you had any sense in that pigeon-brain of yours, you would have been terribly incensed. That man was deliberately uncouth!" The lower-ranked woman sputtered, completely forgetting to whom who ranting was befalling.

"You forget yourself, Mademoiselle Tabitha!" Navali admonished tightly. "My father may have charged you in assuring him that I make it to Dareknay and my betrothed, but never make the assumption that bestowed you with the right to insult me as well."

"Your father gave me the right to see you chained to the center pole of this tent if I so chose!" The woman unwisely continued her tirade, and a sneer twisted her lips at what she perceived was the princess' arrogance towards her and she strove to break the younger woman's spirit as she had so many other young girls in her care. "And how will he enjoy hearing his daughter does not mind the bawdy ribaldry of his menial laborers? Do you think he will consider her a woman of loose character?"

Navali took one step closer to Tabitha, until they stood nearly nose to nose, and then spoke very gently and definably so that the woman could not misconstrue what she was about to say. "Never presume to threaten me again, mademoiselle, lest I take exception to your manner. My father may have given you permission to do with my person as you see fit, but he will never countenance abuse. Indeed, he has taken great pains to guarantee that I am able to dispose of any physical coercion that may come my way. Do you understand what I am implying?"

The once blazing blue pools of malice Navali had been staring steadfastly into cooled considerably at her words, and Tabitha blinked rapidly before backing away.

"I understand, your highness."

"Good, I would hate to have to lend credence to what I just explained." Navali found she almost wished the woman had given her sufficient cause to see her well and truly chastened. But that would have called more attention upon herself than Navali desired to attain and she let the incident pass, knowing full well, that though she may have won a battle, the war still raged on.

Later that evening, after they had partaken of their meal without any additional altercations occurring betwixt Tabitha and Eugene, the king bade them all seek their own pallets, unaware of the further tension that had arisen between Navali and her sleeping companion.

"Good eve, Navali," King Naran wished her and she halted her steps, turning to face him from where she had just been about to enter her temporary canvas dwelling.

"It could be, Father," she agreed, hoping to obtain his permission to sleep without the hated manacle that Tabitha had so eagerly expressed a desire to utilize. "If only … that is—I…."

"What is it, daughter?" he asked, uncertain as to why she was suddenly hesitant.

"I just cannot bear the thought of Mademoiselle Tabitha employing the use of such a harsh and unjust treatment as the shackle. Have I not complied with every order you have placed before me? Even if it is something I sincerely dread?" she asked, and observed him closely as he considered her logic.

"You have indeed, Navali." He dipped his head in a single nod of agreement. "I shall instruct the maidservant Tabitha to desist with the chain this eve."

"Thank you, Father."

"'Tis not I you need to thank, Navali. It is your own conduct which has decided the matter, and let that be a lesson to you. Now you know the importance of always comporting yourself with grace and serenity. Everything goes much smoother and more to your liking that way."

"'Twas a mere lapse of memory before, Father. I shall not soon forget." No, indeed she would not, as these words could very well be the last ever spoken between them. At that contemplation, Navali felt a sudden sadness wash over her, but it was quick to fade in the light of her realization that this could likely be her only opportunity to escape the monstrous marriage her sire had arranged for her.

In such short order that Navali was almost shocked at the rapidity with which it occurred, the camp grew quiet and still. The only sounds to be heard from within Navali's tent were those of Tabitha's evenly paced snores, and Navali quickly and silently changed into the dark cloth breeches she had acquired for this very occasion. Then, creeping carefully to the flap, she peered out into the scarcely lit night, her lips curving in a tiny satisfied smile at the landscape that was revealed before her.

If she could have hand-picked a more perfect eve to disappear she could not have chosen better. For a mist curled gently about the many tents and pallets of the camp, and the light of the stars and moon had been dampened by the thick clouds that encompassed the black sky. So much so, that Navali wanted to dance a celebratory jig at her good fortune. But she reined in the ridiculously frivolous urge and settled for merely slipping unnoticed through the shadows. There would be time to express her triumph later, after she had obtained her liberty.

Navali had nearly reached the protective cover of the woods when she sensed a presence behind her. She took off at a sprint, nearly able to taste the sweet brew of freedom now.

The sudden vicious sting of Tabitha's riding crop slicing painfully across her upper thigh caused Navali to stumble briefly, the very breeches she had so delighted in acquiring for this venture afforded her only the smallest measure of protection against the thin leather whip, and it felt as though lightning had been unleashed to blaze agony across her limb. But it was the woman's beefy hand seizing her arm that forced her to halt just a few feet from her woodland goal.

Navali barely stifled her initial cry of pain and then bit down hard on her bottom lip to still any whimpers that threatened to expose her anguish as the woman's strong, blunt fingers formed a manacle of flesh about her slender arm and delved deeply into her tender skin.

Hauling Navali back to her tent by way of the painful vise that comprised her grip, Tabitha then proceeded to clamp Navali's ankle into the padded shackle on the end of the thick chain that extended from the center support of their shelter.

"You were amply warned of what would be the consequence if you so chose to defy your father," the heavily-built woman reminded, standing triumphantly over Navali's seated form. "Did you think that I would not be fully prepared for just such an occurrence of rebellion?"

"I really couldn't say what I think of you, Tabitha. I'm sure it would be much too vividly colored for your delicate sensibilities."

"As you wish, your *high*ness." Tabitha smirked indelicately, putting paid to all of Navali's sarcasm. "And don't bother complaining of this incident to your father. He approved my methods ere he acquired my services."

"So you have gleefully informed me time and again, you shrewish old hag!" Navali partially arose from the ground, as a tigress would when stalking her prey, and the older woman took a cautionary step back in the face of her fury. "And if you ever contemplate for one moment loosening your vigilance of me, mademoiselle, remember my words prior to this event, and think long and hard on what could befall you if you ever dare to confront me alone again. For I will only underestimate you this once, and I never make the same blunder twice."

Tabitha did not need to reply to such an impassioned speech for her response was plainly written in her shock-widened eyes, and Navali promptly turned away and sank onto her pallet, hiding an involuntary wince as agony raced over her leg once again.

The pain was encompassing enough that Navali did not thereafter concern herself with Tabitha's actions. Instead she lay back on her furs and closed her eyes tightly against the tears that had arisen upon the sudden reflection of her recently failed attempt to liberate herself.

Though if the princess had cared to observe Tabitha at that precise instant, it would have perhaps lifted her spirits tremendously, for she would have been gratified to discover her promises of retribution had come to some form of fruition. As the elder woman now clutched her crop tightly to her ample chest as she lay watching Navali's every move from her own pallet. And, though it would have surprised her to discover it, Navali was the only one to experience any kind of slumber in their tent that eve, even if it was of the emotionally and physically exhausted variety.

CHAPTER THREE

A blaring of trumpets rent the misty night air as the Dareknay sentries atop the capital's battlements heralded the arrival of the Lynarian king and his daughter. The servants frenziedly moved about the castle as last minute activities and preparations were hastily concluded in their ambition to be the first to glimpse their high prince's betrothed.

A full fortnight had passed since that eve when King Avar had discussed the arrival of the Lynarian king, and Ashyre now stood stalwartly watching the procession of torches that dotted the darkened horizon like fallen stars as they ushered his fate ever closer.

Shyre, as he was known to his loved ones, raised one finely sculpted, muscled arm to rest against the frame of the leaded glass window of his chambers and, leaning his weight upon it, heaved a resigned sigh as he reflected on the imminent death of his bachelorhood.

Though some, if there had been any witnesses to the deed, would have likely attributed the release of breath to the mere thought of matrimony, it was not that which disturbed him as he had expected the event would likely befall him one day. But Shyre had not anticipated an arranged marriage. Instead, he had envisioned a loving union, the like of which his parents enjoyed. A union where each party was assured of their besotted regard being duly returned to them, not the frozen state of rigid matrimony he was currently promised with the unfeeling Lynarian as his bride.

But he would do as his honor and duty to his country dictated and meet his fate with nary a whisper of his desire for something more.

Apart from his twin, who was the only person to whom Shyre ever voiced his grievances as he carried no hope of ever keeping a confidence from him anyway, there was none other that would ever know of his roiling discontent with his present lot in life. At times the gift the twins had of reading each other's thoughts and feelings was a blessing and at other times a curse.

Today, it was a curse, Shyre decided.

He felt the air in his chamber stir as Ashtyn entered quietly and then closed the dark, heavy oaken door behind himself. Shyre did not bother to turn and greet him, but continued to stare pensively out the window.

His brother strode across the chamber to join him, glancing down to see what so enthralled his twin, and took note that the advance Lynarian scouts and ambassadors were presently riding across the drawbridge into the bailey beyond. Ashtyn did not utter a word to break the silence, nor did he intrude on Shyre's thoughts in any way as he waited patiently for his brother to confide in him.

"The ambassadors say she is particularly comely," Shyre stated. His green gaze never wavering from its fixed stare as the clear, blue waters of the moat reflected back the images of the Lynarians as they traversed the expanse.

"I've heard that as well," Ashtyn agreed, watching with his brother as one Lynarian scout, too young in Ashtyn's opinion to be given the responsibilities of a soldier, tripped over his own feet. The lad would have surely fallen to the dusty earth if not for the brawny hand that caught him securely by the clothing at the back of his neck and restored him gently to his feet. The young man gave King Avar's chief general, Ivan Titek, a brief nod of gratitude before joining the other scouts in tethering their mounts to a post that stood sentry outside the stable.

Studying the clumsy youth, the two identical men standing at the window above released guffaws of laughter as the young man's step indicated he was a little more sore from his saddle than was comfortable. Still grinning, the brothers turned away from the sight and looked at each other. A sudden thought gripped Shyre, one Ashtyn would never actually contemplate, but would give Shyre the opportunity to avail himself of a puckish pleasure.

"You know when we were younger and would play at switching places?" Shyre began. His brother nodded at him warily. "How 'bout it?" he asked flippantly, though only half jesting, his green gaze locked on Ashtyn's bright gold one as they widened incredulously.

"You can't be serious!" Ashtyn sputtered, before he caught the jest in his brother's voice, and a sly smile stretched across his face. "Don't tell me the Great Prince of our people is scared of one slip of a girl?" he goaded, feeling the need to lighten the tense ambivalence that had of late attached itself to his twin like a dark shadow, knowing as he did so, that Shyre did not need sympathy right now, indeed he needed a strong draft of ale and perhaps a swift kick to the arse. But the amount of liquor needed to dull his older brother's senses was vast, and Ashtyn felt it would not be the wisest of choices to present a drunken bridegroom, not to mention one who was loudly proclaiming that he had been recently walloped on the behind, to meet his future wife and her people. So that notion was out, leaving only his quick wit to distract his brother from his melancholy attitude.

"Ha!" Shyre rejoined bitingly. "You're a 'Great Prince of our people' as well. And there is nothing in the book of laws that states *I* have to be the one to marry that frigid princess."

"Whoa, hold up," Ashtyn commanded, wondering how he had just lost control of the formerly lighthearted atmosphere, and feeling a sudden need to be the voice of reason before his brother decided to venture down a rash course of action. "Just because her people do not show emotion doesn't mean they don't feel it," he stated wisely. "Those are but rumors. And besides, Shyre, when have you ever heard of a woman not being emotional?"

His brother raised a skeptical brow at his logic and Ashtyn overheard the thought that those had not been Lynarian women, before Shyre actually spoke it.

"All it takes is for them to see a brand new baby and they all tear up. Guaranteed," Ashtyn finished quickly, not adding that he felt it was more the ripeness that was oft to be found wafting about the little poo-makers that evoked the moisture in their eyes rather than anything else. No need to let his brother in on that contemplation.

"I heard it anyway," Shyre grumbled, giving his brother a wry glance.

"Doesn't matter if you overheard it or not," Ashtyn replied with an easy smile, now that he felt he had the situation back in hand. "You still have to marry her. The book of laws does state that the firstborn must marry first, and Shyre, I hate to be the bearer of bad news, but that's you. Not I—thank the good Lord." A relieved expression crossed his face. "Better you than me."

"Who cares about a law our senile ancestors put into account?" Shyre countered, a grimace crossing his face as he began pacing furiously.

"I care," his brother responded. "Immensely at the moment. I'm not going to let anyone saddle me with a wife yet, I'm far too young for *that* responsibility."

"If you're too young, what does that make me; ancient? Don't forget, I'm only six minutes your elder," Shyre pointed out defensively as he braced his feet apart and stood resolutely.

"Shyre, I'll have you know, that I am extremely grateful for those six minutes," Ashtyn said with a smile. "You have no idea *how* grateful."

"I think I can imagine," Shyre replied dryly as a brisk knock sounded on the chamber door.

"Enter," Shyre called out, giving his brother a last disgruntled look. The brothers then watched as their tawny-haired mother swung open the portal and gracefully swept into the room, before drawing to a halt in front of her eldest son.

"She's almost here," Queen Kalista said rather helplessly, her gold gaze riveted to her son's face, as Shyre grimaced slightly and turned away at her statement, walking swiftly to the window to look out into the torch-speckled darkness. Kalista felt nearly despondent. How she had so desired for her children to have the same happiness she and Avar had in their marriage, and she was now not in the least bit assured of that coming to fruition with Shyre. Not when he was marrying into the cold-hearted Lynarians.

Shyre had not spoken a word against the idea of marriage when the council had suggested an alliance between the two countries. Not that Kalista had really expected her son to pro-test his duty, but that might have been better than the awkward silence that would often befall their family in recent days when someone mentioned a comely maiden in Shyre's presence. The queen prayed they were doing the right thing.

When Shyre turned back to his mother and brother, his face reflected calmness once again, and Queen Kalista glanced worriedly at her second son, only receiving a perplexed shrug in reply. Apparently Shyre was not giving his brother any glimpses into his thoughts on the matter either.

"Shall we?" Shyre offered a forest-green, armor clad arm to his mother. But Kalista ignored it, instead wrapping her slender arms about his lean muscular frame, hugging him fiercely until he returned her embrace.

When his mother's hold loosened, Shyre gently set her from him, giving her a small grin of reassurance, as he slipped her bejeweled hand into the crook of his arm. He gestured faintly for Ashtyn to go before them and then straightened to his full height as they left his private chambers to traverse the wide stairway that led to the great hall, where the rest of their family converged upon them.

Adam was the first to give Shyre a reassuring clasp on the shoulder as he held little Kiriah securely in his left arm. She was sleepily playing with the thin braids mixed into his brother's long, thick blonde hair with one hand as she sucked the thumb on the other, and Shyre gave her a quick chuck under her chin to evoke a smile. The rest of Shyre's brothers repeated Adam's supportive gesture, their gazes quietly sympathetic, though to their credit they endeavored to disguise it behind rakish and outlandish grins.

Addison's slap on Shyre's shoulder was a little more enthusiastic than the rest, and sent him stumbling into his mother, who gave him a somewhat alarmed glance.

Shyre grinned sheepishly back at her in response as the royal family made their way out into the well-lit courtyard to await the arrival of the Lynarian king and his daughter.

A cold chill abruptly raced down Shyre's spine as the sound of screams swept through the open portcullis. The hair on the nape of his neck raised in apprehension as he and his brothers shifted their stances to stand protectively in front of their mother and younger sisters.

Navali shifted uncomfortably on the lavender squabs of the coach as their caravan neared Chimea, the capital city of Dareknay. Her time for escape had come and gone long ago, leaving her with no other alternative but to accept her defeat gracefully, a fact which her father would have been terribly pleased to hear, if Navali had been of half a mind to enlighten him to it.

The reason for her reticence reared its ugly head as she reflected on the thick silence that had descended between them and she firmly endeavored to forget, yet again, the night Mademoiselle Tabitha had left her mark on her upper thigh. Needless to say, after her *companion,* Navali applied the title loosely to the woman, spoke of the incident with her father, Navali had never been given the opportunity to flee again.

It was a wonder she was still breathing with how close her father and Tabitha had deemed was a safe distance to ensure she would not again try to evade her nuptials. The crone had even been given authorization by her father to see to the searching of Navali's chests of clothes and baubles. Where, upon discovering the princess' precious hoard of coins and confiscating them for herself, Tabitha had conveniently experienced a limited lapse of memory and failed to inform the king of them.

How she loathed them both! Navali thought sourly. *The smug sow,* and *her self-righteous father!*

While Navali silently railed against her father, King Naran sat stoically, deeply regretting acquiring the services of such a harpy as Mademoiselle Tabitha. His lament of his hasty decision had begun when he had been informed of the harrowing incident of his daughter's escape attempt, and how Tabitha's crop had left a large welt on Navali's delicate flesh.

Upon hearing this, Naran had needed to forcibly restrain himself from ordering the woman's flesh stripped from her own back with the selfsame whip. Instead, he had clenched his jaw tightly and turned his face away from his irate daughter, for his gaze would have surely given away the anguish he felt for having to go to such drastic lengths to guarantee her obedience. He could not have her thinking that she would always get her own way—even if she had received it for most of her life.

Reflecting that he had indeed spoiled her incredibly when she was little, he had firmly directed his line of vision out the coach's small side window. Where, staring out unseeingly at the passing scenery, he had proceeded to inform Navali that it was her own fault for attempting to disobey his edicts, and if that was not appalling enough, edicts that had been her king's as well.

The words had nearly strangled him as they left his throat, and he had felt the evil tyrant when his daughter had allowed her gaze to turn cold with hatred towards him.

Navali had briefly displayed rebellion and sullenness before, but she had never hated him with the intensity that flowed from her now. Naran was distinctly aware that once a person began down a particular path, it was best not to withdraw from it in the last legs of the journey. And so, Tabitha remained with the caravan, though Naran was careful to never let her alone with his daughter again.

How he wished they could turn back the hands of time and relive the moments when Navali had been his little princess and he had not had to contend with the debilitating matters that had arisen within his own race. They could not return to them though, and those happier and simpler times were far gone, swept away on the fickle winds of change. Navali would simply have to learn to comply with the hand fate had dealt her, just as he had needed to learn that lesson in his younger days as well. He sighed at what his world had come to, and desired, not for the first time, that Navali's mother were there to help raise their daughter.

His heart softened in his breast as he conjured an image of his wife in his mind's eye. Lily had been full of life, so like the young woman sitting across from him. A life that had been cruelly snuffed out far before her time.

She had been absolutely stunning, not only of face and figure, but of virtue, grace, and character. The young Naran he used to be had never met anyone like her. She had mystified him and drawn him like no other woman had before, and he had quickly fallen deeply in love with her.

Their feelings for each other were a clandestine adventure the two of them had shared, never letting another soul discern its existence. Naran's father, if he had ever found out about their emotions, would have had Lily declared a traitor of Lynaria and swiftly banished to some distant land, while his only son would have received a severe punishment for having the foolishness to indulge in such a flighty experience as love.

King Nigel had been a dark blight on the earth, one that fate had deemed fit to dispose of half a cale after Naran and Lily met. By that time, Naran had already determined he wanted the beautiful young woman to be his bride, and his father's timely demise could not have come too soon for the young couple.

They were wed on the next full moon and had been deliriously happy for the next nine cales. But neither one could have foreseen Lily catching the very epidemic she had fought so hard to eradicate in the Wanderers encampment.

She had died three days after coming into contact with the debilitating illness. And, though Naran had survived, his heart had never felt the same again.

Why Lily had insisted on helping those ill nomads that night he would never know. Why she could not have waited for one of the more skilled healers to come back from an outbreak and take care of them plagued him no end, even after the twelve cales that had passed since then.

King Naran promptly slammed the door shut on his memories before they could rise up and drown him as the coach lurched over a hump in the road and brought him abruptly back to his surroundings.

He fleetingly glanced over at his daughter, who now reminded him so much of his late wife as she sat motionless in the flickering glow of the lantern swinging gently from the ceiling, and he had to fight the impulse to order the driver to take them back to Lynaria. For despite all of her willfulness and present anger, he was going to miss her.

He felt old all of a sudden, and he had to force his shoulders to not slump against the back of the squabs in exhaustion. It would not do for Tabitha to glimpse the defeat washing over her king. Naran could not allow weakness to settle in now, he had to remain strong for his people, a steady presence they could always rely on. As King Naran composed his features once more into the mask he let the world see, he heard a mysterious rumbling noise above the thunder of the unicorns' hooves.

Forced to look around the broad woman sitting on his left to peer out the window that was partially concealed behind her, the king's eyes widened at what he beheld.

He lunged for his daughter, the swiftness of the oncoming threat giving him no time to shout a warning, and hastily crushed her beneath him on the floor of the coach, covering her body protectively with his own.

The screams that had reverberated through the bailey a moment before had barely ceased before a guard from the oncoming convoy rode hell-bent over the drawbridge, the hooves of his sweating horse clattering heavily against the wooden planks and its sides heaving with every panicked breath.

The Lynarian scouts rushed to subdue the frightened steed as the rider's white, blood-splattered form slid down the animal's side. He tottered forward a few paces on legs that barely held his weight and then fell heavily to his knees on the ground before the concerned King Avar.

"Ambush!" the rider cried, frantically pointing one fatigue-trembling arm through the gate and out into the foggy night.

"Who man? Who?" King Avar questioned as he grasped the man by the front of his shirt, and gave him a small shake to revive him.

"The Pitan!" The rider gasped, his eyes rolling back in his head as his body slumped in unconsciousness. The king swiftly lowered the man to the hard-packed earth of the courtyard.

"Fetch the healers," King Avar ordered one of the gawking servants who stood behind him as he straightened abruptly and hastened towards his sidestepping chestnut stallion.

"We ride!" he shouted, his sons and warriors already following his suit and racing towards their own steeds.

Shyre swore violently under his breath as he left his mother and sisters to their personal guardians who were rushing them back up the stone steps and into the castle. He vaulted into the saddle of his golden stallion, Swift Justice, in one fluid move.

He may not have desired to marry the Lynarian chit, but neither did he wish to see her in the hands of the marauding Pitan. No woman deserved to experience such a hideous ordeal as that, for that particular race were the embodiment of evil. The devil's spawn on earth.

The Pitan were known to practice ritual sacrifices on those they captured. First torturing their victims into a state of near madness, before securing them between two rabid, starving dogs on a raised platform. Then the demonic masses that had gathered watched in fascination as the screaming and bloodied being was torn to shreds. It took a very long time for the unfortunate captive to die. Their blood running from the raised stone slab in rivulets as the frenzied mob below frolicked in the red liquid to the accompaniment of the victim's screams and their own crazed chants.

To be fair though, not all of the Pitan race were demonic. The lower classes and slaves were rumored to be quite normal and sane. But under the higher-ranked individuals and their satanic king, Krinar, they did not have too many choices and privileges, and most were said to be starving.

Shyre had met a few good Pitan and many an evil one in his days as an elite Drocunian and he did not curry any hopes that those who had attacked the Lynarian caravan were simply desperate Pitan who were stealing because they were starving.

Nay, the multiple wounds and lacerations on the Lynarian rider bespoke the ghastly tale. These were the Pitan Elite-Horde, the worst of the men who obeyed King Krinar's rule, the ones who killed indiscriminately and in the most horrifying manner, their preferred method of destruction consisting of numerous small wounds that agonized and weakened their adversary until they begged for clemency or death. The Horde's absolute goal was the begging. The pleas for mercy excited them and made the fiery feeling of power streak through their veins.

As the Dareknay king and his Drocuns raced to defend the unemotional and cold Lynarians, Shyre felt sure the coming battle would not improve his standing in his betrothed's eyes.

The princess probably already believed him a wild beast, and if she saw the way the Drocuns fought, she would be almost justified in thinking him that way. His training was not conventional and, for the most part, though they fought honorably, the Drocuns were not afraid of resorting to trickery and dirty fighting to win the war.

That was something the Lynarians had never been able to understand or agree with, as they believed all things should be honorable and fair, even in times of war. And that was something Shyre could not stomach. Men did not prance about like priggish idiots trying to gauge where to land the best debilitating blow. They went onto the battlefield and came out victorious no matter the personal cost. Shyre expected to do no less tonight, and if by chance he managed to spark a tiny flicker of grateful feeling in the princess' cold Lynarian heart, that was just an additional benefit.

A few moments before the Dareknay men heard the alerting screams, a massive tree crashed down the hill next to the royal Lynarian coach and burst out of the shadowed foliage, slamming violently into the side of the elegant conveyance.

Chaos ensued as the coach tipped, rocking precariously up onto its two right wheels. Releasing the reins, the coachmen leapt free of their padded seat on top with a shout of panic. The lines then became entangled in the traces that imprisoned the unicorns to the dangerously listing conveyance, and the animals screamed in terror, hooves pawing at the ground for purchase.

Navali's own scream mingled with those of the unicorns as she felt, and heard, the impact of something large crash into the coach. Her father's body pressed heavily down on her and she grasped at his shirt with shaking fingers, seeking something to anchor herself to as her whole world tilted crazily to one side before righting itself with an agonizingly painful jolt.

She felt her sire's weight ease as he rose swiftly to his feet, and then felt his hands on her upper arms tugging her to a more upright position, her legs shaky and unsteady.

"Navali, are you all right?"

Though she heard her father's voice, the words barely registered, and it took a few moments before she finally managed to raggedly gasp that she was unhurt.

Then he was gone. Throwing open the still working door in the right wall of the coach, the king stepped down, demanding to know what had been the cause of the tree's descent.

Hearing a moan, Navali looked to where Mademoiselle Tabitha, looking dazed by the recent activities, sat crumpled on the floor. Though she acutely disliked her unwanted warden, she could not leave her in a heap before her feet.

She grasped the stout woman under her arms, and with their combined strength, managed to help hoist the maidservant to where she had been previously seated before she had been so rudely thrown to the floor.

"Thank you," Tabitha begrudgingly muttered, and then shrieked as she looked out the coach door King Naran had left open in his haste.

Her beady eyes widened with fright, and Navali spared a quick glance over her own shoulder as she saw the terror displayed in Tabitha's expression. Navali swiftly faced the gaping portal as her gaze filled with the unwelcome sight of dozens of half-naked men hurtling themselves out of the thick underbrush of the forest to attack her father's men.

Pitan!

Navali's ears rang with the harsh sounds that emitted from their attackers as the Pitans' jagged and dirtied swords and knives met the polished steel of the Lynarians' weapons, and she watched in horror as one lumbering savage caught sight of her from where she stood in the inky blackness of the coach.

A leering grin spread across the blackguard's craggy face, parting the matted hair of his coarse beard, and he gave a fierce bellow as he began making his way towards the glittering conveyance in the flickering torchlight.

A gleaming sword swung at the Pitan's head, but his stride remained unbroken as he swiftly dispatched the Lynarian soldier with ruthless ease, delivering numerous cuts and slices as he walked on. Blood dripped freely from his jagged blade and the malicious grin never disappeared from his lips as he moved with an unholy purpose to lessen the distance between himself and the coach door.

Navali realized then, as she was faced with an impending assault, that the only tool of defense she had at her disposal was the small stiletto blade strapped to the inside of her calf muscle. And she unquestionably did not want to allow the brute close enough to give her a chance to use the thin weapon. Navali spun on her heel, frantically searching the darkness for a weapon of some kind and, much to her despair, discovered none in the coach.

Returning to her place at the open door, she peered cautiously out, espying a fallen Lynarian soldier lying a fair distance away in the midst of the fighting. If she could get to the body before the huge brigand did, she would perhaps be able to use the sword still clutched in the dead man's armored hand.

As she quickly reconsidered the fact that the advancing man had just swatted off a Lynarian guard with no more effort than he would have given to squashing a mosquito, Navali swiftly abandoned the idea.

What she needed was a bow, and given the size of the beast bearing down on her, a few dozen arrows. But the time to find such a weapon had clearly dissipated as the Pitan placed one grimy paw against the outside of the coach and leaned into the interior. Navali rapidly backed up and tripped over her skirts as she did so, falling backwards to land on the narrow expanse of flooring in the coach.

The scent of his unwashed state struck her nostrils harshly and Tabitha began screeching hysterically from behind her. The brute spared not an ounce of acknowledgement to the ruckus the old crone was putting up. Instead, he grabbed at Navali as she shrank farther away from him, scratching and kicking at the offending appendage attempting to ensnare her.

"What do we 'ave 'ere?" He chuckled deep in his throat at her resistance. "Ah no, ya don't, li'l butterfly. Ye're mine naw," he said almost gently and beckoned to her.

At her refusal to obey him, he grew swiftly irritated. "Coome 'ere, Princess!" the blackguard barked, as he finally managed to snag one of her arms, pulling her body against his. Navali ineffectively kicked and hit at him as he manhandled her out of the dark interior to stand in the doorway of the conveyance where he could get a better look at her in the torchlight.

"They was right, ye're a tasty morsel o' flesh." He hefted her more tightly against him to still her struggles, and Navali gasped for air as her ribs compressed with the constriction of his arms. "Ye're a wench I'd kill ta 'ave." He ran one beefy paw down the side of her body, clearly delighting in the feel of her curves, and squeezed her buttock painfully as he leered at her. "Too bad they's got 'eir mind's set on 'aving ye fer themselves. But I'se can al'ays 'ope they'll let me take ya first fer my reward."

Navali's senses grew hazy from lack of oxygen as the mongrel yanked her off her feet and out into the open air of the night.

An arrow suddenly whistled past Navali's head and she could not help but flinch reflexively as it narrowly missed her ear and pierced the brigand's exposed throat. Blood spurted from the wound and a gurgling noise emitted from the man as he released his hold on Navali and fought desperately to rip the lethal shaft from his neck.

The huge Pitan fell to his knees as his chest heaved like a blacksmith's bellow to draw breath through his punctured larynx, then his torso met the ground with a sickening thud, his eyes widened in shock at his own death.

Gasping for air herself, Navali wavered as she spun around to face the archer who had shot the deadly missile, and met the burning gaze of her father.

"Navali, hie yourself inside the blasted coach, and shut the damn door!" He shouted down at her from where he stood stalwartly atop the coach. She froze at the harsh sound of his voice. *Her father never sounded like that!*

"Now!" her sire roared, when she did not move from her shocked stance, and then he raised his bow and aimed at a target behind her.

That commanding shout jolted Navali from her stationary trance and she did not again hesitate in obeying her father. Hurriedly gathering her skirts up, she sprinted for the relative safety of the dark interior she had previously occupied. Once inside, she slammed the door shut and fumbled with the small flimsy lock that wouldn't prove much of a deterrent for a determined boy much less a blood-lusting savage, before closing the curtains tightly over the windows for good measure.

Sitting heavily on the seat across from Tabitha, who was still shaking and moaning in the other corner, Navali pressed against the far wall, feeling the coldness from the hard surface invading her skin.

She would gladly freeze if it would forever banish the memory of that brigand's foul hands on her person. Shuddering at how close she had come to disaster, she swallowed hard at how helpless she had felt.

Navali had always thought—foolishly, she now realized—that she would be able to defend herself against anyone intent on causing her harm. But she had been mistaken—pitifully mistaken.

The Pitan's arms had easily encircled her torso, trapping her own against her sides, and stilling all of Navali's frantic attempts to free herself. The princess hated the fear that had coursed through her body when the man had her in his malicious grip, and tiny aftershocks of the emotion still sparked throughout her senses and she felt very fragile at the moment—almost as though she would break if someone touched her again.

She was weak. Even the thought made her cringe. Lynarian royalty were supposed to be strong and unconquerable. But that was not how she had felt with the brigand, and it was not how she was feeling now as she cowered in the dark corner of the coach. She had been weak, and the Pitan had proved it with how easily he had imprisoned her. Now, after she was free from that beast, she was weak with relief that she had been saved from a fate far worse than death.

Navali sat very still, listening to the blood roaring in her ears, trying to force herself into a state of calmness, and attempting to free her mind from those helpless, depressing thoughts. To do this, she concentrated on how her father had saved her and felt warmth bloom inside her, comforted with the knowledge that although she was at odds with her father, he would not let any harm come to her—not if it was within his power to stop it. If it was not, come what may, she would just have to defend herself.

Hiking up her silver skirts to reveal the black leather sheath strapped to her leg, she withdrew the long thin blade held securely to her calf and clutched it tightly within her grasp. She would not be so easily taken next time.

CHAPTER FOUR

H ellfire!" Shyre cursed under his breath, as he, his father, and the Drocuns rounded a crook in the road not a full mile from the castle, and were greeted by the sight of the few Lynarian soldiers that were still alive striving valiantly to protect what was once a sparkling coach pulled by four magnificent unicorns.

The sides of the conveyance were now blood-smeared, and the unicorns, frantic in their attempts to flee the battle, were screaming in fright and tossing their magnificent heads, their spiral horns gleaming scarlet in the faint light from the blood of those unfortunate enough to have stepped, or stumbled, too close.

Several dead bodies lay draped over the roof of the coach, arrows protruding from each white-clad form, as their blank, staring eyes reflected the battle taking place a few feet below them.

Forced to dismount as the overhead branches hindered their movements, the Drocuns rushed headlong into the fray of bloodthirsty Pitan, their broadswords flashing in the torchlight, serving death to those foolish enough to stand in their way.

Shrieks echoed from within the coach as one of the two Lynarian guards left defending the entrance of the conveyance was beheaded and a few of the savages rushed forward to wrench open the thinly wrought door.

Shyre glanced up at the sound, his sword dripping with blood from the man he had just delivered into the clutches of the underworld, to see the first burly savage reach into the dark cavern, only to be welcomed by the point of a knife thrust into his eye. The man did not even have time to scream as the knife met its mark. Dying instantly, he collapsed halfway into the portal, forcing his companions to drag his body out of the way before they shot a few barbed missiles into the entrance.

Several thuds and pain-strangled screams followed the action as more than a few of the arrows found their target. Shyre fought harder, his gaze barely wavering from its mark as the slavering Pitan dragged two inhabitants out and hurled them to the ground.

He noted one Pitan cruelly laugh as he caught the younger woman by her silvery blonde hair, his meaty hand twisting the woman's locks around his fist, and forcing her head back until he could steal a kiss.

Shyre, already intensely frustrated at his inability to reach the coach, beheaded his current adversary, only to have another hinder his way.

The woman, dressed in an elegant silver gown, bit down hard on her captor's smirking bottom lip and jerked free of his tight grasp as he drew back sharply.

Shyre saw, rather than heard, the woman gasp in pain as the arrow lodged in her shoulder hit the brute's massive chest as she shoved away. Blinding agony washed over her beautiful features as she went down hard on one knee, before forcing herself unsteadily to her feet and turning towards the shelter of the surrounding trees.

The diamond and pearl encrusted circlet on her head winked in the meager light as she glanced over her uninjured shoulder, her silver eyes suddenly clashing with his deep green ones.

Shyre knew at that moment she was his.

He wrenched his gaze from the escaping princess, only to see the Pitan man, his face contorted in pain and rage, recover from his shock at the female's audacity in time to reach out and snatch her fleeing form back against his gore-soiled chest. Shyre swiftly realized he would not be able to reach his betrothed in time to save her from the brute's wrath and released a piercing war cry, hoping to divert the savage's attention.

The blood-curdling sound faded ineffectively into the night as the sadistic man viciously grabbed the arrow protruding from the princess' flesh and twisted it, evilly yanking it from her slender shoulder. Princess Navali collapsed back against the monster, her silver eyes closing in unconsciousness.

Shyre reached them just as the burly Pitan slung his troublesome burden over the short pommel on the saddle of his mangy beast. The fiend deflected Shyre's sword with his war ax and, kicking the prince back with one giant foot, quickly mounted the horse behind the princess, spurring the creature to a gallop.

Before Shyre could regain his feet, the savage had disappeared into the foggy covering of the woods, ducking the hail of arrows the Dareknay warriors let loose on him.

The high prince whistled sharply for his stallion and Swift Justice galloped towards him. Shyre grabbed the reins as the animal reached him, and mounting on the run, urged the golden horse to greater speeds as he pursued the fleeing man into the woods. Dodging tree trunks and limbs, Shyre's eyes scanned the darkness, straining to glimpse the back of the huge man who rode swiftly away with the light-haired woman.

Crude horns suddenly blared from the pitch black of the forest, signaling retreat, and the Pitan began fading into the surrounding trees, many reaching a timely end afore they gained the sheltering foliage.

"Drive them from our lands, Drocuns!" King Avar shouted from atop his destrier as he brought the prancing animal back under control. "Make them rue this day above all others!"

Mounting their horses, the warriors rode into the covering of the trees, and each one reached behind his left shoulder to pull a piece of leather from its mooring, revealing a golden tattoo which the Dareknay women had carefully tapped into their flesh. The circular knot of lightning, branding the soldiers as Dareknay men, glowed brightly in the shadows. The mysterious light it emitted was visible only to their kinsmen's eyes, though the tattoo itself could be readily discerned by others not of their race.

The archers sprinted into the woods moments behind the horsemen, their aim careful as they searched for something that moved and did not bear their country's glowing symbol.

Aakin glanced over his shoulder at his twin, who was murmuring to the frightened unicorns. Aaron's smooth baritone calmed the animals' frayed nerves and his hands soothingly glided down their sweat-soaked necks as he sensed his brother's anxious gaze. His eyes met those concerned brown orbs and he bitingly, though silently, ordered, *Get your damned arse moving and chase those bloody savages to the underworld from whence they came!*

Just a might testy, are we? Aakin rejoined, as with a quick sarcastic salute, he took off for the forest, withdrawing his partially serrated sword as he and his mount were swallowed by the trees.

Aaron looked to his father as his brother disappeared from sight, and found King Avar's brown gaze locked on the figure several Drocuns were carefully lowering over the side of the elaborate coach. The man's brilliant blue cloak was heavy from the weight of the scarlet liquid staining the edges, and it caught on an embellishment jutting from the back of the coach.

One of the Drocuns cursed the frivolity of the conveyance ere he finally succeeded in his quest to see the blood-soaked material freed from the crystal spire. Lowering the older man the rest of the way, the Drocuns laid him gently on a travois rigged between two of the Dareknay war horses.

Aaron's attention abruptly returned to the reins he was holding as one of the unicorns began sidestepping, accidentally putting one of his hooves directly on top of Aaron's left foot. It hurt like hellfire and he swore vigorously under his breath.

"Blasted flighty creatures."

The unicorn looked at him from the corner of his eye, and Aaron was sure he glimpsed a mischievous intelligence there.

"*Beautiful*, flighty creatures," he quickly amended, and the majestic beast settled down once again, removing the offending hoof.

Shyre rode as if his very life depended upon it.

Though it was not his own, a life—that of the stunning princess who had fought so courageously to be free—*did* actually depend on it.

As his horse cantered through the trees, Shyre came upon a straggly, fleeing Pitan, whom he grabbed by the clothing at the back of the man's neck. The Pitan yelled curses at him and clawed at Shyre's hands, attempting to free himself from the fierce grasp that held him enslaved.

Shyre did not waste his precious moments trying to get information from the man, for he knew it was useless. One could not reason with a foul-smelling beast. Not one that would gladly see Shyre's head on a pike before he ever gave any truthful answer.

Instead, Shyre grasped the clothing harder, then flung the man head first into a sturdy tree as he kept his stallion's speed at a breakneck gallop. There was a resounding crack as the Pitan's hard skull struck the intended target before he slumped lifeless against the thick trunk, his sightless eyes staring after the prince.

Shyre disposed of several other Elite-Horde in the same fashion as he raced through the woods and then along the edge of a steep cliff that led to the only bridge into Pitan territory. The stallion thundered on and he ducked low over the animal's neck, avoiding the low-lying limbs that reached over the cliff's edge and attempted to unhorse him.

The Dareknay border buttressed the Pitan lands, and a long chasm ran the length of it. In the past, there had been several stone bridges spanning the distance, but now there was only the one bridge left standing to cross that deep ravine, and Shyre had to reach it ere that filthy Pitan carried *his* princess over.

Though the marauding Elite-Horde had never dared set foot on their land since the time of Shyre's great, great grandfather, apparently they had now deemed the risk well worth the price of the lives they had lost this night, and Shyre wondered briefly what they hoped to gain by such a rash action. But all thoughts, save vengeance, fled as he caught sight of one burly man making his way gingerly across the crumbling stone bridge. For slung over one beefy shoulder was the burden Shyre had been so frantically searching for.

A burden that was swiftly changing into something far more desirous for him than a woman he would simply have to marry for the sake of his duty to his country. For, after watching her valiant struggle with a man twice her size, he thought she could not be all ice, that there must be some fire inside her as well.

That contemplation began to override his discontented feelings about his upcoming nuptials, and he actually felt some anticipation at the prospect, now that he had seen some spark of life in a face he had not thought would be expressive. Perhaps there was hope for a happy marriage and life together after all.

He abruptly brought his mind back to the task at hand. They would not be enjoying any type of life together if those bastards tortured and sacrificed her like they did their other victims.

He jumped from his destrier as Swift Justice started to slow, a slight limp becoming known as one of his horseshoes clanked loosely against the rocks. Shyre could not spare any thought on that now and barely glanced at his enemy's winded nag that had been ridden to near death and then abandoned at the edge of the ravine. Stepping onto the decrepit bridge, he withdrew his sword from the jewel-studded leather sheath at his side, and stalked cautiously towards the man picking his way across the expanse.

Suddenly, seemingly out of the very trees, a hail of barbed arrows began raining down on Shyre from the foggy, gray dawn on the far side of the ravine. He ducked and then rolled to the side, forced to seek sanctuary behind the only sheltering refuge to be had, a small wagon that had been abandoned to the elements of nature long ago.

He lent very little thought to the previous owner, except when he became conscious that he was practically lying on what remained of the man, and that a Pitan dagger protruded from the right eye of the skull.

Those dogs, he thought, as he scrunched his shoulder farther out of the path an arrow had recently taken. It barely missed sinking its poisoned, barbed teeth into his flesh, and he cursed his lack of a longbow to return a volley of his own arrows.

Those cowardly, sniveling dogs!

Shyre was condemned to watch, like a desperate prisoner in a dungeon cell watched his last hope of salvation depart, as the evil berserker who carried the princess finished his trek across the bridge, to be welcomed by a small army of Pitan Regulars, who waited on the far side to take charge of his valuable cargo.

Once the princess was transferred to one of the soldiers riding a mangy-looking horse, the apparent leader of the band signaled his men down a faint path leading farther into their malevolent lands.

The arrows clattering down around Shyre were not showing any tendencies to slow or halt in the near future and he began wondering how long he could lie there with the smell of the rotting corpse beneath him.

"Mayhap I should just say a quick prayer and make a run for it," he muttered to himself and shifted his weight again, attempting to hold his breath as long as possible to give his sense of smell a relief from the putrid stench.

"But that would only result in your being employed as target practice for the Pitan, and we can't have our mighty prince end his magnificent existence in such an inglorious manner." Shyre suddenly heard his twin brother call to him from where he, several Drocuns, and most of his other brothers were standing behind the shelter of some trees on the ravine's edge.

"Then hasten yourself, Ash. Lest I expire in that manner afore you kill even one of the bastards," Shyre retorted back and then jerked and cursed as an arrow embedded itself into the leather of his breeches, causing fire to race up his leg as the teeth of the sharp tip punctured the flesh of his thigh. Shyre grasped the shaft and removed the Pitan arrow. His brother had better make haste, those bungling savages' aim was improving!

"Ruin all the enjoyment of coming to your rescue, why don't you?" Ashtyn called lightly, despite the urgency of the situation, from where he was standing safely behind a tree and notching his own arrow. "You need to realize this is an adventure we rarely get to experience," he continued tightly as he whipped from behind his cover and aimed, letting loose his poisoned harbinger of death. He was almost instantaneously rewarded for his efforts by a piercing shriek and a crashing sound as the unlucky offender dropped from a branch high up in a tree on the far side, his body flopping to the ground like a dropped ragdoll.

"Well, if I left you all ample enough time to fully enjoy it, I would be stuck here till doomsday and back again!" Shyre rejoined bitingly, glaring back at him from underneath the cart.

"Fire all!" His brother yelled at that very moment. *Most likely not even hearing his comment,* Shyre long-sufferingly thought. His twin did that to him sometimes.

His father's men quickly vanquished the enemy archers, who had far less success with their short bows and inaccurate aim. Meticulous warfare and disciplined practice was never a Pitan strong suit, slashing and hacking was more to their liking, and they fell like leaves before a strong breeze against the Dareknay's superior methods.

"The least you could say is thank you for saving your worthless hide," Ashtyn said, grumbling good-naturedly as he strode confidently across the bridge shortly after the volley of arrows had ceased. He lent his strength to helping his brother pull himself up from beneath the rickety cart.

"Thank you for saving my arse. Was it as enjoyable as you thought it would be?" Shyre asked, rolling his eyes at his brother's unserious attitude in the face of danger, as he accepted the assistance. Though Ashtyn was only trying to lighten the atmosphere of darkness surrounding them, the attempt was not extending far enough to allow Shyre even a small reprieve from his worry and agitation for his intended bride.

Ashtyn fingered the torn leather of his twin's breeches, as Shyre brushed debris from his chest and arms, and then probed the skin around the long gash left by the Pitan arrow.

"Cease!" Shyre wrenched his stinging leg away from his brother's less-than-gentle hand.

"You need a few stitches back at the castle. As well as a healer to remove the poison that was in that arrowhead," Ashtyn informed his now scowling brother.

"It's naught but a scratch," Shyre replied carelessly, though he could already feel the poison's effect and knew he would have to do as his brother advised.

"Stephen!" he abruptly called to one of the Drocuns that had come to his rescue. The young man quickly loped to the high prince's side.

"Yes, my lord?" he inquired.

"Take two men and track those accursed Pitan, I'll be following as soon as I can so be sure to leave a trail," Shyre ordered, and the man nodded in response before moving to do as he was bid.

"I hope your bride is not bothered overmuch by the appearance of scars," Addison commented to his elder brother as he walked across the crumbling stonework and cast a discerning eye over Shyre. "You're going to have more than a few after tonight," he observed.

"If they do disturb her, she'll quickly learn to appreciate them. After all, he received some of those scars on her behalf," his twin, Adam, stated in defense of his eldest brother as he joined the growing group of brothers standing on the bridge.

"You lads don't know the first thing about the female gender, do you?" Aakin asked with a chiding shake of his head as he approached Addison from behind and then ducked the backhand the larger man aimed at him.

"Enough, let's get back to the matter at hand, shall we?" Shyre quickly brought the conversation back to order before the three could engage in a competitive bout of fisticuffs or verbal jousting.

"My betrothed's wellbeing is my responsibility. But I request that some of you join me in seeing her safely returned to our lands," Shyre paused, and with a glance at Ashtyn finished. "It is your choice what you do."

"You don't even have to ask." Was Ashtyn's way of stating his intention to go. "Nothing could keep me away." His golden eyes lit with the excitement of an adventure and the promise to strike back at the people who had dared to bring warfare to his beloved country.

Shyre looked to the two blonde giants standing to his left, and they both nodded simultaneously. His eyes then found those of his youngest brother's, who had just changed his eye color from brown to the same green as the stare now directed at him. "We go as well," Aakin spoke for himself and his twin. "And Aaron says he'll thrash you in the lists for even daring to think we'd not join in on the excitement."

"He can try," Shyre said, accepting the challenge. "I don't know how much excitement there will be, but I'm sure if there is any to be had, you two will find it."

His demeanor changed to one of all seriousness as a bout of nausea swept through him from the poison making its way through his bloodstream. He took a deep breath to clear his head and braced himself with an arm on his stallion's saddle, a squire having fetched the animal a moment before. He placed his boot in the stirrup and then swung himself atop the horse.

"Mount up."

King Avar paced before the mammoth-sized fireplace in the great hall as he awaited his sons return from their hurried preparations for the dangerous journey into Pitan territory, clenching his hands together behind his back as he reflected on how his firstborn had been wounded.

By the time his sons had reached Chimea, Shyre's face had been pale and drawn, his jaw clenched tightly as his breath labored in his chest from the poison wreaking havoc throughout his body. The only way he had even managed to ascend the massive stone steps without weaving unsteadily had been with the help of his twin. And now, just as soon as the healers declared Shyre fit enough to ride his stallion without doing himself further harm, he would be venturing into one of the most unpredictable countries on all of Yria.

The Pitan region was literally unexplored by anyone other than the natives of that ghastly country and Avar was loathe to send any of his people there, much less his own flesh and blood.

The lands themselves were not causing the king's vexation. For, from what could be seen from the Dareknay side of the border, they were beautiful. Mountains covered in verdant green forests were rampant and the twinkle of blue light in the midst of those trees promised fresh water.

It was the *inhabitants* of those lands that had the Dareknay king gritting his teeth in frustration. He yearned to accompany his sons to assure himself they would be safe, but it was impossible for him to leave his country after what had befallen the Lynarians. His people needed their king near to feel secure, not venturing into the unknown. Resting his right hand on the mantle in consternation, Avar leaned closer to the warmth of the fire and stared deeply into the flames.

A discreet cough echoed from the doorway, bringing him back to the moment at hand, and he glanced up from his study of the hypnotic glow of the fire to find his chief general standing in the portal.

Ivan Titek, a mountain of a man with long brown hair and a full beard, had been by Avar's side for as long as he could remember. They had grown up together, fighting imaginary dragons and pirates as boys, and as young men racing their horses against one another and chasing after every pretty woman in sight.

They were yet young men serving in the Drocun ranks, when their friendship had first been put to the test. Avar's elder twin brother was discovered in his chambers with his throat cut, leaving him the sole heir to the throne and therefore ineligible to retain his status of simple Drocunian.

The camaraderie he shared with Ivan was what saw Avar through that bleak ordeal, and shortly thereafter Avar met Kalista and Ivan his Portia, and the two couples had married within the cale. But where Kalista delivered twins the following winter, it was many cales afore the other couple were overjoyed to welcome their only child, a daughter, Livai, into the world.

Livai had been a very sweet and beautiful little tomboy. She played with Aaron and Aakin, the boys closest in age to her at three cales her senior, as they ran after their elder brothers and mimicked their actions. Though she was very petite, she had possessed a determination and drive that allowed her to keep up with the boys' much longer legs, and she followed them everywhere, to the stables, the practice yard, even the docks.

Everywhere, in fact, a young lady should not be. But that did not faze Livai, for she simply dressed herself in breeches, cut her red curls so they were cropped close to her head, and staunchly followed the boys anyway, much to her mother's chagrin. All the while, her father merely shook his head in affection at her antics and let her do as she pleased.

No one could deny her anything she desired.

Then one day, on her fifteenth birthday, as she and the boys were racing their thoroughbreds across the sandy beach at sunset, while their parents waited back at the castle for their return so they could celebrate with cake and gifts, she was taken from them.

Aaron's black stallion had been thundering down the beach, neck and neck with Livai's own red gelding, when out of the sand arose three figures. One struck Aaron from his horse and proceeded to strangle the prince, using his superior girth to hold Aaron down as he struggled valiantly to free himself and protect Livai.

The petite firebrand was screaming in fear for her life and Aaron's, as the other two men dragged her into the thick underbrush of the forest that lined the beach. Aaron's last glimpse of her was of her captors snapping shackles over her slim wrists and throwing her over a horse. Just as blackness consumed his senses, his brothers rode back around the bend to see what was keeping Aaron and Livai.

When Aaron awoke four days later, King Avar told him what had happened after he lost consciousness. Shyre had jumped from his horse at the sight of his brother being strangled and had dragged the man away, beating the brigand until his hands were so bruised and cut from hitting him that the pain had finally driven Shyre back to his senses. It was not until then that Shyre noticed the man lie still and unmoving, and that he had killed him in his rage at the evilness of his actions in attacking two unarmed youths.

Shyre had profusely apologized to Aaron after he awoke, but the lines and dark circles beneath Shyre's eyes for many days after the attack attested to the fact of how truly distraught he was for not protecting them. Aaron had forgiven his brother without hesitation, for he knew it had not been Shyre's fault the men had assaulted them on the beach and abducted Livai.

Avar thought of Aaron now and how he had chosen not to speak for many moons after Livai had been taken, opting instead to let his twin act as his voice. Aaron telling Aakin in their own way of silent communication what to say in all of the conversations he was forced to participate in.

Livai's mother, Portia, had never been the same since her daughter was lost to her. After the incident, she never left her room and never acknowledged another person's presence. She just retreated from the world and sat gazing out the window in her chambers awaiting her daughter's return. No amount of persuasion could coax her to rejoin the land of the living. Six cales later she still had not uttered a single word, not even to her husband.

General Ivan had insisted on going with the search party, where he sought Livai's abductors with frenzied determination. Two days later and twelve miles from the Pitan border, the searchers chanced upon a bloody campsite deep in the forest, where it was obvious by the deep finger marks in the earth, dried dark blood, and the human hair left behind, that a prisoner had been staked to the ground and cruelly tortured.

A crude shallow grave sat close to where a small campfire still simmered with a tiny plume of smoke.

King Avar had ordered his men to dig up the body, trying to force his friend to look away as they uncovered the remains. But the distraught father could not be forced or ordered to look away, and Avar had been helpless to watch as horror overcame the other man's expression when the soldiers digging uncovered a woman's body.

It had been impossible for anyone to tell by the woman's face or garments if she had been Livai. The remains had been burned beyond all recognition and all that remained to identify her was the tiny gold-flowered necklace around her neck. The same necklace that Livai's parents had gifted her with when she had awoken on her birthday just two days past.

Ivan had been inconsolable. He believed he should have been more firm with her, should have ordered her to stay at the castle and act like a lady, never leaving the grounds unless accompanied by an armed guard. The man had searched in vain for her killers ever since, the only way he had to identify them being a small eating dagger carved with Pitan inscriptions.

General Titek had hated the Pitan with a rage that was unsurpassed and ever increasing since that day.

Now, looking at the burly man striding over to where he was standing, Avar knew, that except for their friendship and trust, nothing was as it had once been. Rage and regret simmered between them, and though the anger was never directed at each other, it changed their relationship.

His friend knelt on one knee before him, even though Avar had long ago forbidden Ivan to ever bow down to him. The king knew what was coming next, that his childhood friend had come to ask permission to join the small band that was venturing into his despised enemy's lands.

He also knew that even if he did not grant the man his request, the general would go without it. Nothing would stop him from seeking his revenge. The king did not even wait for the other man to utter his petition.

"You know I cannot deny your unspoken request. You may go. My only regret is that I cannot join you, my friend, on your quest for vengeance." He watched the other man rise with obvious relief. He knew Ivan had thought he would be forbidden from going.

The king continued, looking pensively into the fire again. "But I have a request of my own. I need you to watch over my sons. See to it they make wise decisions, and bring them back to their mother." He sighed deeply. "And myself … safely."

"With my life," Ivan replied simply to his king's request and nodded his head with conviction.

King Avar straightened to his full height at the man's words, then turned to face the general. "Very well, we shall not discuss this again. Are you ready to depart? The men will be leaving shortly."

Ivan Titek's brown eyes were intense, the rage revealed there barely leashed. "I've been ready since I first had word of the attack. I knew Dareknay would retaliate on such a gruesome assault."

As Ivan finished speaking, the king's sons arrived to seek their father's blessing on their forthcoming journey. Their mother trailed slowly after them with a handkerchief clenched tightly in one fist, her eyes suspiciously moist, and the tip of her dainty nose red.

"Father," Shyre said fondly, as he slowly and carefully crossed the room to shake his father's hand, his knees still a bit unsteady from the lingering effects of the poison.

The older man used his son's hand to pull him into a warm embrace. "Stay safe, my son. Protect your brothers." The king spoke low so he would not be overheard by the others.

"You know I will." Shyre let go of his father and then asked, "Was King Naran indeed traveling with the entourage?" Shyre had not taken much note of anything else that was occurring in the battle, as his whole being had been consumed with reaching his betrothed before she was abducted.

"Aye, we found him on top of the coach. He's still alive, but we had to rig a travois to bring him here," the king stated. "We have our finest healers caring for him, though they are unsure if they can bring him back from the darkness that claims him."

King Avar contemplated his own words as he continued with his explanation of the Lynarian king's wounds. "He took two arrows, one to his left shoulder and the other to his abdomen, and his right temple took a blow from the handle of a Pitan war-axe. For some unnamed reason the mongrels weren't trying to kill him, just maim the man. The other woman in their convoy was not so fortunate. She took her last breaths ere we entered Chimea's gates."

Shyre did not know anything of the other woman, but he certainly did not relish the idea of informing his future bride of the disturbing news that the woman had been killed. A thought

struck him suddenly as he contemplated that at least he would
not be bearing news of the Lynarian king's death as well as the
woman's.

"Father, *why* would the Pitan not want the Lynarian king
dead? He was their fiercest enemy. The Pitan are always at war
with the Lynarians," Shyre waited as the older man formulated
a reply.

"I'm not certain as to why they would do such a disadvanta-
geous thing as to keep him alive. The only reasoning I can think
of, and the thing that concerns me most, is that perhaps the
deaths of the Lynarians weren't what those bastards were after.
Mayhap abducting the princess was their foremost intention, along
with getting us to follow them to the border. After all, they did
retreat as soon as they had her in their clutches and there were
archers waiting in the trees to slay you. It's possible they want
us to retaliate. Though I do not know the why of it." The king
shook his head in confusion. "Not yet anyway."

"Perhaps I'll discover their intentions while I'm there," Shyre
suggested.

"But not if it costs your life," the king stated firmly as he
peered at his son from beneath drawn brows.

"Not if it costs my life," Shyre agreed with him and nodded,
a small grin on his face at the protectiveness of his father. "Don't
be troubled though, I'll not fall so easily into their traps again.
I'll keep my wits about me."

"See that you do." The king gave him that last command with
another stern look as he moved to bid farewell to his other sons.

Shyre watched his father as he embraced Ashtyn, and then
looked towards his mother who was holding Aaron and Aakin,
her youngest sons, close to her in a fierce hug. He knew how
hard it was going to be for his mother to bid farewell to them
all when she knew they were venturing into certain danger. His
assumptions were proven correct when she met his eyes over the
top of Aakin's shoulders and then glanced swiftly away.

Nevertheless, in that brief glimpse, Shyre still caught the glitter of tears in her golden eyes. He wished he could reassure his mother that everything was going to be all right, but he did not have enough time to do so now.

There was the pitter patter of tiny feet in the hallway, and moments later three little heads peeked into the great hall.

"What are you three doing out of bed so late? Didn't your mother already tuck you in?" King Avar inquired, striving to look stern with his three youngest, but failing miserably. He knew his daughters were worried about their brothers, and he did not have the heart to order them back to their beds.

He looked at his wife for any suggestions on what he should do, but she only shrugged at him in reply. He sighed. "Come in, girls, and wish your brothers farewell."

He watched his youngest offspring run into the room and vault themselves into Ashtyn and Adam's waiting arms. They were the closest to the double doors and wasted no time in hugging the little girls close and kissing their baby-soft cheeks.

Avar observed his eldest daughter as she came to stand before him without wishing anyone good-bye. She had her head tilted to avoid his gaze and he could not see her face, and he waited patiently for her to find the words she was so obviously looking for.

"I'm sorry, papa," Kyturah began, and finally raised her eyes to meet his. He saw tears pooling in her blue-violet gaze and thought his heart would break at the sight of them. Kyturah did not cry very easily, but when she did, she always had a good reason.

"Thinking of them being gone, I just couldn't go to sleep. What if they are wounded and we're not there?" Her voice hitched, and she glanced away, blinking back tears, before lifting her eyes to his once more. "Who will take care of them?"

Kyturah was not really searching for a response to these questions at the moment and continued before her father could give her an answer. "I *needed* to be here to see them off. You understand, don't you, Papa?"

"I do indeed, little one. I do indeed." King Avar opened his arms to his daughter and she stepped into them, her head coming to rest trustingly on his wide chest. He held her close and whispered, "General Titek will take very good care of your brothers. No harm can come to them without having to go through him first," he assured her.

He tilted his head to be able to look at her face again and was relieved all signs of tears had vanished. Kyturah was the strongest willed of his daughters and he knew she would be fine as she moved away from his embrace, her eyes now shrewdly assessing the general. Avar hoped she came to the conclusion that the older man was worthy of the job before him, for it would set her mind at ease.

The other two little girls had finished their good-byes, including General Titek in their hugs and farewell wishes and both were now requiring his attention. Turning to them, he scooped each girl up in one arm, and smiled at their precious faces as they wearily laid their heads against his shoulders. Avar felt his wife place her hand on his back and he turned slightly to look back at her.

Queen Kalista gave him such a teary-eyed look of love that his breath caught, and he wished they were alone so he could wrap her in his arms and hold her close for as long as she needed. That would have to wait, he realized, as he saw Kyturah give a last hug to Adam, smiling hugely and giggling softly at whatever he whispered into her ear.

His sons then left the great hall to enter the bailey where their horses awaited them, and King Avar thought this arranged marriage was beginning to be more troublesome than it was worth. *All this, just for a few more trade routes,* he reflected disgustedly, then felt guilty at the unkind thought. The poor girl promised to Ashyre was in the arms of merciless, demonic butchers, and all he desired was for his sons to not have to travel into danger to save her. Avar felt like a complete arse after admitting that to himself.

Sometimes he detested being king. He would love to be selfish and just send word to the Lynarians and let them worry about recovering their princess, while keep his elder children safely near Chimea where he could watch over them.

Avar did not know it then, but his wife's thoughts closely mirrored his own and she had to strive to keep her composure as the royal family walked out into the courtyard and looked on as the men who were going on the journey swung onto the light riding saddles strapped to their impatiently prancing horses.

Shyre took a last look at his parents and sisters standing on the steps in front of the convoy of men about to depart, and sighed. He ardently wished that the previous evening had turned out differently. He would far prefer to now be wed to a beautiful, unemotional stranger than to have had, instead, the tragedy that had taken place.

Glancing to the east, where the sun was steadily climbing over the tops of the mountain range, he felt tired. He had not realized how exhausted he actually was until he had mounted his freshly shod stallion a moment before. Having to swing his leg over Justice's back had reminded him of the poisonous wound he had received and even more of when he had last slept.

The adrenaline rush of battle was wearing off, to be replaced with a steadfast determination to see this mission end as soon as possible. With that same determination driving him, he straightened in the saddle and signaled with a raised hand for his troops to depart.

They were going hunting for dogs. The breed that walked on two legs.

CHAPTER FIVE

Navali barely stifled a whimper of pain as she awoke. Her head was dangling in an uncomfortable position and it pounded fiercely with the blood that had rushed to it, while her entire body jostled with the movement of the horse she found herself presently slung over.

Hearing the sounds of rough voices and base cursing, Navali forced herself to lie still. She did not want to alert the men surrounding her that she was aware of what was going on. Though she fervently prayed they would call a halt soon and remove her from her downward position on the horse, else she was liable to be sick all down the side of the already miserable creature.

The man seated in the saddle behind her unexpectedly shifted his weight in the stirrups, and ran a desiring hand freely over her rounded bottom.

The swine! Navali thought furiously, wishing the soldier would suddenly keel over dead. She did not dare move even a single muscle, as the brigand left his hand on her rear after he had stopped his vile stroking. She turned her head slowly away so that no one would see her grimace of revulsion, and her nose pressed against the coat of the horse. The smell of the beast, combined with the small pommel of the saddle she painfully lay over, made her want to retch, and she breathed shallowly through her mouth to prevent such an occurrence from happening.

The horse beneath Navali suddenly stumbled and the man behind her cursed as he removed his offensive touch from her person and grabbed the reins with both hands. Navali could not bite back the cry of pain that left her throat as the smelly beast tripped over a stone. She thought he, for at her angle she could undeniably identify the animal as male, was the most clod-footed beast she had ever had the misfortune to ride.

Not that she was exactly riding in the conventional manner! she thought with disgust. Her bottom was up in the air for all to see and the oaf who sat in the saddle kept rubbing it and laughing lewdly as he realized she was conscious.

The men surrounding them on similarly mangy animals began making crass comments and suggestions, and Navali's face flushed at their words. She had never been subjected to such foul language in all her life!

One of the brutes went so far as to ride closer and grab her hair in his fist, forcing her head up so that he could leer into her face. "Lookit how she's blushin', mates. Do ye think that's cause we're such a 'andsome lot?" He asked, his eyes dancing evilly.

The blackguard let go of her hair as his horse shied away, and Navali was thankful he had, ere she was forced to add several bald spots to the list of damages wrought to her person at the Pitans hands. Though she was not entirely certain she did not already possess any from his rough handling of a moment before.

"Methinks a kiss from a prop'r man could rosy up her cheeks just as much as the sight o' yer pretty faces. An' we all ken it's gotta be better'n what she's been gettin' from those cold fish lips o' her countrymen," the brigand's voice continued, and Navali felt panic suffuse her being. It was swiftly sinking in that the outcome to this conversation was not going to be to her liking.

"Who wants ta be th' first ta teach the fancy wench 'ow to kiss a man prop'r like?"

The men pressed forward, their voices' raising in excitement, as they all gleefully imagined the prospect of having the princess at their mercy for even a few moments. The ruffian who had so odiously suggested the kiss in the first place laughed at them, and then imperiously selected a hoary man of medium build from the crowd.

"Ye gets to be th'one!"

Navali's stomach dropped in dread at the same time her gorge rose as the man chosen for the task of 'instructing' her urged his horse closer to where she was held captive. He grabbed her hair in one hand and then grasped her chin harshly in the other, raising her body just enough to be able to reach her lips.

"Nay!" Navali cried, scratching at the wrist that held her jaw with one hand, as she turned her head this way and that to evade the man's repulsive intentions.

Laughter erupted from the gathered men as they watched her struggle desperately to avoid her fate.

"Ere now, stop that!" The hoary man ordered and, when she did not, slammed his fist into the side of her head.

The world whirled crazily about Navali as a sense of surrealism raced over her, and she lay stunned as the man's lips closed over her mouth and his odious breath washed over her face. The feel of his wet lips crushing her own had barely penetrated the enveloping fog in her mind, before the disgusting deed was done and Navali slumped to hang limply over the horse as the man finally released her.

Navali's wits slowly returned to her and at that moment, she hated men. All men.

Loathed them with a single-minded devotion as she had never despised a single thing in her entire life. Though Mademoiselle Tabitha ran a close second, and Navali was only all too thankful that woman was not there to make her life any more miserable than it already was. At least Navali fervently hoped the hefty heifer was not there. But she had not glimpsed another woman in this motley group and Navali thought that perhaps she was at least saved from that ordeal.

If Navali deliberated too long on the subject of hate, she would come to the eye-opening conclusion that the trip to her betrothed's had awakened all manner of emotions she could not seem to hold back. She did not care though. From this minute on, she would cry, scream, or rage to her heart's content. No one would gainsay her, not even the oaf who had decided he was not getting enough of a reaction from his now awake and placid victim, and suddenly gave her bottom a brutal, lascivious squeeze.

She was going to kill him! She really was! Navali thought, her sight blinded by the red haze of rage sweeping through her and she began to struggle violently. She kicked and hit, ignoring the stabbing pain in her shoulder and the pommel digging agonizingly into her middle as she attempted to bite the skinny thigh that rested close to her head.

She, who could never stand anyone being hurt, wanted the man to die a horrible death. And she wanted to be the one to deliver the fatal blow!

Followed by an eternity in hell! Navali nearly snarled the sentence out loud. The mongrel soldier had just given her backside a pinch that could have rivaled a horse's bite and she wanted to cry at the humiliation, shame, and pain coursing through her entire being. No matter how much she struggled, the man easily kept her pinned across his filthy, bony lap.

An idea occurred to Navali and she forced her body to limpness yet again, though her shoulder throbbed from the arrow she had taken last eve and the blood had dried on her clothing, making it stiff and uncomfortable.

The savage slapped her rump a third time and when he did not get a response, he dragged her to an upright position by grabbing a handful of the back of her dress and hauling her up, nearly strangling Navali in the process.

"'Ere now, wench!" He grabbed her by both shoulders, letting go of the hold he had on the neck of her dress and shook her, his foul breath wafting over her while his mouth gaped open in a leering grin. Navali struggled not to gasp air into her now unrestrained lungs. "I likes th' ones what fight. 'Tis much more pleasur'ble when ya hafta tame 'em!"

A torrent of agreement rang out amongst the other soldiers as the one who held her captive, brutally grasped her left thigh in his bony fingers and forced her to straddle his thighs. Her skirts were indecently raised above her knees in this position, exposing the pale smooth flesh of her shapely limbs to the soldiers' ogling stares and Navali decided she had waited long enough to make good on her plans of escape! As she was now pressed firmly to the lecherous cad's gaunt chest, she reared back from his encompassing hold and spat full into his face. The loathsome soldier was so stunned at the crass audacity of the lady, he froze.

That moment of stillness was all Navali needed to spring into action. She threw her weight back against the bobbing neck of the horse, breaking the man's hold and, reaching behind her body, grabbed fistfuls of its dirty mane. Pain shot through her injured shoulder as she braced her weight more firmly and brought one leg up to kick the brigand squarely in his shocked face. Losing his seat, the soldier toppled over the side and rump of his mount to land ungracefully on his bony backside in the churning dust.

Turning swiftly, her hands finding the knotted reins, Navali wheeled the animal to the left, while her slender heels pressed to its sides urged the beast to a gallop into the forest. Hearing shouts and the crashing of other horses entering the thickly under-brushed trees, she did not dare glance back as she kicked the horse to greater speeds as the sound of pounding hooves echoed closer.

The woods ended abruptly and Navali yanked back hard on the leather reins clutched tightly in her grasp.

The animal skidded to a halt, one hoof dangerously close to the edge of a steep cliff. The horse screamed in fear, the whites of its eyes showing, and stomped its hooves fiercely against the rocky soil of the cliff's edge. Stones skidded and clattered over the side and Navali glimpsed the green-blue of the water below as she brought the animal back under control.

An elegantly dressed man in dark violet and gold attire, with an ornate shield embossed in gold on the right breast of his long cloak, leisurely rode a magnificent white horse out of the dense forest to her left and Navali whipped her head in his direction, her breath escaping her lungs in frantic gasps.

If it were not for the evil, demonic gleam in the man's limpid, hazel eyes, he would, quite simply, appear as if he were a handsome prince or king coming to her rescue, much like the handsome prince whom she had glimpsed the previous evening. However, this man's cold gaze revealed his true nature, and she tugged further back on the reins of the mangy mount beneath her.

There was nowhere for her to go, she realized desperately as her erstwhile pursuers rode out of the trees and surrounded her. Nowhere but down, that was. Navali swallowed hard as she glanced once again over the steep wall of the cliff to her right. The current of the wide river crashed violently over the jagged rocks at the bottom, and she knew, even if she somehow survived the plunge itself, the rocks below would surely fracture her body upon impact.

"It's a very long way down, do you not agree, your highness?" the regal man queried in clear, calm tones, as if he were bored with her and the situation they currently found themselves in. His eyes betrayed him yet again and Navali grew aware, that whoever he was, he wanted her alive. And he desired it greatly. Especially, she thought, if he were the one who had gone to all the trouble to have her abducted in the first place.

"Do not approach me further!" She practically screamed at him, completely unaware that her voice had risen higher than its normally genteel octave and betrayed the anxiousness she was feeling as his horse took another step closer.

Navali's own mount shied backwards, even though she had not meant for it to do so. But she was soon thoroughly grateful for it when the darkly handsome man drew his horse to an abrupt halt. She knew she was not strong enough to deliberately kill herself by backing her horse over the edge of the cliff, but he did not know that, and that was to her advantage.

"Come, my dear, you wouldn't want to die that way," he told her and shook his head as if he were trying to reason with a distraught child. "It would be very messy and excruciatingly painful."

"I don't want to die at all, you miscreant," Navali retorted under her breath. She was not certain how long she could hold the brigands at bay with the threat of throwing herself over the cliff, but she was not ready to admit defeat yet. Her mind raced as she scrambled to formulate an escape plan. The horse beneath her pranced nervously and she was forced to focus most of her attention on quieting the anxious animal, ere he stumbled over the side and resulted in killing them both anyway.

If she had not been so preoccupied with her mount, perhaps she would have been more aware of her surroundings, and of the nefarious plot to reclaim her that had just been put into play. But, alas, she was woefully unaware of the tall lanky man behind her withdrawing a length of rope from his saddlebag and making a large loop in it.

Bringing her horse back under her control once again, Navali glanced up just as the elegantly attired man nodded at someone behind her. She twisted around in her saddle to look and felt coarse rope suddenly encircle her torso, pinning her arms to her sides. The dirty man who had thrown it yanked hard on the end he was still holding and she was dragged from the saddle. Her skirts twisted around her legs and she hit the ground before she could get her legs beneath her.

She landed hard on her bottom and the air left her lungs in a painful rush of breath. She felt the earth tremble beneath her and forced her head up, meeting the gaze of the smugly grinning man who rode closer on his smartly bedecked stallion.

"Now, my dearest guest, that wasn't very considerate of you to try and leave without first greeting your host." Two men came out of the trees at a flick of the man's bejeweled hand, and grabbed her arms, painfully hauling Navali to her feet before him.

"Good day," she allowed the polite, wholly untrue, phrase to be spat out in distaste, then commanded regally. "Now release me at once."

Her captors chuckled quietly to themselves at her show of haughtiness, fully aware their king and leader did not abide with sharp-tongued women who were accustomed to giving orders. Their king had his ways of keeping any shrewish wench silent and obedient.

The men holding Navali took the liberty of running their filthy hands down the length of her white throat and the flesh visible above the neckline of her gown, already assessing the womanly bounty before them in anticipation of the order that was sure to follow her words. Any captive who insulted their king could expect nothing less than to be given directly into the care of their none-too-merciful hands, and they could barely contain themselves until they were awarded the pleasure of instructing this silver-haired vixen of her proper place in a man's world.

Navali fought not to squirm at the feel of their filthy hands traversing her body so familiarly, and she stood stoically awaiting what would next befall her.

To the two men's ultimate surprise and disappointment the order never came. Instead they were commanded to place her back on the same horse she had ridden when she had tried, and nearly succeeded, to evade and escape them. They glanced at each other askance at the directive, but the order that followed the first one, calmed the disquiet rising amongst the filthy men, and they tied her hands to the pommel of the saddle with spiteful relish, pulling the crude rope taut over her slender, white fingers.

Refusing to let any emotion show on her face as they bound her hands and wrists to the point of unrelenting pain, Navali focused instead on where the Pitan were leading her horse.

The soldiers had aligned themselves behind the nattily at-tired man who was so obviously their leader and they followed him down the rocky path she had inadvertently stumbled upon as it wound its way down to the shore of the river. A flat craft drifted in the still, blue water below them while several soldiers meandered upon its sodden planks.

The troops surrounding her picked up their pace in anticipation of reaching home. When, suddenly, a small dog sprinted out onto the overgrown path in front of them and skidded to an abrupt halt, barking furiously at the horses bearing down on its little body. A young boy burst out of the woods shortly behind the mangy mutt and, scooping up the growling, shaggy creature in his arms, turned and raced back for the cover of the trees as the horses thundered within reach.

The elegantly dressed man in the lead thrust out a foot as he came upon the boy, his boot connecting solidly with the small back, before he drew his mount to a halt. The young lad let out a yelp as he went down and then lay still in fright, his little body trembling so violently that Navali could see it from several paces away.

The boy was obviously terrified of the soldiers and their leader, as he did not even glance up to see who grabbed his arm as he lay on the ground. He kept his head down, his long blonde hair shielding his eyes, the arm the soldier was not grasping clenched tightly around the bundle of fur that was now frantically squirming in a bid for freedom.

The man who held the lad's arm hauled him to his feet and gave the slim child a fierce shake, then pulled the boy towards the man who had kicked him to the ground. The leader grabbed the boy's hair, yanking his head up so he could stare furiously down into the young, frightened face.

Navali's heart caught at the sight of the huge tears welling up in the boy's wide blue eyes, and she could have applauded his tenacity when he blinked rapidly to withhold the moisture. Navali briefly wondered where his parents were, for there were no villages or people in sight, but such thoughts were cut short as a shrill voice intruded upon them.

"Boy! You and your animal dare to stand in my way?" Completely outraged, the man in purple shouted into his small upturned face. The boy's lower lip began to tremble, but he did not utter a word in defense at the man's accusations. "Kill the mutt!" The leader cruelly and suddenly ordered, and for a moment Navali feared he meant the boy. She was vastly relieved however, but no less saddened for the boy, when one of the soldiers came forward and tore the growling bundle from the lad's arms. Navali watched, unable to give comfort or help in any way, as the boy's beloved pet was flung over the side of the cliff and into the raging river beyond.

She could not see where the little dog landed, if its body smashed onto the jagged rocks below or managed to land in the water. But she hoped, for the boy's sake, his pet had landed unharmed in the water and could swim back to shore. Her attention was abruptly pulled from her inner thoughts about the dog and back to the boy as she heard the leader screaming harshly at the devastated child.

"Cease that detestable crying now, brat!" The man's handsome face was taking on the same purplish hue as his clothes. His features twisted in a macabre mask of fury, and he backhanded the sobbing lad, knocking him to the ground again where he lay stunned from the sharp blow and trying to stifle his cries.

"Garrick!" The leader shouted and waited for a huge man to make his way through the soldiers eagerly awaiting to see what would befall the boy. "My army desires more soldiers. Take the boy to the back of the column and see what you can do with him. I trust he will learn discipline and how to show the proper respect due his king under your care."

"I live to serve, your majesty," the brutishly, ugly man responded with a slight bend at the waist.

Navali very much doubted that Garrick served anyone but himself, as she watched him take his cue from the king, and grab a fistful of the lad's long blonde hair and haul him to his feet.

Where he alternately pulled and dragged the boy to his place with the soldiers at the rear of the line.

Princess Navali had come to realize with the man's words that the leader before her was the Pitan king, Krinar, whose cruelty and savagery were known the world over, and she proceeded to call herself every type of fool for not reaching that conclusion earlier when he had ridden out of the forest. As she finished her self-directed tirade, she took a moment to consider the intentions the Pitan king had concerning her, and the only certain conclusion she could muster were that they were sure to be nothing short of unpleasant.

Navali fervently prayed for a miracle to occur as she reached that result, one in which Krinar was only after her father's money and she would be ransomed soon. Nevertheless, the sinking in her heart testified that such an appealing outcome was sure to be nigh unto impossible. King Krinar had never been known to ransom his captives before and she highly doubted he would begin now.

She was going to die. A strange calmness and acceptance washed over her at what her fate was most likely to be, and she felt resigned and helpless, as though there were no longer any reason to hope for rescue or escape. Her shoulder throbbed painfully in time with her despairing thoughts, adding to the depth of her misery.

No! Navali suddenly and fiercely shook off the melancholy gripping her. She would not allow herself to feel that way! She had to find a way to freedom, for her father's sake and for her own. She would not be so easily defeated!

She would portray herself strong and unbroken, and make these men rue the day they had ever dared to abduct a Lynarian princess! Navali relished the heady thought of revenge for a very brief moment, before reality once again intruded. Her hands were bound tightly to the pommel of the saddle in front of her, her shoulder had started to bleed anew and the healing of the wound was taking far longer than normal, while the few coins she had sewn into her skirts, that Tabitha had not found, were not enough to bribe a saint, let alone a foul Pitan. How was she supposed to get free, let alone wreak havoc among the soldiers?

She morosely watched the men around her as they loaded their horses onto the flat watercraft they had just reached and knew she would not find an ally among their motley numbers. There seemed to be no way to save herself.

Her eyes unknowingly alighted upon the boy they had just taken, and she watched as Garrick kicked him with one giant boot from where the lad had slipped and fallen to the water-swollen planks. Hope rose anew in her breast. If she could not save herself, perhaps she could at least save the small lad who was now painfully picking himself up from the deck of the boat.

Surely her captors could not keep her tied to the saddle forever. They would need to release her when they made camp tonight, for the Pitan capital city was far from the Dareknay border, and they would certainly have to halt to give the horses a rest ere they reached their destination.

She twisted a scant inch to the right and, as her horse was led to the front of the ferry to stand next to Krinar's magnificent beast, discreetly glanced back at the boy to see how he fared. She would free him, she promised the lad silently. Nothing would deter her.

Tonight, when they made camp, she would liberate him or die in the attempt.

CHAPTER SIX

Ashyre's men had been riding hard the entire first day of their mission, only calling a brief halt to water their horses when it became necessary. They ate from atop their saddles and rarely spoke, as conversation seemed ill-befitting the seriousness of their current undertaking. Instead, they turned their minds to the matter of what might happen when they chanced upon their first skirmish with their enemy. Would their opponents be the Elite-Horde, the Pitan Regulars, or just a band of desperate and pitiful peasants?

As to whom they would first encounter, they had absolutely no inspiration to draw from, for they had yet to come across a single soul. Which, in and of itself, could have been numbered among the infrequent blessings they were presently receiving. But, instead, it bordered on the strange and bizarre, seeing that they had been traversing the Pitan territory for quite some time now.

Even though the Dareknay's had not opted to journey along the main thoroughfares, they did chance upon the occasional cleared shepherd's path, and yet there was nothing. No sign of anyone living nearby. The main roads themselves did not even boast of a great many merchants or travelers passing along their broken cobblestones, as the plentiful weeds and bushes pushing through the many cracks would have afforded nearly as much cover as the forest path the Dareknay's now traveled along.

Shyre's head was beginning to pound with the rhythm of the horses hooves against the earth when he called a halt late in the evening.

"Shall we make camp, your highness?" one of the two young squires they had brought along asked.

Shyre nodded. "Aye, and light a small fire to keep the night predators away." He was not wary of their position being exposed to the Pitan by the flickering light of the fire on the night sky, as he had not glimpsed any signs of civilization all day, nor any other fires glowing on the horizon now.

As his men and brothers moved wearily about arranging their pallets for the night's rest, Shyre walked the perimeter of the clearing he had chosen, rechecking for any signs of human activity. Just as there had been before, there were none.

Shyre thought it odd that he had not seen any people that day. Not a single village had his warriors chanced upon. Surely the entire Pitan population could not all live in the capital city? How would they have enough farmland to provide food for all the people?

The Pitan did not allow trade with any other countries and there were no seaports anywhere near there. He knew Krinar, the Pitan king, was cruel and unjust, but he could not be so evil as to think they could survive for long without food. Or mayhap he could. After all, he had ventured onto Dareknay holdings and dared to ambush a peaceful caravan on their lands. That, in and of itself, should have spelled suicide for any intelligent person.

Shyre moved farther away from the glow of the crackling firelight and into the trees. He wanted a few moments alone. His thoughts had been consumed with his future bride throughout the day and he needed to rid himself of the incessant distraction. If he did not get hold of his wayward mind, he would be no good to the men under his command.

Hearing movement from behind him, he glanced over his shoulder, unconcerned about an enemy coming upon him. He had drawn his sword when he ventured into the trees and only a fool would mess with a warrior holding a wickedly gleaming, silver sword.

General Ivan stepped through the brush and into his line of vision. "Prince Ashyre, might I have a word with you?"

"You don't even have to ask, Ivan." He turned to face the general and sheathed his sword.

"Are your thoughts to journey as far as Krinarn?" Ivan spoke of the capital city of Pitan, whose conceited king had named it after himself.

Ashyre lifted his shoulders in a shrug. "I'll traverse half the known world to reclaim my betrothed if need be."

"What if that is no longer an option?" The general asked, his eyes glinting with remembrance. This reminded him so much of when his daughter was taken. "What if they've killed the princess already?"

Lifting a brow at the older man, Shyre commented. "You're full of many questions tonight, general. Do you doubt our purpose here?"

"Not I, my prince. I'd willingly march on the city single-handedly if asked and kill all the murdering Pitan swine I could ere I was struck down," Ivan stated, his blue eyes glittering fiercely in the dark. "But first, I must think of the Drocuns accompanying us, and not be selfish in my desire for revenge."

"I *am* thinking of the men and my brothers, Ivan. Else I would not have made camp this night. I'd have ridden my stallion into the ground afore stopping, however foolish that may sound," the prince finished, his eyes troubled. He had never felt such an intense urgency to assure one woman's safety, and felt the imbecile to have so quickly fallen under the princess' enchantment.

"Not so foolish, Shyre." The older man finally desisted with formality and placed one large hand on the high prince's shoulder. Ivan's eyes conveyed his understanding and Shyre was relieved. Things had never been strained between him and the man he loved like a second father, and he had been concerned the general now doubted his abilities and saneness of mind, and did not think him fit to lead. "I would do the same," Ivan stated, and Shyre knew he spoke true, for he nearly *had* done the same.

Looking at the general's strained features, the high prince wished now, just as he had done at the commencement of their travels, that this journey would not prove to be too taxing on the general. Not because the man was over thirty cales his senior, for Ivan was incredibly muscular and fit, but simply for the reason that some of these people had murdered his daughter. And if the man felt a certain connection between the two incidences, Shyre would not begrudge him for wanting any kind of revenge he could finally have on the Pitan.

In fact, Shyre would help inflict it, if he could, and he knew his brothers would be at his side all the way. Livai had been like a little sister to them, and they all grieved her loss.

Shouts from the encampment suddenly reached the two men now standing silent in the darkness, and they turned abruptly toward the noise. Then hurriedly drew their broadswords from their tooled leather sheaths as they raced back to the men.

Their camp was in an uproar when they reached it. Several bodies lay strewn on the ground and Shyre prayed it was not any of his own men.

He ran to where Adam was besieged by three men and grabbed the first offender's arm, realizing as he swung him about that the man was nothing more than an overgrown boy. He swiftly changed his grip on his sword, not wishing to kill the lad, and landed a blow with the hilt of it instead of the blade's edge. The youngling dropped like a stone and stayed there, his eyes closed in unconsciousness.

"Are they all this young?" Shyre asked Adam, glancing around at the attackers as he helped fend them off.

"Or younger still," Adam replied, and growled as he took a hit in the side from the flat of one boy's blade as he attempted not to behead the youth.

"Try not to kill them!" Shyre ordered loudly to his men.

"What do you think I'm about now, Shyre?" Adam grunted in exasperation, and grabbed the unskilled lad's arm as he made another swing. "Though I do not exactly enjoy the bruises I'm receiving for my efforts!" He wrested the sword from his youthful attacker and flung it aside. The lad's eyes grew round in fright as he faced the mountainous man unarmed for the first time.

"Be off with you!" Adam bellowed at him. A whack on the backside with the flat of Adam's blade accompanied the outburst and the boy turned and fled towards the trees.

"Lay down your arms!" Shyre heard a young, high voice shout. "We have you surrounded *and* outnumbered!"

Shyre scoffed softly. Just because he did not wish to kill any of the young lads attacking them, did not mean he was going to surrender anything to this gaggle of children playing highwaymen. The lot of them needed to be spanked and sent home to their mothers. Where were their parents anyway?

He made his way towards the voice that had spoken, and saw Aaron being held at bay by a long bow notched with a fatally aimed arrow.

The young lad who held the weapon looked to be no older than fifteen and, as soon as Shyre managed to get his brother out of the scrape he had stumbled upon, he would tease Aaron unmercifully. A tall, grown, muscular man held captive by a slip of a boy without any hint of whiskers. It was laughable and would only be fair retribution for all the ribbing Shyre had received from his younger brother in the past several weeks. But first, this young lad needed to discover the error of his ways, and Shyre was going to give him a lesson he would not soon forget.

The high prince had come upon the boy from behind and now touched the razor sharp tip of his sword to the lad's neck, directly below his small right ear. The young brigand froze.

"What did you think to attain by attacking an encampment of Drocuns, my young thief?" Shyre asked.

"I'm not a thief, you ogre! Now remove your sword, or I will loose the arrow I have trained upon your brother," the lad fearlessly stated, his aim never wavering from where it was centered on Aaron's chest.

"We are at an impasse then. For you see, I will not remove my sword and surrender. My men have traveled long and hard, and they need their food and rest. What right do you have to steal it from us? If that is indeed what you want." From the bedraggled thinness of the younglings desperately fighting a losing battle against the trained warriors, Shyre was sure they needed more nourishment, though he was not about to let them steal it.

Stealing was a punishable offense where Shyre hailed from and could get them all killed if they ever came up against someone who would not temper their blows, as Shyre's men had done.

"It's a person's right to survive, isn't it?" The young leader brazenly asked.

Shyre thought seriously about the answer to give him. He did not like the thought of children starving, but yet, he could not condone what they had tried to do as a way to get food. What kind of parents would allow their children to fight grown men?

He did not have time to think about it overlong, as what the lad had first said suddenly hit him like a fist to the gut. He dispensed with all negotiating, and grabbed the boy's arm, yanking it up as he did so. The arrow notched in the bow went wildly up into the air and then down to embed itself harmlessly into the ground some yards away.

Tearing the weapon away from the lad's fingers, Shyre spun the surprised boy around. "How did you know he was my brother, whelp?" He shook the boy, demanding answers, his hands firmly grasping the thin arms. No one but his own countrymen would know such a thing. He and Aaron did not look that similar for someone who did not know his family to be able to see the resemblance between them.

"Who betrayed us?" Shyre growled into the boy's dirty upturned face.

"N—no one, my lord," the lad hastily replied, his teeth chattering as his head whipped back with the force of the shake. All of a sudden, Shyre was seized from behind and forced to release the lad.

Dropping to the ground, Shyre rolled away from his attacker and, rising swiftly to his feet, came face to face with Aaron. Shyre halted his movements and stared incredulously at him. What was his brother about?

"Shyre, it's Livai!" Aaron exclaimed, black eyes wide in shock as he pointed to the boy's face.

"Hellfire, Aaron, I could have killed you!" His brother's words registered moments later. "Livai?" Shyre moved closer to the scowling figure Aaron held entrapped in one strong hand. The high prince studied the face before him and found the likeness to the girl he once knew incredible, though he would never go so far as to believe this was actually Livai. He hoped his brother was not taking his own guilt over the way she had been taken too far and seeing things that were not really there and were impossible to begin with.

Before Shyre could say anything, Aaron spoke. "What happened to you, Livai? Why didn't you come back?" Aaron's eyes held an urgently pleading light and Shyre winced. His brother *did* believe this to be Livai.

"I—I don't know what you're talking about." The boy—nay, the youngling was definitely female, wrenched her arm away from his brother and signaled her followers to dispel into the forest. The girl's eyes held a fearful light in them and the two brothers did not move to stop her when she turned and raced for the cover of the trees. Neither one wanted to scare her, for she looked too much like Livai, and, even if Shyre did not think it was really her, they would not have frightened her for the world.

"I know you think I've gone mad, Shyre." Aaron looked at him sideways after the young brigands had disappeared, his shoulders slumped.

"I do no—" Shyre began, but his younger brother cut him off.

"I'm not though, I really believe that was Livai."

"But, Aaron, why wouldn't she return to us *or* her parents?" Shyre asked his brother incredulously. "Its been six cales, brother. If she's leading a band of young children to fight for food, why wouldn't she bring them to Dareknay where they could have all the food they desired? Tell me that."

"I know not," Aaron said and his face took on a determined look. "But I do know that was her, I can sense it to the very marrow of my bones."

"All right, Aaron, I believe you," Shyre gave in, not wanting to distress his brother any more than he already was. "But I don't think it would be wise to tell Ivan what we have seen tonight," he told his sibling.

The other man straightened to his full height and said, "I agree. Until I know for certain, beyond a single doubt, that she is Livai, I won't say anything. It would only break his heart again if I'm wrong and it really isn't her."

Shyre clasped Aaron's left shoulder briefly. If he could take away his brother's guilt and pain, he would gladly shoulder the burden for him. But he could not. Not for all the wishing and trying he had already done to accomplish that feat.

"My lords," Ivan greeted as he approached the two men.

"Ivan." Shyre nodded to him and shot Aaron a quick look, which the other man steadfastly returned. "Any men injured?"

"Only Kaiphus, and it's severe. He took an arrow to the chest." The older man's eyes were concerned.

Shyre swore violently. Kaiphus was young, barely out of his Drocun rights. If he had known the little cutthroats had managed to ruthlessly damage one of his own warriors, he would have never let them depart. "How did it happen?" Shyre was already striding to where several of his men were huddled around a figure on the ground.

"He was on guard to the north. Those young bandits shot him to keep him quiet. It came to no avail though, Kaiphus shouted a warning before he gave in to unconsciousness. He's proved a valiant lad," General Titek murmured as he followed in Shyre's wake.

The high prince reached the young man lying on the ground and crouched beside him. Kaiphus' right shoulder was drenched in blood and his eyes were glazed and dulled by pain.

"My prince," Kaiphus slurred as he struggled to rise from the ground.

"Nay. Stay where you are, Drocun." Shyre stayed him with a hand on his uninjured shoulder. "You showed yourself true and strong this night. I'm grateful for your diligence."

The severely wounded Drocun relaxed under Shyre's hand and a small grin played about the tight-lipped mouth.

"Aaron," Shyre spoke quietly and then waited until his brother knelt beside him. "I need you to take Kaiphus swiftly back to the castle. I fear he won't make it otherwise."

The order was not one that Aaron would appreciate, but he was Shyre's fastest and most capable rider. If anyone could get the young warrior to the castle in time to save him, it was Aaron. Shyre also knew his brother's focus was now compromised and it could get every one of his Drocuns killed. He needed to get his younger brother out of Pitan territory, even if it left him feeling the treacherous asp for sending him back.

Aaron looked at him with a mixture of betrayal and wisdom shining in his black eyes. "I will see to it," he solemnly vowed.

Knowing he would need to have a private word with Aaron before he left, Shyre glanced over at his twin and Ashtyn nodded, telling him that he was right in his judgment and commands. Shyre released a breath, at least he was not dreaming up disaster where there was none. Shyre knew he could count on his twin's rational discernment of the situation.

The high prince needed all his warriors focused and sharp if they were going to survive this mission into enemy territory. He could not have every one of the men peering around trees and in caves for a girl that could or could not be Livai, no matter how personally disappointed he or his brother were at not being able to immediately put to rest this new mystery.

Having gathered wood before the attack began, several Drocuns started a fire, while Adam set about immobilizing the injured man's shoulder and staunching the heavy flow of blood. Adam was not a healer by nature, but he had more knowledge about wounds and treatment than any of the other warriors, thanks to his penchant for reading anything that happened to be at hand.

Aware that it would be mentally impossible for Aaron to keep what had happened from his twin, while Ashtyn had already seen the whole incident in Shyre's mind, Shyre gestured for Aaron, Aakin, and Ashtyn to join him at the edge of the firelight. Though sometimes it was a nuisance not to be able to separate one's mind from your brother's, at this moment Shyre regarded it as a blessing. He would not be standing alone in his commands this night.

Ashtyn would have made a more superior high prince, Shyre reflected. His twin was always level-headed and never acted impetuously. On the other hand, Shyre would be the one most likely to get into trouble, by thinking and making his decisions too quickly. But he knew that Ashtyn did not covet his role as heir to the throne. His twin was perfectly content to stay on the edge of the crowd and observe, giving his advice and ideas when he felt they were needed.

"Shyre," Aaron began. "I understand why you're sending me back. I don't like it, but I will honor your decision, if you promise me you'll continue to keep alert for anything pertaining to Livai. I've already told Aakin of what has transpired." Aakin nodded his head in assent to Aaron's sidelong glance. "He has agreed to be my eyes here."

Though Shyre knew his brother had absolved him from all guilt, he needed to explain his orders. "I'm sorry, Aaron. I would prefer to keep you by my side, but I cannot afford anyone being distracted. And, even without the incident tonight, you *are* my most capable rider and I would have sent you anyway."

"I know and understand that as well. I would be distracted," Aaron confessed. "And not much help to anyone." There was a pause and his younger brother's voice became very firm. "But I should make myself clear as well. If you don't see Livai again, I *will* come looking for her once the mission to recover the princess is successful."

"I don't blame you, brother. I'd do the same." Shyre's green gaze glinted with determination and he amended his statement. "I *intend* to do the same. I'll join you on your quest when the time comes, and I thank you for accompanying me on mine." Shyre held out his arm to his younger brother and Aaron firmly clasped his wrist in response.

"Until you return victorious," Aaron gave his farewell.

"Godspeed, Aaron. May your horse take wing," Shyre returned.

The four men then strode to where several warriors had made the preparations for Aaron's urgent journey. Two horses awaited, both saddled, one stood directly behind the other and between the two animals a litter made of soft leather and two long poles had been attached. Sleeping as though one dead, Kaiphus was already ensconced on the litter, having been given a strong sleeping powder, one that would also slow his heart so it would not pump as much blood throughout his body. The young Drocun would need to conserve as much of the thick red liquid as possible to make the hurried flight back to the healers alive.

The brothers clasped Aaron's shoulder in farewell as he mounted the lead horse, murmuring lowly to keep the animal calm.

"Till we meet again." Aaron nodded once more to the men surrounding him. He kicked the animal lightly and the muscular beast moved in a smooth and even clip out of the circle of firelight and into the dark woods.

"Aaron will get Kaiphus there in time," Aakin promised the men around him. He went to sit and stare into the fire, his mind on the nearly solo journey his brother was undertaking.

Shyre knew Aakin would stay connected with his twin and give them frequent reports. He watched Addison move to Aakin's side. The giant man could make anyone smile at any time and he would distract his youngest brother from his concerns and worries.

The warriors were laying out their bedrolls and several were cooking rabbits that had been caught in snares on a spit over the fire. It would be quiet tonight with everyone absorbed in their own thoughts. Shyre would need to eat, and then sleep for a few precious hours, before his shift began on the early morning watch. He was grateful for the time alone to get his mind back in order for the task ahead.

He sighed as he settled on the hard ground. It had been a most eventful evening.

The brutish, mangy soldiers scattered around Navali were in different reposes of sleep, some snoring loud enough to keep the night-creatures away and others breathing silently. As she waited for the perfect moment to liberate the captive boy, she noted a few of the men even slept with one eye open. Navali had never seen this before and found it most strange and unbecoming. It was rather frightening the way that one orb glittered in the dying firelight, and she prayed they could not really see what she was about this eve.

The dogs Krinar had brought with him were thankfully silent on the other side of the far reaching camp and Navali hoped they would continue to be so, as she struggled desperately to free her hands from their agonizingly tight bonds. She had been so mistaken in her opinions earlier, for her captors had not bothered to untie her hands from the pommel of the saddle when they had made camp for the evening as she had first supposed they would. They had merely removed the saddle from the horse and dropped it to the ground, where she had been forced to sit for the past several hours. The brutes had not even bothered to give her any food and her stomach had long ago quit its noisy complaints and now silently ached from the lack of it.

Navali was nearly frantic with turmoil. She needed to get free and whisk the young boy away from the care of that huge, vicious beast of a second-in-command as fast as she could possibly manage. What she would not give to have a dagger. Her wrists and hands were bleeding from her hopeless efforts to liberate herself and a blade would have greatly eased her travails. Though she considered herself lucky indeed that she could not feel her hands anymore, as she was sure they would hurt something fierce when the bonds eventually came off and the blood was allowed back into her fingers.

Her shoulder was another matter entirely, for it throbbed and burned, though thankfully the wound had ceased bleeding several hours ago. Navali had nearly swooned that afternoon from loss of blood, but she had forced the blackness edging her vision into submission and managed to stay coherent, if not fully alert, for the rest of the day.

Her body should heal miraculously fast as it had in the past, thanks to Navali inheriting some of her mother's healing abilities. Though Navali could not ascertain why she seemed to be able to heal herself and not others, as her mother had been able to do. She was not about to quibble about it now either. She was just grateful that by tomorrow morning the pain and wound would be nothing more than a pink scar and an agony-filled memory.

It was hopeless, Navali realized with a deep sigh as she ceased her attempts to free herself. There was not any way she could devise that would cause the coarse bindings on her hands to loosen this night. She quietly groaned in resignation, rising ungracefully to her feet, her rear in the air once again, as she tried lifting the saddle. It was not that heavy, just unwieldy, but it made her shoulder scream in pain and she hoped she could manage to carry it to where the boy sat.

She glanced about once again to reassure herself that all of the men were asleep. The Pitan king had not assigned guards for the night, secure in his belief that nothing would harm them when they were on their own lands, and he now slept secure in this knowledge in a huge vaulted pavilion in the center of camp.

Navali had observed men carrying large buckets of hot water through the open flap of the cloth structure and knew he had indulged in a bath. She would have done almost anything to be back home and able to take a long, relaxing soak herself, while cleansing away the blood and stiffness from her once soft skin.

It seemed the only way that event was going to occur was if she could free herself. Her own escape would not happen this night though, not with the bulky saddle tied to her hands, but she was determined the boy's would.

Staunchly ignoring the agony in her shoulder, Navali crept closer to the huge tent in the midst of the sleeping men. Garrick had laid his pallet near the entrance to the king's quarters and he now lay upon it, his thunderous snores enough to assure her that he was well and truly unconscious of the world around him.

Navali stealthily followed the curve of the pavilion and halted. Placing the saddle on the ground to allow her arms and shoulder a small rest, she peeked around the fabric to the boy.

The lad was looking at her as if she had gone completely mad, and Navali stifled a ridiculous and untimely urge to giggle, as she would surely be killed or worse if she was discovered in front of the tent. The boy was the only other person, besides herself, who appeared to be awake, and she thanked God for small blessings.

The lad was not tied up, which was another miracle, and he sat quietly and very close to his new master. A few blows from that man's mean, beefy fist had convinced him not to fight his fate anymore, but his blue eyes pleaded with Navali nonetheless. He wanted to go home. She could see that desire as though it were written there.

She beckoned him to herself with a motion of her head, and saw his gaze shift fearfully to glance at the ugly, sleeping giant next to him. Turning to her again, he shook his head helplessly. Toadwarts! She would have to go and get him herself.

Picking up the unwieldy saddle, Navali stood and slouched over, slinking towards the terrified little boy as best she could. She was pleasantly surprised when she reached him and he got to his feet, hunching over like she had done. He seemed to be ready to go with her, now that she was by his side, and she crept back to the pavilion.

It was closer to the savage king, but the dark, peaked shadows created by the structure would give them a little cover as they made their break for the woods.

Then, leaving the concealing shadows behind, the pair raced on quick, silent feet to the edge of the woods and disappeared into the sheltering underbrush. Navali stumbled a few yards in and halted abruptly, her shoulder screaming anew in agony. She bent so that she was eye level with the young boy. He was gazing at her with a kind of awe in his deep blue eyes and her heart turned over strangely in her breast at the sight. This was probably the last time she would ever see the adorable lad.

She hoped his family lived close by, for this was as far as she could manage with the saddle strapped to her hands and the aching wound in her shoulder. She would not risk the boy by going any farther with him, as her injury could begin bleeding again with her efforts, leaving behind a crimson trail for the

Pitan to follow. It would be safer for him if she returned to the brigands' camp. Surely they would not give chase to one little, unimportant boy.

Mouthing the word 'go' to him, Navali gestured with her head the way back to the river. He shook his own blonde head in response and, gripping her skirt in one small hand, lent evidence that he did not want to leave her.

"Everything will be well," she whispered, her voice barely making a sound above the cool breeze. "I'll escape in a few days. Don't fret about me. Go now, before any of those evil men wake up and discover you gone."

He shook his head more vehemently this time, and Navali could have cried—something she never did. The lad needed to go now! He was wasting precious minutes standing here with her. "What are you called, darling?" She used a term of endearment she had heard one other time in her life, and prayed the boy responded favorably to it.

"Peter." His voice was just as quiet as hers had been, his blue eyes large and luminous in the moonlight.

"That's a very strong and noble name, Peter. I am Navali. Now listen closely to me, I need you to leave and go to your family this very moment. I cannot make it very far tonight when I would have to carry this saddle with me. It is wiser if you leave now and I escape later." She looked intently at him, her eyes pleading for him to understand.

Peter stared into the translucent, silver depths for a moment more and then nodded, his small frame straightening in determination. He released the fabric of her dress and took a single backwards step. An owl hooted in the night and he turned from her, his legs carrying him swiftly away. But, just before disappearing from view, he turned one last time and gave her a gap-toothed grin, waving to her in thanks.

The lad grinned to himself as he ran, picturing the shocked looks on his family's faces when he made it back to his home and told them of what had transpired. A beautiful angel had saved him from the devil, his king.

Carefully making her way back to where her captors had left her, Navali set the saddle down and laid her head wearily on its seat. All the moving around had managed to somewhat loosen the bindings on her hands, allowing the blood to rush back into them, and they throbbed in time with her heartbeat, tingling and prickling as though a thousand needles were attacking them. The wound in her shoulder pounded, spreading anguish throughout her body, and she felt unwelcome tears prick her eyes at the intense pain. She stifled a moan, at least it was not bleeding again, she did not think she had enough blood to spare in her body for that.

The sky was beginning to turn a dove grey, the stars disappearing with the meager light, dawn was arising.

Navali normally loved this time of day. Now all she wanted was to hide her head and go to sleep forever. There did not seem to be much hope left in her, and even less fight. But she refused to give in to despair. A Lynarian princess had to be stronger than the circumstances around her and she was determined to make her country proud.

Navali could not seem to keep her eyes open any longer though, and she closed them, instantaneously recalling a pair of green eyes in a chiseled face. She admired the handsome visage of the man her mind brought forth and kept her eyes tightly shut, unwilling to release the image. Even with the gruesome and uncouth men snoring and snorting all around her, she managed to drift into a deep sleep, her dreams filled with a green-eyed prince coming to her rescue.

ALEXA E. WOODIWISS

CHAPTER SEVEN

Ashyre awoke to Adam nudging his shoulder with a boot, and he rolled over with a hoarse groan of disbelief that it could be his watch so soon. It had been a long day yesterday, one that Shyre was thankful did not herald another visit from their youthful highwaymen of the night before, but even without that added tension, he still seemed unable to glean a peaceful rest.

Getting up, he vacated his warm bedroll to Adam, and stretched in the predawn grey of the sky. In a couple of hours the other warriors would start to stir and break camp. They had been able to bring down a deer the night before and the leftover meat would fill their bellies well this morning.

Strolling around the small meadow they had chanced upon late the previous evening, Shyre smiled grimly to himself. They had been lucky so far in their travels. They had not come upon any enemy soldiers—only a few deserted villages, and absolutely no trouble beyond their first night's scuffle with the band of youthful brigands. That luck was bound to wear out soon and Shyre could hardly wait. He was spoiling for a good fight, for a way to use his muscles and purge the frustration he was feeling at his inability to recover his betrothed in the timely manner he had anticipated.

He wanted the blood of the dogs who had whisked away his bride, wanted to avenge the honor they had tried to strip from his people. They would pay. Shyre would see to it. No Pitan would dare step foot on his lands to wreak havoc again. He would make certain of it.

A woodlark trilled, breaking into his thoughts of vengeance. He knew it was not fair of him to judge all of Pitan by their king and his consorts. The few refugees who had made the journey to Dareknay lands had been kind and generous. However, he would need a very good reason, one he had not yet seen, to spare even one of the soldiers.

The sun was coming over the horizon, its warm rays heating the ground below. Last night had been very cool, and winter was rapidly approaching. They would need to hasten their pace to an even faster degree if they hoped to be home before the first snow of the season. Dareknay climate was lush and warm, and Shyre could hardly curb his impatience to leave this cold country. There were rumors a man could get snowed in here, and he did not like the idea of having to stay in this unfriendly region during the cold season.

General Ivan shifted in his bedroll, drawing Shyre's eyes to the older man. He hoped this mission purged the man's soul of the anguish he had felt for the last six cales.

The general's eyes opened at that moment and met Shyre's gaze. He stood up and stretched briefly like the warrior he was, before rolling up his bedding so it could be strapped to one of the pack animals.

After he was done he strode over to wake the others, his voice loud in the quiet hours of the early morning. "Arise, slugabeds, the sun's been up for nigh half an hour already! Get your lazy hides up and moving."

Soon, he had all the Drocuns rolling their pallets and stretching out their kinked muscles as they moaned in good-hearted exhaustion at his jibes at them. It would not do for the famed Dareknay Drocuns to be caught by the enemy with cold and cramped muscles, and they worked them more from habit than thought, their bodies running through the stretching paces they had been trained to follow since early childhood.

They were the greatest fighting force of their world and they took great pride in their exceptional abilities. This pride could have led to arrogance but their leaders taught them to stay humble. Arrogance and pride could get a man killed on the battlefield and none were willing to take that chance. Life was far too precious to squander.

The warriors ate with their usual gusto, laughing and jesting with each other as they sat before the small fire, Shyre and the other sentries joining them in breaking the night's fast. It felt good to have something solid and hot in their stomachs before they finished packing up camp, storing their weapons within easy reach, and buckling on their long swords. Some of the Drocuns strapped their swords to their backs, while others preferred to secure them around their lean hips.

Shyre did not have a preference, buckling the heavy sword wherever it felt comfortable that day. This morning he opted to wear it secure against his back. His men were ready for a fight this day and he could feel their eagerness for the coming confrontation. Swift Justice pranced beneath him, reacting as well to the anticipation coursing through his own master, but Shyre kept him to a brisk even canter as he gave the signal to move out.

He calculated roughly, and to the best of the sketchy knowledge he had been provided with, that they would reach Krinarn today and he hoped to get a good look at the battlements and defenses it possessed before night fell and darkness reigned. Mayhap he would even be fortunate enough to bribe a Pitan guard into letting them gain entrance into the fortress.

They were not planning all out war with Pitan, at least not yet, and not with the few men Shyre possessed at the moment. But if presented with half an opportunity they would willingly and readily spill Pitan blood and, most especially, that of their demonic and savage tyrant king, for they knew what Krinar was capable of.

The few times one of the Dareknay people had dared to venture onto Pitan territory, they could be found days, weeks, even moons later on the steep cliffs bordering their two countries, where spears had been run through the unfortunate's body and he had been pinned to the edge of the precipice. The Pitan left the corpse to rot there as a reminder to others to never trespass on their lands, but the Dareknay always recovered the bodies. No citizen of their country was going to hang from the cliffs like a common murderer.

Under the shadow of the moon they crossed the bridge and freed the body to be properly burned to ashes and then buried. No animal was given the chance to prey upon their own kind, only enemies' corpses were left to the night creatures outside the perimeter of the capital.

At noon, Shyre's men reached yet another small deserted village, one of many they had come upon that day, but this one was different and evoked the memory of just how cruel the Pitan could be.

As they rode down the hill and into the village, they were greeted by animal corpses lining the thoroughfare. A horse, several dogs, and numerous chickens were scattered about the main road leading down the middle of the thatched huts. Not a single person could be seen, but the place held an eerie feel, as though death itself resided there.

The hair stood up on the back of Shyre's neck and he glanced over to his twin. Their eyes met and the silent conversation they had was not pleasant. The corpses of the animals were mutilated and fresh, the stink nearly overwhelming. What person could commit such a monstrous act? Were the people here truly demonic?

Shyre's eyes conveyed the message to move slowly and his brothers each raised a hand. Not a whisper of sound carried on the wind. Rags of curtains and the leather used for doors waved in the breeze, startling some of the warriors' horses and the men dismounted to guide them as they walked.

A distraught moan echoed suddenly from the depths of a hut and Shyre signaled his men to a halt. He, Ashtyn, and two of the other Drocuns crept to the small thatched building, following the trail of blood leading the way. Ashtyn and Harry had their bows at the ready, and Lance and Shyre gripped their swords tighter. Their breaths sounded slow and steady within their chests as Shyre peered through the tattered strip of leather hanging from the open doorway.

A young girl sat before the cold fireplace, her hand tenderly stroking the hair of the dead woman beside her, and Shyre gave the signal to move in. The girl was so besieged by grief that she did not even take notice of their entrance, nor of when they searched the only other room the hovel possessed.

She was whispering a song to the old woman, her voice low and choked with emotion. The four men who gathered around her could not understand what she was saying, but it did not matter, they were aware people grieved in different ways for the loss of loved ones.

Shyre noted as his twin went to the door and gestured to Addison to come inside. The big man moved carefully into the room, his steel-gray eyes seeking out his eldest brother. Shyre dipped his head in the direction of the girl, and the gentle giant nodded and crouched beside where she sat on a three-legged stool.

Addison held his body at the ready. There was no telling what the girl would do when she realized there were other people in the room with her, and strangers to her no less. He did not know if the girl could be concealing a dagger or not, though if he had to take a guess he would wager on the latter. She did not look as though she would become violent at the slightest provocation.

Her hair hung in sodden, gold ringlets down her back and her lips were blue from the cold permeating the room. How long had she been sitting there?

Shyre watched as his brother laid his big hand soothingly over the one she was stroking the dead woman with, stilling the repetitive movement, and her brown eyes fluttered up.

Her tortured gaze bespoke the agony she was feeling, and Addison moved her small, frozen hand away from the woman's matted hair. He gripped it in his larger one and took the other hand that lay still in her lap. He turned her trembling body away from the woman's, so she would not be able to see as the other warriors carried it out and hurriedly buried it. The Dareknay had not known her, but no one deserved to die in such a cruel manner, for the body was mutilated as much, or even more so, than the animals' had been.

As soon as they had the body buried, Shyre sent Adam to get his twin and the girl. Addison walked out of the hovel with his arm around the young woman who was now wrapped in a thin blanket, and Shyre saw she was resting her head trustingly against him in exhaustion. The high prince did not know what he was supposed to do with the girl now. He did not feel comfortable just leaving her to fend for herself, but neither could he take her with them on their mission.

At the sudden sound of shuffling feet, Shyre swiftly faced what could possibly be an oncoming threat, but his gaze landed on that of a young man walking apprehensively towards the girl held up by Addison's arm. The Pitan moved to stand before the giant man, and then cautiously reached his arms out to the girl, all the while eyeing the large Drocun with equal amounts of trepidation and defiance glittering in his brown eyes.

The young village girl hitched a choked breath and stumbled into the young man's arms. The villager pulled her to him fiercely in response, his voice rough with emotion as he whispered, "Adele! I thought ye'd surely been taken by 'em! How'd ye escape?"

Shyre stepped closer in order to hear their conversation.

Careful, Ashtyn cautioned, employing the mind link he shared with Shyre, his hand coming to rest none too casually on the hilt of his blade, *there are more hiding in the trees.*

I noticed as well, Shyre silently commented back, *I am prepared.*

Adele shrugged helplessly as she responded. "I hid in the weeds by the creek when I 'eard 'em comin'. I didn't know what else ta do. Ye always say ta hide in the water iffen they've brought the dogs with 'em."

"It's so cold out today. Ye could have frozen ta death!" The young man exclaimed in concern and rubbed her arms in a belated attempt to warm them.

"She very nearly did." Shyre finally interrupted their private exchange. "What happened here?" The high prince's voice sounded soft, but held a firmness that brought the young man's head up.

"Krinar," the villager spat the name out, as though the taste of it was foul in his mouth. "'E rode through our village at dawn. The out-watchers was changin', and missed warnin' us o' their comin'. Most o' us escaped though. But the old woman refused ta leave 'er hut. Said she'd rather die than flee like a coward."

Shyre heard the self-disgust in the young man's voice. "She must have been a courageous woman, but what could she have hoped to gain by staying? Those soldiers are trained to kill ruthlessly, and villagers are not. There was nothing you could have done to deter them from taking and doing whatever they wanted here."

"I should've done something at the very least! Instead o' hiding in the trees like some half-grown lad!" The young man burst out, his eyes wild.

"Nay," Shyre told him in no uncertain tones. "They would have slaughtered any who stood in their way. A brave and intelligent man knows when to pick his battles."

Laying a hand on the younger man's shoulder, Shyre asked before the man could berate himself again. "What were the soldiers after?"

"Nothin'."

Shyre squeezed the thin shoulder gently, hoping the action would prompt the young man to explain.

"They never want anythin'," the villager finally expounded. "They ride through all o' the villages ta see iffen they're still deserted. No one's ta live outside o' Krinarn's walls. The king demands it, and iffen ye're caught outside o' them, ye're put ta death. We usually have time ta hide our presence from 'em, but this time they were 'pon us afore anyone could utter a warnin'. Our blasted king rode afore the murderin' band as pleased as a rooster in a hen house."

"The king?" Shyre's eyes met Ashtyn's over the youngling's head. Perhaps they were not that far behind the ones who had abducted his bride. "Did you see a woman with them?" He demanded urgently of the man.

The young villager looked back at him with a perplexed expression. "They've always gots women with 'em."

"This woman you would remember. She would be different from all the others. Elegantly dressed, has silver eyes and her hair is very light blond. She would probably be bound in some way," Shyre informed him.

The Pitan looked suspiciously at him, and asked a question of his own. "I know ye aren't o' these lands—" He passed a critical eye over the prince. "Who are ye and where do ye hail from?"

Shyre realized as he returned the man's steely gaze that he probably would not answer any more inquiries until he was satisfied with who they were. "I am called Shyre. My men and I are from Dareknay. To whom am *I* speaking?"

The young man's eyes lit up at the answer, and he forgot to give his name as hope entered his bleak expression. "Dareknay, ye say? What are Dareknay doin' in Pitan? Have ye come ta slay the evil tyrant, Krinar?"

"If we have the chance, though it is not our main reason for traveling here. The young woman I asked about, was she with the soldiers?" Shyre firmly returned the conversation to his original line of questioning.

"Aye, I saw a woman o' which ye speak," the young man admitted, his arms still around the softly crying girl. "Long, blonde hair, she had, and she was wearin' a tattered silver dress with lots o' blood on it. Her hands was bound ta the saddle in front o' her, and she'd a large bruise on her cheek, too." His hand gestured to his own unblemished right cheek.

"Aye, your description aptly fits her. Though for her sake and her captors, I hope she is treated more kindly than you say. I do not tolerate abuse well." Shyre's green eyes glinted with fury and his voice emitted in a low growl. He would not countenance *any* abuse towards his betrothed.

"My lord, wh—"

Shyre interrupted the lad. "I am not your lord," he said, not unkindly. He did not want the young man to know who he really was and did not dare let the lad call him lord, someone might realize that he was more than that. They might remember he was a prince. The high prince, in fact.

"Ye look like a lord." At Shyre's stern expression the man gave it up with a resigned sigh. "Then what's she ta ye, sir?"

There was an emphasis on the last word and Shyre smiled at the inflections in the man's voice. Shyre was not fooling him, but the young villager had obviously decided to go along with the ruse. "She is my betrothed."

"Betrothed? Then why's she with Krinar?"

"Because she was traveling to our wedding and the Pitan Horde ambushed her caravan." Shyre was becoming frustrated with the man's incessant questioning and it reflected in his tone. "Now, farmer, what is your name?"

"I'm not a farmer!" The young man stated fiercely, clearly indignant at the title. He straightened to his tall, gangly height. "I'm a shepherd. And me name's Tucker."

"Tucker, then. What is the quickest route to Krinarn?" Shyre did not mean to waste any more time talking. He needed to get his men moving once again. For the first time he was optimistic they could reach the blackguards before they entered the city walls. The urgent light in his green eyes gave him away to Tucker, whose look became eager and conspiratorial.

"I know of a faster way than the one King Krinar'll take. No one knows these hills better'n I do, 'sides old Finnias," Tucker jerked his head in the direction of where an ancient man was suddenly stepping forth from the coverage of the trees, leaning heavily on a twisted wooden cane as he walked closer.

"How much will it cost to tell me where the path lies?" Shyre's hand went to the flat pouch that concealed his gold in his belt.

"Not coin," Tucker replied, briefly glancing at the girl under his arm, before raising his other hand above his head, palm open and exposed. "I'll show ye the way iffen ye give me yer word ta take us back ta Dareknay with ye."

"All of you?" Shyre asked, incredulously looking at the twenty-some villagers who were now emerging from the forest. Some looked so old he did not think they would survive the journey.

"Only the ones what wish ta go," Tucker told him.

"And how many is that?" The high prince inquired.

Tucker again motioned with one hand, and everyone stepped forward a single pace. He shrugged unconcernedly. "I guess I was wrong, sir. It seems ever'one wishes ta go."

Frustrated with this turn of events, Shyre looked around at the village. He couldn't take them with him! But as his gaze fell on the thatched huts surrounding him, he knew they would not prove warm enough for a mouse to live in through the coming winter moons, let alone a group of furless humans. There was no way he could feasibly leave them behind either and live with his conscience after the deed had been done.

The high prince looked at each of his brothers. Ashtyn's face was resigned. His twin knew they were going to have to take everyone with them, no matter the cost to their mission or themselves. Adam's face was stoic, he would do whatever Shyre decided. Addison was looking at him in determination, the big-hearted teaser would not leave without all of them, not without a fight at least.

Shyre finally looked at Aakin. His youngest brother's face was carefully blank. Aakin could be the most ruthless of them all, but Shyre could see the reluctance gleaming from the white-studded black eyes Aakin had adopted in the absence of his twin.

"I will take all who can be ready to depart in a quarter of an hour," Shyre looked back at Tucker and the villagers and then turned away to face his brothers again.

"Addison, Adam?" Shyre spoke quietly so only they would hear him. "I'll need you to lead the villagers back to Dareknay. The rest of us will follow as soon as we have Princess Navali. Take Lance and both of the squires. See if you can find a cart or wagon that you can repair to carry the old ones and the children. Move the people as fast and as silently as you can."

Adam slashed a hand through the air in a downward motion, and questioned Shyre. "And what of you, Shyre? You'll only have nine Drocuns left, including yourself. I do not like those odds."

"Neither do I, Adam. But if Tucker can get us to the miscre-ants before they enter the city gates, we will have a fair chance of accomplishing our mission alive." Shyre was not really pleased with this new course of action, for the decreasing number of his warriors was indeed weighing heavily on his mind, but he was not going to tell them that.

Ashtyn joined the conversation, having read his twin's thoughts. "We'll be fine. One Dareknay man is worth eight Pitan savages on the battlefield. There will be no opposition worth mentioning."

"Don't let pride be your downfall," Adam warned sternly.

"It isn't pride, it is confidence," Ashtyn smugly assured him.

All the brothers had a good laugh at his response and then Addison and Adam went around to the villagers, ordering them to take only the necessary items. They quickly located a dilapidated cart and harnessed one of the Dareknay warhorses to it, though the horse balked at having to pull the conveyance, unfamiliar as it was with the menial task.

Tucker swiftly mounted behind Aakin as soon as he was bid, and the rest of the Dareknay warriors swung atop their own destriers. The young villager then waved farewell to the young girl, who the Drocuns had discovered was his sister, and pointed in the direction they should take.

The shepherd's path they embarked upon was narrow and overgrown, and the Drocuns had to use their swords to hack their way through the thick underbrush. The pace felt slow and unmoving and Shyre began to feel restless and wary.

What if the man, Tucker, was really a spy? What if he was leading them to their deaths? He reined in Swift Justice and waited for Aakin to draw alongside him, then spoke to the young man seated behind his brother. "Tucker, if you lead us into a trap, you will be the first to die," he stated clearly and then made the youth a solemn promise. "Aakin will see to it."

"I'm not takin' ye ta a trap. I've no reason ta, ye've already agreed ta take care o' my people, and fer that, I'm right grateful." The young man looked at the prince solemnly. "I swear ta guide ye peaceful-like."

Shyre nodded to him, before directing his horse back to the lead. He was satisfied with the man's answer, for now at least. He would trust the peasant only as far as he could toss him, which, in the man's pitifully starving state would be a fair distance.

As the woods closed around them, Ashtyn followed closely behind him, for there was not enough room to ride abreast of each other. Shyre felt himself losing his sense of direction and hoped Tucker was not a complete halfwit. He could no longer see any kind of path before him and he could not fathom anyone being able to find their way out of the trees and overgrowth.

Tucker had better lead them as he had sworn to do! Otherwise Shyre was going to take it out of his hide *before* Aakin killed him.

A few hours later, Shyre and his men were pleased to see Stephen, the man Shyre had sent to follow the Pitan, riding out of the cover of the trees in front of them.

"Stephen," Shyre greeted, clasping the man's wrist in welcome. "Where are Alan and Wesley?" The prince asked after the two men Stephen had taken with him.

The slim Drocun jerked his head in the direction from whence he had come. "Keeping an eye on Krinar and your princess."

"I heard the Pitan king had joined the soldiers who had abducted Princess Navali. Exactly when did that happen?" Shyre inquired.

Stephen pointed behind Shyre and then reported. "At the large river we had to cross. He's been journeying in style and it wasn't very hard to keep track of the foul band after he joined them. They didn't seem to be too concerned about any kind of threat from us and have been moving rather slowly," he paused, and then with a grin asked. "They don't know our ways very well, do they, your highness?"

Shyre's mouth quirked in a half grin. "No, they don't. Shall we show them the error of their thinking?"

"It would be a pleasure." the young man replied and swung his horse about, readying for the coming confrontation. "After what I have seen them do this day, I would gladly send them unto judgment."

"So would I, Stephen. So would I," Shyre agreed. He reached for the sword strapped to his back and, gripping the hilt firmly in his callused hand, unsheathed it in one smooth move. "Ready, men?" He asked those closest to him and they nodded in response, their weapons now also held at the ready.

Ashtyn flashed him a grin. "More than ready, it seems, brother."

"Then what are we dallying here for?" Shyre asked, just as eager to confront the savages. He did not think he had ever been more ready to spill a man's blood than he was this day, and he swung his sword in a broad arc in anticipation. "Let us go and retrieve what they have stolen from us."

"For freedom...." He vowed.

"And honor!" His men rejoined as one voice.

CHAPTER EIGHT

B arely containing her squirms of discomfort, Navali shifted wearily in the saddle. The mongrel savages had not untied her hands once since they had bound them two days ago, except for, and for which she was most heartily grateful, when she had to see to the necessities.

She would have protested her treatment to King Krinar but she already knew in what manner that would be received. Though he had not delivered the blow personally, her right cheek burned as though on fire, painful evidence left behind from her last interaction with that vicious, royal man, and it caused her to be silent more than any fear could have accomplished.

Garrick had smashed his huge fist against her face shortly after she had been rudely awakened by some of the men yesterday. Therefore releasing, on the nearest and most helpless recipient he could find, the burgeoning rage he had felt at the realization that the lad, Peter, was gone. He had not a speck of proof that she had helped the boy in any way, but she had soon learned, to her dismay, that he had not needed it. For his king, Krinar, had sat on his horse during the entire incident between she and Garrick, and chuckled sadistically, as though they were a comedy performance put on for his benefit.

Navali hoped someone cut out his tongue for all the cruel mutterings and sounds that emerged from betwixt his lips. The man was ghastly deranged, and needed to be removed from the face of the earth before he further infected the world with his venomous evil.

After Navali and her captors had been well underway to completing, what she now knew was the last leg of their journey to Krinarn, she had been witness to one of the most malicious acts of depravity that could be visited upon mankind. They had ridden through a nearly deserted village about midday, and Krinar had brutally, and without provocation, ordered the death of every living thing that could be found there. Malnourished animals were quickly slain and mutilated, but what was the most disturbing, and what had Navali nearly retching in remembrance now, was the death of an old lady they had discovered there.

The Pitan king had decreed it justice to murder her, he informed Navali. The woman had broken the law of not living in Krinarn and the penalty for disobeying her king's edicts was death in any manner he could devise at the moment.

Navali shuddered violently at the vision that swam before her eyes. The soldiers had grown excited when they had found the elderly woman in her hut, and Navali, having been alerted by their sudden eagerness, had glimpsed her briefly through the torn leather of her door, where she sat beside the cold fireplace in the rundown shack that was obviously her home, her hands occupied with stitching a patch onto a pair of worn trousers.

The Pitan king had ordered her dragged out, where he had commenced to set his dogs on her as soon as she fell to the ground before him. Navali could still hear the old woman's agonized screams echoing through her mind, and she remembered her own screams as they had joined the woman's. Navali had swung herself to the ground where she had struggled desperately to be free of her bonds as the dogs tore chunks of flesh from the old woman's arms and legs.

The Lynarian princess had fought, pleaded, and even begged to no avail. And she had considered it a cruel mercy, but a mercy nonetheless, when Garrick had ridden into the frenzied fray of fur and blood and thrust his sword through the woman's thin, heaving chest, instead of letting the dogs finish what they had begun.

Navali would never forget what these soldiers had done and allowed.

Never.

These Pitan soldiers and their king deserved to die, every last one of them.

Navali was amazed at herself when she hoped she would be around to witness the event. Even more shocking, she knew she would cheer on the men responsible for bringing about their demise. She even wanted to stomp vigorously on the Pitan graves to make sure they were packed solidly enough, or, even more pleasing a thought, just simply leave their dirty, rotten carcasses to feed the night-creatures that roamed the lands.

It was surprising how these blood-thirsty thoughts calmed Navali. She would not have thought it possible with her unfeeling Lynarian upbringing, but the very notion of revenge upon these men was strangely thrilling and exhilarating, and it energized her as nothing else could have possibly done at that moment. She would—somehow, and God willing—see their comeuppance bestowed upon them for the evil they had wrought their entire lives!

The horse Navali rode chose that moment to sidestep, and she cursed him viciously under her breath. If she wanted to see them pay, she would first have to devise a way off this stinking, clod-footed animal! The only problem with that plan was she had been unable to free herself so far and no other opportunity had arisen for her to escape.

After Peter had been discovered gone by Garrick, dratted King Krinar had decreed she would have to sleep in his own opulent tent. Now Navali knew more about that man's anatomy than she would have ever wished to become acquainted with. If she had ever possessed any questions before her captivity about the male physique, they had all quickly, and without the slightest regard to her innocent state, been put to rest.

Navali did not understand how a man who looked so handsome and muscled with his clothes on, really boasted the belly of a drunken sot, thin, flabby arms, and the scrawniest legs she could imagine, without the aid and benefit of his richly-dyed garments. It was astounding, and she thought she might have gone a little blind as the very white skin beneath the vast layers of cloth had been slowly revealed to the night air.

Thankfully, Krinar had retained the use of his breechcloth as he slept. Too much of an anatomical education would have surely ruined Navali's tender sensibilities. Though with all the crude language and foul gestures exchanged betwixt her captors, she really did not have that many left.

What Navali found far worse than the bare body parts and the foul language were the smells! She swore they had not had a bath in the last several cales! And the additional smells that emanated from them after they ate, were simply too grotesque to put herself through the remembering!

She needed to be around gentlemen again, or even people who just minded their manners and had a care for their personal cleanliness.

Every last one of her abductors ate with their fingers and wiped their hands, noses, and other running parts of their bodies on their sleeves or the clothing of the person next to them. It was disgusting! How could anyone bear to live like that?

However, she could not expound too vigorously upon their inadequate cleaning rituals, when she knew her own toilette was lacking. Hers was forced though. And the mongrels surrounding her could not lay claim to that same excuse. They had been following a river for the past two days and, if any man had desired to do so, they could have taken a brief dip in its chilly waters to remove the very top layer of encrusted grime that enveloped them.

Navali comforted herself about her own lack of a bath with the fact that, at the very least, the dirt and dust that covered every inch of her skin and garments did not reek like the others' and she was extremely grateful for it.

She did not think she could have forborne gasping through her own odor for every single breath she took as the Pitan soldiers now certainly did—or mayhap they did not even notice the ripe aroma that wafted from their bodies every time they twitched a limb.

Her dress was in much the same atrocious condition as the rest of her. The hem possessing numerous slashes, one of which made riding modestly difficult, as it was slit nearly up to one shapely hip and Navali had to make certain she sat on both of its frayed edges to keep it closed over her smooth flesh.

Not an easy feat to achieve with one's hands bound to the saddle in front of oneself. But Navali unceasingly saw her modesty preserved in that respect, for there was no need to provide these men with any more ideas or visions than they already had. It was embarrassing enough to have to see to the necessities of life with them a few feet away on the other side of some measly brush.

The wound on her shoulder had completely healed within the last day and now only afforded her the slightest twinge of pain every now and then. She could see the faint, pink scar through the small tear the arrow had left in her gown. But the smallness of the scar and the lack of pain were not of particular comfort to her right now, for her heart was not feeling very light no matter what kind of blessings she was receiving.

The truth was, she could hardly think beyond her need to return to her own home.

And to her own bath, her pristine gowns, her attendants, good, nourishing food, and gentlemen! Female companionship would be nice as well, of course. Even Tabitha the Terrible's presence would be welcome at this very moment. Anything at *all*, to feel she was not the last person on Yria who possessed a shred of decency and kindness, would be most welcome and appreciated.

Not that she would really be going home anytime soon, Navali realized. Not even if she was rescued, or managed to escape, would she be returning to Lynaria, for she would still be forced to continue on to Dareknay and marry their barbaric prince.

Although, she considered, if he resembled, in any way, the tall Dareknay she had noted the night of her abduction with the swirling green eyes, her fate would really not be so detestable as it had once seemed. Even if he smelled and acted halfway like a gentleman, it would be a vast improvement over her present company.

Navali let her mind wander from the horrors of her current predicament and wondered what being married to a warrior of his magnificent features and physique could be like. She was not acquainted with a large number of warriors, so it was nigh impossible to draw a comparison from any of the men she already knew.

Her father knew how to wage battle against an opponent, but fighting was not what he did for a living. He was not a warrior by trade, he was a politician to the core of his being, and Navali could not quite imagine what it would be like to marry into the warlike race her father had promised her to.

A warrior for a husband, she mused. Muscles and tanned skin, a stubbled chin and callused hands. What a seemingly breathtaking combination!

However, she was inclined to consider that there was a possible flaw to the whole warrior persona. Would he be aggressive towards her or any children they might have? She prayed not, for she would then be forced to flee from that country as well as the one she was now captive in. Navali knew her father would never let her come back home, perhaps a visit now and then would be welcome, but never for good. That could be a dilemma if she had to flee Dareknay, for she would not know where else to go.

Or perhaps her husband would be everything her father was not—that was how she pictured the man with the green eyes as being. Affectionate, and loving, lots of laughter, and touching, someone who would truly care if she was happy or saddened. Someone she could share her feelings and innermost dreams with.

Navali had dared not tell anyone about any of those things in Lynaria, for she had not had many friends in the castle, and she now mused to herself that it would have been marvelous to have been able to speak her desires to someone without fear of repercussion.

The Dareknay did not have any stipulations on emotions that Navali was aware of, and though she dreamed of what it would be like to share her innermost thoughts and feelings, it made her more nervous than she felt comfortable with.

Shifting in the saddle in the wake of that particularly embarrassing emotion, Navali grasped the pommel a little tighter in anxiety. She had never been around unleashed emotion and displays of affection, and she wondered what that would feel and be like.

The handsome man she had seen the night of her abduction had certainly looked very pleasant, his eyes had been kind and reassuring, before a good deal of alarm had flashed in their green depths when the monster of a Pitan had yanked her back against him.

Navali sincerely hoped she would see that particular Dareknay again. Even if he was not the one she was betrothed to, she would still like to know his name and a little bit more about him.

Not that her barbarian husband would allow her to seek out information on another man. He would probably keep her locked in their room until she was as far gone with child as he could hope for. By that time she would not be seen as attractive by any man, let alone the most handsome one she had ever been blessed to lay eyes on.

And he had possessed such thick, lustrous, dark hair. Navali sighed wistfully in remembrance. No Lynarian had hair that color. Her people only boasted hair the color of sunshine, white gold, or silver-blonde like hers. His, though, had been rich and silky looking with a touch of burnished gold in the torchlight.

A lock of Navali's own hair fell into her face at that moment, disrupting her daydream, and she blew it away impatiently. Why did she have to be cursed with such unruly hair? She had never seen anyone with such riotous curls as she had been born with. They were not the tight ringlets she had seen on some of the Selenacan women. They were large, loose curls that tended to tighten at the very ends of her hair, and the strands knotted unbearably when exposed to the slightest hint of a breeze.

Just then the convoy of soldiers ahead of Navali halted, and her horse followed suit with an uncomfortable jolt.

What now? She startled and glanced up from her contemplative stance, before staring in stunned dismay at what lay before her. They had crested a steep ridge in the earth and the trees that had surrounded them their entire journey had abruptly ended, yielding the sight of Krinarn stretching for miles below their position. A dark, malevolent haze hung suspended over the city, and Navali thought it resembled a cloak of shrouding evil.

She could barely make out what appeared to be crude spikes and cages at the front gate, and thought sarcastically of what a wholesome and uplifting greeting they were going to receive from the corpses rotting on the long pointed spires or the ones locked in those steel contraptions.

Vultures and other carrion swarmed the skies over Krinarn, and Navali couldn't quite suppress the shudder that raced through her body at the sight. She did not want to think about why the dirty birds were there, and what part they held in the animal kingdom. They were good for one thing and one thing only—cleaning up someone else's mess.

Navali's hands tightened beneath their bonds on the pommel of the saddle. The reins of her horse were in the hands of the skinny soldier who had fondled her backside the very first day of her captivity, and she groaned quietly in dismay. There was going to be no escape for her, she could feel it. At least not when there would be a chance of disappearing quickly into the thick woods and mountains behind her.

Even the sparsely trained soldiers surrounding her would be able to rout her in a city with that many defenses. Besides, the people who lived there would probably give her over to the soldiers if they found her first, as she did not have much coin to offer them to help her escape.

Navali desired a good cry at the feeling of hopelessness that swamped her body. *How was she going to escape now?* She blinked back the moisture that rapidly sprang to her eyes, suddenly furious at herself for the loss of control they bespoke of.

She would not let these foul beasts see her weakness! She would not let them have that final satisfaction over her. She was the High Princess of Lynaria, and she would show herself as such.

The line of men in front of her started down the steep incline of the rock-strewn road to the city, and Navali felt that much closer to despair. Less than a few miles to go and she would be imprisoned, perhaps forever, in the thick, crumbling walls of Krinarn.

Lowering her head, Navali let her hair slide forward to hide her expression, she could not seem to control the emotions roiling through her and tears seemed to be imminent. She desperately gasped air into lungs constricted by panic. *This was not happening! It couldn't be! Not to her!*

She was supposed to have been wed two days ago, not abducted by vicious fiends! Even marriage to a barbarian would be better than her present fate.

An anguished groan abruptly rent the air and she brought her head up as her horse jerked to the side as the man who held its reins captive fell sideways off his own mount. She glanced briefly down at the body, noted an arrow had pierced the man's chest, and quickly turned her face away from the sight.

Chaos reigned as more arrows found their mark and human screams accompanied the sounds of frenzied, panicked horses. Battle cries joined the cacophony of screams and Navali watched transfixed as three Dareknay Drocun's kneed their horses out of the woods on the left side of the convoy, while others could be seen faintly through the cover of the trees.

The three muscular men rode with supreme skill towards the savages who were now still and nearly silent in their currently cowed state. Drawing to a halt, two of the Dareknay waited silently as the third rode to the line of hulking soldiers surrounding the Pitan king and shouted, "What is mine, stays mine! And what belongs to me I guard, protect, or recover with single-minded diligence!"

The magnificent golden stallion beneath him pawed the air and ground until he brought it ruthlessly back under control with one hand. "If you wish death today, resist my Drocuns. If you wish to live, call off your men. We only want that which is ours."

Navali's heart skipped a beat in hope at the warrior's words. Surely he meant her! These warriors were here to save her! she realized with a wash of pure joy. She could love their entire barbaric race just for this one act of true heroism.

"Come, come, Krinar," the Dareknay leader coaxed in sarcasm as the Pitan king glanced about himself, clearly hoping for a means to defeat this unexpected turn of events. "I do not have all day to wait upon your decision, and my men are growing impatient. You must make your choice now, or face the consequences of the fate I will *relish* choosing for you."

Krinar stared in maddened shock at the muscled Dareknay leader. At his hesitation, an arrow suddenly whistled from the tree line and the soldier to Krinar's right let out a scream and collapsed heavily against the Pitan king, who pushed the bloodied, arrow-pierced carcass away with frantic movements.

Realizing how close he had come to dying, Krinar's voice rang out, high-pitched in fear, but strangled with fury. "I yield the battle …" The word 'today' slipped quietly from his lips with the Dareknay none the wiser. Then Krinar held up one deathly-white, bejeweled hand. "Soldiers, stand down!"

The Pitan men were obviously reluctant to do as their king commanded. But, nevertheless, grumbling and cursing the

Drocuns, they lowered their weapons and stood still, glaring as fiercely as they could manage.

A lithely muscled, redheaded Dareknay broke from the tree line and rode swiftly to where Navali sat captive astride her horse. Drawing to a halt, he jerked the reins of her mount from beneath the body of the dead guard, and then kneed his horse back to the relative safety of the trees, leading Navali's nag behind him.

Another warrior met them in the cover of the woods and slashed the bonds from her hands with a dagger. "Keep silent, and we may make it out of here alive."

Navali had not had any intention of making noise, but the man did not know that, and she nodded her head in response to his order. She wanted to live as much as any of these men.

That was not to say she wanted to *live with* any of them either, but that was best left to discuss at another time—one that was not so fraught with peril.

The leader of the rescuing band of men was backing his horse away from the enraged Pitan soldiers. His eyes never wavered from the savage king, and his strongly, chiseled features never betrayed any anxiety or emotion he may be feeling.

He held himself erect in the saddle, his sword arm held out from his side. From the wicked gleam of the blade, a man would be a fool indeed to challenge this warrior. When he reached the edge of the trees he continued to back the horse into their sheltering foliage until he was swallowed by the dark shadows.

Navali watched from her place between the two Dareknay men as the leader turned the animal he was riding and headed in the direction of his men.

The warrior on her right kicked his horse in the leader's direction and the man holding her horse's reins joined the others as well, her mount reluctantly following in his wake.

The Dareknay Drocuns traveled at a fast clip down a faint path. The forest grew darker and more dense. The horses steps were muffled by the vast sea of green leaves under their hooves, not a sound revealing their swift passage through the forest.

They kept on with the brisk pace for several hours until they reached a small clearing in the brush. Then their leader rode back to where Navali was seated. "Good day, Princess," he greeted.

The deep, seductive timbre of his voice rolled over Navali, and pleasant shudders suddenly raced down her spine as she stared, mesmerized by his masculine features.

Now that his face had been fully revealed to her, a startling realization swept over her. It was him! The one she had been daydreaming about! Green eyes smiled at her in amusement as he awaited her response.

"It is now," she quipped, and could not believe the audacity that had so easily sprung from her lips. She fought the flush that arose to her cheeks and managed to give him a serene smile in return, knowing as she did so that it was probably one of the hardest things she had ever done in her life. Why did this man have to be so handsome? And kind? And gentlemanly?

Were those not the same characteristics she had so longed to see exhibited but a few hours past? Navali admitted to herself that they were. Now if only he were a different race than the dreaded Dareknay, then she could have actually allowed herself to like him fully. But, alas, there was nothing she could do to change his heritage.

"Aye," he replied. "I do believe you would think it better after the ordeal you've been through." His very attractive face was a mask of concern. "I must ask, are you all right? Did those savages harm you in any way?" The hard look in his green gaze gave away the question he was truly asking.

"The bruises and cuts that are visible are the only damage they have wrought this journey. No wound even remains to be tended from the arrow I took in the ambush. And yourself?" she inquired.

His green eyes flashed with amusement. "None the worse for wear. Not even a scratch."

He held his bare, muscled arms out for her inspection, but Navali barely glanced at them. She could not seem to tear her gaze away from his green one. What was it about this warrior that drew her, like a moth to flame?

"Who are you?" Navali asked suddenly, and rather bluntly, completely overwhelmed by the presence of the man she had allowed herself to so girlishly dream of every night of her captivity.

The Dareknay was as handsome as a sinfully dark night, his eyes shining with the delicacies that could be found there. Any man as handsome as this one probably had the arrogance to go along with the chiseled, good looks, and she tore her gaze away from the magnetic, green depths of his eyes. She was not about to stroke his ego any more than was necessary by revealing the deep attraction she felt for him. Doubtless he had droves of women who already heightened his sense of self-confidence, and Navali was determined not to be counted among their heavily-perfumed and twittering ranks.

"Don't you already know, little one?" His eyes were twinkling at her, the different greens swirling enigmatically as the very corners wrinkled with his amused smile.

"Should I?" Navali countered rather snippishly, for she did not like feeling as though he were reading her like an open book. She was determined to sound bold and strong in front of this man. She tilted her head to one side, making a show of slowly inspecting him from the top of his dark head to the tips of his leather boots.

When her eyes met his again, Navali was taken aback to realize that he had conducted his own perusal of her person. But where she knew her own gaze revealed a distinct coldness and stilted formality, his green gaze glowed warmly and appreciatively.

"Apparently not," he said. A glimmer of disconcerted surprise suddenly flittered across his handsome features and his warm gaze cooled a degree before he turned serious. "I am Ashyre."

He voiced the statement with complete confidence, as though it were supposed to mean something to Navali. But, no matter how she wracked her brain for the answer, it did not. She allowed one eyebrow to raise quizzically, and he clarified his answer.

"Your future husband."

Navali gasped in surprise, her luminous eyes widening without her knowledge or permission.

CHAPTER NINE

The announcement of his status as her future husband had not been exactly what Navali had expected to hear. The man of her fantasies to be her husband?

She straightened to her full height in the saddle and tilted her chin to a rather haughty level. It would not do to let him see he had unsettled her.

There was only one good thing about the man's introduction, Navali thought, and that was the fact she now knew her betrothed's name! Though she could not be more pleased that she was not set to wed a man of ogre countenance, she was disconcerted that he was the very man she had been dreaming about! What was she to do now?

Navali did not think she could ever grow to be truly comfortable in his presence, not after allowing her imagination to run shamelessly wild. She would probably blush to the roots of her hair every time he set foot in the same room as herself, and that would not do at all—not for a staid and supposedly composed Lynarian princess!

No wonder her people, especially the women of her race, kept their emotions under lock and key. It was so much simpler to not let those unruly feelings cloud your mind and turn your body to warm mush at the thought of a man's strong arms holding one close.

Certainly she had wished to know more about the man who had so intrigued her, but that was before she knew she was going to marry him! If she reacted so strongly to him now, when she did not even know him personally, and he had not even touched her, she would likely react ten times stronger when she did know him, and he did touch her! How was she supposed to keep her feelings and emotions a secret from her people then? They would surely want reports on how she was getting on, and her father probably had spies aplenty in Chimea!

Her eyes flashed silver fire. She would not fall for the prince. She would not let herself. Her people need never know the brief moment of weakness she had allowed herself in being attracted to her future spouse.

The prince shifted uneasily in his saddle at the look of defiance and determination that fleetingly crossed his future wife's delicate features, before she smoothed it into an unreadable mask. The princess had not spoken a solitary word since he declared himself her future husband.

What was so wrong with wedding him that it struck her speechless?

He did not think she found him hideously unattractive, but her silence was beginning to make him seriously doubt the women who had previously admired his looks and it was making him dashed uncomfortable.

Shyre had to admit to himself though, that even if she did not think the same of him, *he* at least found *her* irresistibly desirable.

Long, curly blonde hair blew gently across a face of infinite beauty. Her silver, iced eyes sparkled with a hidden heat that he wanted desperately to uncover. And, although her clothes were as ragged and dirty as those of the villagers he had come across earlier that day, the smooth calf she painstakingly kept covered with her torn skirt revealed a creamy expanse of skin that stole the breath from his lungs.

Shyre exhaled roughly as his eyes traveled leisurely back up to her face, and he searched her closed expression for a glimpse of emotion to tell him what she was thinking.

Navali blinked her eyes once before swiftly recovering her composure. She still did not know what to say to the strikingly attractive man next to her, but opted for the formalness that was oft exchanged between two newly introduced acquaintances. Even this rapscallion of a prince could not find fault with that. She swallowed nervously, at least she hoped he could not anyway.

"It's a pleasure to finally make your acquaintance, your highness."

Her statement was met with a frown as his eyebrows snapped together.

Finally? he thought. *How dare she infer that he had not done his duty and come for her as swiftly as possible?*

"I'm sorry I was so long in coming to your aid," he snapped back bitingly. "If you are unfortunate enough to be abducted again, I will make certain to ride to your rescue more swiftly."

Navali did not know what she had said to upset him. But she was not given the time to ask him either, for he wheeled his mount about and rode to the opposite side of the glade.

Her future husband lifted one hand and signaled his men forward, and the Drocuns enclosed her and her scraggly mount within their protective ranks.

The men whispered amongst themselves as they directed their horses swiftly across the terrain and occasionally glanced at her with disapproval shining in their eyes.

In confusion, Navali wondered what she had done to cause their enmity and kept her eyes downcast, striving not to meet any of the dark stares that were shot her way.

"You should not have said such a thing." The man stationed to her right told her in a deep, hushed tone several hours later, long after Navali had given up hope of discovering what she had done wrong. She had glanced repeatedly in the high prince's direction, but his stiffened back made it more than clear he was still upset with her. He had not even glanced back once in all that time to give her any indication of a softening towards her.

Navali glanced up now in surprise at the voice sounding so close to her ear and her jaw nearly dropped in surprise. The man next to her looked exactly like her intended!

Her betrothed's double continued to speak, his face taut with disapproval. "We traveled as fast as we dared to reach you, and yet you greet us with snide comments?" His words pattered out in his fury and he glared at her in disgust.

Navali came to the obvious conclusion that her betrothed and this man were twins, and she suddenly found the subject quite fascinating, for there were never any multiples birthed in her culture, only singly-born babies. But there was something vaguely different about this man. Navali allowed herself to peruse his features more closely, what was it?

The brother's eyes glittered in anger as he awaited some kind of response, and she suddenly realized what it was! His eyes were of a light golden hue and not green in color!

His words finally registered. "Snide comments—? What snide comments?" She inquired, completely confused. "He's the one who rode away so abruptly when I was only being pleasant," she haughtily informed him. His brother was the one who had been rude and deserving of a dressing-down, not she.

The man looked at her with a question lingering in his eyes before those golden orbs abruptly cleared. "You were only being pleasant?" He asked, a small amount of doubt still coloring his voice.

Navali was nonplussed as to how her social graces pertained to anything, but, nevertheless, she responded to his query. "I was only observing the niceties that are to be expected when meeting one's betrothed for the first time."

This was met with a brief chuckle as the man looked first at her, then at the back of his leader's head. A robust laugh soon joined the chuckle and it continued on for a few moments as if he found what she had said extremely amusing.

As she allowed a look of stern quizzicality to cover her face, he explained. "We—" He gestured to everyone around him and at the leader. "All thought you were chiding us on taking so long in coming to your rescue."

"Why would I do something as foolish as that?" she asked, the stern look dissolving, and her brow creasing in confusion. "I was extremely grateful to see you all coming out of the trees. I thought I was going to be in captivity in Krinarn for eternity—or worse, sacrificed to their bloodthirsty god. Why, of all things, would I castigate my rescuers?"

"That's the very same thing we were all contemplating. We thought you an extremely spoiled, self-centered, and pampered princess," he said, his eyes now glowing warmly and with a hint of good humor. "By the by, I am Ashtyn. Your betrothed's twin brother."

"I noted the resemblance," Navali stated dryly, and then observed as he chuckled in amusement at his own inane introduction. "Unfortunately, you are all probably right about my being a spoiled, pampered princess. Though I sincerely hope I'm not completely self-centered."

Ashtyn studied her for a serious moment. "I think we were wrong about the self-centered part," he finally admitted aloud. "And probably the spoiled part, too. Otherwise you would not have survived as long as you did with the Pitan. They are not known for their winning ways and courtly manners," he teased her, giving her a wink, and then gestured with a nod in the direction of his twin. "I think I had better go explain things to your intended before he stews himself into a real fury."

"I take it that is not a real fury then?" She asked him and permitted her eyes to widen in wonder. The high prince's face had been dark as a moonless night, his lips compressed into a flat line, and his eyes had shot green fire as he had left her presence.

"Nay," Ashtyn assured her, though the word held no comfort for Navali. The truth about her betrothed's fury was one fact she could have lived her entire life without. "Not many people have seen him when he is truly enraged."

"Then I sincerely hope never to," Navali decided aloud. "And I hope never to be the cause of his rage as well. I will strive to keep my emotions more under control so we do not have any more conflicts," she ended graciously, straightening her spine visibly, thinking the brother may need some reassurance that she would be able to conduct herself as the Lynarian princess she had been born to be.

"That is all well and good that you do not wish to cause him to lose his temper, my lady, for you would not only have to deal with *his* rage, but mine as well. What affects my brother, generally affects me," he stated, a warning light encompassing his golden gaze.

Navali understood perfectly. If she angered his brother unnecessarily, she would most likely anger him as well. Navali nodded her head in response to his warning.

"As to the part about keeping your emotions under control," Ashtyn had gentled his voice and expression and now continued. "It would be wise not to cry and fuss all the time as women are wont to do, but our people do not hold stock with not showing *any* emotion. In fact, we prefer to know exactly what the other person is attempting to say, and emotions help us fully figure that out."

Navali looked at him with only a hint of doubt on her face and Ashtyn realized he would need to give her express permission to show her feelings. "You'll find we are a very teasing and loving family when we accept a person into our close fold."

Fear and trepidation flashed across her silver gaze before being quickly subdued into nothingness. Ashtyn did not think he had gotten very far in his attempt at reassuring her and could have kicked himself at the even more guarded look that now graced her face.

He sighed. He would have to tell his twin to reiterate the message to his intended himself. Glancing at the Lynarian princess out of the corner of his eyes again, Ashtyn thought his brother would perhaps need to repeat it more than once before she felt completely comfortable. At least there was hope that she would be able to show her feelings in time and that she was not completely devoid of any human emotions and frailties—well, when she wanted to be, he amended to himself.

Dipping his dark head in Navali's direction, Ashtyn kneed his beautiful white stallion to his brother's side. He knew he could tell his twin what he had discovered about Navali's earlier comments by way of the special link that connected them, but Ashtyn would not have taken anything in exchange for being able to see Shyre's face when he heard the news.

Ashtyn had seen the look of instant attraction and interest that had flashed across his twin's face and he wanted to question his brother about that as well. By the time he made it to the front of the line, his youngest brother had joined him and now rode a comfortable distance from his elder brothers.

Aakin was not about to miss overhearing this particular conversation. He had seen Ashtyn talking with the Lynarian princess, and when that man had laughed he knew something interesting must be afoot, and he dearly loved to know anything of interest.

Before Ashtyn could open his mouth and reveal his purpose for leaving his post beside the princess, the brothers were joined by the Drocuns Shyre had left behind to keep an eye on the Pitan.

"My lords," Harry greeted as they drew alongside their princes.

Shyre and Ashtyn nodded in response at the same time.

"What is your report?" Shyre queried, ignoring his brother for the moment.

"The Pitan entered Krinarn immediately after you departed. Then, a little more than an hour later, scouts were sent out in every direction." Harry replied.

"What were they after?"

Harry quirked a grin at the other scout and Shyre guessed that money would soon exchange hands from the loser of whatever wager the two men had made.

"We knew you would be asking us that, your highness, so we snatched one of them in the woods."

Shyre's own mouth twitched at the corners, it seemed his men already knew what he would have done in that situation. "Very good," he praised. "And what did you discover? I assume you got some useful information from him?"

"Very useful," Harry snorted. "These Pitan aren't that tough. We had him talking in less time than it takes all of the castle back home to know of a scandal. It seems Krinar doesn't make a move without first consulting his little witch, the High Fayrah. The scout said that no one has seen her for several days and that they do not know when she will return, so Krinar sent them out to find her and bring her back."

Shyre nodded as he thought about the implications of that, and then realized the two scouts were waiting for a more verbal response. He looked at each of them in turn. "You did well, men. Ride far behind the column and make sure we are not being followed. I do not want unexpected company if they happen to find that witch any time soon."

The two men gave brief salutes before kicking their mounts to a trot and disappearing back into the woods.

Shyre's eyes met his twin's, and found that Ashtyn was looking at him with a twinkle in his golden gaze.

"Well Ashtyn, to what do I owe this sudden visit?" Shyre asked, his voice an icy growl of displeasure, better to just go ahead and get it over with now. He knew his brother had talked with his betrothed, though he had purposefully not bothered to listen in. He did not wish to know what Princess Navali had to say about their earlier encounter.

"Not your good attitude, that's for certain," Ashtyn had the gall to answer. "It must be due to my unending patience and diligence instead," his twin cheekily informed him.

Shyre glared at his brother in warning. "If you wish to observe true diligence and unending patience in action, Ashtyn, I will happily oblige you in the lists when we reach Chimea."

"No… no, that's all right, Shyre. I wouldn't want to mess up your face anymore than it already is. We wouldn't want to scare off your betrothed so soon after we have just recovered her, would we?" Ashtyn answered, his grin wide.

"I don't think it's *my* ugly countenance you should be concerned with, brother," Shyre responded. "For if *I* am unattractive to women, *you* are surely much more undesirable. What with your odd colored eyes and all."

Aakin laughed uproariously at the comments slinging between his two eldest brothers, before being quickly shushed by General Ivan as that man rode to see what so interested and amused him.

"Quietly, lad. We are not clear of the Pitan yet, keep your voice down." Ivan shifted his attention and his mount closer to Ashtyn. "Just what are you saying to your brother to make him scowl so?"

"I was not trying to make him scowl. However, it is most amusing to see, do not you agree, Ivan?" Ashtyn asked the general and that man's gaze swung between the two.

"If you weren't trying to make him frown, then what did you wish to accomplish?"

Ashtyn, glee evident in his dancing eyes, replied. "I was attempting to inform my brother of several mistaken assumptions he has about his betrothed."

"Mistaken!?!" Shyre kept his voice to a low, menacing rumble. "About the princess? I don't think so." He snorted ungentlemanly in his twin's direction. "She is a spoiled, ungrateful chit, who is badly in need of a spanking!"

"After she was only trying to be pleasant and make conversation with you?" Ashtyn asked him with mock incredulousness, shaking his head in exasperation. "That would surely cement in her mind that you're a savage, uncouth barbarian."

"Uncouth barbarian?" Shyre nearly roared and made a swipe at his double's grinning face. General Ivan shot him a pointed look and the high prince settled once more in his stirrups.

"She is as *pleasant* as a thistle beneath my saddle," Shyre said in more moderate tones, though they were spoken from between clenched teeth. "The princess is insulting in the extreme and—"

He broke off as Ashtyn started shaking his dark head in a now serious response. "You are wrong, brother. She was only attempting to be polite to a man who had just informed her he was her future husband. How did you think she would take the news?"

"With a great deal more aplomb," Shyre stated.

"Well, she tried. You, and the rest of us, thought she was being ungrateful for her decidedly poor choice of words. I do not think it is every day a woman is told so forcefully and abruptly that she is looking at her new betrothed." Ashtyn attempted to make his twin see reason.

Shyre sighed, feeling resigned to the fact he had acted as a complete bastard. "She really was not trying to find fault with her rescue, then?" He asked Ashtyn, and that man again shook his head in response. "So I suppose I should go back to her and *apologize* for my quick judgment and rotten behavior?"

Shyre really did not like the word apologize, but he grated it out between clenched teeth.

His twin again replied nonverbally, this time in the affirmative.

"Would you please *say* something? Instead of just shaking and bobbing your head about like a halfwit!" Shyre's patience could only take so much at the moment and his brother was not helping in the slightest.

"And what would you have me say?" Ashtyn asked curiously.

"I don't know. Anything!"

"Well," Ashtyn shrugged. "Your attitude hasn't gotten any better for our conversation, you're still being a bastard," he replied, and the quickly strangled laughter around him nearly made him lose the battle to withhold his own smile. His brother was in this deep, very deep. It should be fun to see how he got himself out of the hole he was digging deeper with every passing minute.

"Never mind, Ashtyn. I've changed my mind. I do *not* want you to speak, I want you to be silent, like the grave," Shyre added as they came into a clearing that housed an abandoned village. Crude graves lined the path and he shot his brother a pointed look.

Ashtyn just grinned and saluted. The look on his face assuring Shyre that he could be silent and still talk to him.

Shyre groaned and rolled his eyes in self-disgust. He had a feeling telling his brother to keep quiet was not the best command he had ever given. It was, in fact, one that would probably cause him a great deal of grief.

Sure enough, his twin wished him luck through their private link as Shyre pulled his horse out of the column and waited for his men to go past.

Shyre looked in the direction of his future wife and nearly groaned again. It was obvious that riding away from her before in a fit of anger had not been the most intelligent thing he had done today either.

He just hoped she did not hold grudges, and forgave him sooner than his twin was bound to. Ashtyn could be incredibly pig-headed about letting him off the hook without first making sure he would not repeat his mistake twice.

Shyre refused to contemplate his twin's retribution anymore at the moment. His betrothed was now closer to him and he could see the questions roiling in her beautiful silver eyes. The mission to win his intended's heart could very well be a great deal harder than the one to rescue her from the Pitan tyrant.

Her mount was now abreast of his own and Shyre nudged his horse to keep pace with hers. Navali did not immediately turn her full attention to him as he joined her and Shyre's suspicions that she was upset with him were confirmed. The entire situation was not going in the direction he had so carefully mapped out on the long nights he had lain awake as he journeyed to recover her from her savage captors.

Savage ….

The word gave him pause. Ashtyn had said she thought him a savage, uncouth barbarian and that, if he were to ever have a hope of a love match in his marriage, would never suit his purposes. From this moment on, Shyre would show her he was anything but savage. He would be her knight in shining armor if she so desired it.

Shyre did not exactly know how he would go about accomplishing that feat, but he would attempt it just the same. It would not be the first challenge he had ever faced in his life. If she needed him to be a courtly and genteel prince, he would do it!

Though it might kill him in the process, he thought with a grimace.

Navali ignored the prince as he urged his horse closer to hers, though it proved to be one of the hardest things she had ever done in her life. The man was a rude, arrogant louse and she would not give him the satisfaction of panting after him like a common trollop whenever he was near.

However, it was hard—incredibly hard—to stick to her resolve as she could not keep from peeking at him from the corner of her eye and drinking in the sight of him. He was truly magnificent. If one man had been made on this earth to set her heart aflutter, it was him.

Why did he have to be so unbelievably handsome? Couldn't he at least have been an ugly toad with rotting teeth or some such thing that would make ignoring him and not falling in love with him incredibly easy?

No, apparently not.

He sat his horse as though he had been born to the saddle and his intensely masculine hands held the reins with firm, gentle strength. Navali did not even have to glance at his face yet another time to recall his chiseled features for they were indelibly etched in her mind.

From his thick wavy black hair to his finely muscled jaw with the deep indent in the middle of his chin, every part of his features were perfect in Navali's opinion, and that was really, very terrible for her.

She could not be attracted to her future husband! She just couldn't! It wasn't possible.

She was the princess of Lynaria and therefore not allowed to feel anything for this man—or any other man for that matter. Worst of all, she was about to spend the rest of her life tied to this all-too-attractive Dareknay! What a nightmare this rescue was turning out to be!

It would be easier to save her heart from the prince if he continued to be an overbearing and unreasonable ogre. Yet Navali had a sneaking suspicion that he was about to apologize, and that just wouldn't do! If he started acting kind and caring towards her, Navali knew she would be unable to keep herself from loving him. He was everything she had secretly dreamed about.

It really was pathetic and trite of her to fall for the man she was being forced to marry, not to mention the one who had raced to rescue her from a fate worse than death. However, she could not seem to be able to help herself. And if he opened his sculpted lips at this moment and uttered a heartfelt apology, she was going to lose all command of her emotions and fall even more in love with him than she feared she already had.

Her people would surely know then that she was defective, that she had always been defective.

When other children were able to disengage their emotions and adhere to the strict moral code the Lynarians demanded, she was still attempting to master her temper, and struggling to overcome her impulses to display her affection for her parents in physical touch.

Her father would most assuredly be ashamed of her if she lost that hard-won hold on her control now. Nothing she could do in front of her people after that would be able to make up for losing her composure to a Dareknay of all persons.

If she could only find a way to not fall in love with the prince, then everything would be all right. No one would feel shamed or betrayed.

Navali felt the prince's eyes on her and raised her chin a scant inch. She would not love him. She simply would not!

CHAPTER TEN

S hyre glanced over at his intended and let out a deep breath. The princess was obviously not going to look at him until he made amends.

"I misconstrued what you said earlier and I wish to apologize for riding off in a fit of anger," he began rapidly, desiring to get the matter concluded as swiftly as possible. "It was not fair to you and it was not right of me to leap to conclusions. I was tautly strung. I know that is not an excuse for my abominable behavior, but I ask your forgiveness, princess."

His future bride did not immediately answer him and he saw her jaw tighten. At her silence, Shyre began to grow irritated with her all over again. *Didn't she realize he did not just apologize to people every day in such a humble manner? Did she expect him to grovel even more?*

Because if she did, a surprise was in store for her.

Mayhap his twin had her wrongly pegged. She did not seem to be trying to maintain niceties between them, and she most assuredly was not being very pleasant at the moment.

Mayhap you should *grovel, brother.*

Shyre knew that was not his own thought, for he never would have had such a foolhardy and embarrassing notion. He shot Ashtyn the image of his twin falling unceremoniously off his horse and everyone laughing at his expense.

Ashtyn merely showed him what Shyre would look like if he truly groveled.

Shyre glared at the back of his twin's head.

Navali's soft voice broke into Shyre's black thoughts of revenge and he conceded the mental fight to his brother. The argument was childish in the first place and he had more important things to do and think about than ways to get even with his immature, younger brother.

"Very well." Navali nodded to him. "I accept your apology."

"Thank you," Shyre replied, his irritation at her fading nearly before it even began, he then wracked his brain to think of something more to say to the stoic beauty beside him.

What did a man say to a woman that he did not know, but was soon to wed?

No thoughts immediately revealed themselves to Shyre and Ashtyn started in, once again, on his campaign to annoy him. Shyre's twin sent him images of talking with Navali about the weather, her family, his family, weapons, and the latest fashion in clothes.

Shyre silently told Ashtyn he would return his brother's merriment at Ashtyn's expense when it was Ashtyn's turn to court his future wife. Nevertheless, Shyre took his brother's suggestion and thought about the options he had been given.

The high prince did not wish to discuss her father. That was something he did not think any suitor would want to discuss with the woman he was going to marry, so that ruled out her family as a subject as he believed that was all the family she possessed.

His own relatives were being somewhat obnoxious to him at the moment, and that struck his family from the list of discussion topics.

The weather was a bleary, drizzly mess, and not at all what one wanted to dwell on, or call attention to, when trying to lighten the mood. And *fashion*? Shyre cringed.

He did not know a thing about it and he honestly did not care. Women wore dresses with frills, flowers, and shiny, glittery things sewn on them. Men were more sensible in his opinion, if one did not count the Lynarian guards and soldiers who favored dressing in pure white on the battlefield.

Shyre favored dark breeches and tunics as the rest of the Drocuns did, and the only embellishment Shyre allowed on his clothing was his personal crest. Unless one of his younger sisters got a hold of his tunics, and then added things he did not even want to think about, when they were practicing the lady-like art of decorative stitching. An art which his sisters particularly despised, and thought everyone should know exactly how much they disliked the properly accepted past-time.

So that left weapons as the only other topic, though Shyre was pretty sure Ashtyn had suggested the topic as a jest of some sort.

However, it was one of the subjects Shyre knew a great deal about, and if he could learn anything about what Lynarians thought of as entertainment, mayhap he could impress his future bride through arranging an event or joust that she would find interesting. And, if it was an area Shyre was skilled in, he might even be able to prove himself strong and able in her eyes.

Shyre brought himself up short, he was beginning to sound hugely ridiculous in his own thoughts, and his twin was bent over double in his saddle as he attempted to contain his mirth.

Blast it! Was there no privacy in this world? His jaw clenched tightly, he was really going to have to strangle his brother for this!

Shyre opened his mouth and uttered the first thing that sprang to his mind, lest his brother think him even more of a buffoon.

"Do you find the quarterstaff to be a tool of great use?" Shyre mentally kicked himself after he spoke, how imbecilic could he sound?

Though Navali looked startled for a moment, she nonetheless answered his wayward question. "I'm not really versed in the art of the quarterstaff, your highness. So I would not be the greatest judge on its usefulness. My father did not permit me to learn how to use one, as I could be injured by a man of greater strength on the practice field."

At the high prince's look of consternation and self-chastisement, Navali decided to take pity on him and expounded on her answer. Though she was determined not to fall in love with the handsome prince, it did not mean their lives had to be completely devoid of conversation or common interests.

"But I have learned a great deal about archery and falconry," she continued, glancing at him with a prompting look, hoping that he would take her blatant hint and continue to converse with her.

"If I remember correctly, you're also able to wield a knife with great accuracy. Or was that someone else who slew one of the Elite-Horde with a single blade?" This was a topic that Shyre could talk endlessly on without feeling the embarrassment the other subjects would have surely brought.

"Aye, your memory is quite accurate. I wielded the dagger that night," she replied with a distant look in her eyes, then pierced him with her silver gaze. "Do you bear any news of my father, your highness?"

Shyre had not really wanted to discuss something that would most likely bring distress to her, but she had brought the Lynarian king up and he would now have to answer her. "Only that which my father informed me of before I took my departure."

Her luminous eyes glinted with alarm, before she fortified her inner defenses. Her horse sidestepped into his, as the animal felt her anxiety and prepared for an attack of some kind.

Shyre reached over and took the reins from her limp fingers, pulling the two horses to a halt. The rest of his warriors followed suit, bringing their destriers to a standstill at a discreet distance from the newly-betrothed couple.

"I assure you, Princess Navali, though gravely wounded, your sire is still alive. My parents are seeing that he gets the best care and healers we have," he quickly and gently informed her, for she had grown deathly pale.

Navali released the breath she had inadvertently been holding and relaxed her white-knuckled grasp on the pommel of the saddle. Relief now shown clearly on her face and Shyre realized with dread that he should probably tell her about the woman who had not been as fortunate as her father.

"However," he ventured cautiously, "The older woman you were traveling with did not survive the attack."

The prince watched Navali's face closely and prepared to catch her if she started to swoon. She did not look to be the fainting type, but he was not about to take any chances after watching her face whiten to such a ghostly pallor.

"There was no love lost between the woman and I," Navali's eyes hinted at something else entirely.

The princess reached for the reins that he had taken from her and Shyre relinquished his hold on them. The column of men then resumed its forward pace and Shyre and Navali were once again swept into its midst.

"I take it you did not care very much for each other." Shyre stated it as fact instead of questioning her about it, his body now flowing smoothly with his stallion's rolling gait. "Differing opinions?"

"Something like that," Navali prevaricated, her voice pleasant, though her face remained stoic.

"And your father? Is it the same with him?" Shyre's curiosity was now whetted and he desired answers. Were the Lynarians really as unfeeling as they wished to appear?

"Oh!" Navali looked at him swiftly, afraid he might draw the wrong impression and believe she did not care for her sire. "I am exceedingly grateful that my father wasn't killed by those filthy animals," Navali assured him quickly and then added as an afterthought. "Though he and I do not always see eye to eye either."

Shyre shrugged, completely unconcerned with that. "I think one may find they do not always agree with their kin. That's how a family is. Sometimes you love them and get along, and other times you wish they would just disappear. Preferably into a dark, dank pit accompanied by someone as incessantly annoying as they are." He shot a glare at the back of Ashtyn's head and his twin's shoulders shook as he chuckled.

The man was listening to every thought Shyre was having and it was getting to be more than a body could take. No man should have to contend with this sort of thing! His brother needed to get a woman of his own!

Navali caught the glare Shyre directed at Ashtyn. "Is now one of those times when you wish one would disappear into a pit?" She asked, truly interested in what his answer would be.

Shyre had not been expecting the princess to look at him, as she had been avoiding his gaze and studiously keeping her eyes trained on the path they were taking as they had continued to converse. So it surprised and startled him when her amused, quicksilver gaze clashed with his green one.

Fire and lightning melded together, meshing in an intricate dance that flared between them, and neither could look away for a very long moment.

"I have forgotten the question." All of a sudden Shyre could not remember what they had been discussing. "What was it you just asked?"

"I—I don't remember either." An embarrassed, little smile crossed Navali's flushed features and she quickly faced forward again.

The magnetic spell broken, Shyre swiftly took hold of his raging emotions. This woman was really too beautiful for his own good. Her silver eyes had been dancing with mirth before he had asked her what she had said and Shyre desired the merry fire to remain there forever. How could he contrive to relight her luminous gaze with laughter again? Before Shyre could come up with a solution, Stephen rode over to them.

Shyre made the introductions, though he knew Lynarian culture typically kept the nobles separate and aloof from the lesser classes, but he wanted Navali to feel more at ease with the men that currently surrounded her. They were her sole protection out here besides himself, and he wanted her to feel that she could trust them. "Princess Navali, this is Stephen of Chimea. A better archer you would be hard-pressed to find," he praised truthfully.

"Stephen," she responded with a nod of her head and smiled, fully aware of the social niceties and facial expressions the Dareknay used when greeting each other.

"Your highness," Stephen replied, and bowed as low as his saddle would permit. The slimly-built Drocun then turned to Shyre. "Are you planning on making camp tonight, my lord? Or will we journey through the night to catch up to your other brothers and the villagers?"

Shyre glanced covertly at Navali and gauged how tired she appeared, for she was his deciding factor in the matter. He could travel for days and catch a few hours of sleep from his saddle, but he doubted that a woman of her station could do the same. The lackluster way the princess was directing her horse and the limp hold she had on the reins, combined with the dark circles beneath her eyes, told him that she was indeed exhausted.

"We will eat and rest a few hours, ere we try to catch Adam and Addison," Shyre decided aloud for the benefit of his warrior.

Stephen dipped his head in response. "The lad, Tucker, has informed us there is a glade in the woods a few miles ahead that should serve well as a resting place. Will that be sufficient?"

Shyre nodded. "If Tucker says so, then it probably is. He has not yet led us astray. Keep a close eye on him once darkness falls though."

"Aye, my lord." The loyal Drocun rode back to the front of the column, stopping on his way to inform Ashtyn and General Titek of the plan.

Navali turned to her betrothed. "If you're stopping on my behalf, you really do not need to. I can make it," she stated after Stephen was out of earshot. Navali had not wanted to seem as if she were second-guessing his plan in front of one of his men.

"I'm certain you could," Shyre responded with a small grin. "But we need to eat and our horses need a rest, as do most of my men. It has been a hard ride these last few days and the Pitan have shown no signs of following us yet, so now seems as good a time as any." He was not about to admit that he thought she looked as if she needed the rest more than any of them. If there was one thing he had learned about women in his life, it was that they did not like their looks commented on, unless it was in a favorable manner, and he was sure the princess would not be any different in that respect than any other woman.

"Oh." Navali was not convinced and watched Shyre closely, not wanting to be more of a burden to these men than she already was. Though she was not certain Shyre was really stopping for his horses and men, Navali decided to go along with his excuse and confessed. "I thank you for stopping then, even if it is not for my benefit. I fear I am feeling rather tired and hungry."

"I am not at my best either," her betrothed agreed with a roguish wink. "You could probably tell that by my brutish behavior earlier."

"Mayhap, just a little." Her eyes twinkled with amusement.

"It was not that humorous." Shyre was quick to defend himself.

"It wasn't amusing at all at the time," she agreed. "However, looking back on the incident, you did seem to be acting rather like a petulant two-cale-old," Navali informed him impudently. She did not have much experience with children, but servants and slaves did talk when they thought she was not listening and they gossiped about how toddlers could be most trying and short-tempered.

"I'll have you know, I *never* act like a two-cale-old." Shyre's brow lowered in consternation.

"Whatever you wish, your highness." Navali allowed a look of pure innocence to appear on her face, enjoying teasing someone who would not accuse her of breaking any laws.

"I was more like a pouting three-cale-old, if you must know," he deadpanned, surprising her with his self-deprecating humor. Navali met his dancing green eyes and laughed when he did.

The high prince was startled by the tinkling laughter that she permitted herself. As she was Lynarian, he had expected something a little more stilted and repressed than that carefree sound.

The two rode in companionable silence for the next couple of miles, each sneaking looks at each other and thinking how blessed they were to be marrying someone who was so physically appealing.

They had not nearly looked their fill by the time they reached a small clearing in the dense wood with a narrow brook babbling alongside the right edge of the trees, and both were slightly disappointed to have arrived at their temporary destination.

"I believe this is where we are to rest for the eve," Shyre said as he turned to fully face her.

"Thank you, your highness, I greatly appreciate the respite." Navali drew back wearily on the reins at those words and her mount came to a slow halt.

She waited as Shyre rode to where his twin and two men were gathering. He spoke with them swiftly before they disbanded. Then, dismounting near her, the high prince let his horse's reins dangle loosely on the ground. The animal did not move as Shyre strode over to Navali and grasped her slender waist. Setting her down directly before him, Shyre belatedly realized that Navali was far closer than he had first reckoned she would be, and his breath stalled in his chest at her nearness. The gasp that escaped her lips caught his full attention and he suddenly ached to taste them.

Were they as soft and smooth as they looked? Would she even receive a kiss from him? Would she perhaps slap him for the attempt? Shyre did not know and at that moment he could not bring himself to care.

He lowered his head slowly, in order for her to have enough time to protest if she so desired, but every thought of politeness or waiting for a more opportune moment fled, as Navali tipped her chin up to him in invitation. Shyre nearly groaned in triumph. Did she even know what that small, accepting movement gave him permission to do?

Shyre's lips were a breath away from Navali's now, and his eyes slid shut as he closed the distance separating them.

A rumbling cough suddenly rent the air and Navali jerked her head back before Shyre's lips could do more than feather across hers.

He was then forced to release the hold he had on her slender waist as she used her hands against his chest to gently push him away.

Totally frustrated at the interruption that had deprived him of the taste of Navali's lips, Shyre glanced over his shoulder. His green eyes narrowed in annoyance as he discovered General Ivan standing behind him. A lopsided grin split the man's bearded face and Shyre mentally groaned. He had not meant for anyone to witness his fast-paced and completely inappropriate action.

It is just as well though, Shyre thought, for she did not seem to be quite as distracted by their near kiss as he was. He had brought his attention back to Navali, only to discover her making her way nonchalantly over to the Drocun he had introduced to her earlier. Navali glanced back at him just as Stephen greeted her with a bow, and Shyre noticed the bright pink hue that dusted her delicate cheekbones.

A self-satisfied grin spread across Shyre's face at the flush revealed on those delicate features. Apparently she was not as unaffected as he had first thought.

A heavy hand clapped down on Shyre's shoulder, but the prince did not bother to turn around as Ivan spoke.

"I don't think you'll have to worry about attraction and desire, my boy. It seems the princess was mighty comfortable in your arms a moment ago." The general was fully aware of the cold Lynarian ways, but then what Dareknay was not?

"Ivan, I love you as though you were my blood uncle, but we shall not be discussing this." Shyre's own face was heating in embarrassment, and he did not want anyone commenting on his attraction for the princess, or hers for him.

Shyre caught several of the men's eyes as he scanned over their heads, and their approving grins made his face redden further. Had the whole blasted world been privy to his actions a moment before?

"I just wanted to put my order in for how many children I think you should give your mama," Ivan replied, moving around to stand in front of Shyre. The prince then watched as the older man shrugged his broad shoulders and lifted his palms up in deliberation. "I think six or seven should do nicely."

Shyre gaped at the man. "We are not even married yet! Do you not think talk of children is a bit premature at this point?"

"Not from the way you were holding her, it's not."

Shyre did groan aloud at that. "Do not discuss this with my brothers, all right?"

"I won't have to." At those cryptic words the general went in search of some warm food and a place to sit down next to the small fire the warriors had quickly built.

Shyre looked over at his men again and Aakin caught his eyes, raising his fist in a triumphal manner. If his men had seen him holding the princess close against his chest, then his brothers had as well, Shyre realized with a groan.

He turned away from the fire and his men, taking his horse and the mangy animal the princess was still forced to ride to the small brook on the other edge of the camp. Shyre knew that if he were to go anywhere near Ashtyn or Aakin the ribbing those two would give him would be unbearable. So, like the coward he felt, he fled to the relative safety of the more deserted side of the clearing. He would face his brothers when the food was ready and their mouths were too full to annoy him with their jesting.

What had he done to deserve his brothers being present for his courtship of the Princess Navali? Whatever it was, it must have been gigantically disastrous.

Hellfire and banked ice! Shyre cursed, he was going to roast his brothers when it was their turn. He would be the most obnoxious person to be found for their courtships. Just see if he was not.

"Stephen?" Navali asked and waited as that man turned to her and bowed low in greeting.

She could not stop herself from covertly glancing over to the Dareknay prince who had so very nearly given her what would have been the first kiss of her life, and found Shyre's eyes already on her. Navali felt the light flush that had already arisen from their closeness of a moment before, deepen to a more rosy hue as she met that disconcerting, green gaze. But Navali was determined not to let that man disconcert her more than he already had, and she pointedly returned her attention to Stephen.

As Navali had earlier resolved to not be a larger burden to these Drocuns than she already was, she was not about to wander around the glade as every other person worked to make their pastime more comfortable and secure. *This Lynarian princess was going to be as much help as possible,* Navali thought, and then said to accomplish that very thing, "I was wondering, Stephen, if I could be of some service in preparing the camp."

"Um ... Well, your highness ... I," Stephen stuttered, unable to think of a task a noble lady would know how to perform, and then unable to formulate a polite refusal that would not offend a princess.

Navali immediately recognized the young man's dilemma. "I know how to cook," she offered. "Perhaps if you were to introduce me to the man responsible for that duty I could endeavor to lighten his burden."

"V-very well, your highness, if you would accompany me, the man is just over there." Stephen gestured with his hand, and then became completely flustered when Navali laid her fingers lightly atop his own.

"You may lead, Drocun," she commanded with a gentle smile, when he continued to look unsure of himself.

"O-of course, wh-whatever you d-desire, your highness," The young man finally managed and, grasping her delicate fingers carefully with his roughly callused hand, led her over to the Drocun in charge of preparing the food.

"Gideon," Stephen caught the man's attention from where he was kneeling on the ground and removing foodstuffs from a worn leather pack. "Princess Navali has graciously asked if she could help you make this evening's meal."

The bearded man grunted in response, before returning to what he had been previously doing.

"That is Gideon's way of saying that he would be delighted to have you assist him," Stephen swiftly, and helpfully, explained.

"Is that what he meant?" Navali asked, her eyes twinkling with mirth. "I am awed that such a small sound could actually be interpreted into so many words, and quite eloquent ones at that."

"Aye...." Stephen nodded, gazing at her in some amazement. He had not expected a princess to weather Gideon's gruffness with such good humor. "Well, I should probably return to my own duties now—that is, if you have no further need of me," he quickly amended.

Navali shook her head with a small smile. "Nay, you have already been immensely helpful. I'm sure I can get on fine now, thank you."

Stephen nodded and then turned uncertainly away, not quite sure he should be leaving the princess to Gideon's tender mercies. But there was no further way for him to detain his departure and he was forced to return to gathering wood for the fire.

"So," Navali interrupted the bearded man's attention again. "What task could you assign me to, please?"

Gideon glanced up and then looked her over doubtfully, before shaking his head in silent disgust and setting several sacks to the side.

He waved his hand toward the sacks and Navali took that to mean whatever was in those pouches was to be her duty. She knelt and gingerly opened one of them, half afraid of what she would discover, and found that it contained nothing more innocuous than flour. Quickly going through the other pouches, she then turned her gaze on Gideon who was now cutting potatoes and putting them in a large cauldron.

"You wish me to make biscuits, then?" Navali inquired and watched as he nodded in affirmation. "Very well, then. What would you like me to bake them in?"

Gideon released his breath in a long-suffering sigh and rose to rifle through another pack. He pulled out a deep, thick pan with an equally thick lid and gestured for her to take it.

Navali did so, and then nearly dropped it, as the weight of it forced her arm to straighten. She quickly grasped it with both hands and hugged it close to her body.

Toadwarts! The pan was incredibly heavy and Navali hauled it to where the men were assembling the fire. Then she went back to gather her supplies and set herself to making the best biscuits these men would ever have the good fortune to eat.

The horses Shyre was tending to were nearly finished drinking, and he straightened from the crouch he had been in since reaching the water's edge. Stretching his arms above his head, he inhaled deeply. He was tired now that they had recovered the princess, and exhaustion washed over him in large waves until all he wanted to do was sleep.

He grabbed the reins of the two animals and led them to a grassy spot a little ways from the healthy blaze of the campfire. And, after brushing and hobbling both animals, Shyre ran his hand briefly over Justice's coat as he walked past the horse towards the glow of the fire.

He reached the circle of men, and one of them handed him a plate full of food. Looking for a place to sit, Shyre found the only place open was on the fallen tree the princess was seated upon.

His men were matchmaking, Shyre realized, but refused to let it faze him as he moved in the direction of the princess, catching Ashtyn's laughter-filled gaze as he took his seat directly next to his betrothed.

Apparently his brothers were as bad as General Ivan was. Every last one of them was playing matchmaker and Shyre was not the happiest recipient of their attentions. He could win his woman without their help. He was not that much of a boor around the female gender. At least not in his own opinion, though he was not exactly sure the rest of his men agreed with that after what had transpired earlier.

Two of his Drocuns pulled wooden pipes from their saddlebags and began a lively tune as Shyre took a bite out of the biscuit that had been placed on his plate. He glanced down in surprise at the biscuit he held in his hand when the bite he had taken nearly dissolved on his tongue. Several of his other men began dancing a merry jig in time with the music, but Shyre was far too engrossed in his next bite to do more than briefly note their movements.

"Gideon has certainly outdone himself with those biscuits this time, hasn't he, Shyre?" Ashtyn asked with a cheeky grin.

"He most certainly has," Shyre agreed, and finished his with a last appreciative bite. The men still seated around Shyre chuckled, and he glanced up in bewilderment. "What did I miss?"

"Gideon didn't make those, you halfwit." Ashtyn rolled his eyes in mocking disgust at his brother. "If you hadn't been so intent on making sure every speck of dust was removed from your horse's coat, then you would have noticed that your betrothed was the one who made them."

Shyre quickly trained his gaze on the woman seated directly to his left. "Is my brother merely jesting, or did you really make the biscuits?"

"I honestly did make them, your highness," Navali admitted, and was exceedingly proud of herself when she did not flush beneath his warm regard.

"It was truly amazing. A completely welcome change, in fact," he stated, his eyes caressing her features.

"Thank you, your highness," Navali graciously accepted his praise.

"Are there any more to be had?" Shyre abruptly turned to his brother and asked.

Ashtyn laughed loudly at that. "Nay, they were gone nearly before Gideon had an opportunity to place them out. You are fortunate he insisted on placing one aside for you, brother, else you would never have known of the wonders your future bride was capable of."

Shyre shot his brother a tolerantly amused smirk and then ignored him to the best of his abilities. He turned to Navali once again. "Now *that*, I know to be untrue," he whispered for her ears alone. "I had very nearly discovered one ere we were so rudely interrupted earlier this eve."

Navali glanced askance at her intended husband and then blushed to find his face so near to her own.

"Mayhap you will grant me another attempt soon, your highness? I would dearly love a second opportunity," Shyre finished, an impish smile playing about his lips when she would not look at him again.

"I think, your highness," Navali whispered, her ire slightly piqued at his forwardness. "That one opportunity should have been more than enough to suffice your boldness."

"Next time it will be," Shyre promised, and then watched closely as his future bride pretended an intense interest in the music and dancing. He had only eaten a few bites of his less-than-appealing stew, but he suddenly discovered that he was not very hungry anymore.

He caught the movement of Navali's right foot gently tapping in time with the music and made a quick decision. Getting up, he put his bowl down on the log and offered his hand to Navali. "May I have this dance, my lady?"

Glancing up at Shyre in surprise, Navali took his hand before she thought and stood when he tugged her up next to him. There was only one small dilemma to dancing with him. She leaned close and whispered near his ear. "I do not know the steps."

"It is not the same as in Lynaria, is it?" Shyre's voice was not nearly as hushed as hers had been.

"Nay, not really."

"Why don't you forget you do not know the steps and let me lead you?" He suggested, raising one eyebrow roguishly as his other hand grasped hers and he pulled her slowly, but surely, towards the other dancers.

"It does not seem as though I have much choice, your highness. Has anyone ever told you that you're a little forceful and demanding?" A sharp gleam reflected in her silver eyes and Shyre had all he could do not to chuckle. This could prove more enjoyable than he had first thought it would be.

No," Shyre said, and bent his head closer to her ear, his lips brushing her blonde curls as he spoke. "They usually tell me I'm *quite* forceful and demanding," he corrected and watched her eyes light with laughter as he swung her away from him and then around.

"Do all Dareknay share those *impolite* qualities?" She asked blithely, though her earlier confrontation with Ashtyn came to mind.

"Alas, I do fear you are doomed to a life filled with crassness and boisterousness," he replied with a grin. "My family may very well drive you mad with their *impoliteness'* once they discover how unconfrontational Lynarians really are."

"I never said we do not like confrontation," Navali protested quickly. "I merely pointed out how much of a man you really are."

"Did you need assurances to that fact?" Shyre asked, his laughing green eyes suddenly glittering with desirous intent. He pulled her against his hard body and splayed his hand across her lower back so that the entire length of her body was pressed to his. "I can give you more congruent evidence if you so desire. It would be to my, and *your,* pleasure, I assure you."

He grinned rakishly as she stared at him with a mixture of shock and disbelief on her face. He abruptly whirled her away from him again, as fierce want rushed through his body. Navali's expression may have been hesitant, but her body had given off an entirely different message by softening for the briefest of moments against his own, and he suddenly felt a need to remove himself from temptation. Shyre may desire the Lynarian princess far more than he had ever wanted another woman, but he did not desire to give his men cause to watch her belly to see if it would grow heavy with his child ere their vows had been exchanged.

Navali had completely forgotten everyone around them during their little verbal exchange, though reality soon crashed over her as the laughter and chatter of the men reentered her consciousness as she was spun away from the warmth and closeness of Shyre's tautly muscled frame. She suddenly felt ashamed of her behavior—not to mention Shyre's! No one had ever dared to speak to her in such a familiar manner!

Navali missed a step as she met the eyes of one of Shyre's men and her face flamed a rosy pink. Surely they had not all born witness to her shocking conduct!

"Now, none of that." Shyre said sternly, as he swept her back to him. "Forget about the others, you're doing fine."

Doing fine at what? Navali thought with a bit of hysterical sarcasm rising to the fore. Fine with the movements of the dance, or—here she flushed even deeper—fine with her actions towards the prince in the last few moments? Navali forced her lips to curve into what she prayed was a pleasant smile and then concentrated on the intricate steps of the dance.

Her smile soon lost the hesitancy that resided there as she pushed all thoughts of the encounter with Shyre to the back of her mind. Her betrothed suddenly released her right hand, though he made sure to keep a firm hold on her left, and Navali realized one of his men was offering his left hand to her. She obligingly grasped it and the six men who were dancing formed a semi-circle and stepped to the right and then the left, jumping and whirling at various times.

The earth tones of their masculine attire began swirling in an eddy of muted color and Navali locked her eyes on Shyre's face, needing something to focus on as the dancers picked up their already quickened pace.

Shyre soon noted the disconcerted look in Navali's eyes and tugged the hand he was holding, gently pulling her free of the line of merrymakers. He picked up his bowl of now cold food when they reached the fallen tree, and then gestured for her to take her original seat, before resuming his place next to her.

"It can get a little dizzying sometimes," Shyre stated as he picked up his utensil and ate a few more bites with nary a hint of that affliction mirroring in his actions. "We are going to be here for only a few hours before we continue our journey. Do you wish to lie down for a while and rest?"

"That would be heavenly," Navali replied, and waited for him to finish his meal before following him to a quieter and darker place away from the fire and the revelers. The music had slowed considerably over the last few notes and the deep resonance of a man's baritone voice singing a ballad could be heard faintly from their position.

Thinking it very relaxing, Navali's eyes suddenly felt heavy with fatigue. She did not know the last time she had had a good night's rest, but it had been a long time. Sometime before her father had made the announcement that she would marry a Dareknay prince. That thought did not hold so much disquieting anxiety anymore and Navali just wanted to curl up on the pallet Shyre was constructing for her and sleep the rest of the night. It really was too bad they were still in Pitan territory and could only camp for several hours and not the whole night through as her exhausted body wanted.

Shyre quickly finished putting together the makeshift bed and then helped Navali down onto the thick blanket he had laid on top of a pile of leaves and pine needles. When she had settled herself into a comfortable repose, he spread another blanket over her and her eyes swiftly closed in slumber.

His betrothed was more tired than she was letting on, he thought with amusement and pride filling him at her spunk and determination. His assumption about her exhaustion had been correct and Shyre was glad he had made the decision to call a halt for a few hours and give her some relief from the jarring ride.

Leaning down, he gently kissed the tip of Navali's delicate nose. Her silver eyes flew open at the sudden touch and he saw confusion and hesitancy fill the luminous orbs.

Shyre did not know why he had kissed Navali and was shocked at the affectionate gesture that had happened so naturally. He could tell she was waiting for an explanation of some kind, but knew he could not explain his actions when he did not know what they meant himself. So he smiled gently at her instead, unable to formulate a verbal explanation. She would just have to draw her own conclusions. Shyre shifted his weight away from his betrothed to settle his back against the fallen tree by the top of her head.

Navali's loose, blonde curls glinted in the moonlight and teasingly tempted Shyre's fingers to stroke and delve into their shimmering depths. He resisted the impulse to bury his hand in the silky strands and firmly set his gaze to a point across the expanse of the glade. Looking at her could prove dangerous for his peace of mind and he needed to keep his focus sharp while they were in Pitan territory.

The night air was chilly now that the moon was at its full height, and in the distance Shyre could hear the haunting howl from a wild dog of some sort. A hoot of an owl echoed along the breeze and crickets chirped, forming a soothing, natural lullaby for his princess now that the singing and music had stopped for the evening.

His princess.

Shyre paused in his perusal of their surroundings. What a novel concept. His. Shyre inhaled sharply, he had never thought of a woman as being his before.

Princess Navali would probably not care very much for the idea as she seemed to be a most independent woman, but the notion of her under his protection filled Shyre's chest with warmth and he let out the breath he had been holding.

The Lynarian princess was not all ice as Shyre had first believed she was going to be, but neither was she particularly outgoing. She certainly did not expose her emotions for everyone to see, and Shyre did not know what she really thought about the arrangement between them. *Did she resent it? Was there some other man whom she favored herself in love with?*

Shyre's brows drew together in a frown. He did not like that thought at all. He would see to it that she forgot about any other man very soon. *If* there was one. Her father was rumored to be overly protective. Surely he had seen to it that she had not formed another attachment of some kind.

Shyre had at first been unhappily obligated himself when his father and the council were making the plans for his arranged nuptials. Now contemplating the decision that he was to marry the Lynarian princess, Shyre realized it was beginning to have great personal benefits for him. He hoped she would think so, too.

The princess was beautiful, of course. But her physical attributes were not the only thing that drew Shyre to her. Her strength, depth, and nobility of character were slowly being revealed to him and he was enamored with what he was discovering.

She was very polite and gracious with all of his men, even during their more uncouth and boorish times. Though there had not been many of the rude and crass moments that were common among the unmarried bachelors in his service, there had been a few, and most women would have cringed and berated them. Instead, Princess Navali had politely turned away and given them a few moments of privacy.

She had even helped Gideon prepare the meal! Shyre could hardly absorb that fact.

He had not known Lynarian women even knew how to cook, let alone be astonishingly proficient at it. He had heard servants and slaves of the Lynarians' households did the cooking and preparing of food for their masters, and had assumed that his betrothed was as lacking in those skills as her other country-women were rumored to be. He was pleasantly surprised when the princess' cooking had been very tasty when compared with his men's more meager cooking skills.

The Drocuns' normal fare consisted of overcooked and charred meat that someone had forgotten to turn on the spit, combined with biscuits that were better suited as rocks. Not the fluffy cloud Princess Navali's biscuits had been.

Now that the princess had shown herself adept in knowing how to cook, Shyre would need to keep a close eye on his men to make sure they did not take advantage of her and ask her to do that particularly disliked chore for them. Although, he really would not mind if she continued to cook, and his belly would certainly agree with him on that score.

Risking a downward glance at the sleeping beauty next to him, Shyre took in the sight of her soft skin and noted her deep, even breaths. What would it be like to wake to that delicately carved face every morning? Shyre could hardly picture it. The image seemed too good to be true.

He settled his body more comfortably against the fallen log and let his head rest back against the rough bark. He needed to not dwell on things like their future together until they were safely in his father's holdings once again and he could actually move to further the intimacy of their relationship. And though he had spoken the truth when he had said the Pitan were not showing signs of following them, there were far too many Dareknay eyes trained on him now for him to even contemplate stealing a kiss from her sweet lips.

Shyre's eyes began to drift shut against his will and he finally gave up the fight with his own exhaustion, letting sleep take him the short distance into warm oblivion. His brothers and men were perfectly capable of keeping watch over the small camp. He had no worries at the moment and what few still remained he let wash away with his fatigue.

CHAPTER ELEVEN

A large hand shook Navali awake and she tentatively opened her eyes to the predawn grey of the sky before the sun rose for the day. She forced herself upright and noted that several men moved about as the person who had awoken her placed a bowl of food in her lap.

Glancing up, Navali thanked Ashtyn. She could tell it was him as his eyes shown golden in the meager light. Her betrothed's brother smiled and gave her a wink before moving away to help the other Drocuns in breaking down the camp. Navali ate swiftly as she glanced about. Most of the pallets were already tied to the horses' saddles and she could see someone had prepared her mount as well.

When she was finished eating, Navali stood and wrapped the blanket that had been laying over her during the night around her shoulders. The air was considerably cooler than yesterday and she did not have a cloak to cover herself with and keep out the morning's chill. Navali hoped it would warm up as the day progressed and that the rest of their journey would not be this cold.

Seeing Shyre leading her horse closer, she quickly picked up the other blanket from the ground and shook it, hoping to remove most of the debris it had accumulated throughout the evening.

"Good morning," her betrothed said cheerfully.

"I did not realize it was morning yet," she allowed herself to grumble, her voice hoarse from sleep.

His eyes warmed at her teasing and a small smile crossed Navali's features as she gazed into the magnetic, green depths. Her lethargy faded as he came alongside of her, and his hands joined hers in folding and rolling the fabric. He tied it to the back of his saddle and then took her waist in his hands, setting her atop her mount.

"Wait!" Navali's voice halted Shyre midstride as he turned away from her. "I forgot to wash my bowl. I need to see to the cleaning of it," she informed him and held out her hands so that he could help her down again.

Instead of assisting her in dismounting, Shyre looked at her and shook his head. "You only had berries and one of Gideon's biscuits. The bowl is hardly dirty at all," he rejoined. "Besides the river is like ice this morning. I will not have you freezing your fingers just to wash something that doesn't really need it." Picking up her bowl as he spoke, Shyre proceeded to shove it into one of his saddlebags, and threw a grin over his shoulder at her gasp of feigned indignation before swiftly mounting his stallion.

They rode at a brisk pace for several hours before stopping to have a light meal of smoked meat and leftover biscuits that Gideon had thrown together earlier that morning. The air had indeed grown warmer by then and Navali had long ago shed her makeshift cloak.

As they resumed their journey, none of the men spoke very much as they endeavored to close the distance between the other Drocuns and the villagers that were making their way to the safety of Dareknay holdings. As a result, Navali did not learn very much about her betrothed during their ride and had only managed to pry the story of the Pitan villagers from Ashtyn when they had stopped for the noon meal.

She had been startled to learn that the village she had rode through the previous day with the Pitan king and his escort, had been the very same one the Dareknay Drocuns had come upon. She was grateful the warriors had deemed it fit to give the dog-ravaged old woman a proper burial. And, after learning that Tucker was one of the villagers found there and how he had helped in her rescue, Navali had sought out the young Pitan and thanked him personally before Shyre helped her mount her shaggy horse yet again.

Suddenly, the Drocun beside Navali coughed and brought her attention back to the present. She had directed her horse too far to the right of the line and was in danger of pushing the man into the trees. She quickly corrected her animal's course and the man beside her gave a brief, thankful smile.

As voices suddenly rose in excitement, Navali quickly directed her attention to the front of the column as they crested a steep hill. Ahead of them, on the opposite side of a little valley, were the Dareknay Drocuns and Pitan villagers they had been attempting to find.

Riding down the hill proved tricky with rocks and boulders giving way and sliding beneath the horses hooves. Nevertheless, they made it to the other side in good time, driven by their desire to assure themselves that nothing had gone amiss since they had split up.

Navali watched her future husband greet two blonde giants with genuine affection, clapping each man on the shoulder and throwing his dark head back with laughter at something one of them said. Ashtyn and the redheaded man who had retrieved her from the Pitan soon joined them and their greetings became even more boisterous.

Not wanting to interrupt their banter, Navali felt at a loss as to what to do with herself. So she waited atop her mount for some kind of direction.

"Your highness?" Stephen asked rather nervously as he offered to help her dismount. Hoping to set him at ease, she gave him a reassuring smile and allowed him to assist her.

"We were—that is—" the slim Drocun hesitated and then finished in a rush. "The men and I were wondering if you would do us the honor of helping with the evening meal again?"

"I think that sounds like a marvelous idea." Navali curved her lips in a gently mischievous smile, so he would see that she was truly fine with the notion and not at all upset with his suggestion. Stephen's eyes caught the teasing gleam in the princess' and he smiled back at her, his shoulders relaxing in relief.

He had probably been cajoled into asking her, Navali realized. She glanced at the other men around her and noted the hopeful expressions that were directed Stephen's way. The Drocun turned and offered his arm for her to take so that he could lead her as he had done yesterday. Navali graciously accepted and could not help but notice the way his other hand lifted and made a discreet gesture of victory to several of the men.

One of them caught Navali's gaze as it landed on his victoriously smiling face and he quickly dipped his head in acknowledgement. His face red in embarrassment, the man hurriedly busied his hands setting up one of the numerous tents that would give them shelter for the night.

As Navali walked with Stephen, she took in the villagers' tattered and worn apparel—not that hers was in much better condition. But where she at least had on light walking slippers, most of them did not even have shoes and were forced to walk about barefoot. The few that did actually have shoes were barely better off than the others, for as they walked, their dirtied stockings and leggings could clearly be seen through the torn leather of their footwear.

The ragged Pitan were of all ages and sizes, small children to elderly adults, slightly thin to painfully skinny. It was very hard to watch as they moved about the camp, gathering firewood and setting up tents from the threadbare materials they had at hand.

Having never witnessed such poverty in Lynaria, compassion struck Navali for the first time in her life, and she wanted to weep at the sight of the little children sitting quietly by the fires or helping the older men and women with their chores. She supposed her people must have some form of poverty, but she had never seen evidence of it and the youngest of the Pitan seemed so filled with hopelessness and despair.

Stephen led Navali to a large fire in the center of the camp and bade her sit down on one of the blankets spread about it. Navali shook her head, declining his offer and the slim Drocun looked at her curiously in response.

"You wouldn't happen to have a ball or something of the like, would you?" She asked, gesturing around at the too stoic children.

The princess had never played with children before, but she had glimpsed them playing outside her castle windows. And surely she could manage a game of kick-the-ball like she had seen those children doing. It could not be that hard, could it? Besides, Navali desperately wished to see the little ones' downcast faces turn into ones filled with laughter and joy.

"Nay, I do not, your highness." At the shadowed look that crept into the princess' eyes, Stephen quickly thought of a solution. "But I think I could construct one easily enough from rags. It'll be a mite heavy but it should do the trick." Navali's eyes lit up and, though her face never lost its composed look, the young warrior knew she was pleased with his idea. "Shall I make one now, your highness?"

Navali hesitated, for the young man probably had other more important duties to attend to, rather than using his time to make her a ball to give to the children. She glanced around at the defeated looks on the young ones' faces again. That clinched it for her. "If you wouldn't mind, Stephen. I would greatly appreciate it."

"I'm at your service, my lady." He began walking to one of the tents and then called over his shoulder as an afterthought. "If you'll just stay there, I'll return in a trice."

Navali nodded her head and obediently sank down on the blanket to await the warrior's return. He was obviously in charge of her protection and welfare at the moment and she did not want to see him chastised for something she had asked him to do.

Holding her hands out to the merrily dancing fire, Navali let the warmth of it flow over her fingers and up her arms. She could use a good pair of woolen mittens to chase away the chill, for she was unaccustomed to her fingers even being the slightest bit cool, let alone being red with cold, and she did not like the new sensation one bit.

Her eyes caught a man and a woman holding hands, their feet bare against the cold ground, and she suddenly felt ashamed. What a complainer she was!

Navali fiercely scolded herself for her selfishness. She wanted gloves, but her feet were not bare and her garments were not worn thin, and they did manage to keep out most of the small breeze that swept up the side of the hill. She would work on that fault in her character, she swore to herself, even if she had to go about barefoot to understand what the peasants felt.

Shuddering at that self-castigating thought, Navali shifted her frame closer to the fire. Just thinking about voluntarily removing her slippers and walking about in her bare feet made her want to cringe. She pushed those unpleasant thoughts aside as she felt Stephen return to her side, and she twisted and gazed up at him before he knelt beside her and offered the heavy, circular shape he was holding out for her inspection.

"It's the best I could do, your highness, at such short notice. I apologize that it isn't a better offering."

"Nonsense," Navali said, giving him a beautiful smile of gratitude. "It's perfect. I'm certain the children will adore it."

Stephen was doubtful of such high praise, but rose to his feet and offered his hand to help her rise anyway.

"Thank you for your assistance, kind sir." Navali discreetly adjusted her skirts, which had become entangled about her legs when she had been seated. Walking a short distance from Stephen, she headed towards a little girl who sat alone at one of the smaller outlying fires. She knew her Drocun protector still watched her curiously to see what she was going to do, but she ignored his look of bemusement as she smiled gently at the child who had just noticed that Navali was coming towards her.

The young girl stood abruptly as Navali stepped closer, and she looked as though she might flee.

"It's all right," Navali swiftly assured the child in a soothing voice. "I was just wondering if you wouldn't mind teaching me how to play with this?" Navali held up the ball in her hand for the little girl to see.

"Don't ye know how?" The little girl's voice trembled in trepidation, but a spark of interest shown on her expressive face as she peered incredulously at Navali.

Navali shook her head. "Nay, I was never allowed to play with a ball when I was young."

The little girl's eyes grew round in shock. "Never?"

"Never," Navali concurred. The little girl took a couple of steps closer and Navali handed her the makeshift toy. The little sprite hugged it to her thin chest and then smiled, her face lighting up with her happiness.

The child's long, dark hair swished back and forth as she shifted on her feet in excitement. "Are ye sure ye want ta learn?"

Navali nodded eagerly, hoping to appear enthusiastic. "Very sure. That is if you don't mind and have the time to teach me."

"I don't mind and I don't have a thing ta do." With that simple phrase, the little girl placed the ball on the ground and kicked it to Navali. "Now, ye kick it back ta me," she ordered the princess when Navali did not immediately move to do so.

"Oh! Of course." Navali felt rather foolish, not knowing how to play something that had looked so simple, and a light uncontrollable blush dusted her cheeks as she did as she was bade and kicked the ball in the girl's direction.

The round contraption veered away, not going anywhere near her intended target, and Navali was horrified at her ineptitude. But the little girl giggled in delight and raced after it, retrieving it from where it had rolled to a stop at the entrance of a tent.

"Ye needs ta practice more." Navali was told with another giggle, and she smiled at the child's infectious laugh.

Bringing laughter and fun back into the Pitan children's lives was what Navali had so wanted to do and she finally started to feel as though she could perhaps accomplish that task.

The crude ball was then kicked to her again, and this time Navali managed to return it in a generally straight line.

The pair of completely mismatched players practiced quietly for a few minutes and finally saw their diligence rewarded when they were able to keep the ball between them. Then Navali kicked the ball with a little more force than she had expected and it veered off to the left this time.

Suddenly, a bedraggled boy raced up and scooped it into his arms. "Can I play?" His brown eyes were a trifle unsure and hesitant as he awaited her response.

"May I," Navali automatically corrected his grammar as all of her tutors had done so, and she could have kicked *herself*, when the little boy asked.

"Aren't ye playing already?"

"Yes, I suppose I am. Did it look like I was?" Navali asked the little girl that had taught her and received a vigorous nod in response.

"You may play, too," Navali then told the older boy. "But I think introductions are in order, don't you agree?"

"Intra-what?" The boy asked, confusion settling over his features.

"Introductions," she supplied and then gestured to herself. "I'm Navali, and you are?"

"Travis, and that there's Bethany, she's my cousin." Nodding his head in the little girl's direction, Travis smiled at Navali before tossing the ball to Bethany. The little girl kicked the ball with force towards Navali and the princess sprinted to catch it and kick it over to Travis.

Hearing their laughter, several more children soon gathered around and Navali motioned for them to join in. They quickly formed a lopsided circle and helped kick the crude ball all around the inside. As more and more children joined in, adults began to gather and watch their enjoyment.

The ball suddenly flew out of the circle as a larger boy kicked it, and Navali and the children raced after it, kicking, throwing, and chasing the contraption around the entire camp. They made sure to steer clear of the fires though and made a point of not horsing around near the sentries Shyre had posted.

A few of the warriors and parents could not resist the gaiety and joined in the fun. Soon everyone was laughing and shouting and cheering, their cares all but forgotten for the moment.

As her breath began to rush through her lungs, Navali fell farther and farther behind the group. The merrymakers took very little notice when she finally halted completely, for their play was taking them towards the far end of the encampment, and Navali braced her hands on her knees as she laughingly gasped for air.

Making a sudden decision to return to the main fire to rest for a few moments, Navali whirled about and smacked hard into a man's chest. Gasping, she wobbled unsteadily on her feet.

"Steady there, love." Prince Shyre chuckled in amusement as he wrapped his arms about his future bride's torso and held her secure against his body.

Startled at hearing his voice, Navali glanced up at her betrothed and his vivid, green gaze ensnared her. His arms tightened about her and she inhaled sharply as she was brought more firmly against him and his masculine scent suddenly added to the heated onslaught of her senses. She spread her fingers wide against his chest, not knowing if she did so out of protest, or out of some primal need to feel every inch that she could of the breadth of his muscular chest.

As his intended's slender fingers flexed against him, Shyre let his eyes slide shut as heat coursed through him at their innocent and unexpected exploration. He dipped his head until his lips were a mere breath away from Navali's, and then he felt her sigh and he knew nothing could stop him from kissing her fully this time. Shyre hungrily closed the distance between them and his mouth settled firmly against hers. Her full, shapely lips were smooth satin and hot silk and they tasted of vanilla and a sweetness he could not define as anything but purely Navali.

Navali could feel the warmth radiating from Shyre and she melted against him. Her eyes flew open as his lips lifted from hers and she watched as they turned up in a small smile of satisfaction before gently brushing her mouth again. Navali was completely lost to sensation now and her eyes closed heavily with the desire to feel as much of him as possible.

Shyre's lips abruptly left her own and Navali felt him gently release her as she opened her eyes again. Her future husband suddenly stepped back and his warmth fled. She briefly shivered in the cold air that now separated them, before she desperately sought to control the reactions of her body.

"Princess, I—" Shyre began and then halted as he worked to control the yearning that beat through him to hang the consequences and make her his that very moment. He watched in a tortured state of longing as Navali blinked rapidly, her silver eyes flickering in molten heat before she finally overcame the dazed look his kiss had put there.

Shyre knew Navali would leave his side if he did not come up with something to say to her and he desperately tried to cool the fire that raged through him as he sought to recall what they had been discussing the previous day. He felt triumphant as he remembered the question she had posed to him and he had forgotten to answer.

"I believe you asked me yesterday if I wished my brother would disappear into a dark pit?" Shyre asked her, hoping she would remember and would continue to converse, no matter how abruptly the question came. But, after the heated moment that had passed between them, Shyre felt he could not be faulted for being unable to formulate a more refined or genteel topic of conversation.

"I think I may have...." Navali looked at him curiously, nonplussed by the random question. She did not wish to explore the way Shyre's kiss had completely transported her to another realm though, and she strove desperately to control the emotions roiling through her and reply coherently. A distraction was exactly what she needed to further her chances of success in that endeavor. And, now that Shyre had brought up the subject of his sibling again, she realized she was quite curious as to the dynamics of Dareknay family life.

Growing up in Lynaria, Navali had been luckier than most children, for her parents had not cared for being absent from their child, as most of their culture practiced, and they had lavished their love upon her from the moment she had been born.

However, that changed dramatically when her mother died. For her father, stricken by a deep grief, had assigned their only child to the care of various nursemaids and tutors and had rarely visited Navali after that.

Navali wondered if Lynarian and Dareknay ways of caring for children were the same. Were they as strict and formal as Lynarians were? Or were they more lenient? Navali could well remember what she had overheard in the kitchens of the palace about their barbaric ways of life. But so far, in her short acquaintance with the Dareknay warriors, she had seen nothing that would justify the gossip.

"Yesterday, I would have greatly appreciated the privacy Ashtyn's disappearance would have afforded me," Shyre replied to her earlier question, startling Navali from her wayward thoughts. "For he was making a severe nuisance of himself. But I would never seriously wish any of my siblings gone forever. I would miss them too much for that. Do you have any siblings?"

He asked as he offered his arm, and then led her back to the fire in the center of their camp.

"No, I am the only child of my parents," Navali replied. "You said siblings; are there more than just Ashtyn?" If so, she wanted to be prepared to meet them. One disastrous introductory remark was enough, and she did not wish to raise the ire of any more of the royal Dareknay line.

Her very Lynarian father would certainly show some form of illegal emotion if she did, and it would not be a pleasant one. Intense irritation would be a nice way of describing what he would display.

"Eight, and they can all be as equally irritating as my twin," Shyre answered as Navali sat down on the blanket she had previously occupied.

Striding over to where he could see the game of kick-the-ball, Shyre suddenly loosed a bellowing shout that startled Navali, and the two blonde, identical men Shyre had been speaking with earlier, came sprinting around the tents.

Shyre returned to Navali's side and helped her to regain her feet when she held up a hand for him to assist her. She did not want to be seated when the giant-sized men came to stand before them.

"These are the next set of siblings in my family, Princess. Addison, the family jester, has the gray eyes," Shyre introduced, and gestured to the man on his right. "And the blue-green eyed one on your left, is Adam, the most studious of my brothers."

Navali did not think these two giants could be anything like the prince's sedate description of them, as they both seemed far too comfortable with the long swords belted about their trim waists.

Adam, the twin on Navali's left, spoke first. "It's a pleasure to meet our eldest brother's intended. Do you like children?"

The forthright, abruptly put question caused Navali's face to heat. "A-aye," She replied in a choked voice.

"How many do you wish to have?" Adam continued to question.

"I-I," Navali stuttered, this time unable to formulate a reply.

"Come now, Adam," the man's twin said from the other side of Shyre. "Don't go frightening off the little filly with all of your accursed questions." He gave his brother a playful shove that would have knocked any other man to the ground. "I'm the better mannered of us, Princess. I assure you." The brazen wink and smile he directed at her spoke otherwise.

"D-did you just call me a ... a filly? As in a female horse?" Navali was not sure if she should be insulted at such a moniker or not.

"Aye, he did. And that just goes to show exactly how uncouth *he* really is," the first twin stated.

Their bizarre conversation was beginning to make Navali's head spin, and her expression must have given her away, for Shyre interrupted their banter.

"Cease and desist with your jesting, you two. Find Ashtyn and annoy and confuse him for a while."

"But Ashtyn's too serious," Addison complained, crossing his arms over his massive chest.

"Mayhap I will be lucky enough to have some of it rub off on you," Shyre retorted.

"That's what I'm afraid of," His younger brother grumbled. "Then I'll be as boring as he is."

"Addison, I highly doubt you, of all people, have to worry about being too serious. You have more of the devil in you than anyone I have ever met," his eldest brother informed him. "And I don't think anything Ashtyn may do or say could ever change you. Now, Adam on the other hand—" The high prince abruptly halted in mid-sentence as the man he was about to comment on reached over Navali and cuffed him on the back of his head.

"Now don't go insulting me, Shyre. I'm bigger than you, remember?"

Straightening to his full height, Shyre rubbed the back of his head, before gesturing to their difference in size. "How could I forget when my ribs still ache from when you last sat on me? You rival a horse for weight and size."

This time, the twin on Shyre's right cuffed him on the back of his head.

"Would you two quit trying to behead me?" Shyre groused at them.

"Poor baby," Adam retorted. He then turned to Navali. "We're very sorry you got stuck having to marry the more feminine and sensitive one of us all."

"That does it!" Shyre growled. He prepared to launch himself at the nearest giant. But before he could move, his youngest brother walked nonchalantly over to them.

"Excuse me, if these two finally get to meet the princess, I get to as well," Aakin informed his elder brother and turned a dazzlingly white smile on Navali. "You've been keeping her to yourself for far too long. Introduce me," he demanded.

Shyre groused a bit more at the blonde set of twins as they walked away to go join Ashtyn, who was standing by a tent at the edge of the center circle and watching them. The three brothers instantly started talking quietly amongst themselves, and Shyre just knew they were conniving against him. Not taking his gaze from his twin, he made the introduction Aakin had demanded. "This is Aakin, the youngest male in my family. His twin, Aaron, had to transport an injured Drocun back to Chimea."

Navali nodded briefly in greeting to his brother, before asking her intended. "How was he injured?" When Shyre did not answer, she felt a gentle tug on her left hand. Navali looked askance at the redheaded man beside her, nonplussed that he had so casually touched her.

"We were ambushed one night when we made camp," Aakin informed her cordially. "It's a pleasure to make your acquaintance,

Princess Navali." He gave her a lopsided grin and kissed the back of her hand as he bowed over it.

"Oh! I apologize. My manners seem to be lacking today. It's a pleasure to meet you as well," Navali said, and then blushed when he did not immediately let go of her hand.

What was it with these Dareknay men? Were they all this disconcerting?

"No apology necessary, Navali." Aakin stroked his thumb over the back of her hand and she saw his eyes glance in the direction of his older brother. "I may, of course, call you by your given name now that we are to be family?" he inquired, his eyes dancing in amusement as he brought his gaze back to hers.

"O-of course, you—" Banked ice! This man moved quickly, Navali thought.

Shyre caught the mischievous look in his youngest brother's eyes and he interrupted his betrothed's reply as his attention returned to his ladies-man of a brother.

"No flirting with my wife," he informed Aakin sternly and without preamble as he recovered Navali's hand from his brother's hold, and then kept possession of it himself.

"I was only being friendly in your absence and distraction, brother," Aakin cheekily grinned back at him. "And she isn't your wife yet. Are you jealous already?"

"Not hardly," Shyre snorted. "I'm sure the princess can tell a jester when she sees one."

"And yet, she has given *me* permission to call her by her given name. Unlike you," Aakin readily informed him with a snort.

"It goes without speaking that I may call her by name. Does it not, Navali?" Shyre's green eyes flicked to his intended as he used her name aloud for the very first time, his gaze swiftly asking her permission to cease with the formality that existed between them.

Warmth spread through Navali at the deep timbre of his voice uttering her name and she could not have denied him anything at the present time. "Yes it does, Ashyre." She smiled over at the man she would soon marry.

At the very least, this marriage would be incredibly interesting, Navali thought, then turned to her future brother-in-law.

"Does your twin look exactly like you as well?" She inquired.

Aakin immediately returned his attention to her, his eyes the green of his eldest brother's. "For the most part, though not nearly as handsome as I am," he teased, giving her a roguish wink.

Navali stifled a genuine smile at his foolishness and nodded as if she believed him, then asked boldly. "I can tell Ashtyn from Ashyre, and Addison from Adam because of their different eye color. Will I be able to tell you apart in the same way?"

"Well, that's a little more difficult to explain." At her lifted eyebrows, he changed the color of his eyes as she watched, startled at what she was seeing. "As you see, I can change the shade of my eyes to whichever color I desire. My mother hates it, as she finds it difficult to tell us apart when we decide we want to look *exactly* like each other."

Shyre shot his youngest brother a pointed look.

Aakin relented. "But Aaron has black eyes with white specks in them, while brown is the color that I typically choose. Individuality is more desirable and all that other nonsense," Aakin informed her with another wink, his eyes now a deep, warm brown.

He then gave a brief salute to Shyre, before striding over to join his other brothers, who were throwing looks of anticipation and amusement back at Shyre.

"It seems your brothers are plotting, your highness," Navali observed with a small smile curving her lips.

"Aye, it does appear that way. I'm sure I'll discover what it is before too long," he smiled wryly and pinned her with a long look, before speaking with deep sincerity. "I meant it when I used your given name. Would you mind if we dispensed with formality entirely and you called me by mine?"

"All right, Ashyre."

"Shyre."

"Excuse me?" she asked, allowing a confused look on her face.

"Shyre is what my family and friends call me, because it's easier to say than my full name," Shyre explained. "Though you may call me whatever you wish." He did not care what name she used, her slight, melodic accent would make anything she called him sound wonderful.

Navali studied her betrothed for a moment, her eyes inscrutable, and then decided. "Shyre, then. It suits you."

Navali liked that he considered her a friend, or part of his family. Although she was going to be a large part of his family soon, it would be nice to also be considered his friend on top of the spouse part. That did not have anything to do with love, did it?

No, she decided, friendship was friendship and she would not confuse the relationship with anything else. She would not let herself.

"I should probably help the others with the evening meal." Navali had seen several of the women and warriors preparing food and withdrawing plates, bowls and eating utensils from their various-sized sacks and she remembered her earlier commitment.

"You don't have to if you don't wish to, Navali. I told my men not to bother you with such chores. They're perfectly capable of making their own food. And if you continue to spoil them, they will never stop hounding you for more." Shyre informed her.

"So, I should tell you no then as well, and let you make your own food?" Navali inquired.

"You could." He smiled with smug confidence as he continued. "But my cooking is just as atrocious as theirs, and I would insist that you join me in partaking of the repast I had worked so laboriously over."

"Very well, then. We wouldn't wish you to have to labor that arduously, would we? So, I'll make your food tonight, if you take care of my horse. Agreed?" She bargained with her own smug smile, extending her hand for him to shake, confident that he would accept her offer.

His expression changed to one of someone that had just been had. "You do know that I'll probably get lice from that sack of bones, don't you?"

"You probably will." She laughed at his chagrined look.

"I think I should devise a plan to get Aakin to do it, since his allegiance has suddenly changed to Ashtyn," Shyre mused aloud.

"Nay." Navali shook her head firmly. "If I make your food, *you* take care of my horse. Your brother was nothing but kind to me."

"Are we speaking of the same brother?" Shyre inquired with a disbelieving grin.

Ignoring his question, Navali suddenly ordered. "Be off with you, I have work to do, otherwise you'll be eating when everyone else is asleep."

"Mayhap I am not quite ready to take my leave, then." Shyre's green eyes became intense. "Would I perchance have you all to myself later if I tarried now?"

Navali's eyes narrowed, surely he could not mean what she thought he meant. "Why would you want me all to yourself?"

"Why do you think?" A heated look entered his eyes.

As she saw that look, Navali knew she should not contemplate that potentially inappropriate question and firmly told herself not to. However, she could not stop herself, as the memory of his earlier kiss flooded her being with warmth. She took a step away from him, her eyes uncertain.

Shyre saw her look of consternation and, realizing he was moving too fast for her, motioned for her to go to the fire where Stephen was cleaning a rabbit. He could feel Navali was not ready to answer his last question and suddenly he did not think he was ready to hear her answer either.

How confusing this whole situation was turning out to be. One minute he thought he could read her and the next, a veil dropped over her eyes and he could not tell what she was thinking if his very life depended upon it.

He watched her walk to the fire and smile at Stephen. Navali's movements were graceful and sure and he felt he could watch her all night long.

His life may not depend on knowing what she felt about him, but his happiness was beginning to hinge upon that very same ability to know her and her fleeting expressions. How was he going to get to know her better with all of his brothers around? Not to mention, the curious eyes of the village refugees?

That was the golden question Shyre pondered as he tore his eyes from the form of his future bride and forced himself to leave in order to find the lice-ridden nag the princess had coerced him into caring for. First order of business when they got back to Dareknay was to see about getting Navali a proper mount. One that was not as nasty tempered as the one he now strode over to.

He dodged the horse's stained teeth as the animal attempted to take a bite out of his arm. Cursing, Shyre reached one vulnerable, leather-clad hand out to grasp the horse's bridle and he twisted it, holding the animal's teeth safely at bay.

Hellfired, rotten nag.

If it were a man he would have slammed his fist into its jaw. However did Navali manage to calm the beast, let alone ride the thing? No answers were forthcoming, and he held the horse's bridle securely with one hand as he reached to undue the girth with the other. Then there was no room for other thoughts as his whole concentration was required on keeping the filthy animal from taking a good-sized chunk out of his flesh.

CHAPTER TWELVE

Night fell quickly, bringing a frost upon the light breeze that accompanied the fleeing sun. The fires outside of the ghostly pale tents were unable to warm the inhabitants inside, and Navali shivered alone in her makeshift tent, huddling deeper into the thick fur that surrounded her body. Strange how it was colder this night than the last had been when she had been out in the open air. But then, now she was without Shyre's warmth lying next to her.

The sharing of warmth was something she envied the married couples traveling with them. They had someone to hold and cuddle next to in the middle of the night, how she wished she had someone to do something like that with. *What an unexpectedly shocking path for her thoughts to be meandering down! She had never imagined cuddling or sleeping next to someone in her entire life. Why would she start now?*

She knew the answer to that question nearly before she finished it and she was not going to allow herself to think too closely on it. It was too dangerous to the fragile grip she had on her emotions. But she just couldn't stop her thoughts from replaying the evening's events one last time.

After the evening meal, the Drocuns had again pulled out their musical instruments, and the villagers danced in revelry at being free for the first time in many, many cales.

Watching from the sidelines with the elderly and infirm, Navali had observed more than a few eyes dampen with tears of joy at seeing the younger set so carefree and truly enjoying life for the first time.

Shyre had not asked Navali to dance that evening and she had wondered about it until she noticed his dark head bent over a map that one of his brothers had laid on the ground earlier. His male siblings were gathered around him and General Ivan Titek, whom she had met earlier during the meal, crouched next to him, pointing at various locations.

Navali had not been able to hear what they were discussing, though she knew it could not have been a pleasant topic by the way her betrothed had agitatedly run his fingers through his thick mane of hair and glanced at her. Their eyes had met and he had looked startled to find her gaze focused on him.

He had quickly stood and excused himself from his brothers and the general, and then strode over to where she was standing, a bemused grin curving his lips. "Are you enjoying your evening?" He had asked her, his voice low and smooth, flowing over her in a most disconcerting way.

"I am, though I don't think you are," she had observed to him. "Is everything all right?"

"It will be. One of the Drocuns accompanying Addison and Adam disappeared an hour or so after we parted ways. My brothers couldn't leave the others alone to search for him."

"How awful. Do you think he's all right?"

"I don't know. If Lance was, he would have made it back to their camp. They've been traveling slowly so that even if he was wounded or lost he could catch up with them." Shyre's brows had knit together in a concerned frown.

"What will you do about it now?" Navali had asked, her voice soft.

"I've already sent out several warriors in hopes of finding him. While a few of them have already returned and reported seeing no sign of human life anywhere near here, the others should return with the rising sun. If they were unable to find him either, we will have to continue on to Dareknay. We cannot stay in Pitan with the refugee numbers growing larger every day. It is just too dangerous for everyone involved."

Navali had touched Shyre's arm in sympathy of the responsibility he must have felt for his warrior's disappearance, and he had covered her cold hand with his own rough, warm one. "You're cold. Here, come with me." He had taken her hand more firmly in his, and even if she had not wanted to, she had no choice but to follow.

If she were truthful with herself, she would admit that she had wanted to follow him very much and no thought of pulling away from his gentle hold had ever entered her mind. Shyre had led her to a tent, not far from the center of camp, and then left her outside as he disappeared into its dark depths, reappearing only a moment later with a thick, brown fur thrown over one arm.

"Here, this should keep you warm." He had reached around her and wrapped the blanket about her body. Before turning her back in the direction of the merrymakers and, placing one arm across her shoulders, pulled her tight against the warmth of his side.

That was the last of their solitude before everyone had decided it was time to retire for the evening. Some of the village women had shown Navali to the tent she would occupy for the evening. And, once inside, they had proceeded to help the princess in mending the slits and tears that rent her silver gown and chemise. All the while, smiling and thanking her for the wonderful blessing she had given them by playing with their children.

They had left as soon as the mending had been finished, which had not taken very long with so many hands helping to sew. And now, grateful though she was for seeing her gown returned to a more modest state, Navali sat shivering and feeling like a shrew for wishing they had not quite caught up with the villagers yet. Because then she would have been able to keep her betrothed next to her and be warm for the night. But she understood all too well that they had to observe the proprieties, now that they were under everyone's watchful eyes, and that did not include sleeping next to one another unless you were wed.

She hoped they would speak their vows soon, otherwise she feared she might freeze ere winter even fully arrived. That thought brought Navali up short. *She* wanted *to be married! To the man she was formerly being forced to wed! And she wanted to be married* now!

Navali groaned into the fur wrapped about her body. This was not going as she had planned. Every defense she had built up Shyre had gone through with unsurpassed success. She was trying to construct new ones daily, but it was not working. He did not even have to struggle to see through her defenses. He merely smiled and she melted.

She was not supposed to fall for anyone, let alone her future husband! Her battle to stay romantically unattached had failed miserably, and she knew she had already conceded defeat in that respect. So, she realized with a small smile of delight, she might as well give in and enjoy the experience. After all, the prince did not seem immune to her either and at least she was not alone in her feelings.

Shaking her head in the darkness, Navali's hair tangled beneath her. *This was ridiculous! She could not fall in love with her husband! Her people would tear her apart if they found out!*

Or would they?

What they did not know ... as the saying went. Perhaps she could keep her emotions to herself. The Lynarians did not need to know about her personal affairs of the heart.

Had she really just thought that!?!

Her father had spies everywhere, he would know in a week's time if she loved the prince. It was hopeless.

But Navali knew that fact would not stop her from loving Shyre anyway. She always did the unconventional thing, why should she stop doing so now?

She could not think of a single, rational reason. She was about to be wed to a Dareknay, which was already unconventional in its own right, who was to say she could not adopt some of their idiosyncrasies as well?

Navali sighed as she turned over on her stomach, and closed her eyes in exhaustion. She now knew what she would have to do, and that was rebel against convention. Rebelling was not that awful when one was already accustomed to it, and the little rebelling she had done previously would certainly prepare her for this new challenge. Navali smiled softly as she drifted off into slumber, completely at peace about the decision she had chosen.

The very object of Navali's formerly tormented thoughts lay directly outside the flap of her tent and he was as awake as a body could get.

Shyre's thoughts were whirling in the same direction that Navali's had been, though without the complication of not being allowed to show emotion and having to rebel against a lifetime of training in proper decorum and convention.

His were more along the lines of, how could he be in love so soon? He had only just met her. A man could not love a woman so quickly, could he?

Apparently a man could, because he had already went ahead and done it. Shyre shook his head and realized that fact without the sharp pang he had expected to feel. He did not even feel foolish like he had thought he would. He was ecstatically, unbelievably, and completely in love! He frowned in disgust at his flowery thoughts, though they did not faze him overly much, for he was very secure in his masculine standing.

However, Shyre did not believe he had ever been so grateful Ashtyn was asleep and not listening in on his thoughts.

Now, if only the woman he loved would return and display the same emotion. That was the crux of the matter. So far, only a small smattering of emotion had flitted across her face at various times, and even then he had needed to watch very closely for those flickers of life, except when she had been playing with the children earlier. Indeed, the day had been an unparalleled success, even with Navali becoming quiet and stoic towards the evening.

Though it was becoming easier to tell what Navali was thinking at certain times, it was still exhausting trying to discern what she was feeling. He thought again of the glorious smile that had graced her face when she had been kicking the ball, and his musings caused a grin to curve his own lips in the darkness.

If he could get her to release her control and composure like that all the time he would not have a single problem in the world.

Except for Lance's disappearance. It was as though the man had disappeared into thin air. Nothing had appeared out of place when the main body of Drocuns had split from the refugee villagers, and Shyre could not imagine what had gone wrong that would cause Lance to leave his post and not return.

The man had always displayed loyalty, trustworthiness, and an ability to follow orders to the very letter. Shyre would not have permitted anyone who did not seem sound in all those areas on the journey, and he had not experienced a second thought when he had chosen Lance to accompany the mission.

Out of the five scouts Shyre had sent out, two had yet to return. The other three had reported seeing absolutely no signs of Lance, but had seen smoke on the late night horizon. It seemed the Pitan were on the move to recover what they had lost.

Speed was going to be the defining factor in their flight to Dareknay now. What had started off as a mission to return the Lynarian princess to safety was turning into a complicated medley of rescue, survival, and lots of frightened and tired people.

The Dareknay were picking up dozens of new Pitan refugees every day. Their numbers were swelling into the hundreds and moving that many people was taking longer than Shyre would have liked. Earlier, Shyre, his brothers, and general Titek had reached the decision to split up in order to divert and confuse the Pitan.

Shyre, Addison, Aakin, Stephen and one of the squires would take the princess and one third of the most fleet and fit of the refugees and head for the Lynarian border. It was farther away and exceedingly more dangerous for the Dareknay men to travel into Lynarian lands, but it was necessary for the greater survival rate it proposed.

Having the princess in their midst should halt any aggressive move on the Lynarian side. But they had to travel through more of the Pitan territory to get there, and that had Shyre concerned. He knew General Titek, Ashtyn, and Adam, with the rest of the Drocuns and refugees, would be fine once they reached the bridge to Dareknay. King Avar would have men waiting for their return to discourage any pursuit on the Pitan's part.

The reception Shyre and his own refugees would have in Lynaria was another matter entirely. There would be no relief force waiting for them. Any other type of force, Shyre would not greatly appreciate, for it would surely not be of a friendly nature. They had no other option open to them though, and the plan the leaders had concocted would be put into effect as soon as the last two scouts returned and reported their findings.

Shyre groaned and stretched his arms above his head before settling deeper into the cloak and blanket he had wrapped around his body. He would need as much sleep as he could get this night. For when he, and the people he would lead, split from the larger group, there would not be much rest for him.

He, Stephen, and the brothers that were accompanying them would need to train the male refugees that were under their care to fight with greater skill and to not run from the enemy like they had previously been doing. It would take a huge amount of effort to break them of that particular habit, but Shyre was determined to succeed.

They would all survive, he told himself firmly. *Because that was exactly what these people had been doing the past several decades.* Shyre closed his eyes and, even though he would not have thought himself capable of it, went directly to sleep and did not awaken until the sun had crept just over the horizon.

Navali awoke warm and fully contented with her lot in life. She would forever have to hide her emotions from her father and people, but she would love her chosen prince with every fiber of her being. Fate had seen fit to fulfill one of her lifelong dreams, and life seemed grand!

Forcing herself out from underneath the cozy, brown fur, Navali shivered in the early morning chill that rushed over her body. She smiled as she pulled her dirty chemise over her head to stand naked in front of a cracked pitcher of water.

The hurried flight to get out of Pitan and the Drocuns light traveling ways did not allow for such luxuries as a full-bodied bath, and Navali was exceedingly grateful for the pitcher of water and a rag, Vanca, one of the village women who was near Navali's own age, had so thoughtfully lent her the use of. Navali supposed the woman could not stand the dirt and stains of mud that covered the princess, anymore than Navali, herself, could.

The frigid water she quickly and thoroughly sponged over her body caused little bumps to rise along her extremities, and she hurriedly concluded her cold toilette, though she gratefully luxuriated in the feeling of cleanliness the water brought. She could face anything now.

Pulling her chemise back over her head, Navali then followed it with her mended silver gown, and laced the sides tight, before tying them firmly. She brought the pitcher of now dirty water with her as she walked out of the tent to greet the day. A few of the women smiled as Navali passed by them to dump the pitcher's contents at the edge of the clearing.

As she poured out the filthy water, she heard a muted groan emitting from the forest and she straightened abruptly, preparing to flee should the need arise.

"Who goes there?" Navali was proud of the fact her voice trembled only slightly when she asked that.

"H-help me-e." A voice gasped and broke over the words, and a man stumbled out of the cover of the trees in front of her. Navali glimpsed multiple cuts and bruises on his face and arms as he fell to his knees, one of his arms catching his upper body before he could hit the ground.

She took in the Dareknay crest on the man's upper left shoulder and hurriedly set the empty pitcher on the ground, before rushing to the man's side. Grabbing his right arm, she set it over her shoulders before grasping his waist with her hands. The man groaned deeply at her touch and she felt horrible for causing him any more pain, but she had to get him back to the camp as fast as she could. There was no telling if the savages who had done this to him were following closely behind.

"What happened?" Navali gasped out as she took most of his weight and began walking towards the camp as quickly as holding up a man twice her size would allow. The tents were not very far from them at all, but they presently seemed miles away to Navali, and she prayed they could make it there without falling.

"Pitan." The word was ground out between his clenched teeth and accompanied by another groan of pain.

They had just reached the edge of the encampment when Addison and Adam suddenly appeared from opposite sides to take the wounded scout from Navali and haul him the rest of the way. She followed closely behind them as the twins placed him on a blanket by the central fire that still blazed in the early morning sunlight.

Ashtyn bellowed for a healer as he and Shyre rushed to the wounded man's side. But none appeared from within the crowd of quickly amassing villagers and Adam ran and disappeared into one of the tents, reappearing a moment later with a bag thrown over one shoulder. Shyre and Ashtyn knelt on one side of the bloodied warrior and Navali stood behind them, her eyes betraying the anxiousness she felt.

"Where did you find him?" Shyre posed the question to Addison as Adam knelt on the other side of the man.

"I did not find him, your betrothed did," the blonde giant answered as he stood at his wounded comrade's feet.

Shyre turned startled eyes to Navali's, and she answered before he could even ask.

"There, at the edge of the glade." She pointed in the direction from whence she had come and his eyes followed the movement.

He stood quickly. "Aakin!"

"Here." Aakin stepped from the crowd that had formed around the injured man.

"Tighten the watch and post more men on the south side of the glade," Shyre ordered. "See that they are grouped in pairs," he finished and then knelt again.

"Consider it already done, brother," Aakin answered and took off at a lope away from them.

General Titek pushed his way through the people gathered tightly around. "Addison, help me disperse the crowd and get them back to their duties."

The big blonde man stood, his eyes transfixed on the wounded man for a moment more, before his gray eyes focused again. "Give the man some room!" He bellowed as he turned and, spreading his arms wide, walked away from the man on the ground, forcefully taking several of the gawking refugees with him.

General Titek did the same and very soon more of the Drocuns followed suit, pushing the crowd back with their arms and ordering them to their chores. The remaining Dareknay allowed Navali to stay and she stood silently as Adam began cutting away the man's shirt. The parting fabric revealed dozens of cuts, ranging in various depths and lengths as they ran across the man's muscular torso.

The wounded Drocun groaned, his eyes clenched shut as Adam sponged clean water over the parts of the shirt that had adhered with dried blood to the deeper wounds.

Ashtyn helped with whatever he could, and Shyre spoke gently to the man, his words soothing and questioning at the same time. The prince would not have asked any questions if he had not needed to and he felt for the man as his cracked and split lips parted in gasps of breath.

"Harry, did the Elite-Horde do this to you?" Shyre urgently inquired.

"A-aye." A breath shuddered out of the man. "S-said, t-tell you th-that death i-is sometimes pre—" Harry's words ended in a gasp and his eyes rolled back in his head, but he fought the blackness back enough to finish the message. "Pre-fer-able," he finally managed, his bloodshot eyes closing in unconsciousness and his body going limp as the last broken syllable left his lips.

"Does he yet live?" Shyre asked, his voice harsh with concern. Adam swiftly felt the man's neck and nodded to Shyre, his hands quickly returning to his work of bandaging, stitching, and cleaning the many wounds.

Shyre stood and ran his hands through his dark hair, pulling at the strands. His green eyes were intense as they stared fixedly upon the wounded man. His forehead crinkled in failed responsibility and an inability to be able to go back and change the orders he had given.

Navali did not like to see him in such distress. It must be hard for a leader to command his men and then for them to get hurt while carrying out those orders. She would not want to face anyone after that, knowing she would feel somehow responsible for their injuries, even if her judgment and commands had been wise.

Her hand automatically extended to Shyre in order to offer comfort of some kind, and she laid her fingers and palm gently against the center of his broad back, directly between his shoulder blades. Her fingers quickly warmed with the heat rolling off his body, but Navali stood as one frozen, completely dumbfounded at what she had just done. She had *never* voluntarily touched a man and had no idea as to what she should do next! Was it wiser to remove her hand and act as though she had never touched him in the first place, or should she let her hand remain where it was until he acknowledged it in some way?

No clues were forthcoming to assuage Navali's quandary and she was beginning to feel rather foolish and more than a little ridiculous. His brothers could even see her affection for him! If they had been paying any attention to her, that is. But that was beside the point!

A flush began to creep over her face and Navali was about to remove her hand, when Shyre turned to face her. Her hand did fall away then, only to be captured by his. He grasped it as though she were his last hope and redemption, and Shyre tugged her to walk next to him as he moved to the tent she had occupied for the night.

"Navali." Her betrothed paused as he stood outside the shelter and faced her. "I need you to gather all of your things together. With or without Lance, we ride within the hour."

"Surely the wounded man cannot be moved!" She gasped in surprise.

"We have no choice left in the matter. We cannot wait any longer. It is not safe here. The Pitan would have sent scouts to follow Harry back to camp. By now they would have nearly returned to their own encampment." His green eyes swirled in intensity, he would keep her safe from those butchers!

Navali was troubled and still very concerned about the wounded man. "How do you expect him to stay in the saddle?"

"He'll ride in one of the peasant carts." Shyre raised his left hand to forestall any more inquiries on her part, his right hand still occupied with holding hers. "But he isn't traveling with us. Addison, Aakin and Stephen will accompany us, along with the fleetest of the refugees to the Lynarian border. The greater part of the Pitan Horde will be after us and not them, giving the others time to escape to Dareknay."

Her eyes widened as she heard the part about them traveling to Lynaria. Even with their forthcoming nuptials her people would not welcome Shyre or his warriors on their land. What was he thinking, had he gone mad?

"You cannot enter Lynaria! They'll cut you down as soon as you set foot on our land!" Navali informed him.

"That's what I have you for," Shyre explained gently. "Your people won't make a move to harm you—their one and only princess—and they wouldn't dare harm your husband and incur the wrath of your father. I hear his punishments for a crime committed are rather harsh—" He halted abruptly and Navali almost missed his last words. "But it shames me to have to stand behind the skirts of a woman." He admitted the last part under his breath, uncomfortable with using a woman as a shield. It was cowardice to the extreme in his eyes and it made him cringe with distaste even though he was going to have to do it anyway.

"We aren't even married yet," Navali pointed out, helpfully. "The Lynarians will see our not being man and wife as an open invitation to thrash you, your men, and anyone traveling with you to within an inch of your lives! They won't show any mercy. They think of every Dareknay as a murdering, pillaging brigand. Our marriage, even if we *were* wed, would barely curtail them as it is." She gestured with her free hand to try and get the thickheaded man before her to understand. Not realizing that her voice was rising in her distress at the thought of him being beaten to a bloody puppet of himself.

"Are you finished with your objections now?" Shyre raised his eyebrows in question, patiently letting her express her agitation.

"Not hardly," Navali groused, displeased with his foolhardy notion of traveling to her father's holdings. "But you may have your say now," she relented, her eyes still glinting and sparking with silver fire.

"Good." Shyre then began to tick off solutions to her protestations. "For one, we will hopefully not see any of your countrymen for the brief time we are actually in Lynaria. And two, if it will make you feel more comfortable with the idea, we can solve the problem of our not being married right now."

Shyre liked the idea of that last point more than he would admit to anyone. *Kill two birds with one stone,* he thought. *No thrashings,* and *he would be able to sleep next to his beautifully fiery princess for the rest of the duration back to Dareknay.* That last was decidedly the best part of the whole thing. Now all he had to do was convince Navali to go along with it. Noting the mutinous expression on her face, he knew that would be easier said than done.

"Oh, don't worry about *my* comfort. You will be the only one suffering if we get caught in Lynaria," she snapped briskly.

"You don't like the idea of marrying me now?" He asked, his eyes widening in mock shock.

"I did not say that." At the triumphant look that entered his striking green eyes, Navali knew she had walked right into that one. "Not that I'd find it particularly agreeable. You are, after all, a brash, hard-headed Dareknay warrior."

Shyre called her bluff. "Race has nothing to do with this and you know it. If it did, I wouldn't find myself so distractedly attracted to a cold-blooded Lynarian woman." Most of his cards were on the table now and Shyre waited to see how she would react.

Navali simply did not. She changed the subject in lieu of reacting. "I think I should get to my packing if we are to leave within the hour."

"And the matter of our wedding?" Shyre persisted.

"We shall see if it's necessary first." Navali turned away to make her way into the tent. But Shyre did not relinquish the hold he had on her hand and she was forced to halt and look back at him again.

"Couldn't it be wanted, instead of necessary?" Shyre inquired gently, his green eyes delving deeply into the depths of her silver ones for the answer he so wanted to hear.

"Is that what you desire, then, Shyre? For me to *want* to be married to you?" Her brow crinkled, no one had ever asked her what she wanted. No one, but her sworn betrothed that was. She liked the thoughtfulness he exhibited when he asked, for it showed he may indeed care for her.

"I desire *you*, as my wife. But only if you desire the same thing," Shyre admitted, stroking his thumb over the soft flesh on the inside of her wrist. Her fingers tightened on his and he knew she was not unaffected by the tiny action or his words.

Navali's breath caught in her throat at the tenderness revealed in the small movement. She would never have guessed that something so small could make her heart beat so much faster. His eyes were a darker green now than she had ever seen them, and she could not tear her own gaze away from his.

What this man did to her insides was surely against Lynarian law. Toadwarts! She was not going to think about laws at a time like this, it would just confuse her even more.

"I-I don't know what I want. How can *you* know?" Navali asked, her confusion and uncertainty at the entire situation written plainly on her face for the first time, and he responded to it.

"My heart," he replied. "Doesn't yours beat faster when I am around?" A shutter dropped over her eyes at his question and Shyre knew she would not be answering. Though silence could be its own answer and he continued softly. "My heart beats harder when you are near to me, and I feel I can almost sense your presence before you step into sight."

Navali took another step away and would not meet his eyes, but Shyre did not relent. "I tried not to reveal all of this to you so soon after we met, but I find that I cannot help myself. You are fast becoming the most important thing in my life. Is it not so with you? If it isn't the same, please tell me and I will keep my affections hidden."

"I don't want you to hide anything—anything at all." Navali finally could not help herself, his words and tone of voice touching a cord in her heart that she had not known existed. This time taking a step closer, Navali looked directly into his uncertain, magnetic eyes and the urgency in her own spoke of her honesty. Raising her right hand, she stroked her index finger across his darkly stubbled cheek. "I'm just not …" Her voice trailed off, she could not remember the objections she had been about to raise.

"Not certain…?" Shyre tried. "Not ready…? Not feeling the same things I am? I need you to tell me what you are not." His voice was firm and insistent. His eyes just as intense as hers, the grip he had on her fingers tighter than before, though just as gentle as it had always been. He did not move away from her touch as she stroked his cheek again, her eyes pools of luminous quicksilver as they followed the path her finger had taken, her forehead drawn in longing and confusion.

"I'm not certain of anything right now," Navali admitted, her throat tight. "I didn't expect to feel anything but duty where you were concerned. I don't know if I'm ready, Shyre, does anyone ever truly know?" Her eyes met and beseeched his for understanding. "And am I feeling the same things for you? All I'm certain is that I've never felt this way in my entire existence," she confessed.

They were still standing beside the flap of her tent, not the most romantic of places, for anyone could walk by and see them gazing at each other and standing so close their clothing brushed.

However, neither Shyre nor Navali noticed or much cared about their surroundings, too caught up in the confessions and intentions of the heart to concern themselves with such frivolity.

The world around them had faded to just the two of them and they were perfectly content. The passage of time meant nothing, even under the threat of the Pitan menace, and Shyre groaned helplessly as he pulled her to him, kissing her with passion. His free hand buried itself in the loose curls at her nape, his palm cupping the back of her head and tilting it. His lips firm and insistent as they moved against her own, but softer and gentler than Navali could have imagined existed in a kiss with so much feeling and emotion behind it.

Her people said that emotion led to violence. If this desire to hold him closer and experience more of his kisses was the violence they spoke of, then she wanted *more* emotion, and *far* more violence of this nature.

Shyre raised his lips from hers, his breath coming harshly as he rested his forehead against her own. His eyes shut, for they would have surely revealed everything he felt, and he knew she was not yet ready for that.

Navali studied the masculine face so close in proximity to hers, taking in the tormented longing that etched his features and squeezed his eyes shut. She did not want to be the cause of any torment and knew her unwillingness to speak of the way she felt for him was causing it, even though she had not meant to. She did not know how to dress such meaningful words in exotic prose and so blunt truthfulness was left to her, and she whispered softly, "My heart flutters every time our eyes meet, and my breath catches when you are close to me like this. I don't know if that is how you feel, but that is what *I* feel."

Shyre kissed her urgently once again at her words, and her eyes slid shut as his lips coaxed hers. He suddenly broke the kiss and pulled her head back so that when she opened her eyes he could stare into their molten depths.

"Close enough," Shyre whispered roughly, her eyes still tightly shut. "It's blasted close enough." He smiled tenderly as her eyes finally opened and met his. Her breath caught at the look in his eyes and she smiled gently at him in return.

Someone in the camp suddenly shouted and returned them abruptly to their surroundings, their own private world receding to include makeshift tents and scurrying people.

Shyre released her head as he glanced away to find a few refugees walking closer. Letting go of her hand, he turned her from him, and gave her a small push in the direction of the opening of her tent. "Go on now and get ready for the rest of our journey. I want to get as far away from the other group as possible before the noon meal. It will be safer for all involved."

Navali saw the wisdom of this and moved with only a little reluctance, and a quick glance back at him, into the tent. She sank down on the fur that had covered her as she slept, her fingertips touching her swollen lips for a moment as her senses slowly returned.

Shaking her head firmly to dispel any lingering effects of Shyre's presence, Navali stood again quickly, her hands reaching to fold and roll anything that she would need to bring with her. She did not have anything in which to put the few belongings she had acquired from Shyre and the villagers, and so was done packing and out of the tent again in just a few moments. Her eyes searched for Shyre or any of his men coming to fetch her.

Peasants were frantically dismantling the fabric tents and shoving everything they could into the few carts they had been able to bring. Everyone was banding together and helping and Navali rushed to join in their preparations for the journey, confident one of the Drocun's would find her when they were ready to depart.

CHAPTER THIRTEEN

S hyre quickly found Adam and received his report on Harry's condition. His brother was fairly certain Harry would pull through with only numerous small scars to remind him of his short, but brutal, time in Pitan hands. Shyre then went over to the cart that Adam indicated and grasped the arm of the man inside.

"Forgive me, your highness," Harry spoke weakly as he opened his eyes blearily and peered at the prince. "Like a fool, I've led them right to you."

"I'll hear none of that," Shyre stated. "All my men are brave and courageous at all times. You just got a chance to prove your mettle to the accursed Pitan, that's all."

The man let out a deep breath and his face took on a relieved expression.

"Next time, though," Shyre said. "If you feel a need to show someone your strength of will, I'll gladly allow you to prove it on the practice fields. Less bleeding that way." Shyre tightened his grasp in farewell and then sent out a mental call to Ashtyn. His brother was at the front of the slowly forming line of refugees and Shyre moved in that direction. Passing Addison and Aakin on his way, he inquired if they were ready to depart.

"Only for the past half hour," was Addison's dry reply.

"Aye, for some reason known only to Ashtyn, he would not let us search for you," Aakin informed Shyre, his arms crossed over his chest as he gave his eldest brother a pointed look. "You wouldn't perchance like to tell us why, would you?'

"Not today, and probably never," Shyre replied, smiling and clapping his youngest brother on the shoulder as he continued to the front of the line, stopping to speak with several Drocuns and peasants on the way.

"Ashtyn."

Shyre's brother turned to him, a smirk on his face. "Well, well, if it isn't Prince Romance himself. You do realize I saved your arse again, don't you?"

"Oh, not to worry on that score, brother. I've already spoken with Addison and Aakin. They told me all about how they weren't allowed to search me out." Shyre stroked the neck of the horse Ashtyn was saddling.

"Hah! Then you haven't come across General Titek yet?" Ashtyn tightened the girth on the saddle as he spoke.

"Nay, why?" Shyre's hand stopped mid-stroke as he looked intently at his brother. "What has befallen us now?"

"Nothing—yet. Did you know that Ivan can be an even worse meddler than all of our brothers combined?" Ashtyn mused to his brother, his golden eyes glittering with suppressed laughter. "I dared not let him out of my sight for a moment. He very nearly eluded me anyway, for he was quite intent on finding you and the princess."

"Thank you for keeping an eye on him, then. Because he certainly would have gotten an eyeful if you hadn't, and I would most likely be back in the drudges concerning Navali." Shyre's hand continued its distracted stroking.

"So, where do you stand with her highness now?" Ashtyn asked and turned his full attention to his brother, resting his arm across the horse as he awaited an answer.

"Very well, I think. Mayhap you'll need to prepare for a wedding before we part ways," Shyre admitted.

"*That* well, hmm?" Ashtyn's voice was smugly nonchalant.

"What? You think *you* had something do with the princess and I getting on so well?" Shyre asked, one eyebrow raised in disbelief.

"Merely think it? I *know* I had a rather large part in it. Thanks to me, you're still in one piece. Or else you'd be up against a hard place with your recovered bride." Ashtyn grinned at his brother's scowling face, as he brought up the very first conversation the betrothed couple had.

"That's enough of that, I won't have you naming my short-comings when I already know all about them." Shyre changed the subject. "Back to the wedding I was speaking about, I wish to arrange it for today, within the hour preferably."

"Within the hour!?!" Ashtyn's face showed his incredulous-ness and shock. "You plan on marrying the Lynarian princess in the midst of Pitan territory, without her father or ours present?"

"Aye. We were to be wed anyway. And I find I am anxious to see the deed done." Folding his arms over his chest, Shyre looked intently at his brother, who laughed, his head bent forward as he fought to catch his breath.

"What do you find so humorous, Ashtyn?" Shyre's eyes narrowed.

Ashtyn sobered somewhat and responded. "You. Four days ago, you could not have tried harder to be rid of the wench, and today you want to marry her even earlier than expected. Are you sure you don't want some time to think through your decision?"

"Nay," the word was said firmly and clearly. "Nor do I want Navali to have time to think it through either. That's the point of the hasty ceremony. She's away from the domineering laws of her people and she's letting herself feel, something that I had not allowed myself to hope for." Shyre had unfolded his arms and hooked his right thumb in his belt, gesturing with the other hand as he spoke.

"Very well, then, say no more. So, when and where is the happy occasion to take place, if I may ask?" Ashtyn inquired. "And does she know she won't be having a wedding gown and all the flowers and fripperies that usually accompany a marriage ceremony?"

Shyre's brow lowered at his brother's words, he had not thought about that. "I don't think she will care overmuch about the frills." He hoped his brother would agree with this idea, but Ashtyn scoffed at his words and muttered something about all women caring about them. Shyre then continued staunchly on with his explanation, ignoring his twin and his words. Navali would just have to do without those feminine things. "The wedding is to take place at the main fire as soon as I find General Titek and a priest...." Shyre paused for a moment as an abrupt thought about what could be the most fatal flaw in his plan flashed through his mind. "You did say there was a priest among the villagers, did you not?"

"I don't think I ever mentioned such a thing, no." Shyre's face reflected his consternation at Ashtyn's words. "But if it will make you feel better, there *is* a priest available to perform the vows."

"Vastly better, Ashtyn," Shyre agreed. "Do you happen to know where this priest and General Ivan can be found?"

"It will save time if I just fetch them myself." Ashtyn spoke the words Shyre had been hoping to hear. "While you, Shyre, my eldest brother, get to go and pick those flowers in yon woods for your lady to hold for a bouquet." Ashtyn pointed his thumb in the direction his twin should take. "It isn't much, but it should smooth a few ruffled feathers with her," Ashtyn haughtily informed him.

"I won't need to smooth anyone's feathers, I tell you. She *wants* to marry me." Shyre paused at his next thought. "Well, she will anyway, she just hasn't made up her mind yet."

"Tell me you're jesting," Ashtyn prompted. "No, on second thought don't. This could prove far more interesting than I would want to miss." Ashtyn grinned and turned away, giving his last advice over his shoulder. "Fetch a great deal of flowers, my brother, you're going to need them. *That* I can assure you of."

"Fetch flowers, my arse," Shyre grumbled at his brother's back. "I shall *not* gather flowers like a lovesick swain."

His eyes lit upon two young girls tucking tiny purple flowers into each other's braids and he grinned suddenly. Mayhap he could devise another way to obtain the flowers needed to placate his bride.

"What!?!" Navali nearly shouted the word, despite her upbringing. "I'm not going to marry you at this very moment!"

"Ashtyn has already gone to fetch the priest, General Ivan, and my other brothers. They will be here any moment for the commencement of the ceremony." Shyre was bewildered by her complete and absolute denial that she would marry him. Although, there had been some objections to their nuptials, Shyre had thought he had put them all to rest and he felt any other uncertainties could be resolved by going forth with the wedding and solving them afterwards.

"Well, tell Ashtyn not to!" Navali demanded. "You cannot think I am going to marry you here in Pitan lands without so much as a clean dress to don?" Navali did not wait for him to respond and shook her head firmly in the negative, she could very well see how he would answer. *In the positive,* she thought in disgust.

She had not had the chance to bathe in so long she did not even want to think on it, her clothes were mended but bloodstained, her hair unbound and unadorned. *She would resemble a filthy doxy! And on what should be the most important day of her life!* Navali groaned under her breath, *everything was spinning out of her control!*

Shyre watched as a stubborn light entered her enigmatic eyes. *He would not allow her to gainsay their wedding!* "What of the Lynarians thrashing me and my men if we are not wed?"

"I'd stand back and tell them to have at it! You don't think you're going to get me to marry you with so paltry an excuse as that, do you?" Her luminous eyes widened in exasperation.

"Paltry? I consider a beating more than paltry, Navali, especially when I'm the one receiving it! Trust me, I would not look nearly so hale and hearty for our planned nuptials in Dareknay a week hence if the Lynarians got their hands on me first. You can avert all that by agreeing to wed me here and now." His right hand had grasped her chin as he spoke, and his eyes beseeched her to agree to wed him now and to not wait until they were safely in Dareknay. Shyre was not overly concerned about the possible thrashing to be had at Lynarian hands, but he would use any leverage he had at his disposal at that moment.

Having not yet revealed the flowers he had obtained for her, Shyre wondered for the first time if he was supposed to have shown her the fragile blooms first so as to soften her towards him. Too late now, he shrugged to himself. Why did everything have to be so complicated unless she was in his arms? Then, everything was smooth and easygoing, no denials or fierce bickering. Mayhap he should try wrapping his arms around her again?

The mutinous expression on her face told him if he tried, he might lose a valuable piece of his anatomy from the thrashing her tongue would bestow upon him. The princess could be a shrew when she wanted and her claws were bared for everyone to see as she glared up at him.

"Come, and be my bride this very moment," Shyre persuaded, soft and deep, hoping to coax her to his way of thinking. He released his hold on her jaw and withdrew the flowers he had been concealing behind his back. "I can't do anything about an elegant dress for you to wear or any proper attendants to wait on you. But if you'll let me, I'll be your attendant for today, my love, and if there is anything that you desire to have, if it is within my power to grant it, I will acquire it."

The steel in her silver eyes softened at the sight of the drooping blooms, and the words he uttered caused her insides to melt and butterflies to take flight. He had called her his love. Navali wondered if that could be true, could he love her as much as she felt she loved him?

Her eyes searched his, and she suddenly knew she would marry him this day or any other day of the week he asked. Even dressed in the worst gown she could imagine, with her hair mussed and tangled, with only Pitan refugees, his brothers, and his men to witness the ceremony, she would stand beside him and pledge her troth.

It would not be the most romantic wedding that had ever been, though it would be the one least forgotten in people's recollections, and what more could a bride ask for than to be remembered? Navali only hoped the remembrances were kind as she looked anything but a royal princess about to be wed.

Her future husband was not in much better shape himself though and that comforted her slightly. Though his clothes were not hastily mended, they were travel-stained, and the stubble on his chin and jaw told of his inability to indulge in a suitable shave. They would match in their grimy look, and she would not be alone in that at least. But she kind of liked him this way. There was something very masculine and strong about his appearance. Something that most Lynarian men lacked at all occasions. Navali did not know what that something was though, and really did not much care to waste her time thinking on it.

Gingerly taking the bouquet from him, Navali held it to her chest, and briefly gazed down at the flowers he had so thoughtfully acquired for her before raising gentle eyes to meet his beseeching green ones.

"Very well," she relented. "I will wed you today—but you must give me a moment to brush off some of this dirt and untangle the knots in my hair!" she protested as he immediately took hold of her hands and began tugging her to where the wedding would take place.

"I think not," Shyre informed her. "I'm not letting you go until we're safely and properly wed. I won't have you getting any more notions in your head about postponing something we both want."

Keeping hold of one of her hands, he suddenly halted and turned to gaze at her in all seriousness. "And I think you're beautiful now, just the way you are."

Shyre ran his free hand down the length of blonde hair that had come to rest over Navali's shoulder. The wavy lock cascaded past her breast to end at her waist, and he gave the curl there a small tug, noting the deep flush that arose to her cheeks, before turning abruptly and resuming his quick stride to the main fire.

More than a few people were gathered around the flames and they parted as Shyre and Navali stepped into their midst. Barely able to make out the top of Adam and Addison's golden heads above the crowd, Shyre pulled Navali with him to the center of the people. Once they made it to the main fire, they saw Ashtyn and Ivan standing by an unfamiliar man.

That must be the priest, Shyre realized. Despite the circumstances the little man looked decidedly delighted to be presiding over such a happy occasion as a wedding. He had probably only been performing funerals for far too long, Shyre speculated.

In fact, *everyone* looked deliriously happy and a cheer rose from the crowd as their newfound prince and princess gained the only clear area next to the fire.

Navali knew that if she had any second thoughts when it came to this unplanned ceremony, they would have to be put strictly aside for the moment. She was also aware that even if the ceremony did not happen now, it would certainly take place as soon as they reached Dareknay. And, looking at all the refugees' smiling and grinning faces now, she could not deny that perhaps this wedding would be good for them all at this time and not after they had reached safety. It was certainly boosting the spirits and morale of these people and that was ninety percent of the battle to survive.

Several of the villagers smiled hugely at her as her eyes alighted on them, and Navali returned their smiles with a gentle one of her own, before her attention was drawn to a short man stepping forward from the crowd.

Shyre squeezed Navali's hand reassuringly. The wedding was probably not at all to her liking, but he was determined their marriage would be. He glanced at her out of the corner of his eyes and saw that her face was calm and serene, and that even a hint of a smile curved her temptingly full lips. This was most assuredly the right thing to do.

The priest began a longwinded introduction and Shyre saw Addison jostle the man gently to hurry him along. The little man looked startled and slightly affronted at the gesture, though thankfully took the hint and proceeded directly to the vows.

"Do you, Princess Navali of Lynaria, take Prince Ashyre of Dareknay to be your lawfully wedded husband?" His voice was louder and deeper than one would have thought possible for a man of his diminutive size.

Shyre strained to hear what his bride would say and could barely make out the 'I do' she must have practically whispered to the man. Drat it all, why did the people around him have to speak during one of the most important events of his life? To be fair, they were not speaking loudly, but even the vast crowd's smallest murmurs were making the mighty voice of the priest hard to hear, much less his bride's hushed tone.

When the priest turned to Shyre and brought him back to the task at hand, he knew his bride must have responded in the affirmative. "And do you, Prince Ashyre of Dareknay, take Princess Navali of Lynaria to be your lawfully wedded wife?"

Shyre was so absorbed in making certain that his words would be heard by all, that his 'I do' thundered out over the suddenly silent mob of people. Navali jumped slightly by his side at the loud sound, and Shyre flushed, running his thumb comfortingly over the back of her hand.

What had happened to all the talking and murmuring that had been taking place a moment before?

It did not matter then, because the priest was announcing them man and wife and ordering Shyre to kiss his bride.

Which Shyre did immediately, and with great pleasure.

A loud cheer swept over the crowd as every man, woman, and child let out a shout and threw their hands up in the air. Aakin and Ashtyn swooped Navali up onto their shoulders while Adam and Addison heaved their eldest brother onto their own broad ones, effectively breaking the kiss that both Shyre and Navali had wanted to last forever.

The refugees and warriors had known about the royal wedding to take place almost before Ashtyn had left his twin to find the priest, and hastily picked flowers rained down from the sky, falling on top of the laughing and smiling newlyweds. Aakin and Ashtyn danced to the right of the crowd with Navali held securely on their combined shoulders.

Navali clasped and touched as many upheld hands as she could reach from atop her lofty vantage point, and laughed merrily at the children's antics to reach her. How different this wedding ceremony had been from any she had previously attended. Lynarian weddings were a mostly sober event with few smiles and even less laughter, and Navali figured those couples' marriages were about the same after the ceremony.

If smiles and laughter at the wedding were an indicator of how many would be shared during the marriage, Navali's and Shyre's was sure to be filled to the brim with happy and joyous moments.

As she glanced across the sea of delighted faces, Navali gasped as her husband nearly tumbled from the precarious perch Adam and Addison had him hoisted to. The blonde twins managed to halt his descent and Navali watched in relief as he threw back his head and laughed at the incident.

Navali realized then that she need not have worried, for even if Adam and Addison had failed to catch him before he hit the ground, the many hands of the refugees were there to steady him.

Gaining his feet, Shyre continued to shake hands and accept congratulatory embraces from the excited men and women who thronged him as he made his way over to where Ashtyn and Aakin held his new bride captive.

Shyre grinned up at Navali, and reached his hands to catch her about her tiny waist. His long fingers nearly spanned the small expanse and he marveled at how truly delicate she was. "Come, love. It's time we took our leave of these rogues."

Aakin and Ashtyn abruptly took a step back at his words, forcing him to let go of her waist.

"Do you think it's going to be that easy, Shyre?" Ashtyn asked the groom with a sly grin. "You have to pay a tax for this one." Shyre's twin lightly squeezed the slender thigh that rested on his shoulder and Navali tugged sharply on his short, dark hair in response.

"Cease, Cad!" Navali attempted to sound outraged, but failed miserably when a merry laugh escaped her lips.

"What was that about a tax you were spouting off about a moment ago, Ash?" Shyre inquired, laughing at the shocked look on Ashtyn's face as his twin rubbed the side of his head.

"I wasn't aware your bride had such definite ideas about a man touching her person. You're welcome to her then, and I wish you the best of luck on your wedding night. You're going to need it." Ashtyn began to bend down so that Navali's foot would touch the ground.

Navali was off balance or she would have given his hair another yank for that last remark.

Aakin laughed at his brother's words as he quickly followed suit, allowing both of her feet to rest solidly on the hard-packed earth again.

"You've gone soft, Ash, if a woman can make you do her bidding," Aakin informed him as he straightened, and the rest of his brothers crowed and whooped at the expression on Ashtyn's face.

"What does that make you then, little man? For you are forever doing the bidding of your current lady-love." Ashtyn retorted with a smirk.

"Intelligent," Aakin replied cheekily, and Adam and Addison slapped him hard on the back in laughing agreement, nearly knocking him over. "I know the way to get what I want is to give them what they think they want."

Navali was feeling comfortable enough around the royal princes to feel a little outraged at his comment. "*Think* we want? I'm assuming you're speaking of *my* gender?"

"Of course he's not, love, he wouldn't dare," Shyre said quickly. Navali could hear the barely contained laughter in his voice and then felt him gesturing something to his brothers behind her and she bit back a smile of her own.

"You'd better stay out of this, Shyre, if you expect to share her tent tonight," Addison warned him with a smirking grin. "Perhaps we will see you at the bachelors' fire tonight. What do you say, Navali, *will* we see him?" He asked with a roguish wink.

"Perhaps," she agreed and then laughed outright as her new husband grasped her about her waist and pulled her back firmly against him.

"Perhaps?" Shyre growled playfully into the shell of her ear.

His breath was warm against her flesh and Navali suppressed a shiver of delight. "Or perhaps not," she huskily replied.

"That's more to my liking." Shyre abruptly loosened his hold about her waist.

"I'm sure it is!" Ashtyn hooted in laughter, and jostled a grinning Adam and Addison.

"All right," Aakin stated as he made an attempt to sober himself. "This conversation is getting too bawdy for even my not-so-tender sensibilities. I think it has something to do with you being my elder brother or some such thing."

"For once, pup, you are right," Adam agreed and winked at their youngest brother. "We'd better finish with our preparations for the journey and leave the two newlyweds to themselves for a moment." He turned to the newly wed couple with a playfully, stern look in his blue-green eyes and shook his index finger at them in admonishment. "Now, no calf's eyes at each other until after we leave, I would still like to have my appetite intact for the noon meal."

"Nothing could dull your appetite, Adam," Shyre scoffed.

"If anything could, the sight of you making eyes at your bride would be the most effective by far," Adam retorted and winked at Navali as he grabbed the nape of Aakin's shirt, and nearly hauled him off his feet as he began walking backwards toward the line of people forming again. "Addison and Aakin will be back shortly to be part of your escort, your highness," he spoke to Navali. "But here is where our paths part till we both reach Dareknay again. Take good care of my rapscallion of an older brother. He bears watching."

"I will do both," Navali smiled at the gentle, blonde giant and stood wrapped in Shyre's arms as his brothers and the few remaining refugees walked away from them, leaving them partially alone.

"It was not the wedding you dreamed of as a young girl, was it?" Shyre asked as she turned in his arms and faced him.

"No," she told him candidly. "It was better."

He grinned at her answer and placed a swift kiss on her softly smiling lips.

"Much better." She sighed as he lifted his mouth from hers.

Shyre's eyes flared with a rakish light and he kissed her again, his lips brushing hers more firmly this time. He was fully aware of their potential audience though and restrained himself from deepening the kiss as he heatedly desired to do.

Raising his head, he feathered kisses along her jaw to her ear and nipped the lobe gently with his teeth. "How much better was it this time?" He asked in a contented baritone as he pulled away to look at her. Her beautiful silver eyes were closed and her head was back and tilted to one side.

"There are no words to describe how much better," Navali nearly purred back to him.

"Good." Shyre abruptly straightened and set her firmly away from him, holding on to her waist until she was able to stand on her own two feet without swaying into him. She was far too much of a temptation for him to keep on kissing when the threat of an audience was so high. "We've got to get moving if you're all packed, and if I know my brothers they'll be back any second with our mounts. Let's go," he ordered and she groaned in response.

"Slave driver."

"Of course. Let's get your things, slave." Grabbing her hand, he tugged her along behind him and they soon disappeared into her tent. *Their* tent, he corrected himself. Grinning like a love-struck fool, Shyre sternly restrained himself from taking her in his arms and finishing what he had started.

Letting go of her hand, he grabbed the fur she had rolled tightly and tucked it under his arm. For a moment he was jealous of an inanimate object as he thought about the downy fur cuddled next to her body and then chuckled silently to himself in satisfaction. There would not be any furs taking his place tonight. *He* would be the one she hugged to herself for warmth.

Shyre glanced at Navali and she caught his eyes. The hot look in the green depths of his gaze caused her to flush and she quickly glanced away from him again. Spinning around abruptly, her hands firmly clasping a rolled pallet to her breast, she exited the tent and rushed to the smaller band of Pitan refugees that would be traveling with them.

Aakin and Addison were already standing with Stephen near there and they grinned at her as she walked swiftly to her horse and deposited the thick blanket behind the saddle. Shyre suddenly came up behind her and laid the plush, brown fur over the rolled pallet, and secured them both to the saddle with leather thongs. Navali remained trapped against the horse in the circle of his arms. The heat of him at her back had her face turning a deeper shade of red and she did not dare glance at his brothers as he placed his hands on her shoulders and turned her around to face him.

Then, grasping her waist, Shyre swung her up into the saddle. Navali was startled at the motion and looked at him in surprise, but her husband only winked at her and moved silently away to his own mount. And she quickly scolded herself. She need not have worried that her new husband would embarrass her unduly by displaying his affection in public. He apparently understood her anxious thoughts on the matter, or perhaps had merely read her expression.

An interesting notion, she reflected, as no one had ever been able to read her expression before and he seemed to do it almost easily.

If Shyre could have heard her thoughts at that moment he would have laughed and been the first to correct her. In truth, he was berating himself for not seeing how embarrassed she was becoming by his nearness.

He did not want to frighten or overwhelm her and he was vastly aware that he was most likely proceeding far too quickly for her conservative upbringing, but he could not seem to slow things down. It was not going to happen either, he knew, for when she was close to him, his heart thundered and he completely forgot about every good intention he had to give her time to become better acquainted with him and his brash Dareknay ways. He only hoped Navali could, and would, be willing to keep up with him.

So far, she was doing a blasted good job of it though and he was proud of her for straying so far from her rigid Lynarian training, but he did not want to push her too hard their first day as a married couple. That could be disastrous and nearly fatal to their fledgling relationship.

Shyre knew he would have to strive harder to slow down more, and that was not going to be easy with the way her eyes went molten silver when he stood close to her. He was quickly becoming adept at reading *that* particular look and it never failed to cause his blood to rise. The woman was a danger to his self-control and Shyre could not have forced himself to care even if he had wanted to. The reward was definitely worth any danger that accompanied it.

He mounted his horse, and the stallion shifted beneath him as they waited for his brothers and Stephen to mount their own destriers. The young and fit Pitan refugees would have to walk as the Drocuns and Navali rode in their midst, but it could not be helped. If a threat came upon them the Drocuns would need the advantages of speed and height to face and defeat their enemies quickly before any harm could be done.

Shyre raised his right hand in a fist as he noted that the few refugees that were to follow him to Lynaria were ready. He opened his hand and signaled them forward, and the Drocuns blended smoothly and efficiently into the column with the peasants. Their eyes were already scanning the boundaries of the trees and they held their bodies at the ready in case of any surprise attack or ambush.

Navali rode beside him and he glanced at her face to find it inscrutable once again. He wondered what she was thinking and reached for the slender hand that delicately rested on the slim thigh nearest to him. He held it gently as they rode together, and his bride glanced down at their entwined hands, before raising her shuttered gaze to study his face. The whistle that someone suddenly trilled did not help his uncertain thoughts about how she felt, but he would not let so simple a thing faze him and force him to release her fragile fingers. He enjoyed the feel of it in his large hand too much for that.

ALEXA E. WOODIWISS

✐ CHAPTER FOURTEEN

Navali did not know what to make of her new husband and his affectionate touches, or the tender and sometimes desirous glances he bestowed upon her, for every action was completely foreign to her. They perplexed her no end, and frightened her a great deal more than she wanted to admit to herself. Though perhaps, she thought, the taking of a spouse's hand and holding it in public were perfectly acceptable in his country, wherein her own, they were totally unheard of.

The touch and warmth of Shyre's fingers did not make Navali nearly as uncomfortable as she first thought it would, and even the uncouth whistle had not overly disconcerted her. Was she becoming a wanton, or perhaps something worse? *Was* there anything worse?

She did not know, but, she realized, she could not have cared less if she were indeed becoming a wanton. Shyre seemed to like it when she let him hold her hand or even wrap his arms around her, and if her handsome husband liked it, she was determined she would get used to it.

What was the point of a rebellion if one did not pursue it with everything one had in them? The answer was nothing, nothing at all.

If Navali was already going to be punished or snubbed by her people for her actions or feelings, she might as well take it to the extreme. The green eyes staring at her in wonder, tenderness, and desire well-merited everything she would have to endure should her people discover her rebellion of their ways.

Just thinking about the Lynarian ways of punishment made the skin on her back tighten in apprehension. Navali quickly shoved those uncomfortable thoughts away and focused on the moment—on the colorful, leafy ground beneath her horses hooves, the clear blue sky she could see filtering through the thick green of the trees that towered over them, and most of all, the feel of her husband's strong, masculine hand gently cradling her own.

Shyre's fingers were wrapped firmly around hers and she tightened her own to show that she accepted and welcomed his touch and the initiative he had taken when he had reached for her. She wanted him to know he would be welcome to do whatever he desired and that she appreciated him taking the lead, for she knew next to nothing of what went on between two people that were just wed.

"How far do we have to journey until we reach Lynaria?" Navali asked, meeting the green eyes that were trained on her face.

Shyre's mouth quirked in a small, lopsided grin as she finally broke the silence between them. He would have wagered coin she would have first commented on the physical affection he was exhibiting, and not the length of their journey. But, oh how wrong he would have been. "About four days," he answered.

"Four days?" Navali was surprised they were that far from her country. She had not fully realized the size of the Pitan holdings. "But are we not almost to Dareknay? Why do we not just enter through a different route than General Titek and Ashtyn?"

"We are indeed closer to Dareknay, perhaps only a day or so away," Shyre said, navigating his horse around the stump of a fallen tree. "But there is only one inlet to my father's lands from the Pitan territory; a stone bridge, and we cannot be certain to get all of the people safely across it ere the Pitan attack us. Therefore, we travel to Lynaria, which we can safely cross at several points without meeting resistance."

"My father has posted many more men along the border since the outbreak of the Pitan Horde attacks. It will be difficult for you and your men to cross when we get there, as they will not easily accept you or let you pass on our lands. How do you plan to handle that when the time comes?" Navali asked, and allowed her brows to draw together in confusion.

"Your father doesn't have enough men to be able to cover all the entry points, otherwise he would not be so interested in arranging a marriage between his only daughter and myself. So we will hopefully find one that is unmanned and won't have to be concerned about any aggression at all. If there are guards posted, then we will simply explain what has happened and that I am now married to you. If that doesn't work, we'll have you order them to stand down." Shyre shrugged his broad shoulders, clearly not perturbed about what could be a very dangerous endeavor.

"Why don't I just order them to stand down immediately?" She asked him. "Wouldn't that be easier and simpler?"

"Perhaps, but we want to portray that I am able to control the situation. After all, I may someday rule Lynaria through my marriage to you and we want to have your people respect my word as they would your father's. If I stand behind your skirts and your authority from the very beginning, they will think me incapable of governing them. The soldiers, especially, would not want to follow my commands after that." He spoke with quiet conviction, clearly having given a great deal of thought as to how he should approach this matter.

His wife's confused expression cleared and she gave a small nod in response to his explanation, and Shyre was relieved that she understood his need to exert his authority for her people to respect and obey him.

Navali then sat quietly atop her horse, who was contentedly, and without her needing to give him direction of any kind, following the lead stallion. She did not know why Shyre thought the animal so ill-tempered, for the horse was always so laid-back and calm for her. And she was grateful for it as it allowed her to reflect on the fact that Shyre was one of the few men in her life who actually explained to her what was going on, instead of thinking she was a pea-goose with only fluff and frills betwixt her ears, incapable of her own thoughts or ideas.

Those other men were louses, every last one of them, and they were all Lynarian too, she realized. What an anomaly the Dareknay were from the other races she knew.

The Vetuai were very pious, religious, and rigid, the Selenacans more like traveling nomads who kept to themselves unless they felt the temporary need to do otherwise. And the Lynarians, well, Navali knew exactly what her own people were like, and she was becoming more disgusted with them by the moment.

It was probably very traitorous of her to think that, but she could not help it. When she saw the way the royal Dareknay brothers were warm towards each other, teasing and talking without fear of reprimand, she could nearly spit on the rules and regulations she had previously been forced to conform to.

She was now very sure that people were not supposed to be without emotions or unable to give or receive affection. How could it be bad to feel and see that someone cared for her? She did not know how her people had come to despise all outward displays of feelings. They said it was dangerous to a person's mental stability, but Navali knew that could not be correct, for her new husband was not ill of mind, or of anything else, in any way.

It was a bunch of hogwash, spoon-fed to their children, who were too impressionable at such a young age to defy or even think to rebel until it was too late and they just accepted everything they were told and became the next generation of stiff, cold, and formal conformists, prisoners of their own society and rules.

Navali liked the feeling of Shyre's hand holding hers and she loved it when he took her in his arms, crushing her to him and kissing her with all the intensity he was feeling. It made her feel cherished and wanted. What a glorious and ultimately feminine feeling to be wanted by a man! And a handsome and considerate one at that!

Shyre's horse shied into hers at a rustling in the underbrush and he released her hand to bring his nervous mount under control. Leaning forward over the saddle, Navali peered curiously around her husband to the bushes that had caused his horse to be suddenly skittish, and her eyes widened at what she saw.

"Shyre!" Navali gasped quietly.

"What, love?" He glanced at her face as he loosened the tight grip he had needed to maintain on the reins a moment before.

She looked straight ahead before saying in a hushed tone, "There was a face in those bushes over there." Navali did not dare gesture to show him the area she meant, as it was likely the other person would flee if she did.

Quickly, Shyre turned his head and scanned their immediate surroundings. He did not see anything. "What did the face look like? Male? Female? Any distinguishing marks?"

"You believe me?" Navali was confused by that. Her father or his men would not have believed her if they had not seen the face themselves. But Shyre seemed to do so without hesitation and he did not seem to think it was just an hysterical flight of feminine nerves.

"Why would I not?" Her new husband asked, perplexed.

Navali shrugged her shoulders delicately, not desiring to tell him the answer to that. It was too painful that her own father did not believe her when he had always been a part of her life and her new husband did after only a few days of being in her presence. "No reason, I suppose."

Shyre gazed at her with a skeptical look in his swirling green eyes.

Navali swiftly answered his previous question before he could ask anything else. "The face was unmistakably female. Ghostly pale, with very long, wild, dark hair. She was staring at you so intensely it was as though she hated you with every fiber of her being. You do not know any women in Pitan that would despise you, do you?"

"Nay." Shyre shook his head firmly. "I do not know any women here other than the ones that are refugees. Until four days ago, I had never set foot in Pitan. You say she stared at me with something akin to hatred?"

"Aye, she had an almost fanatical look on her face while she fingered something about her neck, and her lips were moving as though she were speaking to someone. It was very strange and I wouldn't blame you if you didn't believe me, Shyre. I hardly do myself, and I was the one to see her." Navali was deeply troubled by what she had seen. The expression on the other woman's face was not only fanatical, but it was also as if she were not quite right in all of her faculties.

Just thinking about the other woman was frightening Navali. *What did she want? Was she following them? Was she dangerous?*

Noting Navali's breath picking up its pace, Shyre reached over and soothingly laid a hand on her slim thigh. "Now, you are not to worry about this. She was probably just some woman who hates all other men who aren't Pitan, and is most likely harmless."

"My prince!" The shout suddenly came from behind them and Shyre and Navali both twisted in their saddles to see Stephen ride up to them at a quick trot. "Some of the villagers say they saw a woman's face in the bushes—a Fayrah." The last word was spoken quietly as he glanced about himself, hoping he was not being overheard by the others.

Shyre's entire demeanor changed. He stiffened and his face became impassive. "I cautioned you never to speak that word in front of the refugees." His voice was harsh with disapproval.

The other man looked chastened at his prince's words. "Forgive me, my lord. I am only repeating what the villagers are already naming her."

"I know, but tis best if they do not hear us utter it," Shyre cautioned and the other man nodded. "Ride with my bride. I must speak with my brothers."

"Yes, my lord." Stephen quickly brought his horse forward to take Shyre's place alongside Navali.

Navali observed quietly as Shyre rode back to speak first with Aakin and then Addison. Both men were calm, their expressions betraying nothing. She then glanced at the villagers to see them avidly watching the men's exchange with trepidation and wariness written on their frightened faces. She did not know what could possibly frighten them so much and why her husband seemed to be so suddenly on alert for an immediate attack.

"Stephen," she began, but the faithful soldier interrupted what she had been about to say.

"I really cannot tell you, your highness. I've been forbidden from mentioning it." Stephen looked at her in apology, clearly uncomfortable with denying her. "You'll have to ask the high prince if you want to know anything."

"Very well, Stephen." Navali accepted his inability to answer her. "I'm sorry I asked you to disobey your orders."

"Don't be, your highness. You did not even get the chance to ask and, in your position, I would have tried the same thing, anyone would," the Drocun assured her kindly and gave her a brief smile.

Shyre rode back to them after only a few minutes of silence had passed between Navali and Stephen, as both soldier and princess were lost in their own thoughts.

"Stephen, bring up the rear flank and make sure we do not lose any of the villagers along the way," Shyre ordered. The other man immediately nodded and wheeled his destrier around to follow his command. "Navali, I need you to be very careful of anyone who asks you to go anywhere with them, even if they say that I told them to fetch you. Do you understand?"

Looking at his hands which were grasping the reins with white-knuckled intensity, Navali answered. "Yes, though may I ask why?"

"You may. However, I cannot answer until we make camp tonight and are out of the hearing of others. I will answer any questions you have about this incident then," Shyre informed her and she nodded obediently in understanding.

Answering questions about a subject he wished she did not have to know about, was not the way Shyre had envisioned spending his wedding night, but it could not be helped now. Navali would have to know about the Fayrah sooner or later, and it was better she know sooner for her safety's sake.

Riding in relative silence for the rest of the day, Shyre scanned the trees and brush every few seconds. Other than stopping briefly for the midday meal, which was consumed cold so that no fires had to be lit, there was no rest to be had until right before darkness fell and they were forced to make camp for the evening.

The atmosphere was very subdued from the previous evening's festivities and, though they tried hard not to show it, Navali could see the fear and terror written in the refugees' eyes.

Five fires were immediately lit upon the decision to make camp, one placed at each of the four corners and another centrally located. After the fires were taken care of, the men worked to erect a few larger tents in which to sleep. Navali and Shyre were the only ones to have a smaller one, and Navali had blushed scarlet when one of the few married women had explained why.

"'Tis fer yer weddin' night, milady." The woman spoke as though she was puzzled by Navali asking who the smaller structure was for.

"Oh! Of course," Navali answered and could have hid her bright red face in her hands for the woman's questioning look. Navali had honestly not thought on the possibilities of a wedding night. She had gotten married early that morning and had not spared a moment's thought as to the consequences a new husband posed to her privacy. What was she to do now?

Not knowing, Navali opted to sit by the fire and wait for the stew she had helped prepare to finish cooking. It did not take long for the appetizing concoction to boil merrily in the many kettles which were hung from makeshift poles over the fires.

Several of the women then poured generous amounts of the thick stew into bowls and passed them out to everyone. Someone had even taken the time to make biscuits, and the fluffy white bread soon joined the food that was quickly disappearing.

The meal was over far too quickly for Navali, for she found that as the meal progressed, her wariness of the coming night quickly mounted. She had not noticed her husband eating with everyone else and she wondered where he had gone, though secretly she was relieved to not yet see him. Addison and Aakin were not around either and she did not let herself worry as the three brothers were fully capable of taking care of themselves and each other.

Reluctantly, Navali entered her tent when the rest of the refugees disappeared into their own sleeping areas, and she quickly removed her tattered gown and slippers, before slipping between the furs placed on the ground in only her chemise. The softness of the bed and the sound of the crackling fire outside soon lulled her to a half sleep and she dreamily watched as the firelight flickered through the tent wall.

Where was her husband anyway? she thought drowsily. He had promised to tell her what Fayrah meant this eve, and she was more eager now to know than she had been earlier, for the word had most definitely set all of the villagers and warriors on edge. And she hated being the only one who did not know. What was so dangerous about an explanation?

Turning away from the flickering shadows, Navali faced the darker side of the tent. Her eyes closed wearily as she waited, until Navali finally conceded the battle to stay awake. Her conspicuously absent husband would just have to explain what a Fayrah was on the morrow.

Much later that evening, Navali was abruptly awakened as a small sound alerted her that she was no longer alone in the tent. Stiffening under the thick furs at what could possibly be a threat to her wellbeing, she warily glanced over her shoulder, and saw the familiar build of her husband.

"Shyre?" She asked, her voice hesitant and husky from sleep.

"Aye, tis me. I apologize for waking you." He said as he turned to face her in the darkness, before setting something down on the ground.

It was not until he had stepped out of the shadows to sit on the blankets to remove his leather boots that Navali realized he had been holding his shirt and that his back was now devoid of all raiment. She sucked in a startled breath at the glorious sight before her eyes. His smooth, tanned skin rippled over his hard muscles, and the very masculine, bronze tattoo on his left shoulder took away the breath she had just drawn.

"Are you well, Navali?" Shyre asked over his shoulder, having heard her gasp.

"Quite," she responded in a choked voice as she burrowed deeper in the covers. Knowing that her voice was not in the least convincing, she expounded. "The covers slipped and it was just a bit colder in here than I thought it would be."

Her new husband finished with the removal of his boots and then gingerly settled beneath the warm furs, lying next to her on his side, naked chest and all.

"Wh-where w-were you after we m-made camp?" Navali stumbled over her words as she attempted to frantically come up with some form of conversation that might distract him as he suddenly reached for her and pulled her stiff body gently against his.

A smile quirked Shyre's firm lips as he responded, "My brothers and I ventured afield to find the mystery woman you saw earlier." Wrapping his arms around her, Shyre rubbed her back to lend his warmth and soothe her.

Allowing her body to minutely relax at his touch, Navali partially arose and rested her head in a propped up hand.

"About that," Navali began, her voice all business, and Shyre knew that the questions he had been dreading all day were about to be asked. "What is a Fayrah, and why do I feel it has something to do with that woman?"

Her new husband groaned softly and released her, turning onto his back as he did so, his head cushioned on his bent arm. "A Fayrah is a witch that is part of a coven here in Pitan."

"And the villagers think that woman was one of them?" Navali inquired, her eyes troubled as they gazed down at him.

"Not just any of the Fayrah, but the head one that Krinar consults before moving his Elite-Horde," Shyre admitted and glanced over at her.

"The head witch," Navali whispered in dread, her eyes holding a faraway look of remembrance. "Does that mean Krinar is close by?" She looked at Shyre and met the gaze he had trained on her.

"It could, but my brothers and I saw not a sign of anyone following closely," Shyre reassured her and cupped his free hand around her neck, drawing her down to gently kiss her full lips. "Enough talk of Krinar and his pet Fayrah, it is not a fit topic for a bedtime tale."

"What?" Navali managed to gasp incredulously as his mouth stole kisses from her own, each one more intense than the last.

Shyre rubbed his stubbled cheek lightly against the underside of her jaw and placed a kiss directly below her delicately curved ear. "You have heard of a tale before?"

"Of course I have." Her breath came faster as his lips and teeth nibbled a path down the sensitive flesh of her neck. "That is how I learned of how beastly your people were."

"Beastly, hmm?" He chuckled lightly as his fingers played about the laces of her chemise's neckline, working to undue the knot that held the edges fastened. "I suppose those tales went something along the premise of Dareknay are demons from the underworld who snatch unruly children from their beds and eat them?"

"You are astonishingly close to the mark." She sighed breathlessly as his lips followed the path of loosening fabric and she frantically sought to keep her wits about her. "But you do not eat them, you just enslave them."

"And have I enslaved you, my love?" Shyre inquired with a wicked grin as he brought his head up to stare into her eyes.

"Very nearly," Navali whispered, and observed his gaze flaring heatedly as she wrapped her arms about his torso and caressed his naked back with her fingertips.

"Only nearly? I shall endeavor to strive harder then, to assure you're fully enraptured within my grasp." He gently nipped the lobe of her ear, before soothing it with a kiss. "Perhaps I will start by weaving my own tale of Dareknay lore." His breath whispered heavily in her ear as his hands gently removed her chemise.

"Once upon a time," he began, his hands playing about the smallness of her waist. "In a land that was not so friendly to them, two people met for the very first time…" A kiss was placed in the hollow of her collarbone. "They wed two days later…." Another kiss landed gently on her bare, right shoulder. "And then lived happily ever after, enjoying many passionate moments such as this one."

Shyre's next kiss completely ensnared Navali in the passionate longing he was mercilessly concocting with his lips, hands, and body. Soon, both were swept up in a turbulent tide of feverish ardor that melded and sealed the vows they had undertaken earlier that day.

CHAPTER FIFTEEN

The next morning Shyre awoke with the dawning of the morning sun, which was accompanied by the quiet, but insistent hailing of his brother from the other side of the tent flap.

"Shyre!" Addison spoke in a low, urgent tone, threateningly tugging on the flap of the tent as he attempted to rouse Shyre.

"I'll be out posthaste." Shyre's voice was hoarse with sleep, and he cleared his throat quietly. Shifting carefully away from Navali, who had lain wrapped in his arms the entire night through, Shyre tried not to awaken her from her peaceful slumber. His slow movements were for naught as her silver eyes blinked open with obvious reluctance, and she gave him a small smile, contentedly stretching her slender arms above her head.

Shyre grabbed his breeches from where they had been discarded beside the pallet and then hurriedly yanked them on, as icy fingers of cold air raced over his bare torso. His bride sat up, hugging the furs close for warmth, and Shyre glimpsed a swath of creamy, bare skin and groaned at his brother's timing.

"What is it? Is there trouble?" Navali asked worriedly, glancing about for her own discarded clothing.

"I know naught, love. But you'd best get dressed. I'll return shortly to tell you of what has transpired." Shyre pushed his arms through his shirt and leather jerkin as he spoke, then reached for his boots and hurriedly pulled them on. He grabbed his sword in one hand and, giving Navali a quick kiss, rushed out of the tent.

Addison greeted him as he stepped out into the crisp morning air.

"What has happened?" Shyre inquired, buckling his sword about his waist.

"It's that Pitan tyrant," Addison reported. "One of the villagers went out for a morning hunt, climbed a tree to get a feel for the lay of the land and saw the smoke and tents from their camp. It's quite a few leagues behind us. There were no scouts out so the man was able to make it back without an alarm being raised, or there would have been hell to pay."

Shyre's brow furrowed as he walked to the fire with his brother and, upon gaining its warmth, smiled and accepted a bowl of porridge and a freshly made biscuit from one of the village women. Another woman handed Addison a filled bowl and a biscuit of his own, and Shyre finally became aware of the way the older Pitan females hid grins behind their hands as the younger ones blushed brightly and giggled, and he had no problems discerning what they were grinning about.

Flushing a bright red himself, Shyre made a mental note to warn Navali about the embarrassment that could prove imminent for her. It seemed they were the topic of the morning gossip. He quickly swallowed the bite of biscuit that had suddenly become lodged in his throat and, turning, fled the knowing stares of the women, his brother following closely behind.

"Where is this man that found the Pitan?"

"There." Addison gestured with the hand that held a half-eaten biscuit.

Finishing his porridge swiftly, Shyre gave the empty bowl to Addison, who scowled but stacked it beneath his and then returned it to the women. As he took another bite of his biscuit, Shyre strode over to the man who sat at one of the smaller, outlying fires, observing as he did so the way the refugee's eyes shifted nervously every few seconds to glance about.

"You saw the Pitan king?" Shyre asked without preamble.

"Not 'xactly, yer highness, I jes' saw his crest on tha big tent o' his. That were 'nough fer me." The anxious man had risen to his feet when the prince approached, and now stood with his arms wrapped about himself, rubbing his cold, skinny biceps with his bony hands.

"Could you tell how many men he had?" Shyre's voice was calm, assured, and firm. He could see the terror written on the hunter's face and he needed the man to calm down before he caused a full-blown panic amongst the others.

"Plenty 'nough ta catch us an' make us pay fer escapin' his rule, ye can be sure o' that!" The man's eyes were frantic in his fright as he relived what he had seen, and he shifted back and forth on his feet, obviously feeling a need to run and escape even now.

"Steady there," Shyre spoke, and clapped one firm hand onto the man's thin shoulder, forestalling any more thoughts of fleeing. "I need you to calm yourself, man, and tell me what you saw. But first, let's start with your name, shall we?"

The man gave a quick, jerky nod. "Me name's Bertrand o' Fieldstone."

"A fine name to be sure, Bertrand. Now, what was it you saw exactly?" Shyre coaxed.

The man hunched his shoulders in worry. "Smoke rising from fires 'round a huge tent wit' Krinar's crest on it."

"Could you hazard a guess as to how many fires?" Shyre asked.

"Nigh 'nough ta warm the hides a three hundr'd men, I'd say. But I ain't so sure on that, on account o' I didn't take the time ta count." Bertrand, obviously feeling less a man for his lack of courage, looked disappointed in himself and gave Shyre a quick, guilty look.

"I'm sure I wouldn't have stayed to count them either," Shyre assured him, though it was a lie. "Did you happen to notice anything else?"

"Aye," Bertrand nodded vigorously, as he suddenly remembered something important. "When I was climbin' outta the tree, I had ta stop sudden-like 'cause I saw a woman in the distance. A dark-haired one, wearin' a black gown wit' twigs an' leaves stuck all o'er it. She was chantin' and wavin' her arms 'bout. Sure as I'm standin' here now, 'twas that Fayrah we seen yesta'day!" The man's voice rose in panic with every syllable of his last sentence.

"Silence!" Shyre swiftly ordered. "We'll not be saying another word of the Fayrah to the others, my friend. Do you understand?" Shyre asked the man, his green eyes locked on the hunter and his hand firm against the quaking, thin shoulder beneath it.

"Aye, yer highness." The man swore his silence on the matter.

"I don't want the women to be frightened, and I'm sure you don't want that either," Shyre continued.

"Nay." The man's face smoothed and his shoulders squared at the thought of being able to protect the women's tender sensibilities with his silence. His courage was now restored with a mission he knew he could accomplish and that would make his new prince proud of him.

"You've done well, Bertrand." Shyre patted him on the back. "Have you broke your fast yet?"

"Nay, milord." Bertrand stared in awe at this unruffled prince as he shook his head in the negative. He did not think anything could cause the high prince to be frightened or wary. Prince Ashyre would not let King Krinar attack or imprison them again, Bertrand was now certain of that.

"Well, you had best see to getting your fill of hot porridge and some of those biscuits the women are serving then." Shyre gave the man's shoulder a nudge in the right direction.

"Aye, yer highness. I'll see ta that right now." Bobbing a swift bow, the thin man scurried on his way.

Shyre turned to Addison, who had stood silent as he observed the entire exchange between prince and peasant. "Fetch Aakin, will you? Meet me outside of my tent in five minutes."

"Aye, Shyre." The big man strode away and Shyre quickly returned to his tent and ducked inside.

"What happened?" Navali asked him from where she was sitting in the middle of their pallet and plaiting her long, blonde hair into a thick braid.

"One of the villagers found the Pitan encampment," Shyre answered as he sat down next to her and, taking her half finished braid in his hands, continued plaiting it for her.

"Did he say how close they were?" She inquired nervously.

"Several leagues away." Navali gasped and stiffened at his nonchalant words. "It's far enough though, that if we travel fast they won't be able to catch up for a couple of days. By that time, we may have reached Lynaria and acquired a few of your father's soldiers to help fend them off," he assured quickly.

"It doesn't look very likely to happen though, does it?" Navali speculated, her smooth brow wrinkling in a frown.

"It's a long shot," he agreed, as he took the leather thong she was anxiously fiddling with and secured the ends of her plaited hair. "But it's the only one we've got at the moment." He ran a hand down the gleaming, blonde braid that fell nearly to her waist. "I've finished with your hair, my lady."

"Thank you, my lord." She looked at him shyly and he took the opportunity to kiss her softly parted lips.

"I love your hair," he huskily confessed as he raised his head and wrapped her braid around his fist, tilting her head back for another deep kiss. "It's long and silken, just as I've always dreamed my wife would have."

"You received your wish, then, my lord." She smiled gently against his lips.

"Shyre," he insisted huskily, longing to hear his name spoken in her softly accented voice again.

"Shyre," she obliged breathlessly, and kissed the firm masculine mouth so near to her softer one, comfortable enough after the previous night's passionate undertakings to seize the initiative and pick up where he left off.

A discreet cough suddenly echoed into their tent from outside.

"Hellfire," Shyre swore softly against her lips. "That would be my brothers. We need to discuss our next course of action." He stood and set her lightly on her feet as he arose. He released her and turned and bent to pull something from one of the packs on the ground.

"Here, I want you to have this." He straightened and extended the thin dagger he held out to her. "Just in case you again find yourself in need of a blade."

"Thank you, Shyre." Navali smiled and gently took the sheathed weapon from him.

"You should probably pack and get something to eat. We shall be departing within the hour." He informed her, and then stepped from the tent.

The cold air he inadvertently invited in as he drew back the flap caused Navali to shiver violently and she hurriedly drew a blanket around her shoulders as she began rolling furs and other bedding.

Finishing with her task quickly, she stepped out into the crisp morning air and, suppressing another shiver, was welcomed by a cold breeze that snatched tendrils of her hair and blew them across her face. It was far colder here than she was accustomed to.

Her people may have preferred their houses and buildings and attire to be cool in color and nature, but Navali had rarely noticed any true coldness in Lynaria. Now, though, she severely cursed whoever dictated their fashion designs. For her toes were quickly subjected to the cold, biting wind as it seeped easily through her thin, silk slippers. She now far preferred how Shyre's people used furs and heavy materials for blankets and garments, as it was much more effective in keeping out the chill of a crisp fall day.

Navali glanced around at her surroundings, attempting to forget the coldness she was experiencing. The mountains that enfolded the little valley they had taken shelter in for the night were glorious with their peaks crowned in purest white, and glinting brightly in the morning sunlight. Mist shrouded the far edges of the camp, and the leaves from the many trees still shown a deep green despite the lateness of the season.

She breathed deeply of the fresh air. All things considered, it was a good day to be alive. Navali just hoped tomorrow would be as good and they could manage to stay alive with the Pitan Elite-Horde so close at hand. Firmly pushing that discouraging thought aside, she made her way to the central fire.

"Good mornin', yer highness," greeted one of the Pitan women.

"Good morning, Vanca. How fare you this day?" Navali inquired of the petite young woman who had befriended her in the short time the princess had been with the refugees.

"Well, milady, and yourself?"

"Hmm...." Navali hummed as she thought of an answer. "Glorious, now that I have a plate full of the food you've prepared."

Vanca chuckled at the small smile that flitted across Navali's face. "You can thank my mother for that, she taught me a great many things." Vanca had told Navali of all the lessons her once genteel mother had insisted she learn in case Krinar was ever defeated and their family was reinstated to their noble status.

"Your highness?" Vanca then asked hesitantly, her hands twisting the fabric of her dress.

Navali glanced up from her plate of food, her expression questioning.

"Did you happen to see a strange woman yesterday?"

The princess did not know how to respond. Shyre had spoken of the refugees' fear of the Fayrah, and she did not want to incite a full blown panic among them if she responded in the affirmative.

"Why do you ask, Vanca?"

The woman's voice dropped to a mere whisper as she took a step closer to the princess. Her words were for the benefit of the princess she had come to care about so much, and not for eavesdroppers. "Because, Princess Navali, if that woman was indeed a Fayrah, she'd be dangerous to everyone, but mostly to you. She would do anything to kill any good in this world. And, pardon my boldness, your highness, but you're as good as anyone I've ever met. Please don't venture into the woods unaccompanied anytime soon, all right?"

It was the very same warning Shyre had given her. "I'll be careful, Vanca, I promise."

"Thank you, Princess." Vanca straightened and a wide smile abruptly transformed her merely pretty features into one of earthy beauty. "Now that the unpleasant part of our conversation is over, how do you like married life?"

Navali blushed at her friend's words. "I think it may agree with me."

"I dare say so. Your cheeks are blooming a becoming shade at the mere mention of it."

Navali joined Vanca in the giggles that suffused her.

Adele, Tucker's younger sister, made her way over from another fire and gave Vanca a confused smile, obviously wondering what had brought on their laughter. Vanca told her and the two shared another laugh as she finished. Navali had never known people who were so candid and open with each other. She liked it immensely though and hoped she could learn to be more like that herself.

Perhaps in time, she reflected, she could even lose her stilted formality and completely relax around them. Navali finished her meal in relative silence, which was only broken by a few merry comments and tidbits of gossip from Vanca, Adele, and the other women who were busily packing utensils, pots, and bowls.

There were not any children traveling with their group now and Navali missed the little ones running around underfoot and laughing, for it lightened the mood and tension that was so often found in their journey.

The families that had been traveling with the Dareknays had been assigned the shorter route directly to their new lands, and she was glad for the fact that they would be protected and secure in her husband's holdings before the Pitan could have a chance to attack them.

Rinsing her bowl from a leftover pitcher of water, Navali then helped the women as they thoroughly doused the fires. The men had packed up the tents as the women finished, and the few horses and carts they had were quickly loaded with supplies.

Shyre found her at the edge of the camp. "Up to another ride, my sweet?" He asked with a wide grin.

"Of course, Shyre. Though I was unaware I had any other choice in the matter," Navali teasingly answered and, as his muscular arm wrapped about her shoulders, slipped hers around his trim waist. It just seemed like the natural thing to do. She picked up the skirt of her gown with her other hand to keep it out of the way of her slippered feet.

"You don't," Shyre agreed. "But I was trying to sound considerate and perhaps receive a kiss for my thoughtfulness."

Instead, Shyre received a poke in his ribs from Navali's elbow and he huffed in surprise.

"What?" He asked, laughing at her indignant expression. "You don't want me to be nice to you?"

"Not if you are just saying such pleasant things to earn my favors," Navali retorted with a playful roll of her silver eyes.

"I don't have to earn them," Shyre growled playfully, stopping and tugging her firmly against his broad chest. "I already have them." He kissed her slowly and thoroughly, leaving her entirely without breath when he lifted his head.

"Aye," she whispered against his mouth. "You most certainly do."

"Shyre! Quit kissing your woman and get a move on!" Aakin called from atop his destrier. "Daylights wasting away and we're all twiddling our thumbs over here, waiting on you two lovebirds."

"You can just wait, little brother." Shyre stole another quick kiss in defiance of his brother's lighthearted orders, and then lifted

Navali to the saddle of the horse Aakin had brought for her. "And where is Justice?" Shyre asked, raising a lofty brow of inquiry.

Aakin jerked his head towards the far end of the column. "Over there. You're fully capable of getting your own horse, brother, but Mother would have my head if I didn't act the part of a gentleman with your new bride."

"My thanks for all your help, Aakin. Mother would be so proud," Shyre replied dryly.

"I know," Aakin quipped. "And you're most welcome, Shyre, old boy." He then turned his horse to take up his place at the back of the line.

"Shall we?" Shyre looked up and asked Navali from where she had settled in the saddle.

"By all means," she agreed with a smile, and he led her horse over to Swift Justice and then mounted the golden stallion.

All of the villagers and Drocuns appeared calm as they once again began their journey, but the attentive way they scanned their surroundings spoke otherwise.

Shyre's hand rested on his thigh, his sword strapped securely around his waist and his bow tied lightly to the saddlebag on his right. All of his weapons were within easy reach, but he prayed he would not have need of them this day. But he especially hoped his wife would not have a need to use the dagger he had presented her with.

He glanced over at Navali and let his eyes wander down the enticing figure he had so thoroughly explored the previous night. He did not immediately notice the weapon on her person, and he scrutinized her more closely. She must have it somewhere though. Surely she did not pack it in her saddlebag!

"Navali, did you remember to bring the dagger with you?" He asked suddenly, and then felt chastened for it when she shot him a pointed look, obviously believing he thought her a complete lackwit.

"You cannot see for yourself that I have it with me?" Navali smiled tauntingly and too-sweetly up at him as she evaded answering his question directly, her eyes now alight with mischievous coyness.

"Nay," Shyre answered carefully. He did not see a bulge of any kind beneath her gown and he had not felt anything either when he had held and kissed her before they had departed earlier. Was he becoming inept?

"Good," Navali replied smugly, but deliberately rested her hand against her upper left thigh and pulled her gown taut against her limb.

He could now see the faint bulge of the dagger's hilt and was thoroughly assured she had it within easy reach. "I wonder what other secrets you hide, my love," Shyre mused, his green eyes searching her face in avid curiosity.

"It will take you a very long time to discover them all, my brash prince." His bride replied haughtily.

Shyre chuckled at her response and Navali's merry laugh soon joined his.

Unbeknownst to them, their cheerful expressions and laughter went a long way in lightening the weightiness of the gloom and despair that had settled over the Pitan villagers under their care, and the refugees faces brightened considerably as hope again began to bloom.

Though their small band was weary after a full day of walking, as soon as the fires were built and the tents erected that evening, Shyre and his brothers ordered the men to the far end of the meadow that was to serve as their resting place.

The Dareknay warriors then instructed the Pitan men in defensive maneuvering. They practiced archery, hand-to-hand combat, and knife fighting—as most of the men had knives at their disposal and were already fairly adept at its usage.

The men were eager to learn how to defend themselves and their women, and they caught on quickly, their attention completely focused on their drills.

Addison called a halt after the sun had completely disappeared and he noticed the women were ready to serve the evening meal. The men collapsed in grateful, exhausted heaps around the fires, very nearly inhaling the food the women offered them.

Exclaiming over the dark bruise that Shyre had acquired during their practice, Navali gently fingered the injured area on his jaw. "You've been wounded!"

"It's just a little bruise," Shyre assured her and caught her hand. "It's not even painful." Settling down beside her on the ground, he began to eat, not giving another thought to his black eye and bruised cheek.

Contemplating the not-so-little bruise her husband now sported across the entire left side of his face, Navali asked uncertainly. "Do you think it wise to teach the Pitan refugees how to fight, Shyre?"

"Aye," he replied after swallowing the food in his mouth, and then gestured around at the Pitan. "If you look closely at them, you can see that just the small amount we were able to teach them tonight has increased their level of confidence tremendously. They're feeling like true men for the first time in their lives."

Navali took a bite of her biscuit and glanced about at the villagers as he bade, noticing the men laughing and playfully nudging each other with easy grins and sly winks, and flirting outrageously if a woman passed by.

One of the married men suddenly gave his wife's rear a playful swat, and Navali looked away with a small blush dusting her features as the woman laughingly squealed and danced away from her husband's hand.

The people around the couple just laughed at the merry exchange, but Navali did not know how a swat to one's bottom could be considered amusing, and determinedly pushed the incident from her mind.

It was not until she caught herself studying Shyre's callused hands that Navali admitted she had obviously failed in that endeavor. *Shyre had better not ever do that to her!* she thought, disgruntled. She had never been spanked in her royal life and did not particularly care for the thought of her new husband starting the barbaric practice!

She firmly brought her thoughts back into line. *Of course her husband would never do such a thing to her!*

"How do you know this is the first time they've felt like true men?" Navali inquired, looking at Shyre's face again and trying to distract herself from observing his hands any more. She did not understand being cowed in any way other than her emotions being lawfully curtailed and suppressed, but that was something she had grown up with, and so lent very little thought to the uncommon practice.

"Men," Shyre began, his clear, green eyes glinting in the firelight. "Who have been under the thumb of a tyrant for long periods of time, can feel as though they can no longer defend themselves. They've usually tried to rebel before, and serious and fatal consequences have been what they've received for those actions."

He paused thoughtfully, and then continued. "If you've been defeated enough times, you wonder why you even bother to rebel in the first place. Eventually you give up the unequal fight and let the tyrant walk all over you," Shyre finished, his eyes losing the faraway look as he stared at the truly happy and boisterous group of people surrounding him. "And that is what happened to these people."

"You think they've tried to rebel before? How can you tell?" Shyre's words made complete sense to Navali and she figured rebellion and consequence were exactly what would happen if one was under the reign of the tyrant Krinar, and she wanted to know how she could identify it in others.

"It's in their eyes," Shyre answered and took another bite of his food before finishing. "In the haunted and wary look they give anyone bigger or stronger than they are."

"Oh." Navali was quiet for the remainder of the meal, lost in her own thoughts as she ate.

"I did not mean to upset you, sweetling," Shyre murmured, taking her now empty plate and stacking it on top of his own before giving both to one of the women who were collecting the dirty dishes.

"You didn't," she quickly assured him after the woman left them. "I was just thinking about what you said—about their haunted eyes. It makes me sad, even though I'm not supposed to acknowledge or admit to that feeling. Do you think all Pitan peasants are this persecuted?" Her smooth brow wrinkled at the distressing thought.

Reflecting on his answer before he spoke, Shyre took her hands in his—just because he had to touch her in some way—and rubbed his callused thumbs over her soft palms. "I think that a good number of them are."

Navali rested her head on his broad shoulder. They were not discussing anything in the least bit of a comforting nature, but his thumbs stroking her palms and the warmth of him was making her drowsy. It had been a long day for them all, though most especially for the men and Navali did not know how Shyre could be so alert and awake.

"I think you need to seek your bed," Shyre informed her in a rough whisper.

Navali stifled a yawn in response to his words. "I think you may be right."

Not letting her rise when she made a move to do so, Shyre instead scooped her up in his arms as if she weighed near to nothing, and began carrying her towards their tent.

"Are you thinking to join me in that same bed?" She asked coyly, brushing the dark stubble on his jaw with one fingertip, suddenly not feeling quite so tired after all.

"That is my most urgent desire," he admitted with a salacious wink, and hitched her higher in his arms. "But, alas, I have the first night-watch and am unable to perform my husbandly duties."

"Duties, you say?" Navali sharply tweaked the flesh between his arm and chest.

Shyre jostled her in his arms and Navali was forced to wrap her arms about his neck to steady herself.

"Aye, duties, wife. You would nigh drive me to exhaustion if I permitted you."

"So you're admitting you can't keep up with me?" She asked pointedly, her eyes narrowed in gleeful triumph.

He smirked down at her. "Darling, I thought I had already proven who was the one that couldn't keep up. Do you need a reminder?"

"If I do, we both know you won't be the one giving it this night." She retorted.

Navali squealed suddenly as he made as if he were going to drop her, and she clutched him tighter to her, inadvertently bringing her bosom nearer his face.

Shyre took the fortuitous opportunity given him and lustily perused the cleavage so closely displayed to him. "Don't be too sure in that regard, I won't be gone *that* long!"

Once inside the privacy of their tent, he set her down abruptly and began hurriedly helping to unlace the sides of her gown and remove her now thoroughly ruined slippers.

His fingers then undid the thin strip of leather holding the ends of her plaited hair, and he unwound the thick strands, gently running his fingers through the loosened locks before burying his face in the light-colored mass and inhaling deeply.

"I prefer it when you wear your hair flowing loose down your back." His voice was a low, gentle growl.

"Do you, indeed?" Navali giggled lightly when he nodded his response with his face still buried in her hair, and then hummed in agreement at the feel of him pressing against her back. Relaxing into him as he continued to stroke her scalp soothingly with his fingers, Navali let him take her weight as her eyes began fluttering in drowsiness.

"Go to sleep, my beautiful princess. I shall be back ere the sun has risen and then we shall see to that reminder you seem to require. Sweet dreams," Shyre said and then turned stiffly and strode resolutely out into the dark night.

Navali sighed at the loss of his warmth as she finished removing her gown and, folding it neatly, set it aside to wear again on the morrow. Lying down, she covered herself with the thick fur that rested atop the pallet, and snuggled deeply beneath it, wishing it was as warm as her husband had been.

She was acutely disappointed that Shyre had to be away for the better part of their second night as a married couple. *But that was part of being married to a warrior,* she mused. They kept odd hours and were usually on guard for danger at all times.

It was a new chapter in her life, and though it was different, she decided she did not particularly dislike it. Truth be told, when she thought about the previous night and the last few days, she rather enjoyed it.

Except for on long cold nights without her husband's muscular arms to surround her and chase away the chill, she grumbled silently, as she shivered and settled deeper into the pallet, hugging the plush fur closer.

Navali's eyelids began to feel heavy as she imagined Shyre's arms about her person, and she gratefully let them slide shut as her body relaxed further into the soft pallet that was now warming beneath her. Her breath slowly evened out and before she could even finish her nightly prayers she was fast asleep.

Nearly running into Aakin outside of the tent he shared with Navali, Shyre's eyes widened as he was forced to halt abruptly.

"Shyre." Aakin's voice was not in the least bit surprised to have suddenly come face to face with his brother. "That's where you've hied yourself off to." The younger man looked about Shyre, as if he were searching for something. He shrugged briefly and returned his gaze to his brother. "Marriage troubles already?" Aakin inquired audaciously.

"Not at all," Shyre responded in all seriousness, not rising to take the bait to banter with his brother. He was tired after a full day of traveling and instructing the men on the latest fighting techniques, and was not willing to use any remaining energy on jesting when he had a much better use planned for it later when he returned to his tent and the delicious temptation that was his wife. "I'm on first watch."

"Blasted luck, Shyre. I don't envy you the duty." Aakin quipped and then sought his pallet as his elder brother strode away to the edge of the encampment. Keeping tabs on Aaron through their mind link was draining, and Aakin would take advantage of every hour of sleep that he could before his own watch started.

Word had just recently come through his twin that the other group of refugees and warriors had reached the border and crossed it with little difficulty or opposition. Shyre and Addison had confirmation of that fact from their own twins and the Drocuns still in danger breathed a small sigh of relief as their tension level eased.

Their brothers were safe, now they just had to concern themselves with getting their own bodies and those under their care to safety.

The two scouts his eldest brother had sent out that morning had caught up to their encampment at nightfall. They had reported the Pitan had roused themselves around mid-morning and traveled with unhurried pace to follow them. Aakin did not know what the tyrant's plan of attack could be to pursue with such slowness and without a single care to conceal his troops, but he did not dwell on the seemingly mad Pitan's motives.

Instead Aakin cushioned his head on his left arm, his right hand resting carefully on his sword which lay beside him on the slim pallet. A cold and hard sleeping companion if ever there was one, but the reassurance of having the blade so close at hand made up for much of the discomfort.

CHAPTER SIXTEEN

Thick obscuring trees hid Shyre from the sight of others and he paced restlessly, the movement keeping his legs warm and his feet from freezing in his now wet and sopping leather boots.

A cold drizzle of rain had begun to fall upon the small camp shortly after Shyre had assumed his watch, and his shoulder muscles bunched tightly as a cold trickle of water suddenly found its way beneath the collar of his shirt and ran down the length of his spine. Rolling his shoulders in discomfort, he hoped to halt the slow slide of liquid down his back. The motion worked nicely, though it also served as a reminder of the stiff aches in his muscles that had not yet faded from his practice session earlier.

He had been wrenched on and pulled in opposite directions as he had helped to instruct the Pitan men in warfare. His arms, legs, and hands were tired and bruised from his efforts. The left side of his face was not in much better condition and he was only slightly comforted that his cheekbone had not swelled up to the size of a melon after the big ham-fisted woodcutter had punched him heavily across the face.

Horrified at hitting the prince so hard, the big man had instantly fallen to his knees in abject horror, awaiting his fate with fearful eyes. Silence had swept over the group of Pitan men as they warily watched the high prince pick himself up from the ground, where he had been so forcibly reintroduced to the dirt previously underneath his feet, and dusted his hands roughly against his breeches.

The men had been thoroughly shocked when the high prince's brothers had only laughed when they learned of what had caught everyone's attention and then strode over to see the damage that had been wrought on their elder brother's person.

Addison and Aakin had slapped their brother's back and gripped his jaw in their hands, each in turn, taking a look at the dark bruise that was swiftly forming. Addison had released Shyre after a careful, but lighthearted examination that had consisted of a few pokes with his long index finger as Shyre groaned in protest, trying unsuccessfully to wrench his head from his brother's firm grasp. Satisfied that Shyre's cheekbone and jaw had not been cracked or broken from the blow, Addison had moved to the frightened man still kneeling on the ground.

The woodcutter had made no plea or sound of protest as to whatever fate would be meted out by these three royal men as Addison strode over to him. He figured he deserved whatever would befall him for unwittingly punching the high prince with all his might and brawn.

"What's your name, woodcutter?" Addison asked, his voice steady and firm, his face abruptly inscrutable.

Silently gulping, the man focused on the prince's dusty brown boots as he answered. "Logan o' Pinecrest, yer highness."

"Logan of Pinecrest," Addison's deep voice repeated and the man cringed, awaiting judgment. "Good show, man!" Addison suddenly laughed and slapped the kneeling man on the shoulder, nearly knocking the huge fellow off his knees.

Logan gaped at the prince's gesture of good humor, shocked that his head was still on his shoulders and the skin on his back had not been flayed into strips by the cruel bite of a whip. "Wh-what?" The man managed to gasp out, his eyes wide, obviously confused with Addison's joviality.

Striding over to stand next to Logan after his own look at Shyre's face, Aakin commented. "It's not every day a man gets a hit in on our elder brother. You've done well! Your talents are totally wasted with cutting trees. You should at least be one of the new militia leaders. What say you to that, Shyre?"

Stepping forward, Shyre stopped working his jaw back and forth with his fingers to offer the man a hand up from the ground. Logan took it and stood tall before the stern look on the high prince's battered face, watching as the prince's expression morphed into a rueful grin.

"I completely agree," Shyre said and a cheer went over the gathered men. "It seems that everyone is in league with that decision as well. Do you accept?"

"Gla-gladly, yer highness," Logan stuttered. As the three princes moved away, the man previously known as a simple woodcutter was swarmed with good wishes and congratulatory handshakes.

Shyre now smiled in the dark at the remembered look of delighted surprise on the big Pitan's face and then winced as the bruised flesh on his cheekbone moved with the grin. It was not swelling, but he would wager the bruise went all the way to the bone. He wondered if Navali would kiss it better as his mother had done so many times when he was a toddler—all maternal thoughts on Navali's part withheld, of course. He hoped it could even lead to a more pleasant interlude, one vastly more carnal in nature.

A creature, unseen in the dark, shrieked a death call as it became a bigger animal's dinner, and Shyre speculated as to what made this forest so gloomy and foreboding from others he had explored in the past. A chill suddenly swept down his spine that had nothing to do with the droplets of cold water.

The earlier sighting of the Fayrah was disturbing to say the least, for it was said they did not boldly attack, but like serpents, slyly insinuated themselves into place and then struck lethally when someone was unable to protect himself.

Shyre had not seen the woman as Navali had, however he believed she spoke true. The tyrant Krinar had a plan, one that was most likely not only of his own making, but that of the witches that served him as well.

As he paced back and forth in the dark and chill of the night, the high prince vowed that no harm would befall his new bride or those under his care as long as he still retained breath in his lungs.

It was very late when Shyre was finally able to seek the peace to be had in the quiet of his tent. He drew the flap back carefully and then stepped into the cozy warmth inside, abandoning his wet cloak to dry on a crude hook protruding from one of the tent poles.

His bride did not rouse from her slumber as he stepped to the edge of the pallet and sat down to remove his boots, placing them to one side. Shyre made quick work on the laces of his wet shirt and breeches before removing them and drawing a clean pair of cloth britches over his cold limbs. He left his chest bare and was soon ensconced beside his bride in betwixt the bed furs.

Shifting closer in small degrees as he felt her warmth invading his limbs, he first wrapped his arms around Navali's soft pliant body and pulled her close, so that she was cradled against his chest. And finally, when he could feel his feet again, he tucked them gingerly against hers.

Navali abruptly sat up as though she had been doused with a bucket of cold water. "Your feet are like ice!" She glared indignantly at him and inched farther away, carefully keeping her warm toes away from him.

"You don't think you should warm them like a good little wife?" Shyre asked, all impishness now aroused.

"Certainly not. I shall play the shrew this evening!" Navali ducked farther away from her playful tormentor as he swiped an arm up to try and snag her closer.

Shyre's green eyes lit at the challenge she was presenting and he grinned rakishly, propping himself up on an elbow and catching one of her wrists in his strong fingers, determinedly tugging her to him. "Come, wife, I bid you lie beside me and share your warmth." Shyre drew her closer to him amidst her laughing protests.

Navali shrieked suddenly and Shyre shot up from his half-prone position, quickly muffling the sound with a barely warm hand over her sleep-plumped lips as he chuckled softly against the delicate shell of her ear, his goal of her snuggled next to him accomplished.

"Shh—do you want to awaken the whole camp? What would they think if they heard you screaming?" Shyre removed his fingers one by one, the last callused digit rubbing gently against the full curve of her lower lip as he grinned roguishly down at her.

Her silver eyes twinkled with merriment. "They would think I really *had* married a beastly toad!" Navali giggled and he grabbed one of her feet, tickling it unmercifully until she breathlessly managed to squirm away.

"If I'm a toad, my lovely princess, you must give me a kiss so that I may become a handsome prince and fulfill your every desire." Shyre was now kneeling on the pallet facing her, his bared chest gleaming like sculpted bronze in the firelight flickering against the material of the tent.

He held his hand out to Navali and she settled herself before him on her knees, bestowing a quick, feathering kiss upon his lips. Her quicksilver eyes narrowed wickedly as she ran her hands—rather tentatively, he thought, considering the heated look she was giving him—over the rippling muscles in his chest and arms.

"Don't you think it a bit much to ask to be a prince, and a handsome one at that, after being such an ugly and atrocious toad?" She asked impertinently, her nose wrinkling in playful distaste.

Shyre suddenly snatched her firmly against him, holding her arms captive as she struggled laughingly in protest. "An ugly and atrocious toad, was I? I'll have you know I've always been considered exceedingly attractive," he imperiously informed her.

"Shall I kiss you again to see what would happen? Perhaps you'll turn into that *exceedingly* attractive toad again!" Navali scrunched her eyes shut as she puckered her lips up at him in jest.

"I think not, wife!" Shyre held his captive slightly away as she sought to bring her lips closer.

"Indeed, little shrew, I shall kiss *you* instead, and we'll see what transpires then." He adjusted his hold on her and her eyes flew open to gaze into the swirling green depths of his, her arms now slipping free to wrap delicately about his neck.

"I already know what will be the result if you kiss me, my handsome prince," Navali whispered huskily, gazing up at him from beneath half-lowered lids.

"And what, praytell, is that, my love?" Shyre's lips brushed hers with every syllable he uttered.

"I'll melt...." she sighed and he kissed her, his lips gentle and firm against hers.

Shyre pulled back a fraction of an inch. "That would not be an entirely loathsome consequence," he mused aloud.

Navali smiled at his words and though Shyre could not see the movement of her lips, he felt it, and the smile shining in the depths of her luminous eyes gave her expression away. "But I may never be able to move again," she protested weakly.

"I have a way to cure that," Shyre whispered huskily. "Though I would have to want to first." He wryly amended in a side note.

"Really?" Navali asked, rather doubtfully. "How do you think you would go about curing it, then?" *Her husband obviously did not know how his kisses affected her!*

"By placing my freezing cold feet against yours in the middle of the night." The statement was given smugly and Navali shoved him, her hands pushing against his muscled shoulders, playfully outraged at his comment.

"It would also earn you that place by the bachelors' fire your brother was speaking of the other day," she told him and sat up slightly in his arms, giving him a stern, haughty look.

"I yield, I yield." Shyre was laughing as he said it.

"Aren't you aware you're never supposed to yield?" Navali shook her head at him as though he were the village dunce and in need of instruction.

"I thought a man could yield to his own wife if the circumstances were too important to risk." Shyre lifted his eyebrows at her.

"And what is so important in this situation that you don't want to risk it?" Navali inquired of him.

"The ever so important place in your bed," Shyre replied with a wicked grin.

Navali scoffed lightly at herself. "I should have known that one."

"You should have been able to guess it at the very least, my deliciously-curved bride," Shyre retorted thoughtfully and ran one hand down said curves.

Grabbing the wandering long-fingered hand, Navali held it captive against her hip, and leaned into him until her lips were a teasing breath away from his. "Then I give you leave to yield to me as often as you wish, husband. For I daresay I enjoy having my own way all the time." Navali retorted impertinently.

"I'm sure not nearly so much as I enjoy the place it earns me, my love," Shyre assured her with a lewd wink and gave her no time to protest his remark as he kissed her with all the tender passion he was feeling and lowered his back to the furs, pulling her along with him.

They were well on their way to Lynaria the next day, the sun shining high in the light blue sky, when Navali glanced, for perhaps the twentieth time, at her husband from where he led the entourage atop his golden steed, Swift Justice. Shyre's back was straight, his dark head moving slightly as he scanned the surrounding area for any signs of danger.

The Pitan had slipped closer in the night, stealthily moving towards the refugees and their protectors under the cover of darkness and the masking rain it had brought.

The scouts sent out before dawn had nearly stumbled over the sleeping soldiers, so surprised had they been at the nearness of the despised king and his consorts.

Stephen had been among the three scouts sent out, and he had hastily returned and reported to Shyre, waking him from the deep sleep he had found a mere two hours before. Navali wondered if they would ever be able to wake naturally again and pondered the fact that if Shyre were not able to snatch more sleep than the short intervals she had been witness to, it would surely not bode well for any of them over a long period of time.

Her stalwart husband had not complained the disruption to his slumber though and, rising and dressing in haste, had stepped outside to listen to Stephen give his report, immediately giving the order to break camp when the man finished.

Navali, having heard the entire conversation through their tent's thin walls, was already half-dressed by the time Shyre stepped back in to inform her they would be leaving within the hour. As he talked, he had swiftly collected his weapons and then departed their tent for the second time.

After Navali had finished packing their belongings, she had drawn back the flap and stepped out herself, nearly being trampled upon as the Pitan villagers moved with terrified haste to get everything in order. She could see Addison and Aakin striving to keep everyone from a full-blown panic and had applied herself to the same cause, speaking calming words to near-hysterical women and soothing them with a gentle hand upon an arm or a quaking shoulder.

Her efforts had proved useful and successful as everyone saw and took heed of the calm and collected princess. Surely they had nothing to be too alarmed about if their new princess was just as cheerful and collected as she normally was and not a weeping mess. After all, she had recently been held captive by the ruthless tyrant, Krinar, and they all knew what could transpire when one was in his nefarious clutches.

Navali had made the decision to not employ the use of her horse as they had resumed their journey, and it had proved wise on her part. Shyre had reluctantly agreed with her wisdom as well. Her presence on foot and mixed in with the group of refugees would indeed help to calm everyone and allay their worst fears.

Navali now forced her legs to keep pace with the peasants surrounding her, when all she really wanted was to run as fast and as far away from the Pitan holdings as she could get. Her face did not reveal any of her desperate and cowardly feelings though, and Navali was thankful, for the first time in her life, of the strict upbringing she had endured as a child. For it was saving Shyre and his men from a great deal of strife that would have resulted if she had not been so cool and calm in the face of one of her biggest fears—the fear of being held captive by Krinar again. Navali knew she would not be so lucky as to evade whatever iniquitous plans the Pitan king had for her a second time, as he would most likely see to them as soon as he had her in his grasp.

Adele stumbled slightly beside her, jostling her from her wary thoughts, and Navali wrapped an arm around the youth's thin shoulders. The girl smiled at her in thanks and wrapped her own arm around Navali's waist—something the princess told herself she would eventually get used to. She was not yet that comfortable with spontaneous physical touch from others and she firmly tamped down her reservations about it. Adele needed the soothing touch more than Navali needed to be comfortable.

At that moment, Adele was thinking that she had never met a more kind or gentle princess as the one that now walked so calmly and confidently beside her. She had also never seen someone exhibit so much strength and grace at one time. Adele glanced over at the other friend she had recently become acquainted with, and observed her keeping up a steady stream of conversation meant to distract the others around her. Vanca's voice was low and soothing to the ears, and the stories she told were always very humorous. These two women beside her were probably the bravest and most kind she had ever had the luxury of knowing.

Everyone was doing their best to be brave though and the men were doing an excellent job of remembering their defensive training, and Adele felt more safe now than she had in a very long time. Her elder brother, Tucker, was walking near Prince Aakin as he sat upon his horse and she knew Tucker would never let anything happen to her if he could help it.

The princess laughed all of a sudden and Adele looked at her in awe again. It always amazed her when the Lynarian princess made that joy-filled sound, it was unlike anything she had ever heard in her young life.

Catching the younger woman's gaze as she observed her, Navali gently smiled into the blue eyes that were so awestruck. The princess did not feel she deserved so much wonder in one person's eyes, but she would not have crushed the girl's illusions for all the gold in her father's kingdom. Navali understood how people needed someone to look up to. She had at one time had someone like that in her own life, someone she thought had surely hung the moon in the sky just to chase away her nighttime fears.

Her mother had been that person.

Thinking on that woman's gentleness and caring made Navali's eyes sting with unshed tears.

Sometimes the world was cruel and harsh to those that lived in it and Navali had certainly discovered that the day her mother died. She had no intention of ever reliving a moment like that again, but feared she was already forming attachments that would hurt as much as that dreadful day had, if her new friends and family were to die.

The young woman tucked securely under Navali's arm smiled at her in return and the spell of memories was broken. Navali was glad of the distraction from her reflections of the past, she had not let herself think on her mother in a very long time, and she was not quite ready to fully let herself do so now.

"D'ye think we'll be makin' it ta yer kingdom t'day, milady?" Adele asked, her blue eyes shining with youthful hope.

Navali smiled, not that it was really *her* kingdom, per say. But who would argue with details? "I pray so, Adele, though I think we may have another day of travel ahead in order to reach Lynaria."

Adele ducked her head in response and Navali felt like a witch for diminishing the hope the girl had been feeling.

"But ye think we'll make it though, don't ye?" Adele mumbled, her voice hesitant and filled with pleading.

"Of course I do," Navali quickly assured her. "I don't believe there is anything on Yria that could deter my husband from attaining his goals." She had added the last part to comfort the young Pitan woman and assure her there were strong warriors concerned with her welfare, but as Navali uttered the words they had a strange effect on her as well, for she had completely believed in what she said. Shyre would indeed see to it that they made it to Lynaria, and not a doubt against that revelation reared its ugly head in Navali's mind.

She raised her gaze to where Shyre led their small band and was startled to find his green eyes fastened on her as well. His quick grin was one of pride and some other emotion Navali could not define and her return smile was one of utter radiance.

Her husband made her feel so completely safe and secure that Navali felt she could sing in contentment—something she had never before done in her life.

Vanca tugged suddenly at Navali's sleeve to get her attention.

"Navali, are you making eyes at that fine specimen of masculinity again?" Her friend asked with a teasing smile, and Navali's face heated at being caught staring at her husband. Vanca had noticed her doing the same thing earlier in the day as well, and Navali was having a hard time believing that she could not keep her gaze off Shyre.

"I probably am." Navali sighed in exasperation. "I just can't seem to help myself, Vanca." Her voice was hushed and she was glad that only Vanca could hear her. Adele was not paying any attention to the two older women as she was engrossed in the conversation she had struck up with a handsome young man who had made his way over to them. The girl's worries were completely forgotten and Navali was pleased that for the moment her young friend was happy again.

"Tis nothing to be ashamed of, my friend, the high prince is indeed blessed with extraordinarily good looks. Though I find my tastes run more towards a certain lean archer." Vanca giggled and Navali looked askance at the redheaded woman.

"What, Vanca?" Navali asked, hardly able to comprehend what her friend was confiding in her.

Vanca's voice dropped even lower and her lips barely moved as she repeated herself. "I said I favor an archer!"

Navali's gaze was drawn back to Stephen. "Anyone I know?" She had seen her friend and the Drocun eating together the night before and now suspected Stephen was the one Vanca was alluding to.

"Don't look at him!" Vanca's face turned a bright shade of pink and her words came out in a high squeak. "Else he'll deduce we've been speaking of him!"

"Well, Vanca, we *are* speaking about him, aren't we?" Navali asked, her eyes now on her friend's face.

"Aye, but I don't want *him* to know that!" Vanca's smile was sheepishly embarrassed.

Navali's own smile was one of sly mischief. "Well, why not? Does Stephen not like you as well?"

Vanca's light-green eyes were wide in incredulousness. "Don't say that so loudly!" The sheepish look on her pretty face was overcome by one of dreamy anticipation. "But I do believe he may notice me as much as I do him," she admitted.

Navali glanced back at Stephen again in time to see the Drocun looking at Vanca in earnest fascination. The archer felt the princess' gaze on him and his eyes met her clear silver ones. He flushed deeply as he quickly looked away and returned to scanning the trees and bushes around them. "I think he may like you more," Navali informed her friend.

"Do you really think so, Navali?" Vanca's eyes were alight with pleasure and she glanced back at the man she was so attracted to. Navali found herself watching Vanca's expression as a beautiful, wide smile spread across her friend's features, and wondered if that was how she looked when she gazed at Shyre. She hoped not, for it was a little amusing to watch her friend flush as her eyes met Stephen's.

"I really, *really*, believe so." The princess murmured wryly as she glanced ahead to her husband and again met his magnetic, swirling green eyes. She smiled thoughtfully, *that handsome man up there might very well just like her more than a little, too.*

A sudden flash of bright red caught Shyre's attention as he tore his gaze from the delicate features of his wife and he quickly scanned the left side of the column, looking for anything out of place. There was nothing. His thoughts drifted to Navali again, his bride was loveliness itself, how could he have ever imagined he might not be happy with her?

Red flashed again, this time on the opposite side of the column, and Shyre drew back sharply on Justice's reins. What was that? He peered intently through the trees and underbrush, but again, nothing.

The rest of the caravan came to a slow halt behind him and hushed whispers sounded loudly in the background. But Shyre was suddenly acutely aware he could not hear any other sound. Even the songbirds were no longer chirping, where before they were as loud as a gaggle of geese Shyre had once scared when he was a young lad. Now the forest was eerily silent, beyond the hushed chatter of the refugees.

Carefully taking stock of his surroundings again, Shyre felt the hair on the back of his neck rise as Swift Justice shied beneath him, attempting to back away from something his master could not see. Shyre steadied his stallion with a gentle hand against its neck and then listened intently as a faint sound carried on the wind.

The whispers behind him abruptly stopped and Shyre was finally able to hear what was disturbing the forest creatures and his mount. An anguished sob echoed out of the trees to his right and Shyre withdrew his sword, unsure if that was the only sound he would be hearing. People did not normally cry unless given good reason, and the Pitan-Horde could definitely induce that sound from anyone if they so desired.

Waving Addison forward to take his place, Shyre nudged Justice into the dense underbrush to his right. As horse and rider made their way past thick bushes, full pine trees, and low-lying limbs they suddenly came upon a startling sight.

A lone man sat sobbing harshly at the twisted base of a large tree. His legs were tucked beneath himself and he cradled one arm against his chest as he rocked back and forth, keening in grief as if he had lost something precious.

Even from this distance, Shyre could see that a great deal of blood was smeared across his brown tunic.

"What goes on here?" Shyre asked, his voice uncommonly loud in the hushed forest. He kept a close watch around him, wary of ambush, as he forced Justice to walk ever closer to the sobbing man.

Finally noticing that he was no longer alone, the man glanced up, and his face paled even further.

Shyre's mind rang out a single word.

"Lance!" he gasped.

CHAPTER SEVENTEEN

Shyre swiftly dismounted and rushed to the once-missing Drocun. This couldn't be the same man he had left Dare-knay with! Not this pitiful shell of a creature with matted hair and uncomprehending eyes!

"Lance." Shyre dropped to one knee before the man, his sword once more sheathed in the scabbard across his back, and he reached one leather-clad hand out to clasp Lance's shoulder. "What has befallen you, man?"

The Drocun seemed so far in despair that Shyre wondered if he had even heard him, until Lance extended the arm he had held securely to his middle out toward him. Shyre was then made immediately and fully aware of what had the man so upset.

Lance's left hand had been cut off!

The prince's expression tightened, his green eyes blazing with fury, as he swallowed hard against the bile that rose at the sight of the bloody stump that remained midway up the Drocun's forearm. Red, copious blood soaked through the dirtied, white cloth that bound the wound, and Lance's arm shook violently at the effort of holding it away from his body before he hurriedly snatched it back, keening deeply in his throat again at the pain.

"Steady there, Lance. We'll get you to help in no time." Shyre quickly stood and retrieved Swift Justice's reins, coaxing the animal closer when it balked at going near the wounded man.

"We must get you back to the others, my friend," Shyre said as he attempted to hoist the wounded man up from where he sat on the ground.

"Nay!" The Drocun protested, his bloodshot eyes wild as he tore himself from Shyre's helping hands.

"What is it, man? We must get you to a healer of some kind!" Shyre reached again to help the man toward Justice so that he could ride back to the caravan, but Lance would have none of it. He kept stumbling away and mumbling incoherent sentences as tears streamed down his cheeks.

"Very well," Shyre relented. They would have to do this the hard way. "We'll walk back, then. Are you with me, Lance?" Shyre held his hand out to show the way he had come and waited for the crazed and injured man's reaction.

Glancing at Shyre out of the corner of his eyes as he gave him a wide berth, Lance began to move in the direction the prince had indicated.

As soon as they stepped from the underbrush and into sight of the caravan, Addison strode forward to meet them. Shyre was grateful his brother made it to Lance's side before the wounded man collapsed. Lance had insisted on staggering along by himself the entire way back, and Shyre had been forced to watch as the Drocun nearly fell several times, only to catch himself at the last moment and flinch harshly in pain. If the prince made a move to catch him, Lance had pulled away as fast and as hard as his wounded body had allowed.

He did not seem to mind when Addison helped him though, and Shyre thought that strange, for he did not know what he could have done to the man to make him so distrust and dislike him. But Shyre really could not blame Lance for his lack of lucidity. He only prayed the Drocun would be all right—as all right as a man could be after losing his hand, and with it, his way of life as a warrior.

Shyre strode alongside Addison as his brother half-carried, half-dragged Lance to a small wagon. The tired nag pulling the rickety contraption snorted as they came closer and, tossing its head, sidestepped, the whites of its eyes showing as its breath rushed hard in its lungs. Something was still frightening the animal and Shyre was not certain what it was.

This incident was entirely baffling—A lone man in the woods with a recent wound, the flashes of red in the underbrush on both sides of the column without anything being there, and now the horse acting up. Shyre looked around intently, what was out there?

When no answer seemed forthcoming, Shyre returned his attention to the wounded man Addison had just hoisted carefully onto the bed of the wagon, and inquired, "Lance, did Krinar do this to you?" He hoped the man would respond, though did not really expect him to.

"N-nay, n-not K-krinar." Lance's response was stuttered and breathless, his eyes rolling up in his head, but Shyre understood every word.

"Then who, man. Who did this?" Shyre persisted.

Not answering as his good hand went limp, Lance's roughly-bearded jaw slackened, unconsciousness steeling away any answers Shyre had hoped to glean from him.

Navali was suddenly at his side and he glanced down at her to find her staring at the injured warrior. "This man is Lance? The Drocun who disappeared?" Her voice carried a concern that she did not bother to conceal.

Nodding, Shyre placed his hand over the one she had rested on his arm and looked to Addison for his uneducated advice as to what should be done for their comrade-in-arms.

"Shyre, I just do not know." The big man shrugged his broad shoulders. "I attempted to ask Adam through our link, but I cannot seem to reach him."

Shyre sighed in frustration. He knew the reason why Addison could not consult with his twin, it was the same reason he could not reach Ashtyn. They were all just too exhausted for their links to traverse the many miles that now separated them.

Navali was the first to utter aloud the solution Shyre had just reached himself. "We could ask if any of the refugees know anything of the healing ways."

Shyre nodded his agreement and then spoke to his brother, "Addison, you stay here with Lance, I'll see if I can find someone with more knowledge concerning this sort of thing." Turning away, he walked towards the huddled crowd of Pitans and felt his wife's sleeve brush his arm as she accompanied him.

He directed a brief, weary smile down at her and her eyes became less anxious as she wrapped her delicate fingers around his bicep. They soon reached Tucker and Logan, the unspoken leaders of the refugees.

Firmly fixing his attention on the task at hand, Shyre inquired of them. "Is there a healer to be had amongst you?"

"Not one I'd trust with me life." This came from Logan.

"Then there is one?" Shyre persisted. The big man looked unsure of the answer he should give and Shyre pierced Tucker with his green gaze.

The younger man caved quickly at the prince's dark look. "An old man was tha village healer."

"And he's here with us now, Tucker?" Shyre was getting frustrated with their evasive answers and he wanted a clear one *now*. Lance did not have time for this foolishness and neither did they if they hoped to remain ahead of the Pitan for much longer.

"Aye," Tucker admitted after he glanced quickly at Logan. "I'll take ye ta him."

"We would greatly appreciate it, Tucker, thank you," Navali spoke for the first time during the exchange and the young man's face became clearer and more relieved as he heard her gentle tone.

"This way." Tucker resolutely stiffened his spine before leading them towards the healer.

Logan opted to go with them as well and, as the foursome drew closer to a covered wagon, Tucker's stride became hesitant.

"He's in there, yer highness." Tucker waved a hand toward the faded door of a wagon Shyre had assumed contained only supplies. When Shyre made no move towards the door, Tucker apprehensively stepped forward and gave it a tentative rap with his knuckles.

They waited outside for a few moments and Tucker began to fidget nervously. "Sometimes he don't ever answer, yer highness." His tone was apologetic and he knocked again, this time with a little more force.

Shyre began to grow angry. He was the High Prince of Dareknay and these were now *his* people. He had an injured Drocun awaiting assistance and some old man was not going to cow him by not answering his summons!

Just as Shyre lost all patience and took two angry steps forward, the door flew open and banged heavily against the side of the wagon.

"What do you want?" A voice croaked from the darkness. The only part clearly visible of the man was a single gnarled hand that rested on the jamb of the door.

It was enough for Shyre that the healer had finally answered his summons, and he felt calmer now that he was able to confront this anomaly. "A healer. And I have heard that is you, old one."

"I am indeed the one you seek, then." A wry, bitter chuckle emanated from the wagon's depths and the hand retreated back into the darkness. "Though I am not yet elderly."

The man stepped forward then, revealing his features to the light, and Navali gasped softly at Shyre's side. The healer's action of stepping forth from the darkness that enshrouded him caused the right side of his body and face to come fully into the light.

Perhaps the young man would have once been considered handsome as the left side of his face and body gave testimony to. However, it was not now true. A badly healed burn completely covered the right side of his face and body, leaving his looks mangled on that side. The flesh on his face and bare right arm was red and shiny, twisted as if someone had taken a thick, hot iron rod and swirled rough patterns into his skin.

The man sneered as he noted the compassion Navali had failed to hide. "I don't need your pity, wench," he spat the words as much as his ruined voice allowed. "Nor anyone else's. Be gone from here!"

Shyre took a threatening step towards the man at the tone he had used with his wife and Navali caught his sleeve, strengthening her resolve against showing her emotions and feelings. She would not show weakness again and this gruff man had probably done something vile to deserve the hideous scar he now wore. He had certainly frightened the villagers for long enough and that was a wide black mark attesting to his lack of character in Navali's mind. No man got away with doing that to her people.

"Don't aggravate yourself," she replied staunchly to the man's terse tone. "It was not pity. I was experiencing a weak female moment and you happened to catch it on my face. It will not happen again," she assured him. "But, nevertheless, my moments are no concern of yours, and that is not why we have come seeking your aid."

When the man drew himself up in the doorway and his eyes glittered warmly at Navali's spirit, Shyre intervened, not liking the sudden interest the other man exhibited. "We have need of a healer. Will you lend your services?"

Glancing towards the wounded Drocun lying in the far wagon, the healer hesitated.

"Will you?" Shyre asked sharply and waited patiently yet again, though he knew it was in vain. He snarled suddenly and turned away, intent on going back to where Addison was unsuccessfully attempting to help Lance. Though he and his brother would never be mistaken for the most knowledgeable of healers—that was not their calling in life—they would at the very least make some sort of effort, unlike the disfigured man who stood in indecision behind him.

"Bring him to me," the healer croaked and turned back to the darkness of his lair.

"Nay, we will not. If we move him, it would only cause him more pain." Shyre's fist tightened on the hilt of his sword and he wondered briefly if anyone would object if he killed the unagreeable man. "You will have to go to him."

"Very well," was the half-growled reply, and the man emerged fully, slinging a beaten-up leather bag over his good shoulder. "Lead the way, princeling." The healer gestured for Shyre to take the lead as he hobbled down the steps, his bad leg greatly hampering him.

Though he greatly despised the new moniker, Shyre nevertheless led the way with Navali's hand tucked in the crook of his arm. It was apparent the healer thought him a prancing peacock, however Shyre could not have cared less what the man thought about him so long as he complied with their wishes and saw to Lance's wellbeing.

Upon reaching the wagon, the healer motioned Addison out of the cart. At Shyre's nod of confirmation, Addison leaped down and then watched the grotesquely disfigured man like a hawk, not trusting the newcomer as he hoisted himself up beside Lance. Reaching for what was left of the wounded Drocun's forearm, the healer held it in his damaged hand and rummaged through the leather bag at his side. Withdrawing a small blade, he slit the makeshift bandage, carefully removing the blood-soaked cloth.

A coarse curse emitted from the healer and Navali felt she could easily have let herself gag at the sight of the wound. Angry and bleeding, the skin torn and shredded, it was not a neat slice left by a sword or sharp axe. Something unknown had done this, something that had been forged to cause pain, great amounts of pain.

Lance groaned as the healer palpated the area immediately above the wound and the man nodded to himself and then turned to Navali. "I need hot water and rags, quickly." He ordered the princess and Shyre opened his mouth to deliver the healer a stinging set-down. Navali tugged gently on his arm before the words left his mouth and he glanced down to find her shaking her silver-blonde head at him.

"I'll get them," she told the healer and removed her hand from Shyre's arm. Going over to Vanca and Adele, who then followed her, the trio of women disappeared into the crowd of refugees to reappear a few minutes later with rags, a clean tunic, and a bucket of water.

"We can start a fire if you require hot water," Navali informed the healer, gracious without fault, although a slight bite edged her smooth, accented voice. "But we thought speed might be preferred and brought it lukewarm from the water barrels."

"Lukewarm will have to do, I suppose," the healer grumbled, the unmarred side of his mouth kicking up into a half-grin at the princess' feisty tone.

Completely ignoring the irritating man, Navali set the rags she carried on top of the tunic that Adele had placed on the edge of the wagon. Vanca attempted to heft the water bucket up into the cart, and was pleasantly startled when her new high prince took the heavy burden from her and easily placed it next to the healer. The young woman smiled at the prince in bemusement, unused to a man, much less one of royal lineage, aiding her in any way.

"Well, wench, aren't you going to assist me?" The healer sneeringly rasped to Navali, and vastly enjoyed the princess' discomfiture when she realized he was speaking to her.

"Now see here, my *good* man!" Shyre furiously grabbed the neck of the man's tunic and jerked him forward until he was half-suspended from the edge of the cart. *The healer had finally pushed him too far!* "You will not speak to my wife in such a casual manner, unless you fancy my fist brought forcibly alongside your jaw! I'll not countenance any more disrespect from you. All we've done is ask for your help and the least you can do is be decent to the women who have helped you without complaint, even if you can't bring yourself to do so with the men. So leave off my wife, before I leave you naked and beaten in the middle of this God-forsaken country," Shyre finished with a growl, and shoved the man away until he landed abruptly on his backside in the wagon. The prince hooked his thumbs into his belt and stood with his shoulders thrown back resolutely. "So what's it to be, Healer?"

His mouth tensing and flattening into a thin line, the man hesitated before turning his hazel eyes to Navali. "I apologize, your highness. I've forgotten all the manners my mother once drummed into me. I ask your forgiveness and also for your assistance in cleaning and caring for this wounded man." The healer then shot a sharp look at Shyre and the prince was satisfied. Both men then looked to Navali for her response.

Hesitating before nodding solemnly, Navali then held up a hand so the man could help her up into the wagon. The man worked to right himself enough to assist her, but Shyre reached her first and, grasping her about the waist, gently lifted her to stand on the opposite side of the wounded Drocun. Taking in the prince's actions, the healer smiled wryly to himself.

Glancing at Navali and the healer, then back to the waiting crowd of frightened villagers, Shyre was unsure of what he should do. He was not fully comfortable leaving his wife with the disfigured healer, but he knew they needed to get moving lest Krinar catch them. He was torn between his duty to his warriors and the refugees and his need to assure himself Navali would not be further verbally assaulted.

"Be off with you." The healer's eyes were on the wound he was now cleaning. "I assure you I'll take the very best care with your princess and I'll even strive to be polite." A devilish gleam had entered the man's eyes and Shyre liked it not one bit, but he knew he had no other choice. They had to keep moving.

Shyre snarled at the situation and then tightly remarked, "you had better, Healer. Lest I show you the punishment the Drocuns reserve for their most hated foes." Snatching up Justice's reins, Shyre stalked off in the direction of the huddle of people, Addison following closely on his heels.

Navali faced the healer. "What do you wish me to do?"

Peering up through his long, straggly dark hair, he asked. "Do you know anything about healing wounds?"

"Nay," she answered. "My father did not allow me to learn after my mother—" Her voice trailed off. She had not meant to say that, but she felt bad that she was so useless in this area. Her father had expressly forbid her to have anything to do with the healers in the castle and their profession, and the healers had not dared go against their king's wishes. Now, as a result of her father's grief, Navali knew nothing of her mother's giftings.

"Well, that's a shame," the healer told her. "I can feel you have the knack for it. I'd say you even have a secret or two that you're keeping, eh?" His hazel eyes never left his work.

"I-I don't know what you're talking about—" Navali broke off.

"Hand me one of those clean rags...." He waited as Navali did as she was told. "Then reach in my bag and get a needle out of the small wooden container and thread it."

She quickly did as she was bid and, holding the threaded needle aloft, Navali watched closely as the healer finished cleansing the wound. "What did you mean when you said I'm keeping a secret or two?" She asked, disturbed that this man might have seen something she had tried so hard to keep hidden. No one else knew that whenever she had a small cut or bruise it healed faster than could be normally expected.

"No time for such idle talk now, give me that small blade I prepared." He held out a bloodied hand for it and Navali placed the hilt in his palm. Cutting the ragged, dead skin away and leaving a clean edge, he then told her to hand him the needle and hold Lance's arm steady. He was about to take the first stitch when Shyre strode over.

"We need to be off now, can you finish with the wound if the cart is moving?" The prince asked.

"I could finish if the whole earth were moving," was the healer's self-confident and slightly arrogant reply.

"I see," Shyre said dryly and then nodded to Navali. "Stay safe," he ordered and, mounting his stallion, signaled the caravan to start.

Although Navali was getting tired of all the commands, she bit her lip to hold back her discontent as the healer ordered her to hold Lance's arm more firmly.

The cart lurched forward before abruptly halting, and Navali would have fallen out of the cart if not for the healer's quick reflexes. Grabbing her arm, he then swiftly released her, turning his head to the front of the wagon and shouting. "I shan't be responsible for any injuries your princess acquires at the hands of our driver!"

Glaring over his shoulder at the healer, Shyre told the man driving the cart to try again. The wagon lurched ahead and then jerked to a halt once more, the occupants jolting forward and then back as the horse pawed the dirt and wildly shook its head.

"I'm right sorry, milord," the cart's driver apologized to the prince. "The horse refuses ta budge." The man was thoroughly confused by the animal's strange behavior and he shrugged helplessly.

Not responding beyond moving his stallion to the nag's head, Shyre grabbed the halter. Pulling on the leather strap, he nudged Justice to a walk, and with reluctant steps the horse followed Justice's lead.

Breathing a sigh of relief, Navali glanced at the motionless healer. A glimmer of respect reflected in his hazel eyes as he stared at Shyre. A shutter quickly fell over his eyes as he sensed her watching him and he returned his attention to the wounded man. He pointedly glanced up at her when she did not move to continue with her duties and the princess gave herself a mental shake and swiftly resumed holding the wounded man's arm steady.

The mysterious healer then took the first tiny stitch.

ow is he?" Shyre asked Navali sometime later. They had briefly stopped for the noon meal and Navali was eating in the wagon beside the wounded Drocun still under the spell of unconsciousness.

"The healer says he should recover well. If he has the will to do so, that is," Navali added the last bit of the healer's comment because she felt she had to. "At least the bleeding has finally stopped."

"Well, that's something then." Shyre sighed, wearily rubbing his hand over his face. "You did a good job helping that man today." He jerked his head in the direction of the closed wagon the healer rode in.

"I'm not so sure of that one." She smiled ruefully. "He says he's going to check on Lance before the evening meal and see how well I've done."

"As well he should. Lance is in *his* care after all and shouldn't be your responsibility." Dismounting with a groan of relief, Shyre leaned against the back of the cart. Folding his arms across his chest, his body tensed as he stared over at the healer's conveyance of choice.

Placing her hands lightly on his broad shoulders, Navali rubbed his muscles gently, a curious heat leaving her hands.

Shyre rolled his shoulders in contentment. "That feels heavenly, my love." His voice had softened considerably and his head dropped forward to allow her better access.

When she finished her unskilled massage a few moments later, she wrapped her arms around his neck from behind and held him close. He tilted his head backwards to rest against her breast as his eyes closed, content for the moment.

Addison's voice abruptly interrupted their brief, quiet interlude and Shyre groaned. Rubbing one callused hand over Navali's arm in apology, he twisted slightly to bestow a quick kiss upon her soft lips. He smiled in exasperation before resolutely giving her his back as he faced his brother and shouted, "Addison, quit your bawling and become your own man! I don't have the inclination or the wherewithal to always come to your aid!"

Addison looked nonplussed at his eldest brother's insults and Navali wanted to laugh aloud in the worst way. The poor man had no idea that he was constantly interrupting their private stolen moments, and that it was beginning to set his brother on edge. She returned to her duties and glanced at the wounded man, observing that he was as before. Sighing, she jumped from the wagon bed to stretch her legs and paced briskly to loosen her muscles.

Catching sight of Aakin giving a refresher lesson in defense to a couple of young refugees, she waved when he looked up. He grinned sheepishly in greeting as one of the two men who were sparring yelped and cursed as he held his suddenly bleeding nose. Shrugging at her, Aakin shook his head, rolling his eyes in response to the man's carrying on.

A giggle nearly escaped and Navali quickly stifled it. She had to remember who she was, a princess of Lynaria. Petulance rolled through her at the thought and she felt cheated for having been born Lynarian. It was not fair that others were able to joke around and have fun. Navali was thoroughly sick of having to pretend that she was not feeling a thing.

Of course, she could always rebel even more. The thought caused her to smile inwardly, and she wondered how much she could push the boundaries that had been a part of her life since she was a child and decided it might be fun to try.

Try? She would do it, she resolved, *and do it well!* A pox on convention. Who needed it anyway? Certainly not the people that she was journeying with. They did not seem to have a problem expressing their true feelings and no wars or battles had yet happened because of it.

Well, if Navali was honest with herself there had been one violent incident because of emotion. It had taken place after the men had come back from hunting and were telling of how they had come across a wild boar. One of the men had taken full credit for scaring the beast off and another had called him a liar and a coward. He had even gone so far as to tell everyone that the boastful one had been hiding farther up the tree than all the rest of them.

The once boastful man had become the resentful man, and he punched the informant for giving him away. The informant had retaliated in kind, and the rest had been history. The result had been a few black eyes, a broken nose, a couple bite marks, and two pairs of bloodied knuckles.

Navali did not really believe that was what her people meant when they said emotion led to war. Although in all honesty, it had looked to be able to turn into a full-scale battle, until Shyre and Aakin had rushed into the midst of the fighters and broken it up. Shyre had given the men a stern setdown and extra duty on watch for their unruly behavior and no further violence had erupted since then.

Shyre's voice bellowing from behind Navali caused her to jump, and startled, she spun around.

"We resume our journey in two minutes!" The words echoed around the clearing and the people began to put away the utensils and foodstuffs they had used.

"And you." Shyre's voice was much quieter than before and he beckoned her forward.

"Aye?" Navali asked, doing as she was bade and taking the one step needed to close the distance between them. "Did you want something?"

"Aye, wife," he informed her, wrapping his strongly muscled arms around her torso and pulling her against him. "But that is a dangerous question and you are never to ask that of anyone else. Is that understood?"

His green eyes were warm in affection and Navali knew he was teasing her. "Is that an order? You should know that I don't do well with those," she impishly informed him.

"I figured you might have an issue with obeying the voice of authority." He growled softly into her ear.

"That?" She giggled and pushed him away. "You sound more like a bear than 'the voice of authority.' How do you expect anyone to take you seriously when you sound like that?"

"I don't usually have a problem with being obeyed," he told her smugly and tugged her back into his arms.

"Of course you don't, brother!" Addison crowed from behind Shyre. "We never question or blithely ignore you at all." The big man sarcastically shook his head, a huge grin creasing his face as he gestured between himself and Aakin, who had just come to stand beside him.

"Aakin's with him, isn't he?" Shyre asked Navali as he had not yet turned around to face his siblings and she was the only one with a clear view of the area behind him. She nodded helpfully in response and he growled low in annoyance.

Hearing the disgruntled sound, Addison laughed boisterously. "There he goes again, 'the Voice of Authority'! What was that, Aakin?" Addison jabbed his elbow into his startled youngest brother, who had not uttered a single syllable. "Were you not aware of our brother's elevated status?"

"Apparently not, Addison," Aakin replied and slyly smiled, though he rubbed the spot in his side where his larger brother had jabbed him. Navali did not blame him one bit, it looked as if it had hurt.

The two younger Dareknays burst out laughing as Shyre released Navali and turned on them, lunging for Addison and catching him around the middle. Both men went down and somehow Shyre ended up on top, but that did not last very long before they went tumbling over each other again and again.

Navali had never seen such a thing and she unwittingly clutched hard at Aakin's arm, until that man caught her wrist and gently pried her fingers from his bicep.

"They're only playing," Aakin informed her with a grin.

Navali looked at him dubiously. "How can you be so sure?"

He laughed. "That one is easy. There's no blood," he ended matter-of-factly and pointed to the two brothers on the ground.

"Aren't you going to stop them?" She asked with widened eyes.

Aakin looked at her as if she were insane. "First rule you should know now that you're a part of our family, if the men are fighting, don't get between them. That's when it could become bloody."

At her look of alarm, he quickly amended. "Not that we'd ever hurt you or any other family members on purpose. But haven't you ever heard to let fighting dogs—" Navali looked at him blankly and he tried a different animal. "Cats?" Aakin winced, not liking the comparison. He hated cats. Still no comprehension on Navali's face. "Stallions?" He said it tentatively.

Her face cleared at that and, breathing out a sigh, he finished. "Let fighting stallions be?"

"I've heard that one from the stablemaster before," Navali replied confidently.

"Well, it's just like that. Don't get between them and no one will get hurt. Do you understand?"

She nodded. "Fully."

She looked pointedly at the still tussling brothers. "Now aren't you going to do something? I'm certain the two minutes are well past and they are now in direct disobedience to their own orders. As you always put it, daylights wasting."

Smiling when he groaned as if he were in pain, Navali watched from a safe distance as he moved closer to his elder brothers and shouted. "Shyre! Addison! The two minutes are up!"

The two brothers that had been wrestling sprang apart and stood up fast, turning their attention on Aakin so quickly that he cringed and held up both hands in surrender.

"It was all your wife's idea." Aakin quickly shifted the blame, knowing it would be more diplomatic to involve the newly-married woman. His decision quickly proved itself correct as Shyre gave one last shove to Addison's shoulder, smiled, and then breathing hard from his previous exertion, strode over to Navali, kissing her on the forehead and lifting her into the cart.

Adele had been standing behind the princess and watching the interaction between the three princes with wide eyes, and Shyre reached for her. The younger woman stiffened, unsure of what he was going to do. But when all he did was grin at her, grasp her about her slim waist, and swing her up beside Navali, she smiled back and thanked him, her eyes alight with adventure.

Winking at Navali as he strode around the cart to Swift Justice, Shyre mounted and glanced behind him. Addison and Aakin were mounted and ready, while Stephen was walking with a pretty little redhead Shyre had seen talking with Navali earlier. As he lifted a hand, the caravan moved forward. By now everyone was used to the pattern of the journey and everything went off without a hitch.

The mountains gave way to a strait of plains and the Pitan refugees gazed at it with relief. There was no walking up and down mountains and hills, and there were not any trees or brush to navigate around. They could see for miles and that was how they liked it.

The Dareknays hated it. The plains were less defensible and they could not melt away into the background as easily as they would prefer. Anyone would be able to see them, namely Krinar. Being out in the open, an easy target, was something every Dareknay dreaded. However, they tightened their resolve and moved across the open plains, not revealing how nervous or anxious it made them.

Crossing the plains in as little time as could be managed, the band of people came upon a steep cliff that dropped into a lush valley. A river twisted through it and fog had settled over the basin like a blanket of misty white.

Navali stood up in the wagon as they came alongside the drop-off, suddenly apprehensive of how far northwest they had traveled. "Shyre," she called and waited for him to ride to her side. "Let me ride behind you for a little while? There are some things I wish to discuss with you."

Glancing at Lance lying wounded and then to her, Shyre nevertheless held out his hand for her to take, showing Navali he fully trusted her and her decisions.

She smiled at him. "I asked Adele to keep an eye on him for a while. She's been keeping me company and knows what to do."

Shyre nodded and shrugged in response. He had not needed the explanation. He would not care what the reason was so long as she wanted to ride with him. Beckoning to her with the hand he still held out, he winked. "Come, Navali."

"My pleasure, my lord."

Shyre withdrew his hand and his eyes glinted with mirth. "Is that how you should address me, wife?"

She smiled wickedly. "Very well, I remember now, *husband*."

"I very much like the sound of that coming from your temptingly lush lips, but there is another name which I adore the sound of even more." He still kept his hand withdrawn from her.

"I was just following your lead," Navali informed him, arching one delicate brow as she rested a hand on her hip.

"I did not know I had wed such a compliant woman." Shyre smirked and then grinned leisurely. "I sort of like it."

"Compliant?!" Navali scoffed. "Where did you ever stumble across that ridiculous conclusion, Shyre?"

"I only uttered such a complete farce because I knew you wouldn't be able to resist the bait, my love," Shyre admitted wryly and shrugged. "And it served a double purpose by coercing you into calling me by my given name."

His smile was self-satisfied and he offered his hand again. She accepted with graceful defeat, but when she moved to swing her leg over the back of his stallion, he tugged hard and she fell into his lap. He shifted her weight until she felt comfortably settled within the circle of his arms.

"Rogue," she accused, raising one eyebrow in a pointed sideways glance.

"I don't mind that one either, my lady," he retorted and she tweaked the muscle on his upper arm. He winced playfully. "I yield!"

She tilted her chin up. "That's better. Although I don't really think you meant it."

"You're probably right, love." Shyre shrugged his shoulders.

Navali rested her weight against his chest. "I like that name *immensely.*"

"You do, hmm?" He laid his stubbled cheek against her silky blonde head.

She sighed contentedly. "Aye, I do."

They rode in silence for a few moments before Navali sat up abruptly. "You completely distracted me from my true purpose of riding with you!"

"Was it not simply for the pleasure of my company?" He asked, all innocence. He had deliberately put it off as long as possible, already having a pretty good idea of what she wanted to discuss.

"Well, I wouldn't say no completely, but this other matter is very important—At least it might be." Her face was serious and without emotion. He hated when she did that stoic, porcelain statue thing.

"Did you know Lynaria is just on the other side of this basin?" Navali asked, her alarm for his safety carefully hidden.

He knew it! He had known to the very marrow of his bones that she was going to ask him that from the moment she had called his name. Sometimes she was just as predictable as everyone else!

"—And, if this is the right one, that my people have been creating traps and tricks in this valley for centuries?" She continued, bursting the predictability he had been feeling.

"Would you please say that again?" He drew Swift Justice to a halt. He was *really* going to listen this time. To *every* word.

"Weren't you listening to what I said?" She asked incredulously.

"Not really," he admitted and shrugged. "Would you mind repeating yourself?"

"About the part where my people have been laying traps and setting tricks in this basin to keep the Pitan out?" Navali asked, both eyebrows raised, knowing he had not been expecting that news, and not quite ready to forgive him for not listening to her the first time.

"That's the one." Shyre nodded and grimaced. "Do you know where these traps and other things are located?"

"Some of them," Navali admitted sheepishly. "But there are far too many to know about them all, and I'm not even certain this really *is* Trickster's Basin."

"Rea—lly." He drew the word out. "Do you have any suggestions on how to get through them if this is the right valley?"

She nodded solemnly though she never opened her mouth to tell him what they were.

Shyre gave her a pointed look of his own. "Are you ever going to tell them to me, or should I just guess? I'm not a foreseer you know."

"Trust me, I am fully aware of that," Navali said dryly. "And I wouldn't recommend guessing, it would probably lead to death or dismemberment."

"Any other advice?" He asked, rubbing a hand over his face. This journey was just getting better and better.

"No—ot really." She shook her head, her loose curls brushing the bare arm that rested behind her back.

"I have some." The man's voice came from behind Navali and to Shyre's left. "And I for one *am* entirely certain that this is Trickster's Basin."

Navali twisted around to see who had spoken as her heart sank in her chest at the confidence of the answer. No one sounded that positive unless they were absolutely certain they were right.

The healer stood beside them, his hazel eyes inscrutable as he gazed up at them.

"And what would that be, Healer?" Shyre asked, hoping that this man had the key to the puzzle, but all the while wishing that it were any other man in the caravan. "Now that we've ascertained which valley this truly is."

"I've lived amongst the Pitan for quite a few cales and there are always stories of people who have tried to cross Trickster's Basin." The healer shrugged. "Not many have lived to tell the tale though."

"What's this idea you have then, oh wise, all-knowing one?" Shyre did not like the man. There was something about him that was off-putting, and it was not his disfiguring scars. It was more that he gave off an innate arrogance, as if he were judging Shyre's actions and finding them wanting.

"Shyre!" Navali gasped at her husband's rudeness.

The prince raised his chin and would not apologize for his words.

The healer's eyes hardened. "If you have a better plan than the one I have, princeling, all you have to do is say so."

"I don't even know what *your* plan is!" Shyre growled.

"Well, if you kept quiet, I would be able to tell you."

Shyre's mouth tightened and a muscle ticked in his jaw. Navali hoped he would be able to hold the temper he was fighting, as he glared at the healer with narrowed eyes, but kept to his present silence.

The healer nodded in satisfaction. "The tales tell of a safe path, one marked by a squirrel in a tree."

Shyre looked ahead of him at the line of trees that ringed the mouth of the basin. He did not even dare estimate how many squirrels could be in the trees. Just how long did these people think a squirrel lived anyway? "Any ideas on what tree that is? Or which squirrel?"

The healer shook his head. "A grey squirrel, with dark markings. That is all I know. Though I wouldn't head down the incline until I found out which one was the right one. The tales also tell of pits of sand that can swallow a man or even a whole cart in mere moments."

Looking at Navali in question, Shyre asked if that were true, and she nodded ruefully in response. He sighed in frustration. "All right." Shyre was exasperated. "We look for a grey dark-marked squirrel in a tree." He looked heavenward, his green eyes searching for a sign of some kind. "Unless a better plan reveals itself."

The healer shrugged. "I haven't ever heard of one."

"That helps," Shyre replied dryly, then peered at the man curiously. "Just what is your name, Healer?"

The man hesitated and then said. "The man who drives my wagon calls me Jace. You may as well."

"Thank you." Shyre did not mean his words as a compliment. He had gotten nowhere in understanding the man.

"Jace." Navali tried the name out softly. "It suits you," she told the healer, and the unmarred side of his face flushed red.

Shyre stared in amazement. If he had needed to make a quick assessment of the healer, Shyre would have said the man was incapable of feeling any kind of emotion. But there he stood, looking very embarrassed and uncomfortable. Shyre kind of liked him that way.

"Aye, well, don't use it too often, lest I not respond," was Jace's response to Navali.

There went the liking part, Shyre thought in disgust. The man knew how to be insulting at the very least. The healer turned on his heel and abruptly disappeared into his wagon. Shrugging, Shyre dismissed the man from his thoughts.

"So, my love. Do you know anything about a squirrel, or a tree?" Shyre hoped she did or they could be looking for a very long time, and with the Pitan tyrant breathing down their necks that would not be a good thing.

"Nay." Navali cringed when she said it, she hated being unknowledgeable in any area. "Although I have heard of the tale he was speaking of."

"Are there any more clues in your version?"

She shook her head in the negative, her blonde curls dancing. "Only to follow the squirrels and they shall lead you safely through."

"Marvelous." Sarcasm dripped from the word. "You might want to cover your ears."

"Why?" Navali asked, confused and not doing as she was told.

Shyre did not tell her as he was already bellowing, "Addison!"

CHAPTER NINETEEN

Navali's ears were still ringing when the caravan halted and the men left to search the trees for a certain grey squirrel that marked the safe path. It sounded an impossible task and Navali knew her husband would not be in any higher spirits when he returned to find they had lost some of the Pitan refugees to fear of Trickster's Basin.

Not to mention, when he found out they had taken a good portion of the supplies with them when they had fled to the 'relative' safety of the Pitan mountains. Navali had not been very happy herself when she had been informed of that, and she had a rough time keeping her legendary cool when that information had been relayed.

Half! Navali thought in disgust. *How could five people abscond with nearly half of their foodstuffs?* True, they had been running low, the men hunting in the evening after they had made camp had offset the need for most of the dry supplies. But now they would have to literally scrape the bottom of the few remaining barrels they had to feed even a portion of their remaining people.

If Navali ever got her hands on those cowardly thieves, there had better not be any weapons present. She paced as she silently fumed, and Adele and Vanca stood to one side, watching the princess' uncharacteristic display of temper. It was better if they just watched and observed for future reference, they told themselves, rather than draw her attention in any way.

Sooner than they had thought humanly possible, Navali recovered and set every woman to discovering exactly how much they had lost and how much further they could downsize on the items they did not need.

Paring down was now a necessary evil, in lieu of the twisted path their journey was about to take. Navali sighed in frustration, *why did all these bad things have to happen to them? Why couldn't they happen to the evil ones on their trail instead?*

Ugh! Life was just not being fair at the moment. Where was the justice in that?

First, she was abducted by the worst people she could ever imagine, then she was forced to marry a man she hardly knew…. A smile played at the corners of her mouth. *That last part had really turned out to be not that horrible.*

She frowned again. *Then there was the part where everyone had to split up and the journey was ending up taking far longer than anyone had anticipated. And now, a couple of dastardly persons had stolen valuable and needed supplies, and Shyre, herself, and the rest of their band of people, had to travel through a Lynarian death trap!*

Life was one unpredictably wild ride! And she was loving every part of it, she thought sarcastically. *What could possibly happen next?*

Navali instantly repented of that thought when she felt a drop of water land on her forehead. *But seriously? Wasn't this journey turning into a big enough nightmare already?*

Apparently not, she huffed in disgust, as a terrified scream echoed from the basin's edge. Snapping to attention, Navali picked up her skirts and raced with the rest of the women to where the sound had originated. Arriving, they found nothing, absolutely nothing to tell them why someone had screamed.

"Is everyone accounted for?" Navali shouted over the din of the women's nearly hysterical murmurings.

Vanca's head whipped back and forth, her red hair fanning out behind her. "All the women are—I think." She lifted her shoulders in a helpless gesture. "There really isn't a way to tell, my lady."

"That wasn't a human scream." The deeply-toned comment came so suddenly from behind Navali that she jumped and her hand went to her throat in order to hold back her own scream of terror.

"Would you please cease doing that!" She admonished the healer, Jace.

"I apologize, my lady." He dipped his dark head to her and Navali nodded her forgiveness. "But in the effort of prudence, we should really move away from the edge of the incline. It is unsafe."

His monotone words evoked the first tendrils of fear in Navali and she was more than happy when he took the initiative and began herding the women back to the wagons.

Navali went immediately to Shyre's stallion and untied the bow and quiver of arrows that were secured to the saddle. The bow would prove a challenge for her if she went to draw it back, for it was not made to bend as easily as her own was. The extra effort would cost her in strength, but she was unwilling to go about as unarmed as she had the night of the ambush. The small dagger strapped to her inner thigh did not have the long range that she desired at the moment.

"Come with me." The order came from Jace and Navali moved to do just that. She halted abruptly. *Wasn't that order the very one Shyre and Vanca had both warned her about?*

The healer looked over his shoulder. "What is the matter?" Jace asked.

Navali asked him a question of her own. "Where are we going?"

"Where do you think we're going? We have to see to the wounded man in that wagon over there!" He gestured his good hand in Lance's direction.

Jace was frowning rather fiercely at her for questioning him and Navali felt foolish. Of course they had to see to the unconscious Drocun! *What had she been thinking? The paranoia of the Pitan refugees was really getting to her.*

Shaking her head firmly to dislodge any and all misgivings and superstitions that had not been there a week ago, she followed closely behind the healer as he went to the wagon and hauled himself into it. Navali grasped Jace's good hand and he tugged her up to stand beside him as if she weighed nothing more than a feather. For all the man's physical afflictions there was nothing at all wrong with his strength!

Kneeling beside Lance, the healer placed the back of his hand against the man's forehead and grunted in satisfaction. "No fever, that is a good sign."

Gripping the wounded Drocun's jaw between his fingers, he turned Lance's head one way and then the next. He shook his own head in confusion. "Though I don't know why he does not wake. There is nothing wrong with his head, leastways, that I can tell."

"He did mumble something a few times," Navali interjected, her quicksilver eyes watching and taking in every move the healer made. "Does that help?"

"Not really," Jace replied curtly. He was not upset, that was just how he was, abrupt, and he was completely unapologetic about it.

Navali realized that and did not let herself get upset about his brusque manner with her.

"Princess?" Adele asked timidly as she walked to the cart Navali was kneeling in.

"Yes?" Navali gave her a reassuring smile, resting one hand on the half wall of the cart.

"P'haps ..." Adele hesitated. "p'haps I could stay by ya fer a bit?"

The young girl's eyes held intense fear and Navali's heart melted. "Of course, Adele, anytime." She held her hand down to help her into the wagon, but Jace grasped her arm, halting the movement.

"You can see to the eating of your meal. There is no more to be done for the man until he wakes."

Navali laughed, a little on the bitter side. "And pray, tell us, what do you propose we eat?"

Jace looked hard at her. *Had the pampered princess finally snapped from all the wilderness surrounding her and the tension emanating from everyone?* "Food." He replied slowly and carefully.

"There is hardly any left. Not enough to feed everyone, at least. And the men haven't had a chance to go hunting as of yet," she finished explaining and mumbled under her breath. "Not that there seems to be any game to hunt in this accursed place."

Having heard her comment, Jace looked at the princess for a moment and then nodded. "Very well, I will just have to share the food I brought."

Navali gazed at the healer with wide eyes. "What did you say?"

"I said—"

"Never mind. I heard you the first time. I was just surprised. You don't seem the type of man to carry about enough food to feed a small army."

"Appearance's can be deceiving," he dryly informed her.

"I know," she mused quietly. "I am very much aware of that now."

This time Navali followed him immediately and without hesitation as he gestured for her to precede him to his wagon.

"Shyre?"

"Aye, Addison?" Shyre responded to his brother's call, suspecting what Addison's next words would be and instantly regretting the opening of his own mouth. Hearing a snicker to his left, he steadfastly refused to look at the blonde giant beside him. *Here comes the belittling,* he thought with a grimace.

"What exactly are we looking for again?" Every man within twenty feet of the princes laughed uproariously as Addison let out a robust chuckle of his own. Shyre did not even need to respond to his brother's last inquiry, that was not the point.

Every man was having a hard, not to mention amused, time believing they were actually climbing trees, scouring them for a little grey animal that could be close to a hundred cales of age. Which of course was impossible, unless you were an insane hermit-healer who believed in folk tales told around the fire by peasants who had consumed one sip too many of the fermented elderberry brew that was concocted in these parts.

Shyre could hardly wait to get his hands on Jace. He would gladly relish adding a few more scars to the many that man already carried. It was not like anyone would notice more anyway and it would make Shyre feel better after chasing a fairytale. But only if he could actually get away with it without Navali hearing of it and forbidding him from their tent.

The healer deserved it for what he was doing to Shyre, making him the laughingstock of his whole company of men. There would be a reckoning, Shyre vowed as Aakin made a comment this time and everyone snickered and hooted in jest.

Shooting a glare at the men closest to him, who instantly quieted at that threatening look, Shyre waved a hand at Aakin, beckoning him closer.

"Nay, brother. I think it wiser to stay over on this side of the tree," Aakin replied, without taking a single step in the direction of his fuming brother. "We want to make sure we've got these trees covered from all different angles. We wouldn't want to miss anything." His youngest brother quipped, and Shyre wanted to set him on fire when Aakin said under his breath. "Like any small, furry, woodland creatures that have dark markings and have lived on this earth a hundred cales."

That was it! Shyre had had enough. He turned resolutely away from the guffawing men and made his way back to the wagons and women. *What a time he was having! Did no one respect him anymore?*

There was a sudden, loud snap and something heavy and flailing abruptly hit Shyre squarely on the back and shoulders and he went down hard, cursing and gasping for breath as the thing landed on top of him.

"*Oomph!*" The thing cried.

"*Huuhh!*" An elbow jammed Shyre in the ribs and he recognized the man on top of him as Tucker.

"Sa sorry, yer highness." The young man was frantically attempting to rise from his position, incredibly embarrassed for having flattened the high prince.

There was a knee to his thigh, and Shyre thanked God-on-high the bony appendage had not been gouged any higher, as Tucker finally untangled his arms and legs. The youth managed to rise and Shyre gave a small sigh of relief. Tucker was a scrawny thing, but with his sharp elbows and knees he was a lethal weapon of jabbing instruments. Shyre would have to see to it that he was fattened up a bit to prevent any other injuries that could be prevalent if the youth ever studied wrestling.

Sprinting over to laugh at Shyre's misfortune, Addison gave his eldest brother a hand up. After he had risen, Shyre leaned over and attempted to catch his breath as he braced his hands on his knees.

Tucker continued to apologize profusely. "I'm sa sorry. Me hand slipped and I didn't 'ave me feet secure." The young Pitan took a deep breath. "Though twas mighty fortunate fer me, ye were walking by when ye did, yer highness, otherwise I'da probably broke me blamed neck."

The prince used one of his hands to wave away Tucker's words. "Twas nothing."

"Nothing?" Addison sputtered, his hands holding his trim belly as he attempted to hold in his laughter. "Twas one of the most humorous things I've ever been witness to in my entire life!"

"So glad I could amuse you, brother," Shyre said dryly and straightened, his breath finally coming easier.

"You did," Addison reaffirmed and walked over to a chuckling Aakin. "Did you observe that?" He asked.

"I most certainly did," Aakin replied, and then turned his grin on Shyre. "Uh, Shyre?"

Turning halfway around to see what he wanted, Shyre gave him a long-suffering look.

"You don't mind if I tell Aaron about this, do you?" Aakin asked impishly.

Shyre rolled his eyes, raising his hands in surrender to his undesired fate. "I really don't give a horse's nugget what you do."

"That's good, because I already told him," Aakin and Addison immediately started chortling again and Shyre decided to leave the laughing imps to themselves. He would seek sympathy elsewhere, for it was apparent his brothers held none for him.

His long strides ate up the distance back to where they had left the women and, suddenly hearing their shrieks of terror, Shyre broke into a run.

Navali had placed her foot on the first step to Jace's wagon when a hand suddenly grabbed her arm and whirled her around.

"What has happened?" Shyre's voice demanded and she gazed up at him in shock. Where had he come from?

"I heard the screams and I—" Shyre paused, breathing hard, his gaze taking in where she had been heading. "And where do you think you're going?"

Ignoring his second question, which did not seem as urgent, Navali addressed the first. "We heard a scream from the edge of the cliff and when we got there, nothing could be found. Jace says it wasn't human." She shuddered in remembrance of the eerie sound. "But it sounded just as though a woman were screaming."

Shyre's green eyes hardened and he looked at her sternly. "Stay away from the cliff's edge."

She nodded quickly and he gently enfolded her in his arms. She was not the only one who needed to touch something solid and tangible. His heart had leapt into his throat at the sound of that scream and he was still struggling to realize that no one had been hurt. Then he remembered where he had caught her.

Abruptly holding her at arm's length, he asked. "And what were you doing going in there?" Shyre jerked his head in the direction of the healer's wagon.

"We had several refugees flee back to the mountains, Shyre, taking at least half of our supplies with them."

His eyes widened at that. "When did this transpire?"

"Just after you and the men went to search for the squirrel."

"That's just wonderful," Shyre replied with a great deal of sarcasm. "But it still does not explain why you were going into the healer's wagon."

She shrugged. "I'm just getting some food for the evening meal, surely you do not object?" She asked him teasingly. Having caught the flash of jealousy in his eyes, her own became alight with mischief.

"Of course not." The reply was too fast to be anything but a lie and Shyre would have groaned if he had been alone. Then again, if he had been alone he would not be having this dilemma. "I was only wondering. Now that I am here, may I help you carry anything?" He quickly offered, trying to cover his faux pas.

Her silver eyes narrowed on him. "Sure you were," she said doubtfully, paused a moment, and then smiled triumphantly. "But I will use the offer of your brawn and make you carry anything heavy," she relented.

"Just point me in the right direction," he replied, flexing his muscles.

Glancing swiftly to the right and then the left, Navali assured herself they were alone and could not be seen. Adele and Jace had disappeared into the depths of the healer's wagon and no one else was around to see them. She impishly turned her attention to her husband and lifted one delicate finger to place it lightly against her lips. "Right here," she informed him.

His eyes lit with fire and he hungrily reached for her, drawing her slight form into his arms and covering her lips with a swiftness that surprised Navali. He kissed her deeply, his lips firm and insistent, before he abruptly released her.

"No more of that until later," Shyre ordered, breathing heavily as he gently took her arm, escorting her to the wagon's entrance again. "You play with fire, my sweet."

She looked up at him from the corner of her eyes. "If my hair would not singe from the flames of your desire, I would play with it all day and far into the night."

He chuckled softly. "That is satisfyingly flattering." He handed her up into the wagon and took a deep breath as he followed her into the healer's lair, his mind not even wandering to the mysteries that could be unveiled within its dark depths.

Stepping inside Jace's private wagon was not as thrilling as Shyre had once expected. The interior was sparse in furnishings, consisting of only a thin bed with fur throws and a large chest that sat at the foot of the cot, its lock gleamed sharply in the meager light that filtered through a small glass window in the ceiling of the wagon. One wooden stool sat pushed beneath a small table on the opposite side of the bed, and a large cabinet running the width of the interior sat on the far wall with a matching one wreathing the door to the outside.

There were no other furnishings or embellishments to be seen and Shyre was disappointed there was nothing to give him any indications of what type of man the healer really was.

Jace was handing Adele foodstuffs that would be of great use to them and Shyre moved Navali gently out of the way when the healer withdrew a large keg of flour. Jace looked at him in surprise as Adele left the wagon with her hands full.

"Healer Jace," Shyre acknowledged the man and took the barrel from his outstretched hands.

"Just Jace," the healer corrected and released his hold on the container.

"My thanks for this, either way," Shyre responded, and gave the man a nod as he turned and looked at Navali. "Where would you like me to put this?" He hefted the barrel in his hands to show her what he meant.

Navali pointed out the door to where the women were stoking a large fire. "Over there by the fire, thank you." Her eyes followed him as he left the wagon and walked over to the gaggle of women.

"He seems like a good man, your husband." The deep voice was close to her ear and Navali gasped and spun around. Jace gave a low chuckle, surprising even himself at the merry noise. "It seems that I am forever startling you."

"Well don't apologize yet, you will probably end up doing it again before the day is through," she informed him, and then her silver eyes turned solemn and thoughtful. "I agree with you, Shyre is a good man—Nay, he is a wonderful man." She gave a small dreamy smile as she said the last and Jace watched as her eyes became alight with love.

"You love him, don't you?" It really was not a question, for Jace already knew the answer. He was not interested in having a personal and intimate relationship with the princess, but he knew she was Lynarian, and feeling anything for the prince could prove disastrous for her.

"W-what? Love him? Whatever gave you that foolhardy notion?" Navali asked, looking disconcerted.

"Your eyes, and the way you watch him," he answered as he sighed. The princess would have to watch her step and her emotions closely once the caravan reached Lynaria.

"That is nonsense." She waved away his words with a delicate hand.

"Is it?" He asked. She needed to face the truth now before they crossed the border. Jace could well testify as to the rigidness of Lynarian society and he did not want anything bad to happen to these two people. They were showing themselves fair and just and that was something that was hardly ever displayed in his world.

Her eyes showing an anxious glint now, Navali nevertheless admitted in a small voice. "Not really."

"Once we reach Lynaria, I'll help you as much as I am able. Just try to withhold your emotions until we are through your country and to Dareknay. Then say hellfire to laws and rules and love him as you please." He offered his advice and help, though he was not exactly sure why he did. He only knew it would not be easy for her, not showing love never was.

"You're right," she sighed. "Thank you for wanting to help."

He nodded and she picked up a few of the items he had set on the table and walked out to join Shyre at the fire.

Sighing, Jace shook his head in consternation and pushed his fingers through his dark hair, tugging at the roots. So much for staying uninvolved and distant, that was something he never seemed able to do. *He truly was a fool.*

CHAPTER TWENTY

S hall we take a walk, my love?" Shyre asked Navali, as the sky painted the many brilliant colors of a fiery sunset over the golden plain.

The men had returned a good hour before and their report had not been promising. They had checked all of the trees to the left of the caravan and found nothing. Whatever secrets the trees seemed to be hiding they were still firmly sheltering them. The caravan had eaten quietly, disheartened by the turn of events, and most had gone to bed already. No one felt like celebrating this night when the threat of the Pitan horde was so near at hand.

"I would enjoy that," Navali replied, and placed her hand in his. They walked toward the setting sun, pausing beneath a large tree some distance from the encampment.

Leaning back and resting against the rough bark behind him, Shyre pulled Navali to him, holding her close against his chest. They were just out of earshot of the caravan, and on this side of the large tree, no one could see them. An owl hooted nearby and Shyre ruefully admitted that no *human* eyes could see them anyway.

Tilting his wife's chin up with one hand, he placed a swift kiss on her lips. "What is the matter, Navali?" He had watched her furrowed brows closely during the evening meal and he had endured enough of that confused look.

She gave a heartfelt sigh. "Nothing, really."

"Hmm-hmm." He waited patiently, he was not going to let it go that easily.

Navali was unsure of how much she should confide in him. Her heart told her to tell him that she loved him with every fiber of her being, but her head told her to wait and see if he returned the feeling, see if they made it through Lynaria before admitting that particular truth to him. *Oh, toadwarts! She would just have to brave through it and tell him!* If Jace could tell she was in love with her handsome prince, surely so could the very man himself.

She took a deep breath and nothing happened, no sound emerged and she felt the utmost coward. She could not force the words through her constricted throat. She laid her head against his chest and he stroked her hair with one hand as he watched the sunset. He was so gentle and sweet with her, the substance of all her forbidden romantic dreams combined.

She could do this! Shyre deserved to know that she loved him! Swallowing, she lifted her head from his chest, looking straight into his inquiring eyes. Then something glinted sharply in the setting sun from above his head and her gaze shot to the faint object. *Was that—? Aye, it must be!*

"Shyre!" She squeezed the hard biceps she was holding and he turned his head to look at what had her so awestruck.

"Navali—?" Shyre turned completely around in surprise and delight. "You found it!"

"*We* found it, Shyre," she corrected and smiled.

There, revealed by the setting sun, in a hollowed knot in the tree above them, sat a stoic stone squirrel. Dark, ancient runes swirled over its head and what could be seen of the body from the ground. Shyre set Navali away from him and then climbed the tree to get a better look. Onyx stones for the eyes glinted in the fading sun and the statue gazed out over Trickster's Basin. Following the direction of that unwavering gaze, Shyre glimpsed a stone ruin in the distance.

"There!" He pointed to the ruins so Navali could see. "That is where we go."

Jumping down, Shyre swept her close. Navali's feet left the ground as he whirled her in a circle, his arms holding her tightly, and she giggled as he laughed in triumph. *They were going to make it! She just knew it!*

He set her down and kissed her deeply before taking her hand in his and sprinting for the caravan. "Aakin! Addison! Get your miserable hides out here!"

"Shyre!" Navali protested in a whisper. "You'll wake the entire camp!"

"Who gives a damn? We've found it! We're going to make it safely through the basin!" Shyre's enthusiasm was contagious and Navali could not help but smile as Stephen, Vanca, Jace, and Shyre's brothers greeted them at the edge of the firelight.

"What is it, your highness?" Stephen was the first to ask.

Shyre clapped his hand on the archer's shoulder. "We've found the squirrel. It shows the way to a stone ruin in the basin. I'd wager we can make it there by mid-afternoon!"

"That's good," Addison interjected. "Because the Pitan are right on our tails." His gray eyes hardened as he looked behind him to the trees that stood sentinel against the edge of the prairie. Against the darkened horizon, white smoke could be seen from what would amount to nearly half a dozen fires.

Stunned at how close their enemy was, Shyre's jaw clenched. He stepped forward, his features now fully illuminated by the fire's glow. "Aakin, Stephen, go swiftly and wake the refugees. See that they stay quiet and only bring the smallest and most important items they can carry with them. Foodstuffs above all else."

The two men left to do as they were ordered, Vanca's hand firmly secured in the archer's grip. The high prince turned to Addison. "Make certain it appears as if we are still here. We do not want Krinar to guess we have flown until we are well on our way. See that the fires are stoked high and will burn through the night." Shyre turned to the disfigured healer. "We must leave all of the wagons behind."

"Nay." Jace's voice was just as resolute as Shyre's. "My wagon goes."

"Don't be a fool!" Shyre exclaimed. "If we take anything that large, the Pitan will know we have left. We have to make it to the ruins before they know we've gone!"

Shaking his head firmly, Jace reiterated. "My wagon goes. They know what it looks like and they won't give a damn about it leaving. They know I'll desert at the first sign of danger. I always do."

"Coward!" Shyre spat the word in disgust.

Looking unaffected, Jace raised his eyebrows in mockery.

"Surely you wouldn't have really left us?" Navali asked. She had judged the man a fair and courageous one for his stalwartness when the villagers pointed at his twisted face and whispered things behind his back. He had not turned and fled for safety then, why would he do so now?

"If I had wanted to run, I would have done so yesterday when we were still in the forest and I could have easily disappeared." Jace raised his chin in defiance and looked at Shyre. "I have made my choice and am fully committed. I will follow you through this journey. Though once it is over, I go my separate way. But my wagon goes," Jace persisted. "The weakened ones can ride inside, we'll make better time even with the cumbersome thing."

"Very well." Shyre almost growled, thoroughly disliking it. However, he knew that it would be better if they did not have to tie Lance to a saddle. "Let's settle Lance in there."

That was something both men agreed on and they moved to the wounded man in the cart. Navali watched as they carefully used a blanket as a huge sling and carried the man between them to Jace's wagon. She rushed ahead of them and threw open the door.

"My thanks, little one," Shyre whispered, as he walked past her and up the steps to the interior. The two men laid the man on the thin cot and secured him to it with a length of rope.

"Navali," Jace spoke to her once they had Lance settled, and she frowned at his familiarity. "You ride in here with him and make sure he does not thrash about."

"Nay." Her voice was firm as she refused. "My place is at my husband's side."

The healer's eyes glinted with something akin to pride at her words and he gave a half-grin as he left the wagon to go speak with his servant, Ephraim.

"Navali, it is indeed more safe in here," Shyre attempted. He wanted her at his side, but not if that put her at greater risk. She was his finest treasure and Krinar had already stolen her away from him once. Shyre would not ever allow that to happen again, no matter what the personal cost to himself.

Navali was shaking her head. "Nay," she told him. "I ride with you."

Shyre could see that he was not going to win this fight and he really did not want to argue with her when things were so unsettled. He would discuss her doing as she was told when they were safe in Dareknay. "I cede this battle."

At Shyre's quietly whispered words, Navali's entire countenance softened and she wrapped her arms around his neck. "I knew you would see it my way."

"Hardly," Shyre scoffed lightly. "I really did not want you so far from me, and I also know when the fight is worth a few wounds, and this one is not."

"That wasn't a very nice thing to say."

"Does this make it better?" He kissed her swiftly.

"Much," she sighed. "But, Shyre, speaking of wounds, if we have to fight Krinar, promise me you will be careful. He's a sneaky dastard."

He looked at her in amusement. "Don't you mean bas—"

She interrupted him. "Nay, I mean dastard, as in cowardly. I'm not as crude as some people are," she directed a haughtily-lifted brow at him.

"Hmm. I'll have to remember that one." She gave him a pointed look. "And yes, I do promise that I will be as careful as possible. Does that ease you?"

"Aye," she whispered, and he released her before he became any more distracted.

"Go see that your friends are prepared to leave, and then meet me by Justice." He turned her firmly away from him.

Navali turned right back and grinned at him, saluting with two fingers. Shyre gave a light chuckle as she whirled away again just as quickly. His heart full, he swatted her backside gently as she left.

Navali was shocked at Shyre's gesture and her face flamed. He had done the very thing she had hoped he would not ever do to her, and what was even more shocking was that she had not really minded. It had not hurt, for it was more like a pat, a teasing touch, and that had her smiling in the darkness as she went to the fire where her friends were huddled.

Vanca and Adele's frightened faces reminded her that this was a solemn occasion and she quickly schooled her features to show Lynarian calmness and self-control.

"Is it really true, m'lady?" Adele asked, her voice trembling. "Is Krinar comin' fer us?"

"Not this night," Navali assured as she hugged the younger girl to her side. "That's why we're departing now, before the sun rises."

"But what about tha squirrel? We haven't found 'im yet." Adele was still trembling, though her voice was less frightened.

"Aye, we did. Shyre and I spotted him up in that tree over there." Navali nodded her head in the direction of the great big oak tree.

"Oh." Adele's voice was small, but relieved.

"Are you all set to go?" Navali asked Vanca.

"Aye," was her friend's ready answer.

Navali nodded. "Then I must go and see if Shyre is ready to leave." Leaving Adele with Vanca, who hugged her close, Navali turned and saw that Shyre was already waiting for her. He held out his hand and she made her way swiftly to him.

As she reached him, he grasped her waist firmly and surprised her by swinging her up onto her old mount.

"I thought—" She gestured to his horse, looking perplexed.

"It is safer if you ride your own horse," Shyre told her. She wanted to protest, and seeing this, Shyre continued. "It is more convenient if I have to fight to not have you against my back."

The words sounded abrupt, but Navali knew they were not really meant that way. He was just trying to protect her. If he had been closer to her, Navali would have kissed him for it, but he had turned away as he said it and mounted his stallion, grabbing her reins and a quarterstaff as he did so. He nudged Justice to a walk, leading her horse behind, and the rest of the caravan began to move silently towards the edge of Trickster's Basin and whatever fate awaited them there.

Navali prayed they would all make it safely. She held her breath and clutched the pommel of her saddle with icy fingers as they reached the tree that held the stone squirrel.

"Wait here." Shyre held out her reins to her and she took them numbly, a bit perplexed as to his reasoning. But as he gave her a last lingering look she knew what he had in mind and her heart skipped a beat as he suddenly urged his horse down the incline.

"Shyre!" She whispered urgently, and her mount pranced sideways beneath her when she inadvertently tugged sharply on the reins in her distress. Shyre did not hear her call him though and he disappeared over the edge. Her heart began a swift beat that matched the whooshing sound of the blood in her ears and Navali nearly lost all control of her anxiousness and fear before her husband finally crested the incline again.

"The path is nearly straight down," Shyre quietly stated to her and his Drocuns. "Make certain everyone follows the tracks I have laid. One false step and they could be sucked in by whatever lies beneath the sand."

"Is that what happened to your quarterstaff?" Navali had just realized he had not returned with it.

He gave her a long look before he answered. "Aye."

That was all Navali needed to hear and she nodded as he beckoned her forward.

"Stay directly behind me."

"At this moment, Shyre, I am the most compliant woman on Yria," she admitted, and he grinned over his shoulder at her before nudging his stallion once more down the incline.

True to her word, she followed very closely, though she was worried her mount might stumble and take his with it when it skidded and slid several times before they managed to reach level ground again.

Finally making it safely to the bottom, Navali let out the breath she had been holding. Shyre left her to go assist the men in lowering the healer's wagon down the side of the basin. The cumbersome thing slipped and slid down the rocks and sand and a few of the women cried out as it tipped dangerously to one side and then righted itself with a jolt. It was close, but the men managed to manhandle the thing down the incline and everyone breathed a collective sigh of relief.

Shyre rode back to Navali to lead the way. Animal cries were abundant and sounded far closer than she cared for. But nothing burst out of the forest to eat them as she and Shyre reached it and Navali took that as a good sign. When she looked back to see how the refugees were faring, all she could see of them were their pale faces eerily illuminated in the darkness.

Training her eyes forward once more, Navali ducked to the side to avoid a branch. Tendrils of her long hair caught in the twigs and she yanked them painfully from their reaching grasp.

They did not have time to stop so she could leisurely free her hair and she did not greatly begrudge a few missing strands.

They continued on for hours. Everything looked familiar to her, as though she had seen it already that night and she hoped they were not going around in circles. The darkness that surrounded them finally gave way to the grayness of early dawn and with it new dangers arose. Krinar and his men would soon be waking to find them gone and then their frantic flight for survival would truly begin in earnest.

Stopping mid-morning to water their horses, they ate swiftly to break the fast of the evening. Cold biscuits and deer jerky had never been more appealing to Navali, and Shyre and Addison chuckled at her when she told them that very thing, but they quickly sobered, their eyes on the far horizon from which they had come.

Miniscule figures were visible along the top of the basin and Navali's heart sank in her chest. Krinar! And he had seen them. The refugees had noticed the same thing and silence reigned in the deafening quiet of dread that overcame them. Everyone watched as a single man attempted to make his way down the rocky side of the cliff's edge. All of a sudden, he disappeared from view, his scream abruptly swallowed by the sand that closed over his head.

Shuddering at Navali's side, Adele hid her face in the princess' tattered skirt. Vanca was on the other side of the frightened young woman and she rested her hand on the thin, trembling back.

Another man was sent down the incline a good fifty feet from the first, and though he made it farther, he still met with the same fate.

Navali looked at Shyre and he grasped her hand. "I'm glad we found that squirrel," she whispered.

He squeezed her fingers. "As am I."

They did not wait to see how many men would feed the sand traps before Krinar found the solid path to the basin's foundation.

Shyre arose and, taking Navali with him, walked swiftly to their horses. "We need to move swiftly, everyone. It won't do us any good to watch and see when Krinar makes it down." He used the word when and not *if* Krinar made it down and that one small word said everything.

The refugees scrambled to quickly pick up their packs and crates, before following closely behind Shyre and Navali. Not a sound emerged from the group, panic clearly written on many of their faces.

Shyre prayed they would not let that panic have free reign. They needed to make it to the ruined stone structure and find that other squirrel before Krinar made it down that ledge!

As the trees opened up suddenly and the ruins lay before them, a faint roar came from the cliff's edge and Shyre's stallion pranced as he whipped the animal around to see what had taken place. The Pitan Horde raced down the side of the ledge, like an army of dark ants, scrambling and falling over one another in their haste to reach flat ground.

Turning resolutely from the sight, Shyre directed Justice through a crumbling wall to the center of the old stone structure. One terrified man raced ahead of Navali and she gave a small cry of alarm.

"Halt!" Shyre commanded, but the man only pushed his legs harder and ran through the open double doors of the old keep that led from the decayed inner ward. Skidding through the doorway, he abruptly halted to look back at them. The man looked down at his feet, where a thin wire wrapped about one ankle, and then gazed in surprise at the ceiling as the thick rocks that made up the portal gave way, tumbling down onto him, effectively burying his body from sight.

Turning her face away from the avalanche of stones, Navali grimaced. That was a sight she would not soon forget, no matter how hard she tried.

That poor man, who was so afraid he just could not help run-ning away from the Pitan Horde, had just been crushed to death! She glimpsed Adele from the corner of her eye and wanted to retch along with the girl. Tucker held his sister to the side as her body heaved, then the younger woman straightened, and clung to her brother as he held her closely. His hands brushed soothingly down her back, his lips moving as he whispered soft words to her.

Facing forward again, Navali quietly asked Shyre. "Where to now?"

"I'm not yet certain. Do you see a squirrel?" He asked in return, his eyes quickly searching for the little stone creature.

Navali looked around as well, desperately seeking something that caught her eye. "Nay." She was forced to admit, as nothing seemed to appear squirrel-like to her. "What are we to do?"

"Stay calm and figure a way out of this," Shyre said and called his men to him. "Fan out and find a squirrel of any kind in the walls or trees or whatever is about." They immediately moved to follow his orders, and Shyre called quietly after them. "And don't touch *anything*!"

Dismounting, he made his way with Stephen to what was left of the once magnificent gatehouse to their right. Navali watched anxiously with the refugees as the men scoured the thick walls for a nook or cranny of any kind that housed a stone squirrel.

"I found it, m'lord!" Came an excited male voice from behind Navali.

Shyre whirled about. "Where?" he demanded of the Pitan villager as the man appeared from behind a crumbling stone wall.

"It's up there!" The refugee man, Bertrand, said as he pointed to a place above the great iron-studded doors of the gatehouse. "In tha battlements on top!"

"Show me!" Shyre took off at a run and Bertrand followed closely behind. Soon Navali could see Shyre again as he walked up a set of stone steps that had more than a few missing. She watched as Bertrand pointed to something and Shyre nodded in agreement before making his way hurriedly back down the ruined steps.

Whistling sharply for his men to return, Shyre led the way to the gatehouse and ordered Stephen to help him as he braced his shoulder against the heavy wood and pushed with all his might. Stephen hurried to help and the other returning men swiftly lent their assistance. Groaning could be heard from the men and the huge doors moaned themselves as they were forced open on rusty hinges. Navali kneed her horse to a walk and went through them, the refugees following closely behind. Nothing but the sight of more dense forest greeted them, and Navali felt close to despair at the overgrown path that they would now have to traverse.

They had to reach Lynaria! They just had to!

Shyre and the rest of the men wrestled the doors closed behind them in hopes Krinar would not know which way they had gone and Shyre joined her at the front of the caravan. Mounting Swift Justice as he reached her, he led them away from the castle ruins.

Glancing over her shoulder, for she wanted to see the stone squirrel that Bertrand had found, she was surprised to find it sitting in one of the square putlog holes that resided in the remaining merlons of the gatehouse. She faced forward again, feeling slightly perturbed with the craftiness of her people. She would have to speak with her father about his neglecting to inform her where these small guardians of the safe path were. That knowledge would have come in very helpful on this trip.

They were forced to a snail's pace as the men had to dismount several yards into the forest and hack their way through the thick underbrush with their swords in order to be able to follow the overgrown path.

Logan, the new militia captain, and a few of the other refugees who had brought axes with them were helping the Dareknays, and that aided somewhat in quickening the slow pace.

The men's shoulder and arm muscles required that they work in shifts so that they could continue on at a steady rate. The exhausting work was beginning to wear on all of them when, a few hours after what would have been the noon repast had they halted for it, a deep rumble resounded from behind the caravan. Though startled by the sound, not a single person glanced back the way they had come. They knew that sound. Someone had just met a fate similar to the one the poor villager had met when he stepped through the old keep's double doors.

All the resting men rose to their feet in one accord as the rumbling sound faded away and rejoined the others in resolutely hacking at the underbrush. Even if they refused to let it slow them down, fatigue was clearly written on their faces. This was their only hope of survival and they were going to give it their all.

CHAPTER TWENTY-ONE

Continuing on as darkness consumed the thick forest, Shyre and the men unrelentingly swung their swords and axes, beating the underbrush back with what remained of their strength. They had made more headway than he would have thought humanly possible, but the Pitan were still far too close to be able to call a halt for the evening. The howling and screaming of the night-creatures punctured the sound of the brush breaking and Shyre wondered what other surprises were out there concealed by the dark shroud of night.

Shortly after the women had passed out the evening victuals the caravan had come upon a small lake completely obscured by trees. Shyre had thought to briefly water the horses there, but instead had found that the water was filled with great beasts that swished their tails viciously and eyed them with hunger. Bones littered the small beach around the water and it did not take much to recognize that some of them were human remains.

Shyre firmly pushed away thoughts of the huge, fanged creatures and prayed they were confined to water and would not follow them to pick the people off in the eeriness of the evening encompassing them. Shadows seemed to jump at them and catch at their clothes, and many of the men crossed themselves and mumbled prayers under their breath as they worked. The women were huddled behind, staying close together and picking up the branches and leaves that fell in the path of the wagon wheels as it plodded forward along the path the men were unveiling.

Exhaustion burned through Shyre's muscles, and the ache that resided there had long ago become an unpleasant one. As darkness fell, rain had begun beating down on them steadily and

Shyre wondered how much further he could push these people. He knew his brothers and Stephen would go on until they collapsed, and would then drag themselves up again to continue for several more hours, but the others were already lagging, their breathing harsh and jagged, and their movements sluggish.

A man to his left suddenly and quietly collapsed, and Shyre knew he would have to call a brief halt before they all died of exhaustion. Although it seemed a futile hope, he would send Aakin and Stephen to scout ahead and see if the brush they fought against cleared soon.

Calling a halt, Shyre strode wearily over to his youngest brother. "Aakin, take Stephen and see what lies ahead. I need to assure my wife's welfare."

Aakin nodded tiredly without uttering a single word, it would have taken too much effort and energy, and moved his aching feet over to Stephen. Shyre watched the two men disappear into the forest and then went his own way. Coming upon his wife, he took in Navali's determined face as he drew to a halt.

"Still bearing up all right?" he asked, concerned. She had not been brought up to do this kind of manual plodding along for hours at a time with no reprieve.

"Well enough, Shyre. And yourself?" She gave him a hint of a tired smile that belied the determined look that graced her features.

"Cannot think of when I've felt better," he responded with a soft chuckle, and tugged the sodden blonde curl that rested over her shoulder.

"Perhaps you would like me to remind you, then." Navali managed to smile with a hint of coyness.

Shyre sighed resignedly. "If you must, my dear."

"Oh, I must." Navali nodded and stepped closer, leaning into him until her lips almost brushed his ear.

He bent closer to be able to hear her more clearly and could have howled in frustration when he instead heard someone come up behind them. He straightened abruptly and turned around with one hand on Navali's arm to find the healer, Jace, behind them.

"I should have known it would be you." Shyre shook his head in exasperation. The man was constantly sneaking up on them during a private moment.

"You should also be aware, princeling, that I sent Ephraim back to scout out where Krinar and his men are."

Jace's voice and words drew Shyre to attention. He strode closer to the man so that the healer would not have to speak so loudly to tell him of what he had learned and possibly frighten the refugees even more.

"My man returned not too long ago. It seems that Krinar has stayed at the castle ruins this night with his pet Fayrah, though he's sent most of his men ahead and they're only a short way from being able to nip at our heels like the mongrels they truly are." Jace sneered as he spoke of the Pitan king and his witch.

"That's unpleasant news," Shyre replied carefully, his blistered hand tightening on the hilt of his sword as the other still gripped Navali's arm.

"Very," Jace agreed, his arms crossing over his chest.

Shyre faced Navali. "Why don't you see if you can find some deer jerky in my saddle-packs, will you, love? I'm starving."

Navali nodded, they obviously wanted to discuss something without her. Not that she would not pry it out of her husband later though. "I'll see if I can find the flask of mead you put in there as well. It will help dispel the chill this rain has brought."

"Thank you, Navali." Shyre observed as she went in search of Swift Justice and the aforementioned saddlebags. He turned immediately to Jace once she was out of earshot. "You said you were good at disappearing in forests."

The words were not really a question, though Jace nodded apprehensively in response anyway and waited for the prince to speak again.

"If a battle ensues this night, will you take Princess Navali to safety?" Shyre asked, the words sounding as if someone were wrenching them from him. He hated having to ask this man for anything. "I won't abandon these people to Krinar and his consorts."

Raising a single black eyebrow, Jace asked. "What if the princess refuses?"

"She won't," Shyre stated firmly. He would make her vow to go with the healer. He could not bear it if she were captured by that repugnant tyrant again. "Though if she does indeed refuse, you have my permission to rend her unconscious. As gently as possible, of course."

"Of course." Jace nodded, and though still skeptical, held out his good hand. Shyre clasped the healer's wrist, sealing the pact between them. The two men went their separate ways after that, both with difficult tasks ahead. One, to find his wife and make her promise to leave if a battle started, and the other, to wrestle with the conscience he never knew he possessed until now.

"Nay, I shan't do it!" Navali exclaimed and tore her hands from Shyre's grasp. "I won't leave you and these people to die! I know how to fight as well!"

"How do you think your staying will help us? You will just distract me from the battle. And no one said we were going to die," Shyre replied as he reached to enclose both of her hands in his again.

"No one had to say you were all going to die! I saw how many men Krinar has with him when they descended into the basin. It would be a massacre if you were caught! I'm not going." Navali shook her head emphatically and avoided his hands. She did not want him touching her at the moment. It weakened her knees and made her mind haze with a brilliant, languid feeling, and weakness and languidness were not something she wanted to feel at the moment. Nay, strong and capable was what she needed to be, so Shyre would see that she was fully able to make her own decisions in this.

"I've given Jace my blessing to set you unconscious if you fight him." Shyre managed to capture one of her hands, and he grasped it tightly in his as she tried to pry it away from him.

"You did, did you?" Navali wanted to shriek the words, but allowed herself to let it out in a low hiss instead. She shook the hand he held tightly in his grasp to no avail. "Unhand me, you arrogant dolt! I don't want you touching me!"

"Is that right?" Shyre asked, his voice a low snarl of displeasure.

"That's right, you overgrown lummox!" She glared at him, her eyes shooting silver fire. "Release me now!"

"I don't think so." The words were dangerously soft and Shyre's arms encircled her body, holding her captive against him. "You are mine. And I will do with you as I please." Shyre dipped his head to claim her lips in a kiss and met with fierce resistance.

Navali shook her head side to side in an effort to evade his kiss. "I belong to no man!" she fumed and continued struggling.

Grasping her jaw firmly in one hand to still her frantic movements, Shyre quickly lowered his lips to capture hers.

"You belong to me," he growled softly. His breath was warm against her lips as his words vibrated strongly throughout her body. He lifted his head a fraction of an inch to speak before resetting his lips hard on hers once more.

Shyre kissed her with a passion that had been unforeseen. His arms were steel bands to bind her more tightly to him. His lips were hot and insistent, stealing away her resolve to struggle against him. Navali could not help but mold herself to his hard contours as his touch melted all of her resistance away.

When he felt her surrender, Shyre lifted his head, his green eyes glittering intensely down into hers. "And you will do as I say."

Navali nodded, because she knew if she did not, Shyre would not soon relinquish and he would then tell Jace to do more than just make her insensible to the world around her. He would have her tied and wrapped up like a goose for the basting and placed in the wagon, forced to await whatever fate had in store for her.

Nodding in response to her agreement with his edicts, Shyre abruptly released her and withdrew a step, giving her the distance she had so desired moments before, but now regretted. "It is settled then. You will stay on your mount, and if the Pitan Horde emerge from the trees, you are to head straight for the healer's wagon. Am I understood?"

"Very." She could not quite quell the fury in that one word and did not really care that he could hear it either.

"Good." His voice was taut with tension, having heard the anger in hers. "Then I must go and see if Aakin and Stephen have returned. Stay among the refugees and don't wander too far from the healer's wagon. We will hopefully be moving on shortly and I don't want you to fall behind."

Nodding in response as the fury she was feeling choked away her voice, Navali watched as he strode to the edge of the foliage the men had been clearing away. *Her husband could be such an insufferable toad when he wanted to be!*

Who did he think he was? She fumed silently. She was the princess of Lynaria and she was fully capable of making her own decisions. She knew her own mind and wants, and did not need anyone telling her what they were. It was certain she did not want to be in Krinar's clutches again. But neither did she wish to turn tail and run like a cowardly snippet!

She knew how to fight if the need called for it. Shyre had already seen what she could do with a dagger. It was greatly bothering Navali that he seemed to not want her with him, even if he did have the excuse of not wanting her to get hurt. *Like she would be safer away from him and with some relatively unknown Pitan? Hah!*

True, Jace was a healer, but he could just as easily betray them. After all, they really did not know much about where the man originated from, nor about how he had come by his burns, and now her husband was asking him to take her to safety? *What a lark!*

Navali stalked further away from the huddled refugees as she paced furiously. Her steps taking her even farther from the accursed wagon that would perhaps soon become her unwanted prison.

The slim dagger that rested in the sheath secured to her thigh brushed her skirts with every step she took and comforted Navali with how close at hand it was. *She could very well take care of herself! Had she not already proved that to Shyre? Did he really regard her as a pampered princess who knew nothing of hardships?*

Her hands may be soft from the lotions her maids were continually forcing upon her, but they were strong on the inside, fully developed by hours of practicing with the specially-made bow her father had gifted her with when she had turned twelve cales of age. Though she was not skilled with the quarterstaff because her father had forbidden it, she knew how to use every other weapon in her father's armory.

She was even proficient in the use of a slingshot, thanks to the ratcatcher that lurked the palace halls and kitchens assuring there were no rodents about. Navali had bribed the older lad when she was but six cales and he almost twelve with the promise of one of the many pearls that had adorned her blonde hair.

The lad had agreed and she had followed him around for as long as it had taken to become as good as he with the sling-shot. Then she had impishly employed the weapon in scaring her nursemaids until they believed that evil spirits lived in the nursery, throwing things at them at night. As a result, she was moved out of the lonely compartments in the far wing and into rooms closer to her father and the many guests he entertained, as had been her original goal.

Thinking on how much satisfaction she had felt the day her trunks were moved into the more 'adult' quarters of the palace, Navali wandered closer to the healer's wagon, not realizing she was drawing ever nearer to her would-be prison. She leaned against the thick wood of the far side out of the watchful sight of the refugees.

She needed the small amount of privacy the cart afforded and let out a deep sigh of relief. She had acted brave and courageous for a great many hours and the reprieve of allowing herself to feel other than those two emotions was nearly overwhelming to her tired body. She wanted to sink down onto the ground and sleep for several hours, for the previous night's lack of rest was beginning to wear on her.

Refusing the urgings of her body, Navali forced her knees to straighten. She would not give in to any womanly shows of weakness that a princess was supposedly prone to. She would show Shyre that she could go on as long as he did! *Just see if she did not!*

The sound of cloth rustling against leaf-strewn ground had Navali starting and she straightened from where she was leaning. *What was that?* She looked around herself and saw nothing, but that did not mean there was nothing to be worried about in the deep woods all around her.

Knowing Shyre would probably test her to see if she had obeyed, Navali decided it would be prudent to head back. She moved her feet in the direction of the horse that pulled the wagon and where she had tethered her own Pitan nag close by, and then slowed in confusion when she did not immediately glimpse her mount.

Had she not tethered the animal on this side? Her brow furrowed as she came abreast of the edge of the wagon and still did not see the scarred rump of her horse.

A hard, masculine arm suddenly seized her about the waist and squeezed harshly, forcing the breath from her lungs. At the same time a rough hand settled over her mouth and nose, cutting off her air supply.

Struggling valiantly, Navali attempted to scream against the stifling hand. No coherent sound emerged, only the rasping gasp of her breath filled the air around her as she tried desperately to draw air into her constricted lungs.

Clawing at the arm that held her captive, Navali reached for the thumb of the man's hand to bend it back so that he would be forced to release her or receive a broken finger for his malicious efforts. Empty air and the material of her own gown met her touch as she searched frantically for the hand that should have been at the end of the man's arm. Dread suffused her mind when she could not find it.

For there was none! Navali knew of only one man who did not have a hand on his right arm.

Lance? The wounded Drocun that was supposed to be in the very wagon she had been leaning on? It couldn't be, could it?

The man was gravely wounded. He should not be able to stand yet, much less be able to drag her off into the woods, while holding her so tightly with his wounded arm that it was cutting off her breath. *It was impossible! It must be some other man,* her logical mind cried in denial. *Shyre would not trust someone who was not loyal to him! He was more intuitive than that. And why? Why would one of his own men seek to harm her?*

Twisting her head from side to side, Navali thrashed about to loosen the hand over her mouth and nose so she could catch her breath and scream for Shyre. Her struggles proved in vain as the hand kept her head pinned tightly to a muscled shoulder. She kicked back with her feet, frantically trying to get the man to loosen his harsh grip in any way as her vision clouded with a white mist that portended the onset of unconsciousness. Navali pushed the red-sparkled cloud away as it became thicker, her struggles slowing as she concentrated on not losing consciousness.

Stumbling as he walked backwards into the trees, the man dragged her with him and the grip on her face eased. Navali took that opportunity to bring her head as far forward as she could and slam it back into the man's nose, hearing a sharp crack as she did so.

Her captor grunted and retightened his grip, but other than those two actions he showed no other signs of injury to her well-placed blow. She felt something hot slide down the side of her neck in a rush and the lightheadedness returned full force. The hot liquid could be nothing else but the blood that surely ran from the man's now-broken nose.

Navali had never fainted at the sight of blood before. However, she was discovering, much to her horror and disgust, that the feel of somebody else's blood sliding down one's own flesh was an entirely different experience.

Blackness was now consuming the white in her vision and she felt the earth sliding away under her feet as she fell headlong into the oblivion that promised relief from the nightmarish attack that was plaguing her.

Shyre had been conversing with Addison when Aakin and Stephen emerged from the thick underbrush in front of them. As a result, all four of the men heard the sudden sound of hoofbeats thundering away.

Looking at one another swiftly, they raced for the wagon. Jace was emerging from the door in the back wall of the conveyance, one hand holding his head as blood flowed freely from between his fingers.

As he caught sight of Shyre and his men, he shouted to them, "The wounded Drocun knocked me out." Jace gasped for breath as he swayed against the side of the wagon. "He was mumbling something about finishing the task of taking the princess back!"

"What?" Shyre asked, confused. "We already have the princess, is he delirious?"

"He could be. But I have a terrible suspicion he may have meant back to Krinar."

Shyre's heart turned to stone in his chest and sank fast. *Surely not—? No, he wouldn't!*

"Where is the princess?" He demanded of the people that had gathered close together at the sound of hoofbeats. Blank looks and frightened shrugs met his question and dread sunk its claws deep into Shyre. "Find her!" He roared as he took off for the dark side of the wagon.

Beginning to search for clues as to where Lance had gone, his mind refused to believe what he was seeing. Blood had dripped down the wooden steps of the wagon, and the dirt and vegetation beneath had been disturbed by something large. Aakin brought a torch as he joined his brother in searching for tracks of any kind.

"Did they find her?" Shyre asked him.

"Not yet." Aakin's words did not reassure Shyre in the slightest. "And Shyre?" His youngest brother waited for him to look up before finishing. "Navali's horse is the one missing."

Shyre's eyes turned blindly to the ground in front of him as his mind tried to process the implications that could have. As his eyes came back into focus, he realized he had been gazing at the site of a struggle. The earth had been kicked at and overturned by a pair of small feet and a much larger, booted track had been clearly pulling the smaller ones into the cover of the trees.

Having just come around the opposite side of the wagon with his own torch, Addison noted the tracks at the same time Shyre did. He strode with his eldest brother to where the human tracks ended and the horse's began. He looked to Shyre with shocked eyes and waited for orders.

"I'm going after her." Shyre spoke quietly to his brother, his eyes never leaving the tracks that had taken his wife away from him.

"Of course." Addison nodded, and turned to go back to the caravan. "I'll get our horses."

"Nay."

The one word halted Addison in mid-step and he turned in confusion to Shyre, giving Aakin a wary look as that man came up to them.

"You just said—" Addison began, and Shyre interrupted him.

"I said that *I* was going after her... Alone." The younger brothers exchanged a look of incredulousness at Shyre's words.

"You cannot go alone!" Aakin exclaimed, grabbing Shyre's arm in a fierce grip. "They're likely to kill you as soon as they set eyes on you."

"I go alone." Shyre reiterated the words as he shrugged out of his brother's hold and went to find his stallion.

"Nay!" This time it was from Addison. "We do this together. As we have always done."

Shyre shook his head without breaking stride as he came upon Swift Justice. The horse snorted, sensing his master's mood, as Shyre caught up the reins in one hand and prepared to mount. Turning before he did so, he placed one hand on each of his brothers' shoulders.

"Krinar will want me alive. I'm father's heir to the throne and he will think that useful in battles against Dareknay." Shyre sighed. "I may be able to get her free without tipping my hand though, if I go alone. Also, I need you two to lead the rest of these people to Lynaria. Aakin, you have reported that it is less than a day's journey out of the basin. You should all be able to make it if Krinar is distracted with me."

His brothers opened their mouths at the same time to protest and Shyre held up a hand for silence. "I'm counting on you both to obey orders like loyal Drocuns and get these people to safety. That needs to be your first priority, after that, I don't care. Just stay safe."

"Hellfire and maggots! Face Krinar alone?!" Addison snapped at him, greatly disliking this new plan. It was better if they faced the tyrant together. But, then, who would see to the refugees safety? And, Shyre was their leader and they should obey him. This time. Addison prayed there would be a next. "We'll be coming after you as soon as these people are safe."

Shyre nodded, not believing for a moment they would be in time to do any good. "I know you will, Addison." He turned away and mounted his horse, checking to see if all his weapons were secure. Glancing at his brothers one last time, he kicked Justice to a gallop as he leaned low over the stallion's withers.

He prayed he would be able to catch Lance before the man was able to make it back to the snake bed that made up Krinar's camp.

CHAPTER TWENTY-TWO

Navali moaned as she was jostled awake by the steadily limping gait of the man who carried her. Someone blew their breath through their front teeth in a hiss as they neared and Navali wished she could force her eyes open to see who it was. *Where was she?*

The previous night's activities suddenly flashed like lightning through her mind and her eyes began to obey her commands to open. Her eyelids fluttered in the early morning sunlight and Navali caught sight of something she had wished to never see again.

Her eyes flickered open to reveal the face of the man who was carrying her and discovered it was Lance. Navali felt no real surprise at seeing the wounded man, but the shock of him striding towards a man dressed in deep purple and gold very nearly got the better of her. Her mind stuttered and everything became very hazy again. Swallowing hard, her vision returned to normal once more and she looked at the man again to assure herself of what she was actually seeing.

No! It couldn't be! Her mind screamed in denial, though no sound emerged from her mouth. However much she wished, she could not change it. The man was indeed the last person she ever wished to see and she wanted to let herself sob in disbelief at her misfortune, but she knew she could not allow herself that luxury.

She was in the clutches of the tyrant Krinar again! And one of Shyre's own men had taken her to him!

"Well, well, my dear. We meet again." Krinar's voice was reedy with satisfaction and he rubbed his hands together with glee. "You should not have run off so soon, we were just about to get to the entertaining part when your prince came for you."

Sitting up as much as she was allowed to in Lance's arms, Navali strived to keep as much distance as possible between her upper body and that of the traitorous Drocun's. Lance disgusted her, after all she had done to help save his life, and this was how he repaid her!

"I do not wish to be anywhere near you when you are being *entertained*, Krinar," Navali retorted. The Pitan king reached out a hand and fingered one of her silver-blonde curls, unperturbed by the venom in her voice. Navali jerked her head away from his stroking fingers and he laughed in delight, the sound evil incarnate.

"Do not worry, my sweet," Krinar purred. Navali liked the nickname a lot more when Shyre was the one using it. Hearing it now from Krinar's lips only made her want to gag. She fought the telltale urge as Krinar clutched a lock of her hair and wrapped it once around his fist, using it to jerk her closer so that he could place a kiss on the silver-blonde curl before releasing it very gently to lie across her breast.

"We will get to play with you later, but first—" Krinar continued, and looked at Lance for the first time since Navali had awoken. "We will see to your much-earned reward, my Drocun friend."

Lance grinned at that and Navali wanted to scratch his eyes out, even if he was wounded. *He had done it for money! The greedy beast!* She glanced back at Krinar and noted the malicious, hungry gleam in his eyes, before her gaze caught on something behind the tyrant king. The sight was that of a lithe young woman dressed in blood-red standing in the shadow of Krinar's tent. Navali watched as the wild-haired woman licked her overly plump lips and smiled, her broken and stained teeth revealed to those around her when she did so.

Other than the mass of riotous hair and horrendous teeth, the woman would have been considered a beauty by many a man. But the way her eyes glittered with hatred and a mix of something

Navali did not wish to define caused her to think that not many of those self-same men, excluding Krinar, that was, would be idiotic or insane enough to call her such.

Navali's heart sped up at the sly look revealed on the woman's face. There was only one woman this could be. The High Fayrah. The evil witch that sacrificed people to her false gods in the worst possible way.

Both Pitan king and witch were gazing lustfully at Lance, as though he were their next meal, and Navali forced herself not to move and draw their attentions to herself. That would be foolish in the extreme, and she really did not have a death wish that she wanted them to take care of at the moment. As she waited for the Pitan king to give whatever reward he had promised to Lance, Navali prayed the earth would open up and swallow her whole, for that would be a far kinder fate than the one Krinar had planned for her.

The king's hazel eyes gleamed and shifted. *Couldn't Lance see the evil way every last one of the Pitan were looking at him?* Navali wondered as she took note of the soldiers flanking both of the Drocun's sides. Hundreds more were gathered around in a rough circle in the inner ward of the ruined castle that resided in Trickster's Basin. Surely he, a highly-trained Dareknay warrior, would notice such a thing.

Glancing around at the many soldiers, Navali briefly wondered how they had managed to not trip any more of the well-laid traps than the ones the caravan had heard yesterday and could not think of a plausible reason. There was no feasible way these Pitan could know where they were, unless the witch really did possess some sort of magical power to keep them from walking blindly into them.

"Put the princess down," Krinar ordered Lance, and Navali returned her attention to the matters at hand. After the Dareknay set her down, Navali wobbled on her feet and then found her balance as Krinar reached a hand out to steady her. His fingers on her arm made her skin crawl with disgust, and she swiftly moved away from his grasp, only to have a soldier seize her and secure her arms behind her with a thick length of rope.

Hardly noticing when his man moved away from Navali, the tyrant ordered. "Kneel, Drocun."

Navali bitterly wondered how long Krinar had desired to utter those particular words. He was probably feeling very ecstatic and triumphant at the moment and Navali wished he would have a stroke right on the spot. She did not really think wishing for his death right then made her evil, for at least the man would die happy.

Lance looked confused and a little apprehensive now as his eyes took in the sight of the hundreds of Horde soldiers gathered around him. He dropped to his knees, hitting the ground hard enough to cause a small plume of dust to rise and whirl about them.

The dirt settled before Krinar reached to remove the heavy golden pouch that hung from his matching gold-studded belt. Navali knew a moment of dread. Lance would not be leaving this place alive with all of that gold in his pocket. They would kill him ere he reached the dense forest.

Lance was despicable, contemptible, and out of all the feather-brained buffoons she had ever met, he had to be the worst! But the way these people could think of to send their victims to the underworld—well, Navali was pretty certain no one deserved to die like that. Except for perhaps Krinar and the witch-woman he kept close at hand.

"Here is your reward, Drocun." Krinar's voice was mild as he handed the bag to Lance. The man grasped it greedily, his brown eyes widening and showing a hint of madness for the first time. There was something not quite right about that madness though, Navali realized, and at the malicious look in Krinar's eyes, she knew it could not be entirely the Drocun's fault for the way he was presently acting.

The Fayrah stepped forward with a golden goblet cupped in both of her dirty, jagged-nailed hands and the king withdrew a step to let her pass.

"Here, drink," the witch purred to the one-armed man. "This will soothe your aches and pains and make you feel more like the old you."

Lance gratefully took it from her in his one remaining hand and downed the contents in three deep draughts, his head thrown back and his throat working greedily. He shuddered once when he had finished and his shoulders hunched forward as his eyes gradually lost the maddened haze that clouded them. Blinking several times, he shook his head, clearly trying to clear it the rest of the way.

Eagerly leaning forward, Krinar and the Fayrah stared at Lance as his eyes became the clear brown they were supposed to be. Navali felt pity and sympathy sweep through her as she realized what the Pitan king and his pet had done to him. The man had been placed under a dark spell.

This man who looked around in astonished dismay must be the real Lance! The one Shyre knew as a kind and gentle man, a good and loyal warrior pledged in service to his king.

As Lance struggled to regain his standing position on legs that shook from the withdrawal of the enchantment, Krinar gestured to two men on either side of the wobbling Drocun. The soldiers clasped his arms fiercely in rough hands and hauled him none too tenderly the rest of the way to his feet. Lance looked at her with sorrow and shame in his eyes and Navali knew he had finally realized what he had done.

The two hulking guards of the Horde held him trapped between them and Krinar pronounced sentence on the Dareknay. "I gave the promise of a reward to a bewitched man loyal only to me. You are no longer him and so my oath is meaningless. My gold, if you please."

Grimacing in disgust as the guards holding him loosened their grip so that he could hand over the heavy-laden pouch, Lance spat. "I don't want your blood-won gold, you avaricious swine. You're welcome to it." He threw the golden bag with enough force that Krinar stumbled back hard as it hit him squarely in the chest.

Coughing lightly to regain his breath, Krinar drew himself up to his full height again, his hazel eyes narrowing in spite. "You shouldn't have done that, you know." He shook his head as if educating a small child and clicked his tongue twice in a berating manner. "Tsk, tsk. Harsh punishments befall those who upset me."

"I'm sure you already had nefarious plans aplenty set in motion for me, Tyrant!" Lance spoke as the two soldiers grasped his arms tighter, irritated that he had gotten the best of them.

Krinar pouted as if the words hurt him. "In times past, I was only going to have you killed quickly. In a show of mercy, you might say." His eyes hardened and the flesh on his face tautened in fury. "But now, I find that I much prefer a more gruesome demise for you." He waved his hands about imperiously. "Shall we see if the portcullis is working properly, my most loyal Horde?"

The responding roar of the soldiers was confirmation enough. The two men holding Lance's arms began to drag him backwards and he began to struggle in earnest. "Nay!" he shouted as two more men grabbed his legs and helped haul him to the gatehouse.

The huge double doors had been thrown open and one of the Pitan soldiers could be seen inside the structure of the building. Navali breathed faster. *What were they going to do to him?* She did not want to watch and turned her head quickly to the side, closing her eyes tightly and wishing she could cover her ears with her palms to drown out the sound as the Pitan men began to chant loudly.

The Fayrah giggled in Navali's ear as she suddenly came to stand beside her. "What, Princess? Are you not enjoying our form of entertainment?" Cruelly grasping Navali's hair in one hand, the Fayrah forced her head in the direction of Lance. He was now lying on the ground on his back, spread-eagled as four soldiers grasped his ankles and forearms, stretching him out as they lay on their stomachs and waited, holding the large Drocun still, each with grins that made Navali want to retch. The portcullis' many sharp, iron-tipped teeth, where time and rust had not consumed the metal, gleamed in the sunlight above the stoic Dareknay.

"Watch, you stupid cow!" The Fayrah shrieked in her ear, not realizing that Navali was helpless to do anything less. She could not believe what she was seeing!

Krinar raised his hand and an ungodly silence swept over the waiting crowd of soldiers. Navali's breath came in hard pants. *Nay! Surely they weren't going to—!?!*

Krinar abruptly lowered his hand and the portcullis was released from its moorings. Navali could not hold back the involuntary scream that left her throat as it fell. A roar of triumphant delight came from the Pitan Horde and Navali felt tears fill her eyes and swiftly blinked them back. She would not let them see her weep!

They left Lance's dead body where it lay underneath the portcullis, and turned their attention to Navali and the woman who still held firmly onto her royal, blond locks.

The hold on her hair tightened and the Fayrah giggled again, whispering as she did so, "Just think what we will do with you, Princess. Your death will be a far more public one than that simple Dareknay's was, I can assure you of that. Perhaps even your father and husband will be there to witness it. Do you think you'll scream?"

"Rest assured, witch, not a single sound would pass my lips." Navali struggled to speak as the woman tilted her head further back upon her neck. "And if my husband and father were there, you would not live to see me die."

The Fayrah giggled. "Is that not sweet, Krinar?" She asked the Pitan king as he strode over to them. "She believes her father or husband can kill us! Do you think we should let her in on our little secret?"

"If you feel you must, Rheema." Krinar's look was one of boredom and long-suffering.

"I must!" The witch snapped at him, her face distorted with rage at his answer. Her features quickly smoothed as she spoke to Navali again, giving the blonde hair she held a sharp yank to punctuate her words. "The gods have assured me that I will not die at the hands of your husband, nor those of your father. And neither will Krinar. We can do as we please with no repercussions from them. Isn't that delightful?"

"Not really. For if I must, I'll kill you myself, witch!"

Navali gasped, but did not allow herself to wince as the woman's hold tightened painfully on her hair.

Grasping Navali's throat with one hand, Krinar applied an almost teasing pressure. "Such words of defiance! They amuse me." He licked his lips and placed a kiss on Navali's cheek. She sought to turn her head away as his lips neared her own, but found herself held immobile. "We will have to instruct you as to who you will be serving in the very near future."

"Never you," Navali vowed and stilled, icily glaring at him in disgust.

Krinar was undaunted at her words and chuckled, his wet lips very close to hers. "There is fire underneath the frigid Lynarian upbringing. How intriguing!"

Raising his lips away from hers, he turned his attention to Rheema, and Navali breathed easier as the imminent danger of having Krinar's kiss forced upon her faded.

"Rheema, do you suppose we should let the men teach it to her first?"

The men watching every move their king and Fayrah made, leaned forward in slavering anticipation of the witch's answer.

Rheema nodded as she shrugged indifferently. "Why not? It will make her agree quicker to aid us in getting our hands on her kingdom." Her fleshy lips quirked in a sneer. "Although I think it wouldn't be quite to your liking when you have to marry her later."

"I don't care," Krinar assured her. "I won't be married to her for very long. You'll see to that, my succulent little peach." The Pitan king and Rheema kissed deeply as they held Navali between them and she forced down the bile that arose at how near they were to her face. They had not ever heard of propriety *or* privacy it seemed!

Rheema moaned deep in her throat as Krinar lifted his head and then turned to his men. "Very well, it is decided. You may have her!" The crowd of men roared and surged forward as one being. "Garrick, you are first, you're captain of the Horde."

The big man smirked at the lower-ranked men as the king summoned him forward. He moved ahead of his cohorts and grabbed Navali by the shoulders. Releasing her hair, the Fayrah laughed at the shudder of revulsion that Navali could not suppress as the big man held her tightly to his body.

"Oh, you'll get used to his odor, highness. In time, you won't even notice it," the witch twittered as Krinar wrapped one of his arms about her waist. "You'll—"

An arrow suddenly whistled past Navali's head, sliced through Garrick's parted lips, and deeply lodged itself in his throat. The big man swayed before falling forward onto Navali, his superior weight crushing down on top of her. Her knees buckled under the pressure and Navali found herself pinned flat on her back under the big brute, her bound hands and arms beneath her.

"You will release my wife, Krinar, lest my next arrow find its mark in your cowardly hide!" Shyre roared his demands for Navali's liberation.

Smirking coldly at Navali, Krinar bellowed. "You are welcome to her, Prince Ashyre. If you can reach her, that is." His watery eyes searched for the Dareknay prince and he subtly nodded his head to three of his men, who silently melted away.

"Navali?" Shyre called from where he was concealed from sight somewhere in the ruins. "I need you to come to me."

Squirming under the oppressive weight of the dead man on top of her, Navali soon realized she would not be going anywhere by herself.

"I'm trapped under this beast's corpse!" Navali shouted, her breath coming in gasps. "He's too heavy for me to move with my hands secured behind my back!"

"Krinar! Have your men remove the body from my wife's person," Shyre ordered, his voice a menacing threat.

"Tsk, tsk," Krinar responded. "You could ask more nicely. Though under the circumstances, I would still have to refuse your request." The tyrant shrugged. An arrow suddenly thudded into the ground near his feet, and he took a hasty step back. "Well! If you wanted it that badly!" Krinar waved a hand to his men and two of them came forward to free Navali from Garrick's weight. She came to her feet without assistance and one of the men withdrew a dagger, slitting her bonds before moving carefully away. Navali started violently when a male scream of agony sprang from the depths of the ruins, but was not too disturbed when she quickly realized it had not emitted from her husband.

Sounds of a fierce scuffle reached them and Navali heard Shyre grunt in pain this time. She raced for the sound, only to have Krinar catch her up short by grabbing her arms and wrenching them once more behind her back. Desperately struggling against him, she found the effort proved useless as he was far stronger than he first appeared.

Shortly after the sounds of the scuffle faded, two men strode through the crowd dragging another between them. Navali stifled the moan of dismay that sought to escape her throat and struggled against Krinar again as she recognized the third man.

"Shyre!" She screamed.

"Now, now, my sweet." Krinar attempted to pacify her as he tightened his hold on her arms. She ceased her struggles and waited for a moment, hoping to catch him off guard. "He's just roughed up a bit, but I'm sure he'll live, at least for a short while longer."

"How reassuring!" She snapped, glaring at him over her shoulder.

"I'm not always so cruel, Navali. I can be kind, if given the right incentive." The Pitan king released her so abruptly that she stumbled forward. Navali looked at him, unsure of his intentions. "Go to him, highness, and soothe the bedraggled and beaten prince."

Rheema giggled in delight, as though Krinar had made a huge jest, but Navali paid them no heed as she raced to her husband. The men holding him upright dropped his leaden weight just before Navali reached him. She took in the ruination her husband had managed to do to their faces with a great deal of satisfaction. One sported a nose so broken it was askew on his face, while the other's eye was bleeding profusely and so swelled shut that one could not tell if the eye still remained in its socket.

Reaching Shyre, Navali knelt and lifted his head, gently placing it in her lap and stroking his brow with her hand.

"Were there not three of you to begin with?" She asked the guards sweetly as she gazed up at them with a hard glint in her eyes. Her husband was good with his hands it seemed—she had already known that from their pleasurable and private interludes, but it was nice to know he could dole out pain to their enemies with those same hands as well.

The two Pitan guardsmen sneered at her in answer and strode away to see their wounds tended to. She noted with no small bit of satisfaction that one of them limped heavily.

"It seems, my warrior prince, that you have given them a few mementos to remember you by," she whispered for his ears alone, though he was still unconscious.

"Not hardly memorable enough for my prolonged comfort," Shyre groaned quietly as his senses returned with her words echoing in his head. "Though I did manage to kill one of the bastards ere they rendered me unconscious."

"Well done, husband." She allowed a small smile to flitter across her face before glancing around at the Pitan Horde surrounding them. "One already dispatched to the underworld—Nay, there were actually two! We mustn't forget Garrick—now only about three hundred remain."

He groaned again at the large number she quoted and shifted to sit up under his own power as Krinar strode over to them.

"It seems *I* now hold the upper hand, Prince Ashyre," Krinar gloated.

"Do not get too comfortable, I'll soon reclaim it," Shyre responded confidently.

"Such hasty proclamations from a man who is completely at my mercy." Krinar leaned over and gazed at the gash near Shyre's hairline with malevolent glee. "Vicious looking cut. Shall I have Rheema tend it for you?" He offered suddenly.

"My thanks, but nay, I'd rather it putrefy," Shyre responded, and pushed himself to his feet, disliking that the Pitan king towered over him.

"Oh, but I insist." Krinar waved a hand at Rheema, and she came forward to stand before Shyre.

Navali quickly inserted herself between Shyre and the Fayrah before the other woman could touch him. The witches were not known to be very careful with men, or so the refugees' tales spoke of. "I'll see to my husband's wounds, if you don't mind."

"I defer to your wishes, Princess Navali." Krinar sounded gracious, though he smirked at her knowingly.

"Do you even know how to help him?" Rheema asked. "I, on the other hand can do wonders with men's wounds." She attempted to reach over Navali's shoulder to prod the gash on Shyre's forehead.

"I have no doubt of that," Navali replied, smiling coldly at the woman and deflecting her hand. "My mother was a healer, I'm sure I can muddle through."

"Darling," the High Fayrah commented to Shyre. "You should have picked someone who could do more than muddle through." She laughed at her own words and then sauntered away, giving Shyre come-hither looks over her shoulder as she disappeared into the king's tent. Navali wanted to rip her hair out. The woman had no right looking at her husband that way!

Turning to Shyre, Navali inspected the depth of the wound as she asked under her breath. "Are you sure Fayrah isn't another name for blood-thirsty demoness? I could have sworn I saw a fang when she saw your blood, and she hissed at me earlier."

Shyre's mouth quirked in a half grin, though his swirling green eyes never left Krinar's face. "One can never be sure about them. It's best if you do not have to deal with them either way."

Navali leaned over and discreetly tore a piece of fabric from her shift, before dabbing gently at Shyre's cut. "I wouldn't be here if I could help it." Her voice turned serious and her eyes dipped to stare at his collarbone in shame. "I'm ashamed for wandering away from the others, Shyre. I was upset and I wanted to make my own decisions."

His eyes left Krinar at that and he tucked his long index finger under her chin, lifting it until her eyes met his magnetic gaze. "You don't need to apologize, my love, I understand the feeling of wanting to make one's own decisions. Though it was a rather pretty apology and I do appreciate it." He smiled into her eyes and she returned it, not caring who was watching them.

"Isn't this touching," Krinar interjected into their private moment. "The lovebirds staring dreamily into each other's eyes."

Neither Shyre nor Navali commented, though their gazes instantly swung in the Pitan swine's direction.

"What, you're not going to stop now, are you?" Krinar crossed his arms over his chest. "I'm sure it was just about to reach the deliciously sinful part." He waited for a reaction of some kind, and when he still did not get one, continued. "Nay? Well, that really is too terrible for words."

His limpid hazel eyes hardened suddenly and he pointed a finger at Shyre. "You have killed Garrick, my chief captain. For that you will have to be punished, Prince Ashyre."

Navali tightened the grasp she had on Shyre's bicep. *What kind of punishment did Krinar have in mind?*

Feeling her tense, Shyre ran his hand down her back in an effort to soothe her.

"I think a traditional flogging with a cane will be adequate." Krinar raised his hand and a very tall, thick man came forward, swinging a thin long stick in the air. "Although I'm going to add another potential element of agony to it. I hope you don't mind, Princess Navali, but I'm going to use you to my advantage."

"I'm sure you wouldn't care even if I do mind," Navali retorted, her face stoic.

"Leave the princess out of this, Krinar," Shyre growled. "She had nothing to do with my killing Garrick. She couldn't have stopped me even if she had been standing directly beside me."

"The whole idea is punishing you, Prince Ashyre. It will be so much more interesting if you have to work to protect your little wife, like you were attempting to do when Garrick grabbed her." Krinar clapped his bejeweled hands together and Rheema stepped from the tent again.

"What's this I hear about a punishment?" she asked, her eyes widened innocently. Krinar leaned over and whispered what he had in mind. "Mmm, I like it. You are so wicked sometimes, majesty."

"Rheema, I think perhaps that is the greatest compliment coming from you." Krinar then turned to face the beefy soldier with the cane. "You! Remove the prince's armor and bind his hands behind his back."

The soldier nodded once and someone threw him a length of rope. Strutting up to Shyre, the hulking man briefly hesitated at the prince's scathing glance, and then settled for closely observing as the royal man removed his own armored shirt. After the prince was finished, the Pitan stepped closer and jerked Shyre's hands behind his back to carry out the order he had been given.

"Tighter, man!" Krinar called lightly. "I don't want him able to move a single finger in defense of himself." He paused briefly, shrugged, and then said, "Or others."

"I'll see ta it, yer majesty." The soldier nodded again, and yanked hard on the ends of the rope, cruelly tightening it before wrapping it around Shyre's wrists a final time and knotting it securely.

Navali watched her husband's face and took in the fact that he never flinched as the ropes became what she was sure was unbearably tight.

"Navali, you stand over here." Krinar took her arm solicitously and led her to the spot that he wanted. "You will be allowed to move wherever you wish." He assured her, then gestured to Shyre as if he were about to direct a dance instead of a torturous punishment. "Shyre, you stand next to her." He took a step back to study his handiwork. "Good. Just the way I want it."

He motioned to the guard again. "I want one of Princess Navali's ankles tied to a stake in the ground. I don't want her able to wander too far away."

"Your majesty?" Rheema broke into his instructions. "May I have that honor? I've always wanted to have a princess at my mercy."

"She is already at your mercy, my peach. But you may secure her if you wish." Krinar waved her forward and snapped his fingers to his men. "Get her a rope and drive a stake into the ground. Quickly, now!"

"Aye, sire, as you wish." The two closest men responded, and one walked tentatively closer to the Fayrah to give her the length of rope he had been holding. It seemed to Navali that the Pitan villagers were not the only ones who feared the Fayrah, that feeling also seemed to extend to the fierce Horde troops.

The other soldier went to fetch a hammer and stake and returned in a few moments with both items in hand. Driving the wooden stake deep into the ground, he swiftly retreated.

Sashaying her way over to Navali, Rheema slapped part of the rope in her open hand. "Which ankle do you prefer, majesty?" She asked of Krinar.

"It matters naught." The Pitan king shrugged.

The Fayrah knelt at Navali's feet and reached for her right ankle, binding the rope tightly around it before moving to the stake with the other end and attaching it.

"There, all done." Rheema wiped her hands down her dress in satisfaction as she gazed at the neat knots that now held Navali secure.

"Your knots are always so perfect, Rheema," Krinar complimented as he gazed at her work.

"I know." Rheema sighed, preening before him.

"You there." Krinar pointed to another soldier. "Fetch another cane."

The soldier immediately jumped to do as he was bid and returned shortly with a thin knotted stick.

The Pitan king grimaced in disgust. "I suppose that will have to suffice in these conditions," he growled at the sight of the makeshift cane, and the man flinched as though he had been struck. Criticism that came from his king was often accompanied by a more physical repercussion.

"All right, Ashyre, here's a brief instruction of the exercise. Both of these men—" Krinar gestured to the two soldiers wielding the canes. One was quite tall and beefy with crossed eyes and the other was a short, thin, rat-faced man. "Will be trying their hardest to hit your wife—" he rubbed his hands together with a sinister smile. "And your duty, if you care to attempt it, is to see to it they don't accomplish that feat."

Shyre straightened determinedly as a low, demonic laugh echoed from the throats of the Pitan Horde. Krinar's expression turned cold at the sound. "Silence!" He roared. "I was not yet finished!"

He turned his attention to the two soldiers who stood apart from the others. "For every time you hit the prince, you will be whipped once with the cane yourself." The men's eyes widened in dismay. "But—" The men's faces brightened at this. "For every time you hit the princess, a lash will be taken away from your punishment. Do you understand?"

The two men nodded eagerly at the king and the rat-faced one licked his lips lustfully. He was small and fast, and he did not think he would have a single problem in hitting the princess. After all, she could not move very far to evade him anyway.

Shyre glanced at Navali and noted that her eyes were shuttered and stoic.

Feeling her husband's gaze on her, Navali glanced at him, giving him a little half-smile to try and reassure him of her strength. She vowed she would not flinch in pain even if they managed to hit her. A welt would have to be the telling factor for these men. She was determined that they get as much punishment as they meted out, even if it was under their king's order, they still chose to serve that evil man, and they should have to pay for the choices they made.

The men moved into position on either side of the captured royal couple and grinned, slapping the canes they held against their thighs and hands in a show of power and anticipation.

Krinar lifted a hand, and Navali knew that when it dropped the 'dance' would begin. Straightening her spine in readiness, she took a deep breath to steady her nerves, only to have Rheema cry out.

"Wait!"

Krinar looked at her in surprise and the witch's lips twisted in evil amusement.

"I have something I must tell the Dareknay prince."

Dark brows furrowing in frustration, Krinar barked. "What is it?"

The Fayrah strode over to the Pitan king and whispered something in his ear. His face cleared and delight replaced the irritated look. "Please, do share that information with him. At this moment, I think he will be less than pleased with the news."

The demonic couple shared a robust laugh over this and Rheema sauntered over to Shyre, swinging her slim hips provocatively, her hands placed lightly on them and a smile curving her overly full lips.

When she finally attained the Dareknay prince's side she stood on tiptoe and leaned into his arm, her mouth reaching only to his shoulder. She tugged at his arm to get him to bend down so she could whisper the news she had for him in his ear, but Shyre staunchly refused, and his spine remained ramrod straight.

Rheema's face filled with fury and her eyes became crazed at his defiance of her wishes. She reached up with one hand and clutched the hair at his nape, pulling on it viciously. Still, Shyre refused to let her affect him.

She kicked his knee viciously from behind and it crumpled beneath him, causing him to stumble and bend over slightly in an effort to catch himself.

Navali saw the witch's smile of victory flash across her face as she obtained her goal and whispered something in Shyre's ear. When she had finished spewing her venomous words, Rheema let go of the hair at his nape and Navali watched in horror as she dragged her index finger down his clenched cheek, leaving behind a thin trail of blood brought on by her jaggedly sharp fingernail.

The Fayrah sashayed contentedly away from Navali's husband and the princess glared daggers at the woman, vowing that one day, Rheema would be at *her* mercy.

These people were obviously not aware that Lynarians could be just as cruel as they were when it came to wreaking vengeance for a grievance done them. Navali would relish teaching this arrogant Fayrah that fact.

CHAPTER TWENTY-THREE

Shyre's blood turned to ice in his veins and his heart beat harder in his chest as Rheema sauntered slowly away from him.

He did not even feel the scratch she had left behind on his cheek, nor the blood that ran down his jaw and dripped off his stubbled chin. His mind raced, seeking to assimilate the words she had spoken, and he alternated between praying that the Pitan witch was right, and begging God that she was not.

For if she was correct, his wife even now carried his child beneath her heart and the punishment Krinar was about to initiate held far more dire consequences than he had originally thought. His child could be killed before it even had the chance to experience the light of day!

Shyre turned his dismayed gaze on his wife, and found her fiercely glaring at the Fayrah as the woman sashayed her way over to stand beside the Pitan king. What was he going to do now? Was there something else he could offer Krinar to make him withdraw his decree of punishment?

Deep within, Shyre knew there was nothing else. The Pitan king cared naught for a trade of any kind when he was about to deal out pain, for that was what he enjoyed above all else. Even though he hated Krinar and his pet Fayrah, Shyre was extremely grateful they had not chosen to reveal the news to his wife.

He knew she would be just as frantic as he to protect the babe and they did not even know if the Fayrah could know of such things. Surely it was too soon for anyone to know, even a witch could not predict that sort of thing, could they? Shyre did not know, and that thought was both a comfort and a torment to him. He vowed to strive even harder to see that his wife was not struck as Krinar lifted his hand again.

"What did that witch have to say, Shyre?" Navali asked in a low voice, barely glancing at Krinar, her eyes on the set look of coldness reflected on Shyre's face.

Shaking his head in the negative, Shyre let her know that now was not the time to ask him such questions.

Her luminous eyes darkened in confusion, but she nodded her acquiescence to his wishes. "You *will* tell me later though," she whispered and he gave her a short, abrupt nod in response. His mind was occupied with other things as the muscles in Krinar's arm tensed as he prepared to drop it.

Lightly shifting his weight to the balls of his feet, Shyre imperceptibly turned his shoulders closer to shield Navali. The two men with canes crouched low and began to circle the royal couple as the king dropped his hand in the signal to begin.

Shyre's jaw tightened in determination. They were not going to make it past him, even if it cost him his life.

The wound near his hairline throbbed in time to the muscle ticking in his jaw and Shyre circled closely around Navali to keep both the rat-faced man and the cross-eyed one in his vision. His eyes darted between them as the miscreants slowly began to close the distance that separated them from their bound prey.

The beefy one suddenly charged with a deep-throated bellow and Shyre threw his weight to the left, catching the heavy blow of the thin rod on his left shoulder. The pain sliced down his back in a diagonal as the big man lumbered away and the little one darted in from the other side. Navali crouched down and twisted out of the way as Shyre stepped in front of her again.

Whistling down, the cane hit him across the right thigh, the one that was presently protecting his wife from being struck. Shyre felt the welts that were left from both blows begin to rise as both men began their slow circling once again.

"Move, you cloddish whoresons! Lest I see you take their places!" Krinar shouted to his men, and the Fayrah screamed her agreement as they avidly observed the slowness with which the punishment was being meted out.

The short one took the incentive and darted in again, but came up short and turned sharply away at the last minute, not even bothering to strike out at them as Shyre stood stoically in front of Navali. The cross-eyed man took the opportunity of the prince's attention being elsewhere to lunge in and make a swipe at Navali with his long, thick arm.

Navali sidestepped to the right and the rope tethering her ankle to the stake suddenly caught her up short and she stumbled hard, catching herself quickly with one hand on the ground. Shyre stepped over her half-prone body to take the blow meant for her to his chest as a second one sliced across his lower back. His wife ducked her blonde head, covering it with her free arm as she avoided the blow that came from behind him.

Shyre grunted as he straightened from the force of the blows and stepped fully over Navali's body to face any oncoming threats, allowing her to rise to a standing position. She placed her hand on his back, careful to not touch any of the welts that raised the cloth of his tunic and soaked it through with crimson blood. Brushing her hand across the width of his shoulders, she let him know she was moving closer to the stake so that it would not again catch her unawares.

The two men slowly circling them darted and lunged in suddenly, again and again, their blows raining down on Shyre in an almost constant torrent of pain. He could not tell anymore if any of them had hit Navali and prayed they had not. But he did notice that his wife was becoming quite adept at twisting and evading their reach, and was momentarily quite proud of her lithe agility.

Feeling horrible for being the cause of Shyre receiving so many blows was beginning to wear on Navali, as at the same time she desperately wanted to make sure these Pitan swine rued the day they ever dared take a cane to them. Navali readied herself to take a couple of the blows as she heard and noted Shyre breathing harder and harder and rapidly blinking away the sweat that ran into his eyes. She would need to give him a respite before he collapsed.

Blood was seeping heavily through his tunic, causing it to turn a dark reddish-brown color. The thin, red cuts on his bare arms gleamed sharply in the sun, the blood smearing over the unharmed parts of his flesh until he appeared coated in red. His thighs and calves had received cuts and welts as well, some of them could clearly be seen where the canes had sliced through his breeches, and others were just thick, raised bumps beneath the leather. Her husband's face remained untouched from the bite of the wood though, and his features wore a stoic look that Navali could not yet define.

She felt Shyre stumble slightly as he stepped over the rope restraining her to take the next blow meant for her waist and he grunted as he regained his balance. She felt the earth tremble beneath her slippered feet and refused to move or even glance back as the beefy man charged her back. Shyre's head whipped around as he felt the danger to her, but he could not move quickly enough to prevent it.

Feeling the searing bite of the wood in an arc across her back and not wincing in pain was truly one of the largest efforts of sheer willpower Navali had ever called upon herself to employ, and she was extremely proud of herself for the effort.

Shyre's face grew agonized as he caught sight of the now-torn fabric on the back of her dress, and Navali laid her hand soothingly on his arm.

Responding to her touch, he brought his pained gaze to meet her eyes and noted the expression of resolve that resided there.

Navali internally measured how many of the blows she could take, not for her sake, but for Shyre's. For it seemed to hurt him even more when she was struck than when he was the one receiving the blows.

She thought it odd he would actually feel that way, though spared not a moment's hesitation on it as she stepped forward and turned around to face Shyre again, at the same time presenting her back to the rat-faced weasel of a man that streaked in. The harsh blow caught her again and Shyre's body jolted against hers as though he were actually receiving the blow with her.

"Stop this at once!" He growled at her, his teeth clenched as he bent closer to her to drive his words home. "I forbid you to step in front of those canes again!"

Navali's eyes narrowed at the tone of his voice and, though he tried blocking her with his body, stepped quickly to his left, keeping her back to the outside and receiving another lash. It stung like fire and Shyre's eyes blazed at her defiance of his wishes.

Even though he was obviously upset at her for disobeying him, Navali felt much better now as his eyes sparked with life again, for his body was responding more quickly to his commands as he spun around her and deflected the next blow meant for her with his own back. She felt great satisfaction in helping him recover by giving him even that small respite from the blows. However, she quickly realized that it was not gratitude or a reprieve that was driving him now as his lips twisted in an animalistic snarl.

It was rage. A pure, indomitable fury drove him now. His eyes blazed with a wildfire of emotion so strong, Navali felt nearly singed by it.

Shyre's eyes narrowed even more as his wife drew slightly away from him as he turned his scorching gaze on her. "Do not *ever* seek to defy me again, your royal highness. Lest I forget all propriety and protective urgings and turn you over my knee to experience the full extent of a reward you have so sorely earned."

Navali's mouth opened in shock and mute denial and she stood as one dumbfounded as he stepped around her, his gaze still locked on hers, and received yet another blow to his already striped back.

She had just been trying to help him! And there he stood not even the least bit grateful of her sacrifices!

Fuming silently to herself, her own fury was abruptly unleashed as Shyre stepped back in front of her and took a blow from the hulking cross-eyed beast of a Pitan.

The little rat-faced man that darted in at the same time but from the opposite side of the big lout, suddenly found himself facing an enraged creature far worse than any he had ever had the misfortune to cross paths with in his time serving the Pitan king.

Navali had caught the movement of the diminutive man out of the corner of her eye and she spun without thought, stepping forward to meet him partway.

The man's squinty little eyes widened in shock as he abruptly came face to chest with the princess' bosom.

Navali caught the miscreant's upraised arm and halted the downward swing of the cane high above his head. She glimpsed the sudden astonishment on his besmeared face and used it to her advantage, lifting her slender knee and ramming it as hard as she could into one of the most vulnerable spots to be found on a male form. The little man abruptly dropped, writhing on the ground and moaning as though he had been gutted, his hand clutching loosely to his cane as he sought to cradle his abused body parts in both hands.

Turning furiously on Shyre, Navali informed him in no uncertain terms, "I'll do the same to you if you *ever* seek to punish me!" She fairly hissed at him.

His green eyes were wide in shock and so were the big Pitan man's who stood still behind the prince as they both stared incredulously at the downed, writhing man. Recovering swiftly from his surprise, Shyre spun and crouched in the same movement, sweeping the brigand's feet from beneath him with one leg and then rising to stand lightly on the balls of his feet and await the next attack.

Shyre was nonetheless completely unprepared for when Navali abruptly clutched at his arm as she fell suddenly. He twisted to discover that the rat-faced man had somehow recovered enough to give the rope that held Navali's ankle a rough yank, causing her to lose her footing and land hard on her bottom.

The little man on the ground began crawling towards the princess, his eyes alight with maddened fury, and his hand clutching determinedly to his cane. Shyre turned fully then and swiftly knelt over his wife, his upper body hovering protectively over her, as the big Pitan behind him took the advantage to whip his cane down with all his might onto Shyre's bent back. The rat-faced man joined in the fray of blows raining down upon the prince, and Shyre bent further over Navali, trying desperately to shield her from his kneeling position. His wife suddenly curled into the shelter of his body and he knew she was feeling some of the blows on her own tender skin as the lashes continued on and on for what seemed an eternity.

The blows abruptly stopped, and Shyre raised dazed, green eyes to stare up into the face of Krinar. Shyre's breath huffed raggedly in his lungs, his damaged ribs shooting arrows of pain throughout his body. Blackness crowded his vision, and he determinedly blinked it back as rapidly as it arose. He noted in confusion that two Pitan soldiers were dragging the rat-faced man away as he kicked and shrieked in insanity and three more were herding the cross-eyed one to the edge of the crowd.

The wounded prince faintly heard Krinar screaming obscenities after them, yelling at them that was not how he had planned the punishment.

Barely making out all of the Pitan king's words, Shyre shifted his gaze down to his wife, who uncurled slowly from the fetal position she had been in and clutched tightly at the front of his bloodied and torn tunic.

Shyre attempted to give her a reassuring smile, but was not sure he had quite managed it as her worried eyes anxiously scanned his features. Swaying on his knees, he sat abruptly in the dirt and gazed at her in surprise, unsure as to how he had ended up there.

Trumpets suddenly blared around them and Shyre saw Krinar's face transform into a mask of sheer panic as one of his men rushed up and knelt before him, uttering words that did not please the Pitan king.

Shyre's hopes for his and Navali's future rose so swiftly at the messenger's words that he felt lightheaded.

"Did you hear that, Shyre?" Navali demanded excitedly, as her eyes scanned the edges of the ruins for a glimpse of King Naran. "Did you?" She brought her attention back to his face and dipped down to look into his dazed green eyes. "It's my father—!"

War cries rang out as brown and green armor-clad warriors raced into the inner ward, and Navali looked up again at the sight. "And your father as well!" She added, her voice disbelieving as she moved around to Shyre's back and began working to loosen his restraints. Making quick work of the knots, she then carefully peeled the rope away from where it had imbedded itself into his wrists, before removing her own rope fetter.

"I felt they would come," Shyre managed to gasp out through the pain. He had sensed Ashtyn was near, though he had thought it impossible.

He brought his legs beneath his body so that he was kneeling in front of Navali and felt the earth tilt crazily to one side at his efforts. "Ash has always been there when I needed him."

"Shyre!" Navali cried as she caught at his arms to steady him.

"I'll be fine in a moment or two." He waved away her concern as he got shakily to his feet. There was no way he was letting his father and brothers observe him wallowing in the dirt, even if his vision did have a current habit of clouding over.

He was determined to stand tall and greet his family like the warrior he had been raised and trained to be, and hellfire to the burning pain in his wounds!

The Pitan Elite-Horde were making their last stand in small, tight groups, while the Pitan Regulars raced around in panic as white, brown, and green-clad men stormed out of the forest and began rounding them up like wayward chickens and herding them out of the ruins.

Shyre saw his father ride out of the trees to his left and beside him an older distinguished Lynarian sat atop a white stallion. Shyre knew that must be Navali's father, King Naran.

Clasping Navali's waist and pulling her surprised form firmly against his battered body, Shyre raised a throbbing hand in greeting. His father kneed his destrier to a halt before his eldest son, a small smile curved the corners of his lips, though his brown eyes held concern.

"Shyre, what has befallen you?" King Avar asked his son as he dismounted and quickly glanced over the many wounds on Shyre's body. He was trying very hard to contain the fury he felt at the lash marks that had been left on his son. He was not one to countenance abuse on one of his own. "You look more ragged than the last time I saw you." He looked at his son, his eyes asking if he were truly all right.

Shyre felt much recovered now that a few minutes had passed. Even the cloudiness that had been plaguing his vision had faded away, and he nodded in response to his father's unasked question. He turned toward the Lynarian king as Naran dismounted and strode over to his daughter, who was holding herself still in the circle of Shyre's arm, completely in awe at seeing her father healthy and hale on a battlefield so soon after being gravely wounded. Though her face remained still and calm like an exquisitely carved sculpture, Shyre felt her stiffen slightly as her father walked ever closer to her.

He tightened his arm about her waist, lending her silent support, and Navali knew he would step in if he sensed she wanted him to.

"Navali." The word was quietly spoken and almost lost in the din of the men moving about them. Lynarian soldiers and King Avar's personal guards formed a circle that completely surrounded them and discouraged the Pitan prisoners from suddenly deciding to try and accost them.

King Naran came to a halt in front of his daughter and Navali saw the concern clearly written in her father's eyes and tilted her head slightly to one side, permitting the unreadable expression in her silver eyes to slip away and turn hesitant. King Naran allowed a small smile of self-recrimination to cross his face and he held his hands palm up to Navali, silently beseeching her to forgive him.

Drawing a deep breath and looking at Shyre with a question in her eyes, Navali was unsure of what to do. *Should she just accept the silent apology in her father's eyes?*

The life he had arranged for her had not been what she had wanted it to be. However, she now knew that it was the best thing that could have ever happened to her.

Nodding in response to her look, Shyre nudged her in the direction of her father and she took a single, hesitant step forward, her eyes alighting on King Naran again. She took another hesitant step and tentatively reached her hands out for him to take.

King Naran's deep blue eyes softened and he pulled her closer so she stood directly in front of him. Leaning down, he placed a gentle kiss on her cheek.

The barest brush of his lips met Navali's skin, but it was enough to know that her father did indeed love her in his own way. It was not the most affectionate greeting that had ever been, but he did love her—in a correctly Lynarian way.

Navali swiftly decided to return his display of affection and lightly kissed his rough cheek in return. The gesture was enough of a make-peace for her husband though, and he rested his hand on her shoulder in support. She smiled at him and released her father's hands so that Shyre could enfold one of hers in his own.

"Father." Shyre turned to King Avar. "This is the princess Navali."

"At the way you're holding onto her, she had better not be anyone else." King Avar teased, his brown eyes alight with laughter. He turned his full attention to Navali and smiled, reaching for her free hand. "It is a pleasure to meet you, Navali. Though I wish your trip to us had been a little more uneventful."

"With the exception of wedding your son, I would have to agree with you, your majesty," Navali replied, a small smile playing upon her own lips as the Dareknay king kissed her hand gently and then released it to stand back and inspect the newlyweds before him.

"Aye...." King Avar mused aloud, nodding his head in satisfaction. "You two make a very fine-looking pair. I can see we are going to have very beautiful grandchildren. Would you agree, Naran?"

The Lynarian king nodded, his eyes inscrutable, the mention of children bringing up memories of when Navali was but a little girl tottering about the castle. King Naran found the thought of being a grandparent suddenly very appealing, and not just because his people needed to find a way to have children, but because he too, could not wait to see who they would favor in looks.

"I hope you had one of my brothers retrieve Justice for me, Father," Shyre commented to King Avar, feeling a need to change the subject. Besides the obvious reasons, why was everyone so interested in them having children? It was as if the entire world were holding its breath, waiting anxiously for a royal proclamation of a new pink-fleshed bundle to grace the Dareknay castle once again. He had never known two men to be more interested in the subject than his father and King Naran.

Hellfire! They were starting to make even him nervous about the whole thing!

"What?" King Avar inquired of Shyre with a teasing spark in his brown eyes. "You suddenly want your brothers to fetch for you?"

Ashtyn stepped through the line of guardsmen at the same time as his father spoke the words and a wicked smile stretched across his face as he joined their little circle. "Father, you're just finding that out now? I could have told you he was a tyrant ages ago," he jested and then turned his attention to his twin, his golden eyes slowly perusing Shyre. "What happened to you, Shyre? Your wife already beating you for your clumsiness?"

"Aye, she's very talented with her knees." Shyre let go of Navali's hand to clasp his brother's wrist. "You'll have to watch out for them, she dropped a man faster than you can spit."

Navali wanted to grimace at the comparison, but her father was standing opposite her and she restrained the urge. Old habits die hard apparently.

"I'll have to do that, then," Ashtyn agreed. "I was scanning your thoughts at the time and I felt the momentary shock when that must have happened."

The two nearly identical men looked at her and chuckled, sounding so much alike it probably should have bothered Navali, but it did not and she let it go.

"I wager you didn't think your brother was wedding a hellion at the time, did you, Ashtyn?" She asked, giving him a wide smile. It was nice to see that her husband's twin had returned to him unharmed.

"Nay, I most certainly did not," Ashtyn replied and astonished Navali by gathering her close and giving her a brief hug. He released her quickly when she gave a small gasp of surprise and he straightened, shooting her another grin as he did so. "But my brother couldn't have done better. Did I ever say welcome to the family?"

"I don't believe so." Navali shook her head in the negative and her curls swayed against her back.

"Well, then. I just said it." They smiled at each other until Shyre very casually laid his arm across Navali's shoulders.

"This princess is mine, seek your own," he growled playfully. The three of them laughed, as did King Avar. Navali's father looked as though he could not quite decide if he should be offended at the implication in Shyre's voice.

"My rapscallion son was just jesting with his brother, Naran." King Avar quickly smoothed any feathers that might have been ruffled by the playful comment. "Now that everything seems under control here, shall we make our way out of this accursed basin and back to camp?" He suggested, and King Naran agreed.

"Most of the Pitan threat has already been contained," Ashtyn informed his father and the Lynarian king as he had overseen the warriors in battle and could provide the necessary information. "And what little resistance remains is being dealt with."

"What of Krinar? He disappeared like a vaporous spirit when the battle first ensued. Has he been found yet?" King Naran asked.

"Not yet, your majesty. It seems he did indeed manage to disappear, though we have not yet discovered how. But I have assigned some of my best warriors to track him and find the answer. He shan't be bothering us anytime soon," Ashtyn replied.

"And the Fayrah?" Navali asked, interrupting the men. "Has she been captured?"

"Nay, we didn't find any trace of the Fayrah either. Though I'll make certain to tell my men to keep an eye out for anything unusual," Ashtyn assured her.

"You told her about the Fayrah?" King Naran looked quickly at Shyre, his face completely smooth as his blue eyes glittered with disapproval.

"I didn't have much choice in the matter. And today she would have found out about her anyway when Krinar and his little witch decided to have some entertainment." Shyre gestured to the marks the canes had left on his arms.

"Hmm." Her father did not exactly look pleased that his daughter had been in the company of a witch. Not that any of them could have helped it though.

"Have you been harmed, Navali?" King Naran asked, allowing his elegant brow to furrow.

Navali's countenance softened at the king's permitting his concern to show so plainly on his face. "The cane caught me a few times, Father, but I'm sure 'twill leave no lasting damage. I hardly feel the marks at all. My husband bore the worst of it." Glancing hesitantly at Shyre, she prayed no one noted how his striving to protect her affected her emotions.

Nodding in satisfaction, her father stoically turned to the Dareknay king, gesturing to the waiting horses as he did so and changing the subject. "You know, Avar, this second son of yours is quite competent. I don't suppose you would consider lending him to me? He would prove quite the asset I need to properly train my soldiers."

"Well...." The pair's voices faded as they turned to make their way back to their destriers. King Naran stopped abruptly, and their conversation paused as he turned back to face Navali. "Did you wish to ride with me, daughter?" He asked, his voice soft with affection.

Navali's lips curled upwards in a small smile and she shook her head gently. "I think I need to assure that Ashtyn doesn't add to Shyre's bruises ere we make it back to camp."

Nodding and looking a little bemused by her answer, King Naran turned to finish his conversation with King Avar. He hesitated before mounting though and Navali wondered if he were going to turn around and ask her something again. She watched, her small smile still in place as he finally gave a shrug, grasped the horse's mane and swung into the saddle.

King Avar saluted Shyre as King Naran nodded regally to his new son-in-law, then both men turned their horses and headed towards the path that would take them out of the Basin and into their camp, carrying on with their discussion as though no interruption had taken place.

Shyre faced Ashtyn as soon as the two kings left. "How did you know to come?"

Ashtyn shrugged. "King Naran awoke a day after we returned from the Pitan territories with the refugees, and he instantly insisted that we make our way to the Lynarian-Pitan border. We at first thought he was objecting to the princess traveling unescorted by a maid and quickly assured him that you were both properly wedded afore we parted ways. But all he said to that, was if we didn't beat you to the border, his soldier's were bound to arrest you—That was if you managed to make it through Trickster's Basin first." Ashtyn's attention shifted to Navali, a bemused smile on his face.

"You know, Navali, I never realized your ancestors could be quite so devious as to think up something like this." He gestured around at the ruins and foliage surrounding them. "I was almost pinned to a tree by a long, pointed metal stake that unexpectedly shot from an outcropping of rock."

Shyre was amazed and scoffed at this information. "What?"

"I couldn't be more serious! I could have died a very gruesome death coming to your rescue!" Ashtyn looked his brother up and down. "Sometimes I think you're more trouble than you're worth. Just look at you, violently beaten by two measly little Pitan. Married life has certainly made you soft quickly, Shyre."

"Soft!" Shyre roared.

Her husband took a menacing step forward and Navali shook her head at their antics, letting them be. There was no way she was going to attempt to break up any kind of masculine fighting these two had in mind.

A man that looked exactly like Aakin, but at the same time completely different, strode over with Shyre's horse, breaking up the imminent threat of a wrestling match. "Ashtyn, don't you think you should let Shyre heal a little from his wounds first, ere you add to them?"

"Aaron!" Shyre exclaimed as he caught sight of his brother.

—

CHAPTER TWENTY-FOUR

Navali moved to one side as the brothers shook hands and Shyre clapped the younger man on the shoulder. "How do you fare?"

"Meeting your new bride would, I'm certain, improve my disposition," Aaron replied with a rakish smile that was reminiscent of his twin and faced Navali. "I've been hearing quite a bit about her from Aakin and would like to meet this paragon of womanhood."

"I'm hardly a paragon," Navali denied as she took a step forward and introduced herself before Shyre could do the honors. "I am Navali."

"It's nice to finally be able to meet my brother's wife, princess. As you have probably already deduced, I am Aaron. The other twin of the last set," he retorted dryly.

"I'm sure you don't suffer much in your status as one of the younger ones as much as your tone implies that you do," Navali teased him lightly, instantly liking him, though she was not sure why. He was obviously just acting lighthearted, for his black eyes with their mysterious white specks held a deep sadness that pulled at her heart strings. What had happened to put that bleakness there, when Aakin, his twin, was always so carefree and boisterous?

That would remain a mystery for a little while longer, Navali realized, as Shyre noticed Swift Justice just then.

"Well, old boy." He carefully stepped over to the horse. "You don't look as though you've been out all night with your saddle on, but I know better." Shyre brushed his bruised hand over the horse's nose and received a soft huff of air in return.

"We discovered him just outside of the clearing where you had obviously tethered him, though I don't think you left the dead Pitan soldier there next to him. That was one snake Justice seemed to have taken care of himself," Aaron commented. "You'll have to make sure he gets an extra serving of oats for that."

"Trampled a Pitan, eh Justice?" The horse bobbed its magnificent golden head as though he understood what Shyre had asked. "Well, then. I wholeheartedly agree that deserves a reward. And a little vacation time in the pasture for both you and me, though I'll have my wife with me, and you'll be all by yourself." Shyre shrugged as if he pitied the horse and his brothers laughed as Justice sidestepped closer and knocked into Shyre's shoulder.

Navali did not have to see her husband's wince to know that shove had hurt more than he was letting on. "Shyre? Do you think we could make our way to the camp now? I feel an ache in my head coming on." She had always heard that a headache was the excuse women gave when they wanted to get away. She had never employed the tactic herself before because it implied weakness. However, Shyre's wellbeing was worth the sheepishness she felt at voicing such a paltry complaint, and his wounds did indeed need seeing to as soon as possible.

Aaron stood to one side, watching the interaction between the new couple and waited along with Navali for Shyre's response. A twinge of shame flashed through Aaron when he thought of how that could have been Livai and himself if he had not been weak and allowed those cursed Pitan savages to take her from him. *What a failure he was.*

He was an acknowledged Drocun, a warrior with few equals, but he felt unworthy of the title. How could one feel like a strong and able man when he let the only person who meant more to him than his family slip through his fingers like sand to be stolen away by the blithe wind of chance? He did not know, and it was plaguing him no end now that he had glimpsed a dirty waif that looked exactly like her.

The nightmares had returned full force since that night, and all Aaron could do was pray that Aakin would not sense them and tell all of his brothers what was going on. That was the last thing he needed. He had a plan and it did not involve his brothers in the least. It was something he had to do by himself, to prove that he was man enough for the job.

Shyre's low, warm voice broke through Aaron's agonized thoughts and he pulled himself from his dark plans, shielding them from Aakin's probe as best he could.

"Of course, my love." Shyre held out his arm for Navali to take, completely unaware of the battle taking place in his younger brother.

Ashtyn reached Navali first and Shyre drew back, fully aware of what his twin was about. Ashtyn was making sure that he would be the one to lift Navali onto Justice so that Shyre did not aggravate his wounds further in the attempt.

"My thanks, brother," he muttered low in his throat to Ashtyn and his twin grinned in response.

"I'm certain you'll return the favor one day, Shyre," was the reply, and Shyre felt the side of his mouth kick up in a returning grin. As he raised his arms to hoist himself into the saddle, Shyre felt the wounds on his shoulders and back stretch to accommodate the movement, and barely kept the wince of pain from his face as burning agony flashed across his torn flesh. When he finally caught his breath, he brought his leg over the saddle and felt Navali grasp lightly onto his waist, holding herself steady behind him.

"We'll see you back at camp," Ashtyn commented as he slapped Swift Justice on the rump. The horse began a smooth walk, hardly jostling his passengers as he moved. "Tucker!" Ashtyn called, and the young Pitan man appeared at his side.

Navali had not realized before that moment that some of the refugees they had been traveling with had fought alongside the other warriors in the battle against the Horde.

"Escort them back to camp," Ashtyn ordered. "You know where it is. And see that my brash brother isn't beheaded by some Lynarian trap on the way, please. He's been having a streak of luck in finding trouble recently and I've only just pulled him from the latest incident. I would hate to have the pattern repeated so soon."

Twisting stiffly in the saddle, Shyre narrowed his gaze at his brother and made a rude gesture with his hands. Ashtyn chuckled deeply and turned away, unconcerned at his twin's antics, and began to converse with the Drocun that waited patiently to give a report of the prisoners.

Facing forward again, Shyre felt Navali settle herself more closely against him. He watched as a grinning Tucker swung up into the saddle of a vacant horse and took the lead, and Shyre allowed himself to relax in the saddle. After following the young Pitan once before, he knew they were in capable hands now. The ordeal of the journey was over and all that remained was to travel with King Naran through Lynaria and back to Dareknay.

Shyre would greatly enjoy it when they were safely in Chimea and he could have his wife all to himself for many days on end for the first time in their married life. He thought a week secluded in their chambers should do wonders to relieve the exhaustion that had dogged him for the past several days. Though he was not quite assured how much peace he would be experiencing once his mother glimpsed the condition they were returning to Dareknay in and began fussing over their wounds.

He grimaced, perhaps he and Navali would stop and stay at the royal family's hunting lodge for a short time ere they finished their trek to the capital. His father could probably be persuaded to give his mother a plausible excuse for their absence, and Shyre felt his wounded body would appear less gruesome to his mother's concerned eyes by the time their sojourn was over and they made it back to the castle.

Yes, Shyre nodded to himself in satisfaction, *he really liked that idea*. He would just have to speak with his father and assure him of the merits such a pastime would surely have.

As the threesome traversed around an outcropping of rock, Tucker suddenly whistled sharply and Shyre was amazed when they came upon Jace's wagon.

The disfigured healer stepped down and waited for them to approach.

"Why are you not at my father's camp?" Shyre asked, his brow furrowed as he gingerly dismounted, ignoring the pain the action brought with it. He reached for Navali, only to find she had already slid to the ground. He looked at her reproachfully and her silver eyes sparkled with a teasing glint. So, she had known how weak he was truly feeling. It was a conspiracy of caring, Shyre reflected with a small measure of chagrin. It seemed everyone knew of his weakened predicament.

"I stayed behind in case someone had need of a healer," Jace replied, and moved closer to the prince as he took in the multiple lacerations that covered his bare arms. "Have you need of my assistance, princeling?"

"I'll be fine," Shyre nearly growled in determination. It was one thing for his wife and brother to know how he was feeling. It was another matter entirely for this upstart of a Pitan healer to have such knowledge as well.

"Shyre." Navali allowed her disappointment in his words to be evident and he looked chastened.

"Perhaps, Jace, you could clean the wounds I cannot reach," Shyre relented, knowing Navali would feel better if the healer looked after the deeper lash marks.

Jace nodded, carefully keeping his satisfaction that Shyre had admitted he needed help to himself. He turned to his man-servant. "Ephraim, fetch the stool in the wagon, get that salve I just mixed up and plenty of bandages as well. Tucker, I need fresh water. You'll find a small stream over there." He pointed to the left, indicating where Tucker should look for it.

Returning almost immediately from doing his master's bidding, Ephraim set the stool down near the wheel of the wagon and Shyre moved reluctantly to the three-legged seat when Jace dipped his head in that direction. His body ached as he lowered himself to a sitting position and he clenched his jaw as the healer took his arm and began inspecting the wounds. Shyre was not even going to argue that Jace was going against his wishes and seeing to *all* of his wounds and not just the ones he could not reach himself.

As she followed her husband's movements with her gaze, Navali thanked Ephraim quietly and sank onto a blanket that man had thoughtfully brought and laid out for her near the fire a few yards away.

She smiled softly at Shyre and he felt an answering grin crease his face. Jace suddenly probed a tender spot and Shyre shot him a quick look, but the man never even took note of it. When Shyre returned his attention back to Navali he saw that she was covering a laugh with one delicate hand and he gave a soft chuckle.

"What's the jest?" Jace asked, surprised by the sound. He halted what he was doing and looked closely at the high prince. Had Shyre been hit on the head by the cane? That could explain any odd behavior on the prince's behalf.

"Nothing," Shyre assured him. "My wife and I were just having a private jest."

Jace nodded, not even wanting to know what *that* was about, and continued his examination of the lacerations. Some of them were deep enough they would need stitches and even more welts could be seen beginning to form. He would need to give the prince a small amount of the powdered root he always carried with him to reduce any pain he would be apt to feel on the morrow. It would be intense, Jace was sure. Finished cleaning the first arm, he moved around behind the prince to look at the second.

An arrow suddenly whistled through the clearing and Navali screamed as the prince fell back heavily against Jace, clutching at the projectile that now protruded from his right shoulder.

"Get down," Shyre snapped through clenched teeth at Navali. She had jumped up and begun racing towards him.

Navali halted immediately, though not from his words, but from the shrill feminine laugh that echoed from the trees.

"I promised Krinar a very long time ago that I would take care of you, Prince Ashyre, and that is exactly what I intend to do." The cackle sounded again as the High Fayrah stepped from her hiding place. "Now I will be able to accomplish that deed quite easily."

She had another arrow notched in her bow and Navali stood as one frozen in ice.

The witch smirked at her. "Go to your prince," she ordered. "I will let you hold him as he dies."

Navali's face tightened in fury. *This little tramp was going to kill her husband? Certainly not! Not if she was still able to do anything about it.*

"Why should I?" Navali asked, willing her voice to sound bitter as she sauntered a little closer to the woman. "He was unable to save me from the Pitan king and the torture he meted out. Tell me why I should care if you kill him?"

Rheema looked shocked and delighted at the same time, her eyes completely wild in insanity. "A woman after my own heart. Never care if a man suffers. I've heard stories of how coldhearted the Lynarians were, but I never believed them until this moment."

She quickly looked Navali up and down and made a quick decision. "Fine, you can stand over there while I take care of these men. I'll see to you later."

Navali went to where the woman gestured and moved a little farther behind her than she had indicated. If she could just get fully behind her then the woman would not be able to see what she was doing. Navali would then be able to retrieve the thin blade that rested against her thigh and remove this threat to humanity that wanted to destroy the man she loved.

Her breath quickened in her breast. She had not even told Shyre she loved him yet and he could very well die in the next few moments if she did not act quickly. Navali vowed that if they both lived through this, she would be a coward no longer and tell him exactly how she felt.

"The other man in that wagon had better emerge now with his hands straight out in front of him," the witch called as she moved closer to Shyre and Jace.

Jace had moved around the prince so that he stood beside him, his body tense with readiness. Shyre knew that any small flicker of hesitancy on the Fayrah's part and the man would spring. Both men were determined to live through this and Shyre desperately needed Navali to quit inching behind the witch. *His wife would give him an apoplexy yet!*

"Why don't you let the others go free?" Shyre drew the insane woman's attention so that it centered on himself as Ephraim stepped cautiously down from the wagon, his arms out before him. "I'm the one you really want. The others mean nothing to you," he tried reasoning with her.

"That one there can be my new pet." Rheema's voice was shrill as she nodded hungrily to Ephraim. "He's too old to fight against me, and I have need of a well-behaved slave for when I'm Krinar's queen."

"Queen," Navali mouthed mockingly from where she now stood behind the woman. She twisted to the side briefly and drew her skirts out of the way as her hand closed over the hilt of her dagger. The woman would be dead afore she was ever able to be anyone's queen if she moved any closer to her husband. Grasping her weapon in readiness, Navali waited for something to draw the witch's attention away from Shyre for just a moment.

Whistling to himself as he strode out of the trees, Tucker was completely unaware of the threat that awaited him in the clearing. He halted abruptly, gasping hoarsely as his eyes grew huge in his face at the sight of the feared Fayrah standing before him, holding a bow on Shyre, Jace, and Ephraim.

The witch's head snapped to the right as she heard Tucker and her bow went in the same direction. Navali moved silently and swiftly toward her, the blade flashing in her hand. *Now was her moment!*

She raised the dagger and the witch turned to her as she heard the rustle of Navali's skirts. Navali cringed as she brought the weapon down on the other woman. It sliced through the Fayrah's throat with ease and buried itself deeply in her flesh.

Rheema jerked and her mouth opened as she gasped for breath, her hands clawing at her throat as she attempted to dislodge the imbedded dagger. Navali took a hasty step back as the woman fell to her knees and turned her face away when the body finally keeled over to convulse silently on the ground.

The threat was past.

They were alive and the Fayrah was dead! Navali let out the breath she had been holding, nearly fainting at the lightheadedness that swept over her. She shook it away firmly and then raced for her husband.

"Shyre!" Navali fiercely desired to throw her arms around her husband and have a good cry, but checked herself just before she did that very thing. The Fayrah's arrow was still buried deeply in his shoulder and she had no wish to harm him further.

Grasping his hand in hers, Navali waited impatiently as Jace inspected the prince's latest wound. The tip of the arrow protruded from Shyre's back, dripping crimson blood from its wickedly curved barbs. Navali forced back a pained expression at the sight.

"That arrow needs to be removed as soon as possible," Jace informed the prince, and Shyre nodded his agreement. The healer took his knife from his belt and began to cut around the shaft directly behind the tip. "Ephraim, grab those bandages I had you get earlier. You'll need to press them to the wound as soon as I pull out the shaft." Jace grimaced as he suddenly snapped the head off the arrow and Shyre groaned at the sharp movement.

Grasping the arrow at the front of the prince with his good hand, Jace braced the other on the wounded shoulder to hold it steady. He looked at the prince's pale face and Shyre curtly nodded, silently informing him he was ready. Jace mentally braced himself and pulled as hard and as steadily as he could.

Navali felt the tears well in her eyes as she held Shyre's hand and was forced to watch as the muscles in her husband's jaw clenched even harder. He gasped and his chest heaved once as Jace finally managed to pull the shaft free.

Jace moved away to dispose of the arrow and dip a clean cloth in the water Tucker had brought so he could clean the wound. Ephraim quickly placed the thick bandages over Shyre's wound and held them to it tightly as the prince's blood soaked into them.

Releasing Shyre's hand, Navali threw her arms around his neck, careful to avoid jostling Ephraim's hold. Of this man's affection she was assured, as she had never been of her father's since her mother had died, and she had almost lost him to the Fayrah!

Though Navali would have liked to hear the words that made her claim on his heart complete, she was more than satisfied with the knowledge that he would rather die than see her in danger. The turmoil in his eyes as she had crept up behind the insane Fayrah had spoken of his caring for her. But if he did not get around to saying something very soon she would, and she did not know exactly how she was going to go about that since she had never, in her entire life, said those three words aloud. *I love you.*

"What did you say?" Shyre asked, and drew back slightly to stare at her.

Navali was instantly appalled. *Surely* she hadn't just spoken them aloud!

"N-nothing." Her answer was too quick and she stuttered the word. *He would not believe that for a second!*

A short laugh escaped Shyre as he saw her shock. She must not have realized that she was speaking aloud.

However, he was not about to let her take them back now.

"It's about time, my love," he teased her gently, and brought his now free hand up to cradle the back of her head.

She gazed into his twinkling green eyes. "It's about time?" She repeated, a bit indignant that he had said such a thing to her, even if it was in jest. "What of you? You haven't ever said that you love me! I was the first to say such a thing, and I am Lynarian."

Navali was exasperated. *He should have spoken the words first, instead of her! He was the Dareknay, after all. They were the ones known to be brash and outspoken, not the Lynarians!*

Shyre gently pulled her toward him and briefly kissed her indignantly pursed lips. "I call you my love all the time, Navali," he told her tenderly.

She shook her head, her blonde curls dancing. "But I thought that was just an endearment you used. Like 'my sweet' or 'little one.' I didn't know it had any special meaning to it!" She searched his eyes carefully, wanting to assure herself that he really meant it.

"Well, it does," Shyre informed her. "I wouldn't call you that if I didn't really love you, even if I am a Dareknay and prone to endearments."

"Oh."

His wife's voice was soft with wonder and Shyre smiled briefly before he tugged her closer, kissing her more deeply this time.

Navali stilled in hesitation a mere moment before laughing softly against his lips and returning the kiss with a passion she had never shown before.

Her love bloomed brighter in her chest than it had ever done, and her lips tingled as her hands heated against the flesh at the nape of his neck.

Hearing Ephraim gasp as he quickly moved away, Navali drew back in shock, having completely forgotten about their audience.

"I—" she began and stopped abruptly.

There was a soft glow emanating from Shyre and she drew back even more. Navali was about to release him completely when Jace caught her shoulder and held her in place.

"Do not let go," he ordered and she tensed, not understanding what was going on. "I knew you had the ability to heal," Jace continued. "I was wondering why you didn't use it with Lance. Did you not know about it?"

Navali continued to look deeply into Shyre's eyes in amazement as she answered Jace. "My mother had the gift. I thought when I healed more quickly than others that was the extent of the gifting in me."

"You were obviously wrong," Jace replied dryly, as he wrung out the wet cloth he had been holding and slung it over a wheel to dry, he would not be needing it now. The wounds that had once covered Shyre's body were swiftly scarring over and turning a shade of light pink, the same was happening to the skin where the arrow had pierced. Jace had seen the gift of healing only once before and knew that even those faint scars would fade away to nothing if the healer held on long enough.

At the way Navali was clinging to Shyre, Jace could safely wager there would be no scars left from his ordeal with the canes, nor from that of the arrow. He heaved a weary sigh as he made his way up the steps and into the wagon to put away the salves his manservant had taken down. No woman would ever feel such love for him, not with the way his face and body had been disfigured, and not with his self-imposed nomadic lifestyle. Jace abruptly brushed those thoughts aside and focused on the task at hand.

Outside, Ephraim nudged Tucker with his elbow and gestured with his head to follow him. Tucker looked confused and refused to budge until the older man grabbed the younger one's arm and roughly hauled him into the trees to give the royal couple a moment to themselves.

Watching the glow begin to ebb, Navali felt the heat slowly leave her hands, and knew instinctively that she would be able to release her hold soon, even though she did not want to. "Shyre?"

"Hmm?" He was busily twisting one of her curls around his long index finger and smiled contentedly at her.

"Do you think—?" She hesitated.

He stopped wrapping his finger in her hair. "What is it, my love?"

"Do you think we could, perhaps, keep our love a secret from my people? I don't think they would approve." Her beautiful face was very serious and her luminous eyes were greatly troubled.

Shyre shook his head gently. "Never."

"What?" She asked, shocked that he would refuse her request. She let go of his neck and made to step away from him, suddenly not feeling a need to be loving towards him. *Didn't he know that she would be shamed in her people's eyes if they knew she loved him?*

His brows drew down as she attempted to put more distance between them and he frowned, tugging her right back into his arms where she belonged. "What I meant, Navali, is that there is no way to hide a love like ours. It's shining from your beautiful silver eyes and I'm very sure it's doing the same thing from mine. Anyone with any sense of judgment of character is going to see it a league off and there is nothing we can do about it. Besides, I don't want to."

He frowned as a thought struck him. "Do you?"

She sighed deeply. "Not really." Shrugging miserably, she whispered dejectedly. "My people are going to despise me."

"No, they're not," Shyre responded matter-of-factly. "They aren't allowed to feel hate."

"Oh!" Navali gave an involuntary giggle at that and then turned serious, her eyes still holding a hint of a smile. "But that doesn't mean they won't feel it." She wanted to see if he could come up with anything to gainsay that. She had not known that

Ashtyn had said something very similar once before and Shyre was ready with an answer this time.

"Perhaps a few will." He nodded. "After all, you are breaking a few rules."

"Laws," she pointed out helpfully.

He shot her a pointed look. "Laws then. A few of those people are bound to be uptight sticklers, but I think you'll find that many of them won't care a whit about it, and the few that do," he shrugged. "Well, we will just have to show them how much better life can be."

Settling herself more firmly against him once more, Navali brought her mouth within inches of his. "Will it be better?" She asked huskily.

"You know it," he growled, swiftly closing the distance between their lips before she could get away. Navali giggled softly as he lifted his head and laid his forehead gently against hers, their breathing mingling together as they gasped for air.

"I do now." This time *she* was the one to kiss *him*.

S hyre!" Navali screeched as she ducked lower in a tub filled with deliciously hot water a few days later. Her surprise at seeing her husband suddenly burst through the door to their chambers in the hunting lodge was clearly evident.

"What are you doing here?" She asked, trying to reach the piece of toweling that sat on a nearby bench, only to discover it was just out of her reach.

Shyre strode over confidently, and she shrank back as he perched on the edge of the tub and had the audacity to slowly run his fingers through the water. Crossing her arms over her chest, Navali sunk even lower, her chin barely rising above the waterline.

"I'm testing the water to see if it is warm enough to bathe in." Shyre answered with a lustful glitter in his green eyes.

"It is," she assured him, and breathed a small sigh of relief when he stood up and turned away. She sat up a little, feeling better now that the imminent threat of drowning herself was at an end. It was one thing to be happily married, it was quite another to have a man in the same room with all of the candles lit while one bathed! Even if that man *was* your husband!

"Good," Shyre replied, and proceeded, in quick order, to remove his boots, forest green shirt, and tan leather breeches.

Navali gasped and hurriedly sank back into the water as he turned around. Her face heated at the magnificent display he flaunted before her. "What are you doing?" She squeaked nervously.

"What does it look like?" He sauntered over to the tub again and she closed her eyes tightly against the sight.

"I'm afraid to answer that," she replied.

"I'm bathing, my sweet," he continued, as he placed one foot into the steaming water.

"This is *my* bath," she said, moving her legs out of the way as he put his other foot in the tub and slowly sat down.

"Didn't your parents ever teach you to share?" He chuckled low in his throat and steadfastly pulled her—closed eyes, crossed arms, and all—into his lap.

"Didn't your parents ever teach you not to be greedy?" She asked in return, peeking at him from one eye, while firmly telling herself not to melt at the sight.

"Nay." His grin was rakish. "While your ancestors were fine with whatever holdings they came into through inheritance, mine were of the mindset that you take all you can get your hands on." He chuckled roguishly as his hands leisurely traveled over the soft flesh of her damp back.

Navali finally opened both eyes and decided to give in to his charm as she saw the sparkle in his green eyes. Wrapping both arms around his neck, she surprised him with a wicked smile of her own. "Well, my barbarian prince, I think we've talked about our ancestors and parents quite enough for the moment, don't you agree?"

Shyre threw back his head and laughed at her words. Navali's merry laugh joined his before he covered her mouth with his own, completely and effectively stalling all sounds coming from her soft full lips.

His hand tenderly brushed her stomach and Shyre remembered the whispered words of the Fayrah and he paused, drawing back until a breath of space separated them. *What if the witch had been right and Navali even now carried his child?*

He mentally shrugged as he returned the kisses Navali was successfully attempting to distract him with. If his wife was with child they would both know soon enough. *And if she was not?*

Well, they would just have to strive to see the deed accomplished.

Navali's delicate fingers tangled themselves in the thick dark hair at the nape of his neck and Shyre grinned as all other thoughts fled.

He would certainly not prove an unwilling participant in such endeavors.

Note from the Author:

Every author who ever writes one of these 'notes,' always says something along the lines of 'this book would not have been possible without the help of' and then they list the names of the very helpful people. Now that I have finished my first novel, I finally realize exactly why every author does it. It is so very true. And now I get to bore some of you while I honor others.

Thank you to Jennifer C, my sister Amber, and Aunt Rosalie—three of my advance readers—you will never know how utterly relieved I was when you returned my manuscript without it being thoroughly riddled with red ink—you gave me the courage to continue on. Thank you to Nicole for letting me exploit your face and figure all over my cover. To Carrie—let's face it, without you, there would be no cover and I would still be floundering about trying to rid myself of those pesky O and W's. Thanks!

To my mom—both editor and wonderwoman extraordinaire—there would be no book without you. The same also applies to my dad, but for entirely different reasons. Thank you both. And this wouldn't be complete without mentioning my last two siblings—Seth and Arienne—because, quite frankly, my life wouldn't be complete without you two!

Finally, my utmost thanks belongs to God—You pick me up when I don't think I can go on and You give me a gentle nudge when I refuse to—Thank You.

And to my grandparents—Glenn and Joyce—who have never scoffed at the idea of my being a writer—I love you both so much! To my Grandpa Ross—though you are not here, you will never be forgotten. And to my Grandmama Kathleen, I would not be an author if it hadn't been for you—I miss you, and will always love you.

Thank you to *all* of you wonderful, helpful people!

Alexa

P.S. I couldn't live with myself if I forgot my Grandmama's fans who actually took a chance and read my book and didn't judge me too harshly compared to the perfection of my Grandmama's writing. Thank you so much! I will now not become a hopelessly ashamed hermit because of your kindness. And to my own readers (I dare not call you fans yet—does that make me superstitious?), you make all of *this* possible. Thank you!